I0660446

ALSO BY

THOMAS M. MALAFARINA:

99 Souls
13 Nasty Endings
Yes, I Smelled it Too
Burn Phone
Eye Contact
Gallery of Horror
Malafarina Maleficarum I
Malafarina Maleficarum II
Fallen Stones
Ghost Shadows
Undead Living (editor)

For my beautiful wife JoAnne who is so incredible, she has absolutely no idea just how important she is to me. Thank you, Sweetheart for being my everything.

DEAD KILL

BOOK ONE

THE RIDGE OF DEATH

Thomas M. Malafarina

SUNBURY PRESS

Mechanicsburg, Pennsylvania   USA

Published by Sunbury Press, Inc.
50 West Main Street, Suite A
Mechanicsburg, Pennsylvania 17055

SUNBURY
P R E S S

www.sunburypress.com

NOTE: This is a work of fiction. Names, characters, places and incidents are the product of the author's imagination or are used fictitiously, and any resemblance to actual persons, living or dead, business establishments, events or locales is entirely coincidental.

Copyright © 2014 by Thomas M. Malafarina.
Cover copyright © 2014 by Sunbury Press.
Sunbury Press supports copyright. Copyright fuels creativity, encourages diverse voices, promotes free speech, and creates a vibrant culture. Thank you for buying an authorized edition of this book and for complying with copyright laws by not reproducing, scanning, or distributing any part of it in any form without permission. You are supporting writers and allowing Sunbury Press to continue to publish books for every reader. For information contact Sunbury Press, Inc., Subsidiary Rights Dept., 50-A W. Main St., Mechanicsburg, PA 17011 USA or legal@sunburypress.com.

For information about special discounts for bulk purchases, please contact Sunbury Press Orders Dept. at (855) 338-8359 or orders@sunburypress.com.

To request one of our authors for speaking engagements or book signings, please contact Sunbury Press Publicity Dept. at publicity@sunburypress.com.

ISBN: 978-1-62006-365-1 (Trade Paperback)
ISBN: 978-1-62006-366-8 (Mobipocket)
ISBN: 978-1-62006-367-5 (ePub)

FIRST SUNBURY PRESS EDITION: May 2014

Product of the United States of America
0 1 1 2 3 5 8 13 21 34 55

Set in Bookman Old Style
Designed by Lawrence Knorr
Cover by Lawrence Knorr
Edited by Angela Wagner

Continue the Enlightenment!

Yeah, I know I'm ugly... I said to a bartender, 'Make me a zombie.' He said 'God beat me to it.'

Rodney Dangerfield

CHAPTER 1

The early morning sun was just beginning to peek over the eastern hills, casting its luminescent rays down across the pockmarked asphalt and gravel surface of Rt. 61 just outside of what was once known as the community of Mountain Springs in Schuylkill County, Pennsylvania. Now, however, the road was in severe disrepair, as were most of the roads in the country, not to mention the world, but everyone understood that no such repairs would be coming any time soon to this particular highway or to many other rural roadways in the foreseeable future. It was simply not cost effective; at least for now for smaller communities; maybe if they were a large city, but that was not the case. Some of the deepest and potentially deadliest potholes had been crudely filled with dirt and stone, likely by armed road workers in a haphazard attempt to keep the highway at least passable. However, despite their best efforts extreme caution always had to be used whenever traveling along such questionable roadways.

An ancient 2013 Toyota Corolla was slowly working its way along the highway; its once beautiful teal green finish was now scarcely recognizable as such because of the numerous attempts at do-it-yourself body repairs which the owner had done over the years just to keep the wreck running. The original shiny teal paint had long since faded to something of a flat looking turquoise color, and its various repairs were easily identified by its random patchwork of colors, which made the vehicle resemble a rolling jigsaw puzzle. The car had rolled off the assembly line in Japan five years before its present driver was even born. That same driver was now thirty-five, and as far as he knew, Japan either might or might not still even exist. The aged vehicle moved cautiously along the highway, its driver zigging and zagging to avoid the numerous craters and other obstructions. He had driven this road many times, and although familiar with most of its obstacles, he was always on the lookout for new ones. Also, because it had been a few weeks since he had last driven on this particular stretch of highway, it was probably a good idea for him to use caution.

This was a fairly straight and relatively flat section of road with fields, woodlands, and the ruins of many abandoned houses on both sides. No one lived in these formerly suburban houses any longer because the properties were located outside of what were considered safe zones. In fact, just traveling these roads whether armed or not could be extremely dangerous; so much so that attempting such a trip unarmed was not only illegal, but it was just plain stupid. Every citizen knew the rules, and as such, everyone always traveled armed.

In the distance was the base of a mountain where the road climbed steeply upward, winding and twisting its way toward the summit, where it passed by the local reservoir located behind a forest thick with trees. Most of the leaves had changed to their vibrant fall colors a few weeks earlier, and many were beginning to shed their foliage in the chilling autumn air. The reservoir was surrounded by a fifteen foot high electrified fence topped with razor wire to keep the water supply safe. Armed guards patrolled the area round the clock for the same purpose. The reservoir provided water for two different safe zones; the Ashton Cooperative and the Franksville Colony.

The driver of the automobile was alert, always on the lookout for trouble as he and everyone else in what was left of the civilized world knew they had to be. The focus of the driver's attention was not just the perils brought on by the questionable roadway, but also the other dangers which quite possibly lurked beyond the highway, in the nearby woods. He was happy to see the leaves fall from the branches, rendering them bare, as this also provided additional visibility into the woods along the sides of the highway. Such an increased line of sight was always welcome.

He understood no one could ever be too careful when driving alone in this brave new world. Something as simple as an automotive breakdown or flat tire could easily prove fatal. There was no guarantee the limited number of government highway police would happen by in time to assist if trouble should arise. This recollection caused him to rest his hand on the 45 caliber pistol located on the passenger's seat next to him. The driver of the vehicle didn't consider himself a daring man by any means; but neither was he anyone's fool.

Jackson Ridge earned his living as a freelance writer and occasional investigative journalist and often worked with several area newspapers as well as other news services located within a commutable distance of his home in the nearby Ashton Cooperative. Most of the time, Jackson found he was able to work from his home office. This allowed him to keep the number of required road trips to a minimum; a good idea for obvious safety concerns.

Jackson could best be described as an average man in almost every sense of the word, and if asked, he would likely agree. He was of average height and build, and had light brown hair and glasses, which gave only a limited amount of character to a slightly pale complexion with no other noticeable facial features. He looked about as nondescript as one could imagine. Likewise, his personality was equally run-of-the-mill.

He did, however, have a good sense of humor, and although he appreciated light-hearted conversation, he seldom if ever told a joke himself. Jackson was not comfortable being the main focus of any conversation and tended to stay in the background in group situations; observing others. If necessary, he could rise to the occasion and participate in discussions but was far more comfortable listening as opposed to speaking. If he had anything to say, he preferred to do it through his writing. His profession brought Jackson many different acquaintances but very few close friends.

Although his chosen profession was journalism, which occasionally resulted in his involvement in controversial issues, Jackson avoided publicity and conflict whenever possible. He had not always been that way, however. Years earlier, he was quite ambitious and had dreams of fame and fortune; but then everything changed, not only for Jackson, but for the world. Now with a wife and daughter, Jackson Ridge had settled down quite a bit, spending most of his time dealing with the business of surviving and taking care of his family. He now thought of himself less as a reporter and more as a writer. Jackson loved writing but often had trouble dealing with the hassles some of his stories brought with them.

Although some might consider Jackson's normality to be a negative trait, for an investigative reporter, it often proved to be a benefit whenever he was wearing that particular hat. He could go almost anywhere virtually unnoticed and could easily blend in with any crowd, gather whatever information he was looking for, and then slip stealthily away with no one being any wiser. Jackson was a good watcher and an even better listener. Those two traits combined with his ability to blend in was what made him so good at his job.

As a journalist, occasionally one of Jackson's stories would be deemed noteworthy enough that he was able to sell it to one of the remaining national publications or syndicated wire service. On these rare occasions he could score a small bonus, but most of the time, Jackson's bread and butter came from working with local news outlets. This is not to suggest the money he got for his work with such businesses was all that profitable, but at least it managed to provide something resembling a steady income.

Sadly, many of the better paying opportunities were becoming few and far between. Jackson was very fortunate, however, that his wife Andrea, a registered nurse, still had a lucrative and much in demand profession, which provided a comfortable income as well as a decent medical plan. This was quite unusual, since such benefits were a rare commodity. His wife often found she had more work available to her than she could ever expect to have enough time to handle. It seemed to be that way for anyone working in the medical, law enforcement, and military professions. Her substantial income helped to make up for those times when Jackson could find little work or work that didn't pay as well as they would have liked. Andrea didn't mind being the primary bread winner and Jackson had no trouble with it either. Such former social stigmas were all but gone now that so much had changed with the world.

The highest paying jobs for Jackson usually came whenever a writer at one of the local newspapers took sick, went on an extended vacation, was fired, or else moved on to that great editorial desk in the sky. Whenever something such as that happened, he would get a call from one of the several temp agencies he used, asking him to fill in for a few weeks, or if he were really lucky, for several months. The work was often tedious, consisting of such mundane tasks as writing obituaries, covering town meetings, and doing the occasional human interest piece; but as he was always fond of saying, money was money. Every so often he would get an opportunity to work on a real story; an investigative piece. Regardless of the assignment, Jackson was always grateful for whatever writing work came his way.

As he drove, Jackson reached down and found his sunglasses, which he slipped onto his face because the morning sun was now high enough to blind him as he crested the top of the mountain. He traveled down the long sloping hill on the opposite side and entered the Franksville Colony. His final destination was the Yuengsville Free Zone office of the Schuylkill Daily News.

Early the previous evening, Jackson had received a call from a temp service with which he often worked. The recruiter told him one of the newspaper's regular staff writers had fallen and broken his leg or some such thing. From what he could determine, the writer would be out of commission for at least six weeks, and because it was an emergency assignment; a last minute sort of thing, they would be willing to pay an additional premium on top of Jackson's normal hourly rate.

One of the things Jackson loved best about temporary work versus direct employment, besides the higher hourly rate, was the fact that he could for the most part; set his own schedule; coming and going as it suited him. Also, once he had built a good working relationship with a client, he was often permitted work from home on certain projects. Traveling the twenty miles one way along the hills of Schuylkill County on a daily basis would put quite the strain on his decrepit old car, not to mention his having to deal with the dangers involved with such a daily trek. Jackson accepted the assignment, however, because he hated to turn down good money. He had worked for "The

Skook," as it was locally known, on many previous occasions and assumed the editor would be agreeable with allowing him to do most of his work offsite as he had done on previously occasions.

Jackson passed through the Franksville Colony without incident after making it past the various checkpoints, all of which were manned by heavily armed guards. Then as he headed south down the winding, one-way hill from Franksville to the former village of Saint Clara, the sun had moved off to his left and his view of the road was much clearer. He was not at all surprised at the lack of traffic; there were few if any cars on the roads these days, especially early in the morning or late at night. If people could avoid driving anytime, they did. Although life within the cities was fairly normal, conditions outside of the cities had not improved enough yet; although everyday they seemed to be getting just a little bit better.

Truckers, for example could often been seen driving their large rigs between cities. With their speed, size, and weight, there was little they had to fear. Also, because of the perils of road travel, truckers were often known to be some of the toughest and most well-armed workers around.

Rounding one of the sharper turns, Jackson saw something along the right side of the road at the base of a hillside. It appeared to be a large mass of barely recognizable remains of some sort. There were several turkey buzzards tearing hungrily at the tattered flesh of the disgusting mess. The hideous birds scattered as his car approached, their massive wings opening to a span of over five feet. "Could be a deer." he thought at first, then as the car got closer, Jackson saw a tiny orange flag mounted on a flexible metal rod sticking out of the top of the indistinguishable pile. Then he noticed a few remnants of clothing and knew exactly what he was seeing.

"Damn!" Jackson swore with frustration, "I could have really used the extra hundred bucks. If only I had gotten here a little earlier." Then looking at the amount of destruction which had been done to the thing he wondered what could have possibly struck it with enough force to cause so much damage. He decided it must have been an eighteen-wheel tractor-trailer rig or something equally as large. He did occasionally see them from time to time in his travels. "Those truckers are driving money-making machines" Jackson thought with additional frustration. "If I were to hit one of those things with this antique piece of crap I'd probably total my car and end up dead myself as well."

A few hundred feet later when Jackson was about to increase his speed, he noticed a road sign. He hadn't driven this highway for a few weeks and the sign must have only recently been put in place. He noticed fresh overturned dirt at the base of the sign pole confirming his assumption. That, combined with the gory pile of mangled highway meat he had just seen by the side of the road made it all too clear.

The sign was a typical diamond-shaped reflective yellow insignia, with a black border paralleling the outside edge. It was similar to those signs used in days gone by to depict deer crossings or in school zones for student pedestrian traffic, but instead of depicting the silhouette of a jumping deer or shadow of a walking child, this sign had a much more ominous symbol. The illustration depicted the black silhouette of something resembling an undead creature. Above the image was the word "Zombie," and below the image the word "X-ING". Just below the triangular sign was a small rectangular white sign, which read "Reduce Speed 35 MPH".

"Wonderful." Jackson said sarcastically at the reduced speed zone. Then realizing what the presence of the sign might potentially mean to him in terms of money Jackson changed his opinion. "Wait a minute. I might be able to score myself a Benjamin or two today after all."

He looked in his rearview mirror to make sure no one was behind him. He was fairly certain the road would be clear, as he had seen almost no other cars or trucks on the road that morning. Jackson immediately slowed his car down to a bit less than the required speed limit. He didn't do this so much out of respect for the law as for his own safety and hopefully financial gain. Then he couldn't believe his luck when he saw exactly what he was hoping to see about one hundred yards ahead, at the place where the highway entered a straight stretch. It was crawling up awkwardly from the wooded area on the left side of the road. "Bingo!" Jackson yelled happily, and then added "Caching!"

This portion of Rt. 61 was a divided highway, and both sides were one way roads. Jackson was traveling in the southbound lane and down over the hill on the other side of the wooded area was the northbound lane. The creature must have somehow successfully crossed the lower stretch of highway, then gone through the woods and now was making its way onto Jackson's road.

As it reached the edge of the highway, the creature stood upright and Jackson was shocked to see the size of the thing. It was most certainly a big one, perhaps six feet seven inches tall and about two hundred and seventy pounds of once well developed muscle. Now, however, most of that muscle had begun to decay along with the rest of its grey rotting flesh. The creature wore only a pair of shredded blue jeans, no shoes, and barely enough tattered material to recognize its flannel shirt for what it had once been. Jackson noticed its right arm was hanging uselessly limp with a long gash running along its length, exposing the glistening pinkish-brown musculature beneath.

"A buck!" Jackson said using the slang term for a male of the species. "And a huge monster at that."

Although Jackson liked the idea of the extra money, the truth was, he hated dealing with the horrible things. He also knew he had no choice. It was every citizen's duty upon seeing one to take it down. Failure to do so could result in imprisonment. If, for example, he chose to ride on and someone witnessed his leaving and reported him, he would likely be severely fined. If the creature went on to hurt or kill someone else than Jackson could be looking at some extremely serious jail time, up to life in prison.

The beast stood by the side of the road, looking around; as if it had no particular purpose, which seemed to be typical of all of these creatures. However, Jackson knew each of them did have one specific agenda, and it was the same agenda; to satisfy an uncontrollable lust for human flesh. This didn't overly concern him since he had been dealing with these former members of the human race for many years, as had anyone who could still count themselves among the living.

"This one shouldn't be too tough to handle." Jackson thought as he pulled his car to a stop directly across the highway from the hulking beast. "The bigger they are, the harder they fall." Never taking his eyes off the creature, Jackson reached over onto the passenger seat and retrieved his 45 caliber hand gun. He eased the driver's side window down as the huge, grotesque monstrosity began to lumber slowly out onto the highway heading in his direction with its one good arm outstretched.

"Oh man! That's so weird! It looks just like that road sign back there." Jackson thought to himself. Then he saw the creature's dead-filmed eyes staring directly him with a look of unrestrained hunger he recognized far too well.

The thing opened its ghastly mouth and uttered a deep guttural groan, the same unearthly sound they all seemed to make. A thin stream of blackish drool trickled down the beast's chin and Jackson saw several yellowish-white maggots falling from the creature's lips. Most of its remaining teeth were black and broken, inadvertently creating a set of deadly jagged-edged tools, which unfortunately appeared as if they would be far too effective at ripping flesh from bone.

Jackson calmly extended his arm out of the window to prevent the deafening roar his gun would surely have made if fired from inside the confines of the car, and without hesitation, he fired once. The bullet tore past the left side of the creature's head, ripping off the top of its left ear and leaving in its wake a smoldering groove in the side of its cheek and hairline. The thing stopped for a moment as if confused, and then it slowly shook off the sensation as a living human might shake off the feeling of being brushed by a fly. A moment later it continued its advance toward Jackson's car.

He tried again and the bullet struck the lumbering creature in the left shoulder. Jackson saw a spray of blood and flesh shoot from beast, as an exit wound hole the size of a baseball blew out from its back. The impact of the round caused the thing to stumble back a few steps and almost lose its balance, but it soon shook off that hit as

9

well and was once again it was back on track, heading straight for Jackson.

Not wasting another second, Jackson took aim trying to keep his now trembling hand steady. He realized if this round missed he was going to have to hit the gas and speed away before the creature got to him. Fine or no fine, Jackson was not going to risk allowing that thing to get any closer. Luckily, when Jackson pulled the trigger this last time the bullet found its mark, entering the horrid thing's head via its left eye, passing through its rotting brain and exploding out the back of its skull in a shower of gore. The force of the blast knocked the beast backward. This time it did lose its balance as its single working arm pin wheeled uncontrollably, as if it were trying to keep itself upright; but it was far too late for that. Then the monster collapsed in a convenient heap onto the side of the road.

"Thank goodness." Jackson thought to himself, seeing where and how it had fallen, "He was a big 'un! And wow! I thought he had me there for a minute. But even though I nailed him, the last thing I needed to do this morning was to have to haul that stinking buck's carcass off the highway." And that was exactly what Jackson would have been required to do. Not only was that the law, but it was the only way he could be guaranteed to receive his money. Jackson reached into his car's glove box, rooted around a bit and pulled out a metal rod about eight inches long with a sharp spike on one end, a flexible spring in the center, and a fluorescent orange flag emblazoned with a digital code; Jackson's own unique citizen's identification code.

Jackson stepped out onto the roadway with his gun still at the ready. He looked around to make sure there were no other such creatures lurking about, and then cautiously approached the fallen beast. Most of its face and skull had been annihilated. For a moment he thought he saw the thing move slightly and considered blowing off the rest of it head. Instead he kicked it hard several times to see if there was any sign of movement. There was none. It would never rise up again. Covering his mouth and nose to avoid the ungodly stench surrounding the wretched thing, Jackson reached down and sunk the spear end of the rod deep into its shoulder, which was now the highest point on the thing's body, making the flag as visible as possible.

As the point of the spear sunk deep into the rotting flesh with a sickening sound, Jackson pulled away quickly and was hit by an involuntary shudder which started at the top of his head and rapidly shot right through his body to the tips of his toes. He stood there on the side of the road slightly bent over with his both hands extended, palms down barely able to hold onto his gun, knees bent and legs trembling. "Oh my God! I hate these freaking dead things," Jackson said with a shudder in his voice. He was so glad he was alone and no one had witnessed his ridiculous involuntary reaction.

Unfortunately, this was something that had to be done in accordance with government mandated regulations. He looked over and saw he was a few feet from mile marker 25.4. Taking a deep breath to regain his composure, Jackson withdrew his communications unit, or CU, as they were commonly called, and snapped a photo of the creature with his flag and digital code clearly displayed. He also made sure to get the mile marker sign in the photo for reference.

Walking cautiously back to his car, ever vigilant for not just other such creatures but also for possible approaching cars, rare as they may be, Jackson climbed behind the driver's seat, started his engine, and closed all of his windows. Holding his CU, Jackson selected the required communication number from his list and after hearing the digital preprogrammed greeting, he left his message, "This is Jackson Ridge, citizen number 132-78-5498. I'd like to report a dead kill on the southbound lanes of Route 61 at mile marker 25.4. I have placed my digital code identification tag into the remains in accordance with regulation DK5479-38. I'm sending a digital image as confirmation of the dead kill. Please forward payment to my account on record. And do not hesitate to call me if you have any additional questions. Thank you."

Then he disconnected, put his car in gear, and continued down the highway to his new writing assignment. One hundred dollars would be transferred into his bank account before the day was over. Jackson was starting to think it was going to be a good day after all. Little did he know the unexpected turn fate would soon have in store for him.

CHAPTER 2

Thunk... Thunk... Thunk. Young Sarah Stanton awoke in darkness. She was disoriented, confused, having no idea where she might be. She could hear a steady, rhythmic "thunking" sound, like that of a leaky faucet dripping water one droplet at a time into a deep metal sink, creating an echoing reverberation all around her. In her confused state, the noise seemed to fade in and out. One moment it seemed faint; barely noticeable. Then a moment later it seemed so loud that it hurt her ears. She knew something was very wrong with her to cause this strange distortion of her senses.

She felt a damp, icy chill, as if some weird mist had settled on the surface of her skin. She was no longer wearing her jacket; she could tell. Sarah smelled an unpleasant odor that was rank, moist, and fetid. She was having a great deal of trouble focusing on her surroundings. It was as if she were coming out of a dream; or perhaps she actually was still in the midst of a dream. She tried desperately to concentrate, wanting to remember what might have happened to her; what she might have done to cause her to end up in such strange circumstances. Her mind was a jumble and everything around her seemed so unnatural.

The last thing she could recall was leaving the Yuengsville library and preparing for the short walk home. Sarah loved the library. It had only reopened about two years earlier after having been closed for almost eight years because of what had happened, but ever since the library was back in operation, Sarah used every opportunity she had to go there. She especially enjoyed reading about how things used to be; how the world was during the time before.

The area surrounding the library; in fact, the entire city, was considered a safe zone. People had the confidence to move around freely with virtually no concerns about any of "them" lurking nearby. The city was surrounded by massive security barriers, and the only access in and out was via one of the heavily fortified and well-guarded checkpoints located at several spots where major highways converged on the city. There was talk among residents that within a few years, maybe ten or less if things continued the way they had been going, it might actually be possible for the barriers to be taken down, but for the present and immediate future they would remain in place.

Most of thirteen year old Sarah's young life, as least that portion which she could still remember with clarity, had been spent behind these walls. She thought she could still recall fragments of memories of the time before, but those moments seemed like a lifetime ago, and in many ways they were. These snippets of recollections were like short, choppy scenes from a movie, one which she couldn't quite recall; perhaps a movie more about someone else's life than her own. She wasn't sure even if these small memories were actually real, since she had only been three years old. Perhaps they were just fantasies brought on by the many historical accounts she had read at the library.

Regarding what she could recall about what had happened to her when she left the library, Sarah remembered it had been just before dinnertime but was already getting dark as it often did in late October. She could recall how the street in front of the library had not been very busy, and for some unknown reason, that particular fact had seemed to disturb her. She attributed the strange feeling to the early darkness. Everything seemed to not be quite right with the world when the days got noticeably shorter. Sarah found this thought somewhat ironic, since things had not been right with the world for almost as long as she could remember. However, during late October, Sarah always felt like the clouds seemed thicker and darker, the moon appeared more effervescent, and the air was filled with a crisp chill that she often imagined might be colder than a grave. Sarah began to shiver more from that particular thought.

As the fogginess began to leave her, Sarah was able to think back to the last thing she could recall. She remembered how she had rounded a corner at the end of the block down from the library and before she realized what was happening, she had felt someone grab her from behind and put something over her nose and mouth. Just before everything blurred and finally went black, she remembered feeling herself being tossed roughly onto the hard metal floor of a van or utility truck of some sort. Then she saw the vehicle's door close. That was the last thing she could recall before the darkness had engulfed her.

Sarah had forgotten that "they" were not the only ones she had to worry about. The walls of the city did a good job of keeping them at bay, but danger came in many different forms nowadays. She had apparently let her guard down for just a moment, and now she knew she was in real trouble. Trying desperately to focus in on her surroundings; Sarah felt as if she were seated in a large wooden chair of some sort. When she tried to move her hands and feet, she was unable to do so, realizing she was bound tightly to the chair. She was fairly sure her shoes had been removed along with her jacket because her toes were cold, as were her arms. She had worn a pair of jeans and a sleeveless shirt to school. Her mother had given her a hard time about the weather being too chilly to dress so lightly. Now she wished she had worn a sweater because it would have helped in this cold place for sure. She tried to shake the chair vigorously in an attempt to get free, but it wouldn't budge even a fraction of an inch. The solid feel of the thing made her understand the chair was either extremely heavy or else it had somehow been secured to the floor.

Squinting her eyes, trying to focus in the darkness, she felt something wrinkling over her eye lids. "A blindfold." She thought. Then she began to panic, wondering for a second, if she had been gagged as well. She couldn't feel anything in or around her mouth, and as such, Sarah breathed a deep sigh of relief. One of her biggest fears in life was to have her mouth restricted. Sarah had been plagued with sinus issues and asthma all of her young life, and as a result she had become a mouth breather. She always feared if she were ever gagged she would have a panic attack, and no matter how unlikely, she was certain her young heart might explode in her chest from fright. Or else the terror of such an experience might simply drive her insane. Just the thought of it made her need to take another deep, cleansing breath to assure herself she could breath and to help keep the rising panic at bay. She could practically taste the dank, mildewed air of the room. She knew being in such a moist place for very long would eventually cause her problems because of her allergies to molds and such, but for the moment she seemed to be all right.

"Kidnapped." She realized with terror. "Someone has kidnapped me." For some reason she could not begin to comprehend, someone had taken her from the pavement near the library and brought her to this damp, foul-smelling place. "Basement! She thought, "It smells like a cellar or basement." She wondered why she had been kidnapped and who might have wanted to take her. She was no one special, and her parents most certainly were not rich. Bad guys only kidnapped the children of rich people didn't they? If whoever had taken her expected to collect a ransom, he was in for a major disappointment, as he would never get much money from her folks, no matter how much they would be willing to pay to get her back. Obviously this all must be some sort of unfortunate misunderstanding. Perhaps the kidnappers had mixed her up with someone else; likely some rich girl.

She knew despite everything that had happened in the world, there were still some people with wealth in the area, people who had power and influence. Her Uncle Frank, the mayor of Yuengsville was one such person, but he was her mother's brother, and since his last name was McKinney and hers was Stanton, she doubted that anyone even knew they were related. It was more likely if a kidnapper was hoping to extort money from her Uncle Frank he would have been inclined to go after one of her cousins; the mayor's own children, rather than a virtually unknown niece.

"Hello?" She asked into the darkness. "Is anyone there?" Then she suddenly realized how foolish it was for her to do such a thing. If someone was in the room with her, he would be watching her and would not be someone she would want to speak to anyway since he would most likely be the kidnapper. Yet she still needed to find out what was going on and why she had been taken. Sarah thought about screaming for help but realized it would probably be useless. If her kidnapper hadn't bothered to gag her, then he was likely not worried about anyone hearing her scream. Also, if she did scream, would he then decide to gag her after all? That was the last thing she wanted to happen. Then she realized with terror that as bad as she could imagine gagging her might be, it was not the worst thing someone might do to her. She was aware that she was a very pretty teenage girl, and she knew what bad men sometime did to girls like her, but she couldn't allow herself to think about such things or else she certainly would be thrown into a panic.

"Hello Sarah" a strange, soft male voice said from somewhere in the room. Sarah couldn't determine exactly from which direction the voice came, as the words seemed to echo and bounce from wall to wall. "I hope you find your accommodations acceptable." The voice sounded almost gentle and kind, but there was something else lurking just below the surface of that smooth voice; something very, very wrong and something evil. She heard the slow patting of footsteps coming toward her.

"He knows my name!" Sarah thought with sudden terror. Because now she realized this abduction was no mistake; she had actually been the intended target of the kidnapping. But why her? Why would anyone want to take her?

Then she felt strange cold fingers gently stroking the side of her face, then gently creeping down the white flesh of her arm which was suddenly covered with goose bumps. She cringed with discomfort as a new chill shot through her body at the stranger's icy touch. She pulled away in disgust as far as her restraints would permit.

"Oh there, there my lovely little sweet pea." The voice said with a strange and eerie calm. There seemed to be an odd accent to his voice like someone from a farm area or maybe someone from the south. She had watched many movies from the time before at the library, so Sarah knew what a good number of different accents sounded like. He was standing close to her now. She could smell something, perhaps his aftershave or cologne. It smelled cheap and too strong. "There's no need for you to be afraid of me, honey. I promise I won't hurt you. You see, you're way too valuable to me. But I should mention that as long as you do exactly I tell you to do and don't go making no fuss, you won't get hurt. 'Cause if you do... well, let's not go talking about that right now. You see, I care very much about you, sweet Sarah. And I promise you in time... well, I'm sure you'll grow to appreciate all the good things I can do for you. You just wait and see. After all, you're going to be part of my little old family for a very, very long time". Sarah heard the sound of a chair or stool scraping along the cement basement floor as the man took a seat somewhere off to her left.

Sarah's stomach clenched with terror. Had she heard the man correctly? What was it he just said? Had he really said she would be with him a very long time? How could that possibly be? Could he really expect her to remain an unwilling prisoner for days, weeks, years? Surely this man must be crazy. This single thought terrified Sarah to her very soul; most likely because she realized just how accurate the thought was. She was in the clutches of a madman.

"Who... who are you?" The Sarah stammered. "Where are we? Want do you want with me?"

The man's voice replied, "All in good time my little darling. I promise you, all in good time. For now, don't you go worrying your pretty little head about that."

"Please." Sarah pleaded. "I'm just a kid. I'm only thirteen. Please let me go. My parents aren't rich. They can't pay very much. I'm nobody special... please just let me go. I won't tell anyone, I promise."

The strange voice chortled with a deep guttural laugh and replied, "But Sarah, my sweet little angel. You simply don't seem to understand. You're so very lovely and so very special. Don't you see? I'm not interested in your parents' money at all. In fact, I have no intention of asking them for any ransom whatsoever. I didn't have you brought to me for any dumb old reason like that, my beautiful little girl. I have much, much bigger things in store for you."

With crippling terror Sarah understood just exactly what that statement meant. This creep was likely a child molester, a pedophile, a pervert, some sort of slimy worm who preyed on young girls. She had heard about such characters. For the first time in her thirteen years, Sarah was sorry she had been born such a pretty girl. It was all well and good when the young boys at school were fawning over her big brown eyes or her long, shiny dark hair, but now she realized her attractiveness was anything but an asset. Now her looks were apparently the reason she had been kidnapped by this sicko.

Sarah heard what sounded like the man standing, once again getting up from his seat. She could hear him walking slowly around her, behind her and off to her right. Her captor said "I think it's time to get this here show on the road, my little darling. So I'm going to have to say good night for a little bit my baby Sarah." A moment later she felt a pinch in her right arm, and soon the world around her began to fade to nothingness once again.

CHAPTER 3

"It's almost time." The pretty, young blonde hospice nurse indicated in a soft, consoling voice to the weeping middle-aged woman named Francine Moore. Francine's mother lay unmoving on what was just a few minutes away from becoming the old woman's death bed. She was barely clinging to what little life remained in her withered, cancer-ravaged body. "You should say your goodbyes now. Then as you know, we'll have to ask you to leave for just a little while." Andrea always hated this part of her job. She and many others in her profession could still remember a time when the bereft were permitted to sit by their loved one's side until the time of the final passing. But that was a long time ago, and things were very, very different now.

"But can't we just stay with her a little while longer." Francine pleaded, clinging tightly to the arm of her husband, Tim. "I can't stand the thought of leaving her all alone."

"I truly understand your concern Mrs. Moore, but I promise you she won't be alone. We'll be with her." Andrea said, nodding in the direction of her nurse's aide.

Francine retorted, "Yes, but you two aren't her family are you? No! You're just here to...well...to do what you have to do... what you're paid to do."

Andrea didn't have what she felt was an appropriate reply for the woman's comment, so she said nothing. After all, the woman was right. This was Andrea's job, her profession, and although she could empathize with Mrs. Moore's grief as she did with all of her patient's families, she wasn't the one whose mother was just minutes from death.

Francine Moore's husband held his wife closely and tried to comfort her in a gentle voice. "Francine, Honey please. I know how much you hate to leave her, but these laws were put into place to help and protect us. I'm sure you want to remember your mother's last moments like this, with her resting peacefully. You don't want to ruin you last memories of her with... with... well, you know."

"Of course I know Tim!" Francine replied with frustration; her voice trembling "Everyone in the whole world knows what will happen for God's sake, but that doesn't make it any damned easier does it now?"

Andrea Ridge attempted to explain with a look of understanding in her sympathetic blue eyes, "Mrs. Moore. I truly do understand your reluctance to leave, but your husband is right. And the truth is I've actually allowed you both to say in here longer than I really should have, all things considered." Then she nodded to Mr. Moore, who looked as though he couldn't wait to leave the room and understandably so. He turned his wife around and guided her away from the death bed leading her out through the bedroom door, her shoulders shaking and her head down as she wept uncontrollably. Andrea could still hear her muffled cries as her assistant closed and locked the bedroom door.

"Damn girl! You're cutting this one way too close." Andrea's nurse's aide, Jyleen said, moving quickly and hurrying to secure all of the necessary restraints. Jyleen Wilson was a short and stocky young African-American woman who had been paired up with Andrea for the day. Although not a regular partner and the physical opposite of the taller, slimmer Andrea, Jyleen had worked with her on several previous occasions, and they had gotten to know each other well enough to have built a good working relationship together. As a result, Andrea was always happy when she had an occasion to be paired with outgoing Jyleen.

Andrea replied, "Yeah. I know. You're absolutely right. I don't know what's wrong with me Jy. Lately it seems like I've been getting soft or something. I never would have let anyone hang around this long in the past. But I have to focus; to go by the book and do my best to stay on task. Right now this sweet old lady is as helpless as a newborn kitten, but very shortly she'll be one hell of a force to reckon with."

"You ain't kiddin', sister." Jyleen replied. "Now hurry up and secure her head before she passes on and turns."

"Got it." Andrea replied. This was always the worst part for her. The old woman was technically still alive, although in a deep coma, but Andrea's experience had taught her that sometimes patients would wake up near the end and would have one brief, final moment of clarity, just before they died. During that momentary time of comprehension, they occasionally would realize they had been restrained. That was never a pleasant experience. Andrea had unfortunately seen it happen several times in cases similar to this one and it was suddenly becoming a very real concern for her with each passing second.

Jyleen said, "I don't know why they just don't let us pop her now; one injection of the right stuff and its lights out; permanently. We all know she ain't never going to get any better anyway."

Andrea said, "I agree with you, Jy. But unfortunately in the eyes of the law, that would still be considered murder. Once they pass on naturally it's a completely different situation. So for now, we have to follow the letter of the law." Andrea smiled at Jyleen and thought about the way the girl loved using street slang on the job and insisted on projecting a no nonsense attitude to everyone she met. She found this appealing because Andrea knew that despite the way the young girl spoke, Jyleen was actually an extremely bright and hardworking young woman who was not only working full-time but soon would be finishing up her nursing degree program, which she had been doing at night. Andrea had nothing but respect for the girl, especially considering the state of the world.

As Andrea tightly secured the leather strap of the cranial device that she had placed over the woman's head, immobilizing it, the woman suddenly opened her eyes in surprise and said in a weak, barely audible voice. "What... what are you doing? Please... please... don't hurt me! Where's my daughter? Where's Francine?"

"Ah man!" Jyleen exclaimed, "I hate when this happens." As Andrea had dreaded, the woman had briefly regained consciousness; likely for the last time. Unfortunately, it would change nothing; if anything it would hasten her passing. In Andrea's experience, when there was this last moment of clarity, the person might be just minutes or even seconds away from crossing over. She doubted the woman truly even understood what was happening to her, but they had to act before she began to scream. If she were allowed her to start screaming, then the daughter Francine would surely try to come into the room through the locked door, thinking some sort of miracle had saved her mother from the grave at the last minute. She would likely stand outside banging on the door screaming, crying and calling for her mother, just causing more confusion, and if that happened then Andrea would have a very unpleasant and potentially dangerous scene to deal with inside. Andrea looked over at Jyleen, who already had the syringe in her hand ready to administer.

"Do it Jy," Andrea said. Then her aide injected the mild sedative into the woman's arm and she instantly fell back into blessed, silent unconsciousness. Now it would just be a matter for the two caretakers to finish securing the restraints and then to get ready for the finalization process. There had been nothing in the sedative to speed or assist the woman's passing; as Andrea said, that would have been forbidden by law, but the drug Jyleen gave her would allow her to peacefully cross over on her own while asleep.

Andrea said, "Good work Jy. Thanks. I was afraid she was going to start bellowing. That was the last thing we needed." As she fastened the final restraint Andrea said, "There we go. That should do. Now we just wait."

"Maybe you should put on that mouth guard thing." Jyleen suggested, looking at the old woman bound in the hospital bed. "You know, just in case when she passes she starts to growl in that horrible way they all do."

"Yeah. You're right again." Andrea agreed. "I hate getting close to their mouths though. I'm always afraid they might come back just as my hands get within biting range. And it's just our rotten luck that Mrs. Charles here still has most of her teeth."

Jyleen suggested, "Here's something new we can try. It's a gadget the mad scientists back at the lab came up with. We got one of the first prototypes to test out. It connects right to that helmet on both sides like the old-style guard did. Here, I'll show you." Jyleen connected one side of the muzzle-like leather mouth guard to her side of the cranial device then passed the muzzle guard over the old woman's face and let the strap fall onto Andrea's side. The mouth guard had a shiny, cone-shaped piece of metal attached to it which slid into the sleeping woman's slack-jawed open mouth. "Now you connect your side."

Andrea did as Jyleen instructed, and in a moment the guard was secured in place. "What's that metal piece attached to the mouth guard for?" Andrea asked.

"That's some new feature they came up with. The brainiaks back at the lab said the metal cone would not only prevent them from working free of the mouth guard like they sometimes did with the old style, but it also gives them something to chew on... besides us." Then she exhaled an uncomfortable burst of nervous laughter. The old woman gave out a shuddering final breath which both nurses recognized as her death rattle.

Then within a few seconds the woman's eyes flew wide open once again, but this time there was no trace of intelligence, no sign of life in the filmy orbs. Instead there was just a fury, a seething hatred, and an unbridled hunger. The now dead woman's body tensed and she tried violently to break free of her bindings in order to attack the two women who were responsible for her entrapment, but she was secured tightly and as such could barely move at all.

As the undead woman thrashed and struggled with strength she had never possessed in life, Andrea took out her stethoscope and placed it on the woman's exposed chest. "No heartbeat. She's gone Jy." The old woman's filmy eyes bugged out of her skull so much so that Andrea feared the might pop right out of her head. She let out deep growling breaths which already had become rancid with a stomach turning stench.

The formerly dying woman, who was now a living dead creature with a craving for human flesh, chomped down savagely on the steel bit inside her mouth, trying to gnaw her way free. Andrea could hear her aged and fragile teeth shattering under the pressure of the steel cone. The awful sound sent a chill down her spine. It was a sound she would never forget and one she hoped to never hear again.

Blood trickled from the corners of the woman's mouth. Andrea was thankful the woman's heart had stopped beating and her blood was no longer pumping through her body or else she might have a real gory mess on her hands. She looked over at Jyleen who was likewise cringing with revulsion from the unbearably horrible cracking sounds. Andrea could only hope Francine was not able to hear the commotion from the other room. They certainly didn't need her out there banging on the door.

"Good Lord save us." Jyleen said. "That was the worst damned thing I ever heard in my entire life. I think the brainiaks screwed the pooch big time on this one."

"Oh man." Andrea replied, equally disgusted. "I don't know what those guys were thinking. I'm going to have to write this up in my report for sure."

Jyleen said, "Maybe they should'a use something like leather or rubber. That might be a better idea."

"I think you're right on the money Jy. I'll be sure to add your suggestion to my report as well." Andrea said.

"Thanks. We can only hope they listen to you more than they ever listen to me." Jyleen replied, "Sweet Jesus! That's a horrible sound."

They both took a moment to regain their composure then Andrea said "Well, I guess it's time for us to wrap this up. Ok? Ready? Count of three, right? You do your side and I'll do mine."

With that, both Jyleen and Andrea took positions near their respective sides of the bed, right next to the cranial device. The old woman continued to struggle against her restraints. There were two buttons located on each side of the head piece along the forehead strap, one red and one blue in each set. The red button was to arm and the blue was to disarm the device. The buttons utilized software which was designed to provide a psychological means to help relieve some of the stress associated with what the hospice nurses were required to do next.

One of the red buttons was useless and did nothing. The other one did what needed to be done. Like a firing squad with one rifle containing blank bullets, this safeguard allowed the hospice nurse to rationalize that it was not her button which fired but her partner's and therefore she would carry out her work with a clean conscience. The active/inactive state of the buttons was randomly decided by a computer and was randomized each time the headset was activated.

They both placed their fingers near the red buttons and Jyleen counted "One... two..." and on "three" they both pressed their respective buttons. There was a second or two delay, as the sensors checked to assure both buttons had been pressed. If one of the nurses had chosen not to press the red button or accidently pressed the blue button nothing happened. Both red buttons had to be pressed simultaneously in order for the process to continue.

Suddenly, with the sound like that of locks releasing, several areas around the cranial helmet sprang to life, two located at the ears, one at the base of the skull near the spine and one at the forehead. Next there followed the sickening squishing sound of the razor sharp needles as they pierced deep into the creature's skull, penetrating its grey matter. A specially designed mixture of poisonous acidic chemicals was simultaneously injected into the creature's brain to further assure the thing was properly destroyed.

After a moment of brief residual thrashing, the horrible creature which had once been Mrs. Mable Charles, mother of Francine Charles Moore, mother-in-law of Timothy Moore, widow of Edmund Charles and most recently a flesh-craving undead horror, ceased movement forever. Then, just as they had done with the red buttons the nurses simultaneously pressed the blue buttons causing the needles retracted back into their ready stations, pulling free from the woman's flesh with a final revolting sucking sound.

With haste, Andrea and Jyleen disassembled the restraints and packed everything neatly away in their appropriate cases and out of view of the family. Andrea wiped a slight trickle of blood from the dead woman's forehead, revealing the almost invisible pinhole; left over from the brain piercing device. She also cleaned up the other tiny wounds as well as the blood-smeared lips. She reached into her medical bag and withdrew a container of flesh-tone makeup. Andrea kept bottles of various hues for the many different races and skin tones she encountered in her work. She gingerly filled in the tiny hole, being sure to smooth out the excess, completely masking the wound. "Ok Jy." Andrea said when her work was completed, "Let's bring her folks back in. They can have one last look at her before we have the squad come and take the body away." And with that, Jyleen unlocked the door and walked out returning a few moments later with the grieving couple behind her. As was always the case at times like this; Andrea found herself distressed over how much things had changed, not only in her profession but in virtually every aspect of everyone's lives during the past decade. With that bit of realization, she exhaled a melancholy sigh.

CHAPTER 4

The sign on the wire fence read "Ashton Cooperative Happy Home Daycare". Behind the fence, a dozen or more children laughed and played on the various pieces of playground equipment as their care providers watched their charges intently, making sure none of the children were playing too rough. The owners of the daycare, Mellissa and Michael Reedy, had an outstanding reputation for safety to uphold, which not surprisingly was a difficult task to accomplish during such troublesome times as these. The Reedys made a point to only hire managers who took that responsibility seriously; and one such person was Mrs. Lenora Johnston.

Short and stout, Mrs. Johnston commanded the daycare with the discipline of a third world military despot. In Mrs. Johnston's capable hands, the daycare ran like a well-oiled machine. She made it clear to all with stern looks from her bulldog face and her equally commanding voice that she would not tolerate any disobedience of her orders. She would not hesitate to fire anyone for even the slightest infraction.

The daycare unfortunately backed up against part of the Ashton Cooperative's northern-most boundary and therefore also served as one of the barriers against unwanted intruders. As such, the backside of the daycare playground was surrounded by a ten foot high chain-link fence topped with barbed wire. This location was a major point of contention for both the Reedys and Mrs. Johnston, who referred to the members of the Ashton Cooperative's board of elders as a collection of "morons" and "idiots". It was difficult enough to keep children safe without placing them so close to the danger zone. They were repeatedly assured by the town elders that this would only be a temporary location for the daycare until such time when a better spot, closer to the center of the Cooperative could be arranged.

Their feeble responses didn't appease Lenora Johnston in the slightest because she knew how slowly such committees and politicians moved. She was surprised people of the cooperative were even willing to send their children to the daycare, but she supposed they had little choice. There was much work to do and few people remaining alive to do it. She also knew the importance of choosing one's battles, and this was one she could never hope to win. She reluctantly accepted that the ancient adage "you can't fight city hall" was as true now as it had ever been, so instead she did her absolute best to keep her children safe. That was how she thought of them; her children. Lenora Johnston and her husband, Walter, had never had any children of their own, and now on the back side of middle age, she knew they never would. So these children were as close as she would ever come to having a family of her own.

All of the children appeared to be busy playing. Anyone who might be watching the children would notice they were playing very much like little children had played for generations before them. One would never suspect that anything had changed in the world, but of course, it most certainly had. Mrs. Johnston began her regular ritual of counting heads, making sure all of the children were present and accounted for.

Unbeknownst to her, one of the children, a young girl with blonde hair, was not presently playing with the others but had wondered away from the group and was standing over near the back side of the playground, staring attentively at the tall wire fence. In reality the girl was not actually staring at the fence itself but was staring at something just outside of the fence.

The girl was four-year-old Kyla Ridge, and she was looking out at someone who had just appeared at the fence, someone who none of the grown-ups had noticed yet. In fact, Kyla was fairly certain the person outside the fence was not so much a "someone" but was more like a "something". And that something was now staring back at her though the fence.

She didn't know what to make of the strange something. Kyla believed it might be a lady, at least it sort of looked like a lady, but then again, it really didn't. It seemed like maybe it might have once been a lady a long time ago, but now it was something else; something different; something not very nice; not very nice at all. Even though she was only four, Kyla knew quite a bit about the bad creatures her Mommy and Daddy called "them". And Kyla had even seen some of "them" on TV.

Her playmates at the daycare called them names like "zombies," or "dead heads," or "moldies," or even "stinkies." The kids would often play games where some of them pretended to be "zombies" while the others pretended to be people who hunted them down. The big people at the daycare always tried to break up these games saying that "they" were nothing to be joked about or to be included in the children's playtime, but as with children's games for generations before, stopping such imaginative play was always a constant struggle.

The workers at the daycare, especially that mean-faced Mrs. Johnston, always told Kyla and her friends to be sure to let any of the big people know if they ever saw any of "them" hanging around outside the fence. Kyla had never seen any walking around before, and never in her young life had she seen one up close like the one standing right in front of her until now. And Kyla had never, ever realized just how awful one of them would smell. She didn't think she had ever smelled anything as bad as the sort-of lady leaning against the outside of the fence smelled. The stinky smell made her tummy feel like she might have to throw up. She backed away from the fence a few more steps trying to put some distance between herself and the bad, stinky lady that wasn't really a lady anymore.

Kyla knew she should probably call out to one of the people in charge, maybe even to Mrs. Johnston herself, but she didn't. Even though the lady smelled really bad, Kyla was far too fascinated with the weird creature looking back at her through the fence. She didn't even notice how the fence was inching closer to her as the stinky lady pushed on it.

The hideous creature was clinging tightly to the wire fence with her fingers gripping between the diamond-shaped metal patterns. She would occasionally clumsily try to shake the wire. She seemed as curious about Kyla as Kyla was about her. But curious was not really the right word. The undead thing bore a look which indicated she wanted to reach in through the fence and grab Kyla. Voracious or ravenous would be more accurate words to describe that wanton stare.

Even though Kyla was just a small child, she understood what that particular look meant. She had heard many different adults talking about "them" and knew exactly what it was the horrible zombies wanted. She had also heard her Mommy and Daddy telling stories about "them" when they thought she wasn't listening. Plus, her parents had warned her about the creatures many times. Kyla knew at one time before she was born there were lots of them, now there were not so many, but when they did come, they were very dangerous. She took a cautious small step backward.

Kyla noticed that the ugly lady's fingers were not like real people's fingers because there were sharp and broken pieces of bones sticking out through her skin in many places. Kyla was smart and knew all of her colors. And she could tell that the lady's skin was not the color of regular people's skin. It was much yuckier; a little bit gray and a little bit green looking. Also, some of the lady's fingers didn't seem to work the way they should, and some even were pointing in different weird directions. Kyla found it kind of gross but also sort of interesting at the same time. But boy-oh-boy, the lady smelled really bad!

Staring closely at one of the strange moving finger bones, Kyla saw one of them wobble and wiggle as the used-to-be-a-lady grabbed harder on the fence, pushing it further inward. She also noticed the lady's eyes were not like alive people's eyes either. Although they were pretty much the same shape they didn't have the same sparkle. In fact, they didn't have any sparkle at all. And there was some sort of gray stuff covering her eyeballs so it looked to Kyla like the lady's eyes were hiding behind a piece of wax paper. Kyla knew about wax paper from craft time at the daycare. One time, they made a musical instrument from wax paper and plastic combs.

Kyla noticed part of the lady's nose was missing too, and she could see into the hole where the tip of her nose was supposed to be. At first, Kyla thought it was kind of funny looking, but then she changed her mind very quickly. This was because there was some sort of gross worm crawling around inside of the hole where the lady's nose should be. The lady also had a really big mouth and most of her teeth were yucky brown or broken or missing. Some greenish black stuff dripped down out of the corner of the lady's big mouth, and whenever her long black tongue fell out of her mouth, more of that yucky stuff dripped off of it. But what Kyla disliked the most was the bad way the lady smelled. It was really stinky; worse than horses, worse than cows, even worse than the big, smelly pigs Kyla knew about from the town's animal pen.

The thing tried desperately to stretch its fingers out though the fence far enough to reach for Kyla, and when she did, one of the digits with the exposed bones broke off and dropped to the ground, landing right in front of the little girl. She stood staring down absently at the rotting gray finger lying in the grass, resembling a slimy juicy worm. It was still wiggling, making it look even more like a worm or maybe a small snake. As Kyla's attention was focused on the wriggling finger, the creature began to push harder against the fence, expanding it further inward, hoping to get close enough to get a good grip on the small girl. The thing's reaching, bony fingers were just a few inches away from Kyla's golden hair nowThen, just when the hideous creature's reaching grasp was but a fraction of an inch from the child's hair, Kyla was abruptly pulled back away from the fence by a pair of strong hands. It was Mrs. Johnston, whose face was red with anger and most likely terror as well.

CHAPTER 5

"Kyla Ridge! What in heaven's name do you think you're doing? You know you should never leave the other children and especially never go near the back fence! And how many times have we told you never, ever go anywhere near one of them?" Kyla noticed that word, "them" again. It looked as if everyone referred to the stinky creatures as "them". "What do you have to say for yourself young lady?" Mrs. Johnston demanded.

"I'm... I'm sorry Mrs. Johnston. I... I never seen one... one of them... up... up close before. I... I.... I was just looking." Kyla stammered.

"You mean you never SAW one before." Mrs. Johnston corrected. Always the teacher, apparently even in crisis mode Mrs. Johnson couldn't help but correct Kyla's English. "And you know Kyla, that's not really a very good answer for why you didn't immediately call for help." It was one of those stupid things kids just did without ever questioning why. The child simply had been curious, although if she had known the word, mesmerized would have been a more suitable description.

Mrs. Johnston took charge as she always did in situations like this and instantly began barking orders to the rest of her helpers. "Get all the children inside the building and close the blinds immediately. You know the drill. There's no reason these little ones need to see what's going to happen out here. Just get them inside NOW!" Then the woman said quietly to herself, "God I can't wait until those idiots on the town council approve a new location for this daycare. I've warned them countless times that one of the children might get hurt someday, but would they listen to me... no! The sooner we move out of this place the better."

Kyla turned and looked back toward the fence as she was being led away by one of the other assistants and taken inside the school. She could see Mrs. Johnston looking at the fence. She was waving her arms and seemed to be talking to herself. The ugly dead lady at the fence had been joined by two other creatures; one was a man and the other was a woman. They were just as strange looking as the first one, and they too were hanging onto the fence making growling noises. Kyla imagined they also probably smelled just as bad as the first one did.

As Mrs. Johnston stood staring angrily at the three living dead creatures she began shouting loudly into the Communications Unit which she carried with her at all times. "Mr. Schwartz, we need you up in the schoolyard right away. This is an emergency! There are three... three intruders by the north fence... I'm sure you know what I mean... three of 'them'... and they need to be eliminated... immediately."

Mrs. Johnston heard the voice respond, "If I heard you correctly Mrs. Johnston, you said there are three stinkin' rotten maggot bags in need of immediate termination. That sound about right?"

"Um... well... yes... yes, it most certainly is, Mr. Schwartz." Mrs. Johnston replied, caught off guard. She was not a fan of the man on the other end of the line by any stretch of the imagination and felt the school janitor was often crass, crude, and generally low-class. She had considered firing the man on more than one occasion, but she had to admit that he was reliable and did his job well, especially when it came to situations such as this. Because of those traits, she somehow managed to overlook what she saw as his obvious shortcomings.

Then she added, "And by all means Mr. Schwartz, please do your best to be discrete... you know... because of the children."

"You got it Mrs. Johnston." Schwartz replied with artificial congeniality. "I'll be right up."

Jake Schwartz was no more a fan of Lenora Johnston than she was of him. After clicking off his own CU, Jake said through gritted teeth to no one in particular, "Very well. Mrs. Lardbutt. I'll rush right up at your beck and call and take care of it, Mrs. Gravityass. I can't wait to do something very dangerous, which I don't begin to get paid nearly enough to do. I certainly don't get paid as much as your over-abundant backside does."

Jake Schwartz knew despite the fact that there were many other jobs available, good paying opportunities with benefits were hard to come by. Also, no matter how much he detested the way mega-butt Johnston barked out orders like his former army drill sergeant, this job was a lot better than the one he previously had. That job involved hauling the rotting carcasses of those same ugly, inhuman things out to the burn piles. The very memory of the stink of those foul, flaming corpses made his stomach momentarily turn over with revulsion. Even though the burn piles had been long ago replaced by crematoriums, the idea of even handling the rotting, dead corpses still made him cringe.

Although he loved to complain about it, if he were to be perfectly honest with himself, what Mrs. Johnston just asked him to do was the probably the part of his job he truly did like the best; one which he didn't get to do often enough. He thought of it as pest control. Despite the fact that he hated taking orders from that fat sow Johnston, he did enjoy occasionally having a chance to do away with some of the rotten, hell-spawned creatures. What was it fat-ass had said? Three intruders? Yes this could be interesting as well as a bit profitable.

Jake grabbed a duffle bag from his locker containing all of the necessary tools he would require and walked up from his room in the basement and out into the light of an otherwise beautiful day. When he arrived at the north fence, he found Mrs. Johnston standing with her fists clenched, one resting on each of her ample hips, staring at the fence as the three undead creatures stood behind it growling and slobbering mindlessly.

For the briefest of moments, Jake had a fantasy. He imagined himself pretending to trip, fall, and 'accidently' bump into Mrs. Johnston, shoving her into the hungry reaching fingers of the hideous creatures. Those sorts of accidents were commonplace nowadays, and no one ever seemed to be prosecuted for such things. The cops were too busy dealing with everything else going on in the world to worry about such menial situations as questionable mishaps. They were ill equipped to handle actual murders, let alone something which could be perceived as possibly having been an accident.

Then, as if time stood still, Jake played out the imaginary scenario in slow motion in his mind. He pretended to stumble, and then reach out with his hands as if to stop his fall. His palms 'accidently' pressed against Mrs. Johnston's back and she tumbled right into the waiting hands of the three putrid creatures. One of the things grabbed onto her hair and held her against the fence while the others used their long broken fingernails to begin slicing off pieces of her flesh. Mrs. Johnston began screaming in terror and agony.

She tried desperately to support herself by holding onto the wire fence. As her fingers slid through the diamond shape wire they would fall right into the creatures' waiting mouths, where they were promptly bitten off one by one as she bellowed with pain. One of the demons got lucky and managed to get a grip on her soft and juicy tongue which he promptly ripped out along with one of her plump lips. Another one put its mouth tightly against the fence and managed to suck out one of her eyeballs, enjoying the sweet taste of the delicious morsels. Mrs. Johnston died screaming her lungs out and for a few pleasant moments Jake had the pleasure of enjoying watching her agonizing torture.

But then Jake's fantasy was ruined when he realized even if someone wasn't watching from one of the classroom windows, the security cameras would likely catch everything digitally. He knew in order to pull off something like that, he would have to act as if he was trying to save her from her fate but he unfortunately had been too late to help. He might even need to terminate one of the creatures while the other two finished her off. But he didn't think he had the acting skills to make it look unquestionably accidental. So with frustration, he decided to abandon his particular train of murderous thought for the time being; perhaps another day, perhaps another time.

"Mr. Schwartz. As you can see we have a slight problem here." Mrs. Johnston said, interrupting his most pleasurable homicidal fantasy. She was still standing with her wide back to him and gawking at the undead creatures before her. Jake wondered how she had even known he was standing behind her. He had approached in a way he thought to be stealthy, yet she had somehow known he was there. He also wondered if the fat witch had read his mind and maybe had seen his murderous thoughts.

Jake thought, "What was that she just said? Did she say we have a slight problem here? That's an understatement if I ever heard one. A clogged toilet is a slight problem. A broken window might be considered a slight problem. But there was nothing slight about this particular problem. No sir-ree. This was a major heap-big sort of el problemo." He realized he would definitely be earning his bonus today.

"Would you be so kind as to take care of these three... whatever they are... for me?" Mrs. Johnson said, wiggling her fingers at the fence dismissively as if she were asking him to flick a bug off of a screen. "I've already called the disposal service and they'll be around within the next half hour to haul away the remains. As usual, the school's account will be credited $300 for these dead kills and also as is typical we will credit your account $25 for each for a total of $75. I assume that will be satisfactory."

Jake reluctantly replied, "Yes Mrs. Johnson. That will be just fine." He truly hated only receiving only a quarter of what these dead kills would be worth, but he knew he had little choice but to take it or leave it. In the beginning of the outbreak, many years earlier, before the ranks of the undead had been sufficiently thinned out, Jake had been able to work full time and earn a very good living eliminating the brain dead creatures and collecting a ton of money in bounties, but once things were under control, that gravy train had become permanently derailed.

Jake being Jake, he had squandered away all of his earnings long before the well of good fortune ran dry. He had not anticipated it coming to an end, but once it did, the only steady work he could find was scraping the dead kills off the highway like rotting animal carcasses for $10 an hour and hauling them to the local disposal sites. In retrospect, perhaps the idea of having the pleasure of occasionally wasting a few of the sorry creatures for a $25 per unit bonus on top of his full-time paycheck wasn't such a bad deal after all. This daycare was really a sweet gig when he thought about it. He didn't have to work very hard and had few hassles, other than having to deal with the likes of that obnoxious wide load Mrs. Johnston.

It never ceased to amaze Jake that there must actually be a Mr. Johnston, and he couldn't come to grips with the idea that someone might actually been willing to sleep with that repulsive cow. It was then Jake realized he had no idea what Mrs. Johnson's actual first name was. For the past year or so since taking the job, he had always referred to her as Mrs. Johnston; at least to her face. He had a library full of many other derogatory names he used behind her back. He assumed he might have heard someone refer to her by her first name at some time but damned if he could recall it. Then his thoughts were once again interrupted by the woman's unpleasant and demanding cackle.

"Mr. Schwartz. I'm going to be heading back inside now to check the children and to make sure they stay away from the windows. I'm certain you can take care of everything out here without my supervision. And besides, you know how I hate dealing with these horrible things." Again she made that finger-wiggling dismissive motion and again Jake thought momentarily of the zombies biting off a few of those stubby, fat sausage fingers one at a time. "As I said earlier, Mr. Schwartz, please use the utmost discretion when dealing with those things and unlike last time, no firearms please. We don't want to upset the little ones."

Jake replied, "Not a problem, Mrs. Johnston. Heavens no. I would never want to upset the little ones. I have just the tools to make this a nice quiet job. And after the retrieval squad gets here I'll be sure to hose down the area like I always do."

"Yes. Well see that you do," she said curtly.

After Mrs. Johnston left, as Jake was rummaging through his duffel bag for the specific tool he needed, he mumbled to himself, "Oh yes Mrs. Johnston. Whatever you say Mrs. Johnston. I can only hope that someday when that extra eighty-plus pounds of hog fat you're carrying around on your enormous carcass causes your black heart to explode in your chest, you're all alone and no one gets to haul your rotting corpse away. Then when you lumber back here as a slobbering, grunting, walking cadaver to visit your precious little kiddies and you're the one clinging to the outside of the fence, maybe I'll be lucky enough to be asked by your replacement to 'take care' of you. Oh yes, you blubber-filled whale. That's the day I live for, Mrs. Johns-ton you worthless pile of pork." Then he decided to get back to the business at hand.

"Alrighty then." Jake said in a cheery voice, to the hungry, growling beasts clinging to the fence. "So the lady says I need to be discrete. Not a problem. Even though, Lord knows I really hate getting too close to these stinkin' maggot condos, a man's gotta do... yadda yadda yadda." He reached down into the duffle bag and took out a long, thin stainless steel rod about a quarter inch in diameter and about two feet long, with a t-shaped handle fitted to its base covered with a rubber bicycle handlebar grip. Jake had fashioned the tool himself, drilling and tapping the handle then threading the rod down inside. He had also attached a special tip which was secured to the business end of the rod and consisted of a multi-blade arrow head with both the front and back ends barbed and razor sharp.

"So kiddies. Who's gonna be first? How's about you little lady?" With that Jake walked cautiously over to the fence and picked what he thought might be the easiest target. It was the first creature, the one which Kyla had seen, prior to the arrival of the other two. This thing was still clinging to the fence and licking the wire with its long blackened tongue, which appeared to be shredded and covered with weeping, puss-filled sores. Watching the creature, Jake assumed someone must have touched the outside of the fence at some point and this ugly beast was attempting to lick some of the remnants of human flavor off the wire. It never ceased to amaze Jake how these mindless creatures could be driven so completely by the need for living flesh. Then the thought suddenly revolted him and brought him back to the task at hand.

"Oh yes, my ugly little worm-infested critter. You are definitely going to be the first." He said.

Then with surprising speed and dexterity, Jake lifted the rod, his right hand gripping the 'T' handle while his left steadied the shaft like a pool cue, and in one quick motion he shoved the razor sharp arrow tip up through the creature's gaping mouth. He felt it momentarily slow down as it cleared the roof of the thing's mouth, but then it easily slid further upward plunging deep into its brain with a sickening squishy sensation. Then just as quickly, Jake retrieved the deadly tool, slamming the creature's face against the fence while pulling out bits of decomposed gray matter and flesh simultaneously. The thing suddenly dropped to the ground like a rock. The other two creatures seemed to not even notice the carnage as they continued to cling to the fence, groaning and trying desperately to reach through.

Methodically, Jake repeated the operation in a similar fashion with the second creature. This time he shoved his makeshift tool through the thing's eyeball, once again feeling it sink into the rotting brain. He heard the eyeball pop as the blade pierced it, then had to suppress a chuckle as he pulled remnants of the things brain out through the socket. The squishy gray matter stuck out of the now empty opening, resembling a baby bird peeking out of the hole in a bird house.

With the final creature, the other woman, Jake chose to be a little bit more creative and pushed the tool up through the creature's nostril. As with the others, when he retrieved the tool a significant clot of brain tissue dangled like an errant booger from the creature's nose. The zombie seemed to stare at Jake for a moment through its filmy eyes, as if unsure of what was happening. Then it too fell to the ground with a thud, joining its defunct partners. Jake was pleased with his work. He believed variety was the spice of life, and he had been feeling extra spicy today.

Not more than five minutes after the deed was done, a truck arrived from the retrieval center, parking on the outside of the fence, and a crew of two gloved-handed workers began piling the bodies into the back of the truck. Jake recognized them as O'Hara and Nolter, two guys he had worked with back when he drove the retrieval truck.

"Nolter! O'Hara! Is that you?" Jake asked.

"Schwartzy!" Nolter replied. "Wow man! Long time no see. I didn't even recognize you in these swanky digs.

What's it been, like a year or more? How's the new gig going?"

Jake replied, "Yeah. The fact is it's been over a year. The job's a job, you know, not that bad. It's a pretty sweet deal. I get a nice steady pay check, the work ain't too hard and every so often I get to collect a bonus when I have to take out one of these dead heads." Jake looked around then whispered, "The boss lady here is a bit of a nagging bitch and a pain in the ass, but other than that the gig's a good one. How about you two? How you doin?"

"Same old, same old. SSDD. Another day, another deader." O'Hara quipped.

"But our business is picking up." Nolter said, using the same old standard joke they had been recycling for far too many years. All three of the men laughed at that until they looked over at the truck piled high with rotting corpses and suddenly it didn't seem quite as funny. Jake could see insects swarming around the vehicle, doing their best to get what morsels they could before the bodies met their eventual fiery fate. Overhead, the familiar, ever-present flocks of turkey vultures swarmed, waiting for the opportunity to pick a juicy bit of flesh or perhaps an eyeball or two for themselves.

The two workers climbed back into their truck without another word and Nolter waved to Jake from the passenger window as the truck began to pull away. Jake returned the wave, let out a sigh of resignation, and then began to hose down the remaining bits of blood and brain matter, content to know he was $75 richer and he had been able to have an enjoyable time in the process. Within the next hour, the children would be back outside playing as if nothing had ever happened. But not Kyla Ridge. When she returned, she stood and stared at the wet grass around the fence and wondered what ever happened to the strange woman and the rest of "them".

CHAPTER 6

The year is now 2053. The world as it had once existed is gone; most likely forever. That particular statement in and of itself might not at first seem exceptionally profound, because at any given time in history, anyone who has lived for half a century or more would likely not hesitate to explain how the world they presently occupied was a much different, much less civilized, and much more of a hostile place than the world that existed when they were younger. Some might say this is because fading memories have a way of providing us with the tools to rewrite our own history, often in a more favorable light and occasionally unrealistically so.

In 2053, however, such a statement would be painfully accurate. Ten years had passed since 2043, when, according to original accounts, the first formerly lifeless individuals mysteriously became reanimated, rose up from their places of recent interment, and promptly began feeding on the flesh of the first living persons they encountered. After the initial reports of these first living dead beings became public, the news media struggled to coin some new term to describe these creatures. However, the public never generally accepted one of the new names. Instead, people chose to stick with the other more popular names as coined in fiction from the past, such as Zombies, Walkers, Living Dead, Undead, and so on. The public even managed to come up with their own new slurs as the public always does, such as dead heads, rotters, stanks, grave tards, and many others. As a result, when it was discovered that an infection was responsible for the reanimation of the corpses, the virus soon became commonly known as Virus Z43 (The Zombie Virus of 2043). The infection had an actual scientific name, of course, but no one had time or desire to worry about such things; so Z43 became the generally accepted name to describe the plague.

A year or so after the initial identification of the virus, scientists were pleased to discover there was a time limitation for infection of just a few days before the initial outbreak took place in 2043. In other words, every dead body in every cemetery in the world didn't suddenly arise and begin digging their way out of the ground. If that had occurred, humanity would not have had a chance of survival. Instead, the scientists learned that someone had to have been infected with the Z43 virus prior to death in order to reanimate. Fortunately, this greatly limited the number of available creatures shambling about the world, but it didn't do much to prevent more of them from quickly making an appearance as soon as any member of the living population died.

Some theorized that the Z43 virus was man made; a biological weapon developed for the military, which had gone awry. Yet others suggest it might have been a natural mutation of some other common strain of virus. Still others say it was Mother Nature herself that spontaneously created the Z43 virus as a defense mechanism against the overpopulation of the planet by the human race. Proponents of this theory noted the similarity of the creation of the way the virus functioned to the way the human body creates antibodies to fight off its infections. Whatever the origin, man or nature, the virus had arrived.

Thanks to overpopulation as well as modern transportation, Virus Z43 ran rampant. In the present, ten years after the initial outbreak, it is understood that the Z43 virus actually resides inside the bodies of every single living human being on the planet where it remains dormant until seconds after a person dies. In its dormant stage, the virus is essentially harmless. However, once the body shuts down completely, the heart stops and the brain dies, the virus becomes active and that particular body quickly becomes reanimated as a cannibalistic living dead creature.

The virus made its first documented appearance in the eastern part of the United States near the city of Pittsburgh, Pennsylvania and immediately began spreading rapidly in all directions. Most horror movie buffs found this fact quite ironic since that particular area of the country was the location for several of George A. Romero's zombie movies, starting with the 1968 classic "Night Of The Living Dead." However, anyone who managed to survive through the previous ten years would agree the movies were far more entertaining than the reality turned out to be.

Since the turn of the 21st century, horror fans had been predicting the coming of a so-called "Zombie Apocalypse" which would eventually result in the destruction of the human race. By the beginning of the second decade the Internet was flooded with predictions of the imminent zombie takeover. There were countless movies, TV shows, and websites dedicated to the subject. Many websites instructed how best to survive the looming zombie apocalypse, and still others actually sold all manner of survival gear and dried rations for storage in zombie shelters.

This mania was not unlike the nuclear scares of the 1960's, when everyone was certain the human race would nuke itself out of existence before the end of the twentieth century. People who could afford it had fallout shelters in their basements or in remote mountain cabins. During that time, many magazines dedicated to surviving such catastrophes sprang up and gained popularity. However, as history recorded, the US won the cold war, the Soviet Union collapsed, and that particular threat disappeared. That is to say until the next alleged threat could be created; and as humans we often have very fertile imaginations for such things. Those of a survivalist mentality always seemed to have a need to find reasons to maintain their shelters and paranoid ways of life.

As a result, in the post-nine-eleven world, some chose to fear the possibility of detonation of dirty bombs or suit-case nukes or perhaps even biological warfare; any one of which gave sufficient reason to have and maintain survival shelters. There had also been the Y2K scare, which claimed computers would go crazy at the turn of the 21st century and the electric grids would fail, bringing with it the end of our modern way of life; essentially throwing us back into the stone age.

Also, let's not forget those really wacky paranoids who, when they couldn't find a suitable foreign threat, chose to believe their own government would come after them and they would have to defend their right to life, liberty and the pursuit of handguns. Of course, none of these dreaded events ever occurred, so those mistrustful individuals who considered themselves among the disenfranchised had to devise a new threat; a new enemy; therefore, whether consciously or unconsciously, people did just that.

Following the success of the "Living Dead" movie franchise as well as the "Resident Evil" video games and movies, not to mention the phenomenal success of the 2010 television series "The Walking Dead," the idea of a zombie apocalypse quickly became the new celebrated threat, no matter how unlikely, which would signal the end of mankind's reign at the top of the food chain. After all, what could humanity do, even with its amazing intellect and technology, against a constantly growing army of the undead? It was the perfect threat; a paranoid's dream-come-true.

Then in 2012, it was reported that a man in Florida was shot and killed by police officers while he was trying to eat the face off of another man. This event sent the zombie enthusiasts on social networking sites into a fit of frenzy and the hundreds of zombie bloggers began writing volumes about the coming inevitable zombie apocalypse. They insisted the incident in Florida was the first documented authentic zombie attack and therefore the end of mankind was just around the corner.

Most bloggers were certain the end of the world would begin as early as December of 2012. This was largely because many of the zombiphiles combined their apocalyptic predictions with those followers of the end of the world theories. They believed the ancient Mayan calendar predicted the world would end on December 21, 2012, but no matter how much fervor they managed to stir up and no matter how much they apparently wanted the end to occur, it never did. Life simply marched on as it had for centuries before.

Eventually, most of the zombie aficionados stopped their relentless blogging and posting on various websites. Soon, such zombie related sites began to disappear one-by-one. Shortly thereafter, zombie movies and books began to lose popularity and fade from existence. By 2018, the zombie obsession was relegated to history as yet another ridiculous fad, but this one propagated by survivalist hysteria rivaled the space alien invasion panic of the 1950's. Then many years later, in 2043, when the actual zombie apocalypse did take place, virtually no one anywhere in the world was in the least bit prepared for the unimaginable horror that followed.

CHAPTER 7

In the spring of 2043, after the first of many creatures had begun rising from the dead, the Z43 Virus began spreading faster than anyone could have possibly imagined. By the end of 2043, things didn't seem at all promising for humanity. The hoards of the shambling dead had grown exponentially to the point where it looked as if they would quickly overrun the human race. In fact, in most underdeveloped areas of the world, that was exactly what did happen. Many countries ceased to exist, their populations either being eaten alive or transformed in to undead, flesh-starved demons.

Many third-world civilizations simply didn't stand a chance. With no sound infrastructure, poor healthcare, unsanitary living conditions, and no effective knowledge as to how to properly dispose of their growing numbers of dead, the humans of such countries were easily overrun and, for all intents and purposes, were wiped out. The plague was so severe that those European and Asian countries that did somehow manage to hold on had to find ways to close their borders while simultaneously fighting their own zombie masses from inside the boundaries of their countries. There were large portions of certain continents which were deemed to be uninhabitable and would remain so until such times when armies of the living might be formed to start slowly winning back some of the occupied territories from the undead.

In more technologically advanced nations, many of the electric grids failed as did dams, utilities, phone systems both land lines as well as mobile Communication Unit based systems, and even nuclear power plants. Catastrophes were everywhere. In some countries, fortunately not the United States, it was reported that several nuclear plants melted down, contaminating large sections of formerly populated areas, killing millions, only to have them return as radioactive undead beasts.

Civilization as it had formerly been known began to break down in a matter of just a few weeks. In areas beyond the reach of surviving governments and law enforcement, robbery, murder, rape, and general mayhem were the new way of life, with neighbors killing neighbors for a crust of bread as many of the cities of the world burned amid the chaos. There was as much to fear from the man across the street as from the lingering undead.

The members of what most survivors thought of as the civilized segments of society had always assumed that those things, which were required for their existence, would always be provided for them. Humans had gotten fat, dumb, and lazy throughout the years. People had lost their "rugged individualism" and had willingly traded their freedoms for a lifestyle in which they chose to be protected, coddled, and cared for by their governments, but in many places in the world, those governments no longer existed, and those which still did were hanging on by a thread. The world was rapidly becoming a Darwinian nightmare of pure survival of the fittest.

Also, with little available electric power, almost no mass communication and a complete collapse of virtually everything humans needed to live; other diseases flourished and spread as fast, if not faster than the Z43 virus itself had propagated. People who a few years earlier would have been considered perfectly healthy now died from things as mundane as the common cold, sinus infections, strep throat, or bronchitis; the sorts of things which a simple antibiotic could have cured. Then, of course, those same individuals would return from the dead as flesh eating monsters. By 2044 more than 60% of the world's population had been wiped out, and it looked as if there might be little hope left for what humans remained. Most survivors were all but certain mankind was doomed. Then just as suddenly, the trend began to change.

Survivors of a like mind began to group together into small cadres resembling tribes or clans. Instead of running from the zombies they found ways to destroy them. As it turned out, terminating the brain or severing the brain stem from the spinal cord as depicted in many of history's zombie movies actually did work to destroy the things.

After that, their remains could be safely handled and disposed of through cremation.

Fortunately, all of the undead were slow and clumsy creatures, and unless they were able to overpower humans by sheer force of numbers, they could easily be brought down. The people of the clans learned to fight and defend themselves. They no longer expected the government to solve their problems, instead they learned to rely only on themselves for their own survival.

Also, they discovered that by eliminating the creatures' food supply - living humans - the undead would gradually begin to degrade and they would eventually fall prey to their own natural enemies; flies, maggots, vultures, and other scavengers who prefer carrion to living creatures. It was not uncommon to see zombies clumsily stumbling about as various limbs simply dropped from their bodies. Turkey buzzards, crows, rats, and other such creatures could often be seen tearing apart any of the creatures which had bccome unable to defend themselves while whatever remained of them twitched on the ground, growling in confusion until eventually they were eventually picked clean and destroyed.

The various bands of survivors found abandoned towns and cities they could make safe and began forming small communities and creating their own new mini-governments. People in these safe zones were able to pool their resources and talents to defend themselves against the horrid creatures. Fences and walls sprang up around some small towns and cities. These perimeters were defended round the clock, and the zombies were soon destroyed by the hundreds of thousands. Where possible, these perimeters were expanded, increasing the amount of land survivors would have available and decreasing the feeding zones for the shambling dead. Soon the mini governments joined forces and new national governments were restored to power.

In places where such governments had arisen, bounties were placed on the undead, which immediately resulted in an army of thousands of hunters all eager to earn a very profitable living by destroying the zombies. There were also squads formed whose sole purpose was carting away the decomposing remains to landfills where they were placed on burn piles and set ablaze. During these early transitional years, most communities had funeral pyres burning round the clock. The stench near those areas was ungodly, and as such, this job was not for everyone. However, if you were of a disposition to withstand the reek of the burning, rotting remains, this was a means of making some money, which in and of itself remained a challenge until economies began rebuilding.

Unfortunately, some of the dead also inadvertently stumbled onto their own means of surviving, either by chance or perhaps by some genetic survival mechanism that remained in effect even after the moment of death. Those zombies that were able to find and eat wild animals managed to survive even longer, eating cattle, small game, and sometimes even larger game. Hunters claimed to have seen clusters of the creatures overpowering and bringing down animals as large as a full grown deer or bear. Thankfully, for whatever reason, the virus remained confined to the human population only, never spreading to wildlife.

Although it had only taken a matter of weeks for civilization to crumble, it was apparent the rebuilding process would take much longer. Yet after ten years of dealing with the plague, humanity had finally begun to consider themselves victorious. Things were in no way like they had been before the apocalypse and might not ever be the same again, but humanity had made great strides and was continuing to do so on a daily basis.

The United States with its strong military presence and over-abundantly armed citizenry was the quickest of all countries to respond to the threat. Considering that on average the general population of one single state in the United States had more guns per capita in the private sector than the entire armies of many smaller foreign countries, few should be surprised that the US was winning the war against the dead much faster than most other countries were. It was a hunter's paradise to have every day declared open season. Plus, having a bounty placed on the creatures made the call to arms even more irresistible. Unfortunately, those countries that had all but disarmed their population were likely regretting their decision as the dead quickly overran and essentially devoured their countries from the inside out.

Eventually, most of the surviving US cities and towns, now known as safe zones, had electricity, clean water and food, and even internet as well as Communications Unit network service. With the exception of the walls, fences, and crematoriums, things were starting to return to a state resembling normalcy; although normalcy was a relative term. As had occurred after the attack on the twin towers on September 11, 2001, the surviving state governments of the US had put a lot of new laws into place to protect its citizens and deal with the Z43 plague. Many of these regulations greatly changed the way most professionals in any fields involving contact with dead or dying did their jobs. There was much to learn and many new stringent guidelines to follow.

The world accepted the fact that the horrible, flesh eating undead creatures were still out there and they would always be as long as people died and their bodies were not properly disposed of. The monsters remained every bit as deadly to any living human as they had been since the start of the plague, but thanks to the various stopgap measures put into place, there were now a lot fewer of them remaining. There were also a lot more safe zones, and by 2050 or so, the creatures had become relegated to being considered more of a nuisance than a serious threat. They were now thought of in a way very much like deer wandering out onto the highway had been ten years earlier; simply an annoying fact of life which must be dealt with and disposed of properly.

The new unified national government of the United States had devised an official procedure, DK5479-45, which the population referred to under the nickname "Dead Kill". The name was actually coined by some quick witted journalist who jokingly suggested that might be what the "DK" stood for. What started as an off-the-cuff remark ended up sticking, and soon "Dead Kill" became the accepted term nationwide. The purpose of the DK5479-45 procedure was to provide a method of rewarding citizens who destroyed the undead they encountered.

The clever promotional slogan for DK5479-45 used in advertisements to promote dead kills was "Why run when you can have some fun? And make money too." Those in authority even came up with a catchy musical jingle to go with the slogan, as well as a cartoon character known as "Dylan Deadkill". He was a muscle bound, superhero type of character armed with knives, a sword, and a semi-automatic rifle, who could be seen hacking off the heads off of hoards of zombies in all of his posters, comic books, cartoon adventures, TV commercials, and video games. There was also a line of Dylan Deadkill action figures. Although corny, over the top, and perhaps embarrassingly ridiculous, the campaign was extremely successful.

Every US citizen was required to apply for a personalized digital code, which identified him or her by what was once called a social security number, presently known as a citizen number, and in the event of a confirmed dead kill, that person could automatically receive a $100 credit in the bank account of his choice; minus the appropriate taxes of course. Not surprisingly, the one thing which had no problem surviving even such an unimaginable holocaust was taxes. This ironically gave new meaning to the old saying from Ben Franklin, "The only things certain in life are death and taxes." Survivors now got to deal with both on a daily basis.

In addition, because of a certain segment of society's less desirable citizens, the government found it necessary to write, apply, and enforce many new strict and sometime radical laws against the use of the living dead in the areas of entertainment, gambling and other games of sport or chance. As with all catastrophic events, there is always a dark, unseemly, and depraved segment of society that preys on the misfortune of others. These merchants of all things illegal had devised gambling games involving misuse of the undead.

Then another even more revolting form of perversity also soon reared its ugly head in the form of both still photographs and videography. It was a warped form of pornography featuring zombies known in the media as Z-Porn. As the term suggested, this type of depravity depicted living humans engaged in simulated sexual acts with the undead. Even more so than the zombie games of chance, Z-Porn was declared illegal, immoral, and reprehensible; and as such was completely forbidden. Punishment for the purveyors of such filth was death; no prison time just real and final death. This was largely because that industry tended to attract the worst of the worst society had to offer; murderers, rapists, pedophiles, kidnappers, sex slavers, and the like. Yet despite the government's best efforts to destroy this foul and embarrassing element of a newly rebuilding society, the unspeakable trade still existed.

Also, the zombie apocalypse did little to stop the other more traditional forms of pornography which were already in existence prior to the start of the plague. Once humanity began to make its comeback, these reprehensible merchants catering to the most debased level of society began to resurface. Now, combining these traditional forms of decadence with the new and even more depraved Z-Porn, the world had most certainly become a very different place than it had been only ten years earlier.

CHAPTER 8

Upon his arrival at the Schuylkill Daily News building, Jackson headed straight for the editor's office. This was his usual routine whenever he reported for the first day of a new assignment. As he walked along the row of windowed offices, which surrounded a farm of cubicles, Jackson could see each of the cubes was populated by workers already busy with their own assignments. The room was awash with the amber glow of incandescent lights and the air was filled with the familiar staccato sounds of rapid fire conversations, keyboards clattering, desk phones ringing, and CU's beeping. They were sounds he knew and loved very well because these were the sounds of his chosen profession.

At times like this, Jackson often thought about how much everything in the world had changed, or perhaps regressed might be a better term, during the past ten years. He noticed the steady streams of billowing clouds of cigarette, cigar, and pipe smoke rising up from the tops of the cubicles. Jackson could also smell the scent of marijuana mixed in with the other burning tobacco products. The bluish gray mixture of smoke hung like a fog near the tops of the high ceilings. As he passed, he looked through the doorways and could see some of the trash containers, which held empty beer cans as well as the remains of liquor and wine bottles.

With all of the changes the world had been forced to endure, many of the previously required social morays as well as many former laws governing social behavior had all but disappeared. In addition, many of the opinions toward vises formerly frowned upon by society and considered dangerous to one's health and well-being had been cast aside. Jackson supposed many people probably figured what was the point of worrying about lung cancer or heart disease in a world where you might die or be eaten alive at any minute? What good was fretting about the sins of our youth coming back to haunt us in our old age when old age was something most people no longer thought about?

Over the previous ten years, people had been so busy dealing with the day-to-day business of survival that many of the previously accepted workplace conventions and proprieties had gone the way of the dinosaur, the dodo, and much of mankind. Those people who remained among the living often found themselves doing the work previously handled by several people, and of course, workers rarely got paid extra to do the additional work; it was just considered the responsibility of any good citizen to help carry the load.

As a result, there was no longer anything such as political correctness, and no one worried about such trivial things as hurt feelings, a hostile work environment, sexual harassment, or any other such concepts from days gone by. The office environment of 2053 more closely resembled the types of workplaces depicted in old black and white movies from the early twentieth century, but without any of the glitz or polish. It was a much coarser and less disciplined environment. Smoking of legal and sometimes illegal substances was commonplace, as was excessive drinking, swearing, shouting and occasional fighting. Whenever a problem arose between coworkers, it was often handled by a quick punch to the face or a kick in the balls, and few employees if any ever got fired for such behavior; it was simply the way things were now.

The other thing Jackson thought about which had changed so drastically was the physical structure of surviving towns and cities. Jackson's own small community of Ashton, now known as the Ashton Cooperative, had become more of a fortress than a town, as was true of most functioning communities. It was surrounded by a variety of brick buildings with barred or boarded windows to provide an effective means of keeping out the undead. Between the buildings and in areas where there were no buildings were generally tall security fences. the original town of Ashton had expanded during the past ten years to include several of the surrounding smaller communities as well as the land in between them. The town of Ashton had once only been about a mile long and about a half mile wide, but the Ashton Cooperative covered several miles in all directions; and the entire area was surrounded by one form of barricade or another.

Wherever feasible, obstructions of whatever materials townspeople could find and salvage were constructed. One end of Ashton had barriers which had been cleverly built from funeral vaults and coffins. There had once been a local funeral supply company in town with a significant inventory of caskets and concrete vaults stored in a nearby warehouse. The residents had confiscated all of the inventory to use for their own protection. Jackson couldn't help but appreciate the irony of keeping out the dead with storage containers originally constructed to house the dead.

Another type of barrier which was quickly gaining popularity was one constructed of steel cubes made from crushed automobiles. This type of wall, given the nickname Legos, not only served as a deterrent to the dead but also kept out those of the living, generally robbers, murderers, thieves, and outlaws, who had chosen to exist outside of the towns and outside of the reach of whatever laws still remained.

These numerous gangs of motorcycle riding bandits, formed during the initial outbreak of the plague still held onto to their love for the uninhibited freedom their lifestyle brought and chose to live away from the so-called civilized world as well as from the confining legal system. No matter how much society had rebuilt and continued to rebuild on a daily basis, these outlaws chose to remain as such. This meant that oftentimes someone traveling alone, outside of the protective walls of a fortified city was as likely to fall prey to a gang of roaming marauders as he might become overrun by remaining clusters of the hungry dead.

During the previous year or so, these outlaws had become somewhat less of a problem thanks to the presence of the newly reestablished military, whose soldiers patrolled the areas between communities, but the problems these violent and wild outlaws caused still existed because the simple truth was there were not enough police or soldiers to guarantee completely safe passage to everyone.

Then Jackson thought of how the Z43 plague had also given way to a new form of criminal underworld teeming with degenerates and perverts who set up shop in the abandoned areas outside of the fortified cities known as the outlands. These outlaws participated in every form of debauchery imaginable. With the limited number of law enforcement agencies available to stop them, this scum essentially had free rein to carry out their trade among the denizens of their dark subculture. Jackson was well aware of such activities taking place on a smaller scale in and around his own beloved Schuylkill County and had even written an investigative piece about it several years earlier.

Walking up to the editor's office, Jackson noticed the blinds covering the large office windows were closed, which was typical. He saw the familiar name stenciled on the window; "William H. McCleary Editor-In-Chief". He knocked on the door while simultaneously pushing it open and was immediately greeted by the pungent odor of burnt tobacco; cigar smoke to be exact. The inside of the office was filled with gray clouds of circulating smoke. Pacing back and forth behind the desk was Big Bill McCleary himself. He held a telephone in his right hand and a glass of whiskey over ice in his left, while a thick, acrid smelling cigar dangled from the corner of his mouth. He was speaking agitatedly to someone on the other end of the line with his desk phone receiver tucked under his chin while simultaneously puffing and drinking. Despite the many technological advances which had occurred in hands-free communications in the years preceding the plague, McCleary still preferred to do things old school, so the antique circa-2011 digital desk phone still suited him just fine.

McCleary was a big, burly sort of a man of Irish decent, about sixty years old, with a thick head of reddish grey hair, which currently was in disarray from his habit of running his hands through it whenever he felt stressed. In Jackson's opinion, based on the perpetual condition of the man's hair, this state of stressfulness appeared to exist almost all of the time. Jackson assumed at some point during the morning, at least one of McCleary's hands must have been free of phone or whiskey in order for him to have caused his hair to become so disheveled.

William Hawthorn McCleary, known to all as "Big Bill," shouted something obscene into the phone then slammed the receiver down hard into its cradle. "What the hell is wrong with those morons?" McCleary shouted as he downed the remainder of his whiskey and set down the glass while staring down at the phone like he might be deciding whether or not to smash it to pieces. He was currently running his free hand through his hair, making it appear even wilder than previously if that were possible.

Jackson had no idea who McCleary had been speaking with or what the problem might have been, and knowing McCleary for as long has he had, Jackson correctly assumed the man's question to be rhetorical in nature, and as such he chose not to respond. McCleary let out a deep, alcohol-tinged breath, then slowly raised his head and seemed to notice Jackson standing there for the first time. Instantly his demeanor changed from that of the proverbial angry hibernating grizzly bear poked with a sharp stick to that of someone actually happy to see Jackson standing there across the room.

"Ridge!" McCleary said with great enthusiasm, reaching out his massive paw-like hand to vigorously shake Jackson's. "Good to have you back onboard again. We certainly can use your help. More than you realize."

"I understand one of your writers had an accident." Jackson said.

"Yeah!" McCleary explained, "That dumbass Sam Edmonds was up cleaning leaves out of his gutters or some other such ridiculous stupidity. He fell off the damned ladder and broke his old fool leg. Can you imagine such a thing? I haven't touched my gutters once in the last ten years. Who has time to worry about such nonsensical crap with dead people walking around eating everybody? Jesus, Mary and Joseph! Two years from retirement and he's out there climbing friggin' ladders! The old idiot should have landed on his damned fool head!"

Jackson stood for a moment as McCleary vented, then after the man took another big drag of his cigar while pouring himself another whiskey – it was only 7:55 in the morning – Jackson asked, "Well, Bill. I guess I should go out to Sam's desk and see what he was working on. That is unless there's something else you have in mind for me."

"You bet your ass there is!" McCleary said, "Hell. For what we're paying you, there's no way you're gunna be working on all that mindless crap we fed to Edmonds. That stuff was just perfect for someone on the downslide of his career like he is. No muss, no fuss. But for your information I already handed that garbage off to some of the newbies we recently hired. No sir Ridge, my friend, I have something much more important in mind for you."

He nodded his head at the door behind Jackson, his wild hair flapping, "Do me a favor Jackson and close that. What I'm going to tell you has to stay between you and me. It can't leave this office."

Jackson was surprised by the sudden serious change in McCleary's demeanor. He was suddenly very interested in what the editor had to say. Although he was somewhat reluctant to close the office door, essentially creating a cancer-producing gas chamber from all of the thick clouds of cigar smoke, Jackson did as McCleary suggested. Despite the many changes the world had gone through, Jackson was still a non-smoker and preferred to keep his exposure to second-hand smoke to a minimum. His curiosity had been peeked, however, as he now realized he would not be relegated to the normal mundane daily routine of writing obituaries for the next six weeks or more. Apparently, Big Bill had some other project in mind for him; something special that no one else was permitted to know about. Yes, to say Jackson was intrigued was an understatement.

He asked, "So, what do you have for me?"

CHAPTER 9

"Jackson... You know Frank McKinney, the mayor of our fair city?" McCleary asked in a voice quieter than was typical of the man.

"Why yes, of course I do. Everyone knows Frank McKinney. Well, what I mean to say is I know who he is. We've never met." Jackson said.

"Well, you'll have the pleasure of meeting him very shortly." McCleary explained, his expression suddenly growing even more serious. "He called me last evening asking for a very important personal favor, and I've have every intention of granting him that favor. That is to say, I have every intention of having you grant him that favor on my behalf."

Jackson looked on without speaking. He knew Big Bill very well and was wondering what he might have up his sleeve. With McCleary, there was always an angle; always a catch; always a reason for everything he did, and Jackson knew sooner or later that reason would rear its ugly head. Bill McCleary would never do a favor for any politician unless he had something major to gain from doing so. Nonetheless, Jackson remained silent, his built in reporter's curiosity had left him chomping at the bit to learn more.

McCleary continued. "Here's a quick overview of the situation; at least as much of it as I've been told. Frank apparently has a sister, Elizabeth McCleary Stanton; married to some guy named James Stanton. Most people who know the mayor aren't even aware he has a sister. I didn't know myself until last night and I've known Frank both professionally and personally for many years. Anyway, Liz and Jim Stanton have a thirteen year old daughter named Sarah." Jackson continued to listen now even more intently as McCleary spoke. "Sarah is missing and based on recently discovered evidence, we know she's been kidnapped."

"Kidnapped?" Jackson asked. Just moments earlier he had been thinking about how for the past ten years, loved ones of all ages had been disappearing on a regular basis; most of whom either ended up as lunch for the undead or had become walking corpses themselves. The list of missing and unaccounted for people was still massive in size.

Within the last five years or so after the various mini governments had joined forces and formed a new federal government, they managed to put together a system to try to locate or identify some of the missing among the dead kills. Whenever a corpse was taken to any of the disposal centers, it was photographed, blood typed, DNA sampled, and fingerprinted to whatever extent was possible. This often proved at best to be a daunting task, as the flesh of the decaying corpses was often too decomposed to fingerprint. Also, since the only way to kill the creatures was by incapacitating their brains, the heads and faces were frequently no longer recognizable, being blown apart ty gun blasts or hacked to pieces. Even blood typing and DNA sampling proved to be challenging. Lab resources were still very limited so some of the testing was backlogged for weeks if not months. Nevertheless, many thousands of missing persons nationwide had been identified and their surviving relatives finally given long awaited closure.

Jackson's expression must have given his thoughts away because McCleary said, "I know what you're thinking, Ridge. You're thinking the chances of finding this girl are slim to none. And you're most likely right. You probably also figure that I'm sending you on some sort of a wild goose chase in order to gain myself some favor with the mayor. Well in that regard you may be at least partially correct. It would most certainly be in my best interest and the interest of this paper to have the mayor of the Yuengsville Free Zone owing me one, but I assure you this assignment won't be a waste of either your time or my money. In fact, this could actually end up being an opportunity for the story of a lifetime for you."

Jackson held back his first response and simply let out an inaudible sigh. He had become quite cynical about such claims since he had heard many of them and other such promises countless times before, but he also knew how to recognize a potentially great opportunity when he saw one, and as a result he was very interested. In addition, he had recently heard that the Pulitzer committee had been reformed and soon they were going to begin giving out the prize once again, after a ten-year hiatus. If he could find the right story, he might actually get a shot at nailing one of the first.

"Ah. So I see I have your attention now." McCleary said with a mischievous grin. "Ok. Here's what I know. Sarah Stanton, the mayor's niece, was walking home from the Yuengsville library as she has done a hundred times before, when she went missing. There were no live witnesses but one of the recently reactivated traffic cams managed to catch a shot of the actual abduction as well as the black van which was used to snatch her. It also got a good shot of the license plate, but unfortunately, they discovered the plate had been stolen from a car down in Berks County, in the Fortified City Of Reading. So the bad news is we have no actual idea who may have taken her, although I suspect the mayor may have gotten more info by now."

"Then I suppose the kidnapper was likely not local." Jackson said. He was already starting to formulate a possible scenario. The population of most small, defended cities had become more like small towns in which just about everyone knew each other, so the kidnapper was most probably not someone from the Yuengsville Free Zone, although he might have connections there. Unfortunately, since state Route 61 headed north from the city of Reading and went straight though the center of Yuengsville, anyone who managed to safely make the trek from the Berks County areas could travel into the city once they were cleared and had passed successively through the armed checkpoints.

"Not local?" McCleary said contemplating. "Yes. I like that, Ridge. Good thinking. You're probably right on the money with that one."

"With the license plate registered in Berks County, the kidnapper likely originated somewhere in that area."

Jackson said. Then he asked, "Am I correct in assuming the checkpoints still don't screen license plates of cars entering and leaving the city yet?"

"Yes you are." McCleary said, "They do photograph them but we don't have the computer software or necessary manpower to do any more than that at this point. We're hoping to be able to start scanning and getting instant ID confirmation in a few years, but for now the main reason the guards are there is to make sure none of the dead creatures make it into the city. The guards also check for anything that looks out of the ordinary. And if they get a specific request from the police department they'll look for that as well. Unfortunately, by the time the mayor learned Sarah was missing and saw the street camera video, the bad guys were already long gone. And as I'm sure you recall, the old Amber Alert system left over from the first part of the century is a long way from being restored to full working order."

"Wow! Talk about your needle in a haystack!" Jackson exclaimed. "What about a ransom demand? Wouldn't someone assume the mayor had money and kidnapping his niece might be a quick way to score some cash?"

McCleary said, "There's been no ransom demand in the past twelve hours, and to be honest with you Jackson I'm assuming there probably won't be one. I don't think this grab has anything to do with the mayor. As I said earlier, even most local folks have no idea Sarah is the mayor's niece. I've sort of come up with my own theory and unfortunately it's not a very nice one."

"I'm not going to like where this is heading, am I?" Jackson asked suddenly suspecting why McCleary had chosen him for the assignment.

"No. I don't suppose you will." McCleary said with resignation. "As a father of a young daughter I'm sure you won't like this one little bit. However, the main reason I want to put you on this one Jackson is because of that story you did a few years ago; the one about the druggies, perverts and such."

"Oh man!" Jackson said in disgust. "I knew it! Dammit Bill!"

He had suspected his past story might be why he was being given the assignment, but he had really hoped it might not have been the case. That particular story may have been one of the best investigative pieces of his career; likely a Pulitzer winner had the award still been given. But the story had taken its toll on him both emotionally and physically. It had also driven a wedge between Jackson and his wife Andrea, one which almost had destroyed their marriage.

The constant threat of danger to himself and possibly to his family was hard for Andrea to deal with. As a result, it had taken a great deal of hard work on both of their parts to bring things back to normal; or as close to normal as a marriage could be in a world such as theirs. Investigating for that story had required Jackson to explore the most deplorable segment of society, to crawl down into the gutter with those who could only be described as the scum of humanity.

"Really Bill? You honestly think that might be where this is heading?"

McCleary said, "I hope to God I'm wrong. But think about it Jackson. As much as we might want to turn our eyes away from the possibility, it unfortunately makes a lot of sense. I'm told Sarah is a very attractive young girl, a real beauty in fact. This is something that wouldn't go unnoticed by those scumbag types. And if what I fear is true then you are most definitely the best person to spearhead this."

Jackson wondered just how much of what McCleary was saying was his honest feelings and how much was simply blowing smoke up his butt to convince him to take on the story. Jackson asked, "But what about the cops? Isn't this a matter for the police? He's the mayor of the city for God's sake. Why get us involved instead of them? I just don't get it."

"First of all as you should know, there simply aren't enough cops available to handle the current problems we have now, let alone trying to handle something like this. I'm sure the mayor will be pulling out all the stops he can but his resources are limited. Secondly, the mayor doesn't want to do anything to alert the kidnappers to the fact that

Sarah is his niece. A major police investigation would likely do just that. He figures if they think she is just another pretty girl they grabbed off the street for these purposes then maybe they won't take any extra precautions to hide her; and that can only help us."

"If the mayor orders his police force into a manhunt to find the kidnapper or tries to pull strings with cops from other areas such as Reading, then very soon every news venue in the area would be hopping on the story. And if that happens, the mayor believes the girl will be as good as dead. Hell, the only reason I'm sitting on this story myself is because I know it'll likely buy me a lot of political clout down the road and will someday pay off when I might really need it.

"Always the humanitarian." Jackson said sarcastically.

McCleary tossed off the insult, "In the immortal word of the ancient scholar Popeye the sailor, "I 'yam what I 'yam and dats all dat I 'yam'. Look Jackson, the mayor will be giving you full access to everything the police have on this so far, but he's keeping them at a distance on the active investigation, until you absolutely need them. I'm not going to force you to take this on Ridge. If you prefer I can give it to someone else and you can go back and sit at Edmonds' desk writing all the boring crap he does on a regular basis; the pay's be the same. But I don't think you'll want to do that. I know this one is right up your alley and is what I believe will be a major story. But it's entirely up to you. You know stories like this one don't fall into your lap every day of the week. Because if they did, you'd be too big for the likes of our small city paper and we probably couldn't afford to hire you. And who knows? Maybe after this is all over and this story breaks, you may be so big we really won't be able to afford you any longer. It could definitely put you into the big leagues. But I'll also admit... as you know, breaking a story with the potential this one has won't hurt the paper's literary reputation or circulation either."

Jackson asked, "And what if I do find her? Alive that is, what am I supposed to do then? I may be a good investigative reporter but I'm not a cop. And I'm most definitely not some kind of superhero. It's not like I can swoop in and take on a gang of murders and kidnappers. So what the hell am I supposed to do if and when I locate her?"

McCleary said, "To be honest, I don't really know. That's something you'll have to work out with the mayor and the chief of police when you meet with them later this morning. However, I'd recommend working out some sort of quick means of contacting them when you get a lead; something that will keep both you and the girl safe. Hell, they probably have something in mind already. And if God forbid, you find out she's dead, then I'd recommend you should try to at least get all the info you can to make sure the cops can take down whoever is responsible. Again, this is something you'll have to figure out with the powers that be. I'm just fulfilling a request and sending you their way."

"This all just seems so strange and so off-the-wall." Jackson said pondering, "I'm just having a tough time believing that getting us involved instead of some law enforcement types is really such a good idea."

"Maybe you're right." McCleary agreed. "God knows I feel the same way about it. Maybe this is some half-baked scheme someone over at city hall dreamed up, but nonetheless I see it as an opportunity for us to get a first-hand account and an exclusive story. And if you think you're interested then it's yours for the taking."

Jackson hesitated for a moment then said, "Alright. Look. I'm not saying I'll do it yet, but I am willing to find out more. So where do you want me to start with all of this?"

McCleary said, "First thing I need you to do is to head over to the courthouse, to the mayor's office, and he'll brief you with everything he knows; which hopefully by now will be a lot more than I just told you. He'll also probably identify the cops who will be working with you. But, be prepared, Ridge, the cops may not be all that thrilled about working with a reporter."

"Are they ever?" Jackson said sardonically.

"No I suppose they're not." McCleary agreed, "But I think since this is a lot more important than your run of the mill investigation, and since the orders are coming down directly from the mayor himself, they might be more inclined to cooperate. Besides, I'm sure you'll find some way to win them over to our side. If all else fails you can use some of that Jackson Ridge charm of yours."

Jackson said, "I'm going to have enough trouble charming Andrea into agreeing with my taking on this assignment. You know what that other story almost did to us."

McCleary said somberly, "But maybe if you explain to her that this is not just a story; it's much more important than that. It's about saving the life of a thirteen year old girl. Surely she'll be able to understand that; especially since you both have a little girl of your own."

"Yeah. Well, I most certainly hope so." Jackson said with genuine concern and a great deal of uncertainty. "But that little girl of ours is the main reason she might be against this." The truth was he had no idea how he would go about approaching Andrea with the idea. He knew he had to find some way to make it work for Sarah's sake, but he also had a responsibility to Andrea and Kyla, and they would be directly affected by any negative results which might accompany the investigation. Everything was much different now that he had a young daughter and now that he and Andrea had worked past their rough patch.

Jackson turned and started to leave the office, and stopped for a second as if in the midst of making a major decision. Then, just before closing the door behind him, Jackson looked back at McCleary and said, "I'll find her Bill. One way or another, I swear I'll find her."

CHAPTER 10

Walking out from the newspaper office, Jackson felt his communications unit vibrating in his shirt pocket, after which it immediately rang with a ringtone he recognized all too well. It was an electronic mechanized-sounding interpretation of the 2040 song by the band The Crystal Pipettes called "She Blinded Me With Science." Most people didn't know their version of the tune was actually a cover of the original 1980's Thomas Dolby hit of the same name; but Jackson did. Even without looking at the screen with the large "II" displayed prominently in a mid-eastern style font, the ringtone told Jackson the call was coming from his sometimes absent minded albeit extremely intelligent friend, Sean "Double I" Patel. Jackson had given Sean his nickname Double I back when they were kids. It came from the fact that Sean's mother was of Irish decent while his father was the son of an immigrant couple from India.

"Double I." Jackson said, pressing the answer button. "How's it going my man?"

Without preamble or small talk, as was typical of Jackson's close friend, Sean quickly exclaimed, "Jackson! I need you to stop by here and see me as soon as you can. It's extremely important!"

Jackson replied sarcastically, "Why yes, Sean. I'm fine. Thanks for asking. And Andrea and Kyla are doing very well too. Your concern and consideration are so greatly appreciated."

"What?" Sean answered, bewildered and briefly thrown off by Jackson's remarks. "Oh... I see. This is another one of your feeble attempts at sarcasm. Very good, Jackson. It's nice to see you're on top of your game this morning. Regardless; here's the situation. I need you to stop by my office... like now if possible. I have something very important I need to show you."

"I'd love to stop by, but I gotta tell you Sean, it's been a crazy day already." Jackson replied, not wanting to blow his friend off but also not wanting to put any more on his plate than he already had. The thing was Sean never called him during the work day unless he had something important to discuss. Jackson decided to hear him out, "So what can this humble writer do for Schuylkill County's most esteemed photographer of all things dead and rotten?"

Sean Patel's actual title was Deputy County Medical Examiner assigned to the Recovery and Identification Unit of the county's Pestilence Control Department also known as the PCD - RIU. The main focus of the department was to attempt to identify as many of the remains of dead kills as possible. With so many hundreds of thousands of people still missing in the state, survivors from all walks of life were eager to learn what might have happened to their loved ones.

At the time of the outbreak of the Z43 virus, Sean had been in medical school, and when the world began to plunge in to chaos, he never had gotten the opportunity to complete his studies. Things had still not yet returned to a state of normalcy sufficient for him to restart his education. Besides, to the best of his knowledge, his former medical college was not even back in operation the last time he had checked. However, fortunately for Sean, he had acquired enough medical knowledge to qualify for an entry-level position with the PCD five years earlier, shortly after the time of the department's inception. Eventually he managed to work his way up to deputy medical examiner with the Recovery Identification Unit (RIU). Sean felt this was not too shabby a position to have in a world that was still working its way back from the brink of extinction.

"By the way, Double I, I scored me a major dead kill this morning. You should be receiving the remains later today I would suspect. He was a biggun. Good luck with the identification. I'm not so sorry to say, I blew most of its numb head off."

"Not a problem, Jackson. As I'm sure you are aware I am extremely good at what I do, and I suspect I won't have any trouble nailing down the identity of your latest $100 trophy."

"I don't know about that Sean." Jackson replied. "He was a real mega mess. He looked like he might have been roaming around for several months; pretty rank and rotten. And the weird thing was he was really huge... I mean massive. I don't think I ever saw one that big before. It was most definitely the biggest dead head I personally ever put down. It took me three shots to do him in. One grazed the side of his head and clipped the top off his left ear. Another sunk into his shoulder and the final one went in through the eye socket."

"Hum." Sean said. "Perhaps you need to work on your marksmanship Jackson. I mean if this fellow was as big a target as you say, one would think you would have been able to hit him on the first shot."

Jackson hesitated for a moment then said, "Ok. Look. I'll admit it. I was maybe a little nervous with this one, his being so big and all. Maybe that threw my aim off a bit. But I'm telling you Double I, he was a monster."

Sean replied, "They're all monsters Jackson. Every single one of them." But Sean was thinking about something else. Some information he had recently learned about but to his displeasure could not reveal to Jackson. So instead he decided to change the subject, "Fine. So when are you stopping over to see me?"

"What makes you think I'm even in the neighborhood, Sean?" Jackson countered. "For all you know I might be three hundred miles away."

Sean said triumphantly, "I may not be world's greatest investigative freelance reporter, as you see yourself my friend; but I am a fairly bright fellow with a few connections of my own. First of all most CUs are only still only good for communications within two hundred or so mile range, so you couldn't be three hundred miles away. Secondly, if you had a dead kill this morning that I will most probably will receive shortly, it means that you must somewhere be nearby. Thirdly, I am well aware that you are here in the fine city of Yuengsville and are currently filling in over at the Skook. Am I not correct?"

"Absolutely." Jackson admitted "Apparently you do have some pretty [good] sources of your own."

"Yes I most certainly do. More than you know. And I claim my right to protect their identity and keep them secret." Sean replied. "So would you care to share what Big Bill McCleary has you working on today?"

Jackson hesitated for a moment then said, "Something big, really big Sean; something special and extremely important. And unfortunately, it's something I can't really talk to you about, at least not now. In fact, I'm on my way to meet with someone about the story right now, so I won't be able to stop by and see you for at least another hour or so. Will that fit your busy schedule?"

"Not a problem." Sean replied. "In fact if I continue to be as busy the rest of the morning as I have been so far, I suppose it would be better if what I have to show you waits until later when you get here. It's not going anywhere anytime soon."

Jackson said, "Well then, it's almost 9:00. What say I stop by your butcher shop around 11:30?"

"I don't find your crass comments about my place of employment very amusing, Jackson." Sean scolded. "The work I do here is extremely important. Perhaps not as glamorous as the action packed life of Jackson Ridge, ace reporter, but I do what I can for the greater good. So I suppose I'll see you at 11:30. And I'll make a deal with you my friend; if you still have an appetite by the time we're finished I'll be happy to buy you lunch. Although I am quite sure when you see what I have to show you, you might feel obliged to buy me lunch instead."

"Most likely knowing you, but the time I see what you have to show me I won't have an appetite any longer. And I'll have to take a rain check on lunch. I have too much on my plate already today. I can do a quick stop-by then I have to be on my way." Jackson said. Yet at the same time, Jackson was getting curious, "Ok. That sounds like a plan. By the way, can you give me some sort of hint as to what you want to show me?"

"No... I don't think so." Sean said, "I would rather wait 'till you get here. Allow me to just provide you with a teaser and say what I have to show you is something which has the potential to lead to a major story for you."

Jackson thought to himself, "When it rains it pours. It must be my day for great potential stories." He had been running through a dry spell for several months, and most of his work had been boring, everyday sort of writing. Now, in the span of an hour he had two possibilities handed to him. Then excitedly he said to Sean, "Ok. Sean, I'll definitely see you at 11:30."

He walked across to the parking lot, got into his car, and headed across town to the office of the mayor. He was both eager and apprehensive to be getting back into the investigative game again. He decided before he went any further with this assignment he had better call Andrea, make her aware of what was going on, see what she thought about it, test the waters and assure her that things would most definitely be different this time.

CHAPTER 11

"Hey Babe. How's the new job going?" Andrea Ridge asked her husband, doing her best as always to be supportive of any new writing assignments Jackson was offered. She often wondered it if really did secretly bother Jackson that he brought home much less money than she did. He claimed it didn't but still she worried. Because of this, she always wanted him to know she was in his corner and that she appreciated everything he did to try to support his family.

Jackson said, "Well. It looks like I have an opportunity for a really terrific story, but it may involve me spending a few days away from home." Jackson figured he might as well get at least some of the worst of the news out there right away because sooner or later he would have to break the rest of it to her anyway.

Andrea hesitated for a moment and the concern apparent in her silence was obvious. Then she asked. "What... what do you mean, time away from home for a few days? I thought this assignment was only a desk job for Big Bill at the Skook right? I assumed you'd be writing obituaries, engagement announcements and stuff like that. What sort of story could they possibly have that would involve sending you out of town Jackson? And for how long did you say... a few days? You know the world outside of the cities is still not a safe place to travel. I didn't even like the idea of you going down to Yuengsville today."

"Honey. I told you not to worry about that. I have my gun with me." Jackson said, not sounding very convincing. "If fact, guess what? I scored a dead kill on the way to work this morning. One hundred bucks before I even got a day under my belt. Pretty cool right?"

"Don't try to change the subject, Jackson. That dead kill is a perfect example of just how dangerous the world still is." Andrea scolded. "So getting back to my question, what's the deal here?"

Jackson waited a beat, released a sigh then said, "Right now all of that is still up in the air. I have to meet with some people in a few minutes and I'll find out more. And I don't have to take the assignment if I don't want to. I can go back to the office and do the sort of stuff we originally thought I would be doing."

"People? What people." Andrea asked. "This all sounds so cryptic to me Jackson. I need some facts here! This is all making me feel very uncomfortable."

Jackson knew exactly what his wife was referring to. She was remembering the other investigative piece; the one he, himself had just been thinking about; the same story that had become an obsession for Jackson. He realized if he were going to get her to buy into this assignment he was going to have to be completely up front and honest with her about everything.

"Listen Honey, I can tell you what I know at this point, but what I have tell you is strictly confidential. You can't say anything to anyone."

"For God's sake Jackson. I'm your wife." Andrea said. "You know you can tell me anything and it will stay between us."

"I know that honey." Jackson said consolingly. "But this is very important and what I tell you could literally mean the difference between life and death for someone."

Andrea said with even more concern now present in her voice, "Life and death? Jackson, now you're really starting to scare me. I don't think I like where all of this is heading. This new story... it's not... you know... a story like that last big story you had is it?"

"Well... I'd really like to tell you it isn't, but I don't know all the details for sure yet. However, it is highly likely that this story might actually be very similar to that other one." Jackson said cautiously. Then he quickly added, "But there's a lot more... much, much more at stake here than before."

"Oh Jackson. No! Absolutely not! Not ever again!" Andrea said angrily, "You promised me you would never get involved in a story like that again. Dammit Jackson, you gave me your word! You know what it almost did to us."

Jackson hesitated, then spoke, "Yes, of course I know. How could I possibly forget? But this time things will be different, I swear. I know I promised to stay away from that sort of thing. And I truly even considered refusing the assignment outright, but then when I found out more about it I felt I had to at least discuss it with you. Look Andrea, I'm not the same man I was then; I'm a lot smarter now. I know what to watch out for. Also, this time it's not just about me getting the story of a lifetime."

Andrea asked, "What is that supposed to mean Jackson? What are you trying to say, it's not just about a story? It's always just about the story with you. You can lie to your editor, you can even lie to yourself; but you can't lie to me."

"No babe, I promise you it's not like that this time. Last time I was different, I was younger, foolish and ambitious. I was looking to make a name for myself, and unfortunately at almost any cost. But this isn't about me or even about my writing or advancing my career. It's much more important than all of that. The stakes are far too high."

Andrea was caught off guard. She knew just how important Jackson's writing had always been to him, and to hear him say that there was something he put ahead of his chance for a great story was a very new idea for her to try to comprehend. She always believed his writing defined who he was. At times she even would have had to admit a bit of jealously; as if writing was his secret mistress.

Jackson said, "I suppose it's because of the way the world is. I don't know; maybe I'm just finally growing up or something. I think being a dad, having Kyla is what's changed me. But I'm telling you the truth sweetheart when I say that under any other circumstances I swear I would have told Bill McCleary to give the assignment to someone else. But this involves helping to save the life of a young girl; a kid."

"A young girl?" Andrea asked. "What are you telling me Honey?"

Jackson proceeded to explain the entire story of his time in Bill McCleary's office and about the kidnapping. He also told her about why it was so important that he find the girl and about how the police would be watching out for him. He wasn't exactly sure that would be the case, but he was hoping it might be.

"Oh my God, that's horrible!" Andrea said.

"Yeah. I know." Jackson replied. "When McCleary told me about Sarah I immediately thought of Kyla nine years from now and felt like throwing up. Someone has to do something to stop these people from hurting her or worse. Maybe I can find out enough to not only to save Sarah Stanton, but maybe to get some of these scumbags into the hands of the police where they belong."

Andrea said, "Yes Jackson, I understand what you're saying and why it is so important. And I know this is going to sound selfish of me but I don't care. What about us Babe? What about Kyla and me? What'll we do if something bad happens to you? It's hard enough surviving in this world with an intact family. You know how rare that is. What would happen if you were permanently injured, disabled, or maybe even killed? We'd be devastated trying to cope without you. I'd be lost without my husband and poor Kyla; what would she do without her father?"

Jackson explained, "I promise you Andrea, I won't get as deeply involved in this story as I did the last time and I swear I will stay as far away from danger as is humanly possible. My goal here is to just take a few days to snoop around, find out what I can, possibly discover what has happened to Sarah, and then call in the authorities. That's all; no more. I learned the hard way that going deep undercover is no longer an option for me. I have too much to lose to risk my life for a stupid story. You and Kyla are the two most important people in my life. You should know that. But that's also why I have to at least try to find out what happened to Sarah. If it were Kyla who had been kidnapped, I'd want everyone doing everything they possibly could do to bring her back to us, safe and unharmed."

Hearing this explanation made Andrea realize that not only was Jackson right, but maybe he truly had changed. Perhaps he had finally grown up at last. And apparently everyone from the mayor of Yuengsville to the editor of the newspaper believed Jackson to be the best man, if not the only man for the job.

The Z43 plague had been responsible for the deaths of so many people that the old idea of leaving the dirty work for someone else to clean up was no longer acceptable. There was simply no one else. She, herself had to admit what she had just gone through that morning at the death bed of Mabel Charles was something she would never have imagined herself doing ten years earlier. Now it had become a daily routine. The world had most certainly changed for the worst, and without people like Andrea and Jackson, mankind might never have survived at all.

"When would you have to leave?" Andrea asked Jackson reluctantly.

He replied, "At this point I don't know. I suspect I'll know more after I meet with the mayor and the chief of police. It's likely they'll want me to head down to the Reading area as soon as possible. I suspect perhaps as early as this afternoon or this evening. I might not have time to come home and pack my clothes and stuff for the trip. But we'll see what's what. I really don't see myself getting to Reading before this evening."

Andrea conceded, "Alright Jackson. Even though you know I'm not thrilled about this, I do see how important it is. I'll pick up Kyla after work at the daycare and bring her home. You do whatever you have to do. I'll explain to her you had to go away for a few days but you'll be coming back home soon. And you WILL be coming back home! The sooner you get on this the sooner it will all be over."

"Thanks sweetie," Jackson replied. "I want you to understand I truly don't want to do this but I feel I have to. I'll miss you and Kyla desperately and I'll do my best to get home as soon as possible. I'll also call as often as I can with updates. I'll tell you what; as soon as I'm finished with my meeting at City Hall I'll call you back and let you know what's going on. Ok?"

"Please do." Andrea said. "I'm taking an early lunch and have to go to another client at around eleven. I'll have a few hours of down time waiting for... well you know what I have to wait for... for my next patient. But I doubt the man will last much longer than that. He's been terminally ill for several months and I just got the call a few minutes ago saying he is fading fast."

Jackson said, "Honestly sweetheart, I don't know how you do this job day in and day out. You're an amazing woman Andrea. No wonder I love you so much."

Andrea replied, "It's like you said. If we don't do it, who will? We have to each do our part to help humanity make it back one step at a time. Just... well... please Jackson... just be careful."

"I will sweetie. I promise." Jackson replied. "And I'll be back home safe and sound before you know it."

"You'd better be. I'm holding you to that, Mr. Ridge!" Andrea said with genuine concern in her voice.

Jackson hesitated for a moment, then said, "You know it, Mrs. Ridge. And I'll call soon. 'love ya."

"Love you too." Andrea replied. Then she disconnected her CU.

She knew her husband and understood he was careful and wasn't in any way daring. But she also knew he would do whatever he had to do to help save the girl. Jackson might not be a big, macho muscle-bound hero, but Andrea also understood her husband would never stand by and see some innocent young girl suffer either. Suddenly an unpleasant feeling began to settle in the pit of her stomach and Andrea was not feeling very confident... not very certain about her husband's future wellbeing at all.

CHAPTER 12

"Good Morning, Mr. Ridge." Mayor Frank McKinney said as he stood and walked purposefully around his large oak desk to greet Jackson with his hand extended. Jackson could see the concern on the man's face as the mayor said, "I'm so very grateful you've agreed to work with us. I assume you've met Chief Holden." McKinney was a tall, well built man with salt and pepper hair and a natural air of congeniality while simultaneously exuding the authority a position like his demanded. Jackson suspected that no matter what position McKinney might hold, the man would instantly command the respect of those around him.

He was smartly dressed in a dark blue suit that would have been considered fashionable some time before things had changed. Now there was no real fashion to speak of, at least in small towns and cities where the luxury of being concerned about such things had not yet made a comeback. McKinney wore a crisp white shirt and a bright red tie.

Jackson could see the mayor's obvious discomfort lurking just beneath the façade of affability. Despite the mayor's best efforts, he couldn't hide his fears. Jackson supposed if it were his niece that had been kidnapped, he would never be able to appear even as much in control as the mayor now pretended to be.

"Yes. We've met briefly this morning, Mr. Mayor." Jackson said respectfully. "And please, call me Jackson."

Upon his arrival at City Hall, Jackson had been met by the chief of police, Brent Holden, who was dressed in a police Chief's uniform complete with highly polished black leather shoes. Brent had remained silent and somewhat aloof while leading Jackson down the long marble-floor corridor toward the mayor's spacious office. He suspected this was because the chief might not be happy about Jackson's involvement in the case.

Jackson was surprised to find the room tastefully decorated and much less ostentatious than the type of surroundings he had expected to find in the county courthouse. He suspected part of the mayor's appeal was the man's ability to tone down the charisma which he seemed to naturally emit, and this seemed to create more of an atmosphere of approachability. This was further demonstrated by the next words he spoke.

"And you can feel free to call me Frank," The mayor told Jackson with a vote-winning smile. "We don't like to stand on formality around here Jackson; especially among coworkers. Isn't that right, Brent? And since you will be working closely with both of us for a while, we want you to feel like one of the gang."

Jackson replied a bit uncomfortably, "Thank you, Mr. May... I mean Frank." Everything was happening far too quickly and Jackson was having difficulty coming to grips with it all. He suspected that no matter what McKinney said, he would never feel like a member of this particular gang. Yesterday he had never even met the mayor, and now they were having a private meeting and he was expected to call him by his first name.

Also, Jackson was picking up a very strange vibe from Brent Holden. He couldn't pinpoint what it was, however. He supposed it might be a bit of a reluctance on the man's part to want to work with an outsider; especially a reporter. He also sensed a bit of tension between Brent and the Mayor. He felt as if he had walked into the middle of something, but what he had no idea. And maybe he was wrong about it. He prided himself on his ability to sense such things based on body language and facial expressions, but maybe he was off base in this case. It was a tense situation, after all, and Jackson decided this might be the reason for the feelings he was getting.

Unlike the mayor, Jackson was unaccustomed to warming up to people so quickly. Most of his work as a writer was done away from the public, and when he did have to interact with people it was always on a formal or professional basis. He had just a few close friends who had managed to survive the zombie holocaust, but far too many of his former friends had not been so lucky. This tended to make his normally reserved personality even less outgoing.

The mayor said, "Bill McCleary at the Skook told me you were the best man for the job. Bill and I go way back, and even though we often find ourselves on opposite sides of an issue, we've managed to maintain a professional respect for each other. Also, I should point out that although I realize you might think this is a bit of an unorthodox approach to take to such an unfortunate situation as that which we now find ourselves facing Jackson, I'm sure you will agree these are not what one would call normal times."

Jackson thought to himself, "Wow! Only a politician could have come up with a sentence that long in the context of a normal conversation." He kept his poker face firmly in place and managed to somehow suppress the grin which wanted to escape. He watched the police chief's face and suspected he was thinking something very much the same.

Next, the mayor addressed Chief Holden and asked, "So Brent, have you had the opportunity to brief Jackson at all as to the latest information we have available?"

"No. Not yet." Holden replied. "I figured I'd wait until we all got together then go over everything."

"That sounds fine with me." McKinney said, pointing to a room just off of his main office. Its door was open, revealing a large, round conference table with a variety of documents spread out on top. "Let's all sit down and bring Jackson up to speed with everything we know."

The three took seats at the table as Brent began sorting out the papers and photos, organizing them for Jackson to see.

Mayor McKinney said, "Jackson, I assume you've been given the basics by Bill McCleary. Is that correct?"

Jackson hesitated for a moment, unsure of what exactly the basics might be, then said, "Yes... I... suppose. Bill told me this morning about Sarah being abducted last evening."

The mayor liked how Jackson had used Sarah's name rather than simply referring to her as his niece. It seemed to make him feel as though Jackson was already thinking of Sarah as a young girl in desperate trouble rather than just another assignment. Although such recognition might seem trivial to most people, McKinney was a politician and as such was accustomed to noticing the smallest of nuances in people. He was happy to see what appeared to be genuine concern coming from the man.

Then Jackson surprised both the mayor and police chief when he announced. "I also suspect it was likely not someone local who took her."

"So you know about the license plate?" Brent inquired.

Jackson replied, "Yes. Bill McCleary told me about it and the fact that the plate was registered to someone in the Reading area."

"Yes. That's true." The mayor replied. Then he glanced over at Brent Holden as if prompting him to say something.

Then Brent said, "But the stolen plate alone doesn't necessarily mean that the perp might not be local. In fact, he very well may be from this area and could have driven to Berks County for the specific purpose of stealing a plate to throw us off."

Jackson felt for some reason as though Brent was not being completely forthright with the statement he had just made, and he also had the impression that Brent might actually be testing him. So he decided to give his opinion of the situation as he saw it and stand his ground. "That could very well be the case, Brent. But based on my limited experience in matters such as this, my gut is still telling me the guy's not local."

The mayor and chief exchanged another knowing glance, then McKinney said with a troubled look, "Well Jackson, it looks like that gut of yours is right on the money. The fact is both Brent and I believe the kidnapper is most definitely from out of town. In addition, we may possibly; and I stress possibly, have a good idea who the culprit might be or at the very least, who he works for."

"That's fantastic news," Jackson said, "If we have that sort of lead, we should at least have a good head start on nailing this guy."

Brent looked from Jackson to McKinney and interjected, "Well... not necessarily I'm afraid."

Jackson examined Brent's uncertain expression as well as the mayor's troubled face and said, "OK. I have to admit, I'm a bit confused. I seem to be missing something here. What exactly don't I know?"

The police chief took a deep breath, sighed with apparent resignation and then said cautiously, "Jackson. We know you've heard of this man before; a very bad character who goes by the name of 'Deimos?"

Jackson's eyes opened wide and his throat became dry as he instantly got a hollow sensation deep in the pit of his stomach. "Did... did you say Deimos? Yes... yes... I'm most certainly well aware of him; at least by reputation. Deimos is something of a legend. His organization, or I should say a subset of his organization, was at the center of a major series of articles I wrote many years ago. But I don't understand why would you even consider mentioning him? If what I understand is true, then he couldn't possibly be the one behind this. The last thing I heard was that Deimos had been killed by a rival several years ago."

"Well." The mayor said hesitantly, "Our latest information... it leads us to believe that it's possible that Sarah...." His voice caught in his throat, which was suddenly thick with emotion.

Brent finished for him, "Um... yes... well... we have good reason to suspect Deimos is actually still alive; and that he or members of his criminal organization may be responsible for Sarah's abduction."

Jackson was shocked and horrified. How could that be? If it were somehow conceivable that Deimos truly was behind Sarah's kidnapping, then the entire situation just took a turn for the worst and the assignment just got about a hundred times more dangerous as it had been previously. He thought he knew as much about that mysterious and deadly maniac Deimos as any living person; especially since most people who learned too much generally ended up dead.

"So you're saying the rumor about Deimos' death was wrong? You believe he really is still alive?" Jackson asked.

"That's correct," Brent replied.

"But what exactly makes you think even if Deimos is still alive he would be involved in this? What interest could he possibly have with your niece?" Jackson asked, not certain he wanted to know the answer and hoping it all might be some unfortunate misunderstanding. He understood that if what they suspected were true, young Sarah might be better off dead than being alive in the hands of that madman.

Brent said hesitantly, "Well. There are several things that have led us in that direction." Then he pointed to a large, slightly blurry photo of the back end of the van used in the kidnapping. It had been taken by a local traffic camera and after enlarging it had lost some of its clarity. "As we mentioned earlier, the license plate for the van used to abduct Sarah was stolen from a car which was apparently parked along a Street in Reading, since an address on that street is what showed up on the registration. We contacted the Reading police about the plate to check out the owner. It turns out she was an elderly woman who has trouble getting around lately and hasn't driven her car in over a year. She's been trying to sell it for some time. In fact, it was still parked out at the curb with the license missing and she had no idea it was even gone."

"Ok. So the plate was definitely stolen from a car in Reading." Jackson conceded, "But I'm still not sure where all of this is going."

Brent said, "And we also learned a van similar to the one in the video was also reported stolen from the city of Reading a few days earlier. As I'm certain you know Deimos is purported to operate in and around the Berks County area, which includes the Fortified City of Reading as well as the surrounding outlands. And when we spoke with our counterparts on the Reading police force, they confirmed Sarah's kidnapping falls right in line with his M-O," Brent added.

Jackson interjected, "Oh man. That means this is gonna be rough. In the past, Deimos was known to keep his operation mobile, constantly moving it from one location to another in the outlands. In fact, from what I learned, he tended to use any one of several dozen locations for his activities at any given time. That's how he has always been able to avoid capture and prosecution.

And with all the abandoned houses in the former suburbs surrounding the city, that constitutes a lot of possible hiding places. It's believed that no one knows his real name or his history; they only know him by his alias. He is essentially a nameless ghost of a man with the financial means to keep himself surrounded by an army of followers who treat him like some sort of god."

"A false god." McKinney said. "Do you have any idea of all the things that madman has been purported to have done?"

Jackson replied as if reading from a rap sheet, "Deimos has been involved in virtually every form of illegal activity you can imagine, from robbery, drugs, prostitution, slavery, pornography to even murder." He couldn't help but notice the way the mayor seemed to cringe at the recounting of Deimos' numerous illegal enterprises. Although McKinney had already been briefed on the activities earlier, hearing them again while worrying about the condition of his young niece probably brought the reality of her plight even closer to the surface.

Jackson continued, "The name he chose for himself, Deimos, comes from Greek mythology and means 'the personification of terror'. The mythical Deimos was the son of Ares and Aphrodite. Ares was the god of war and Aphrodite was the goddess of beauty, love and sexuality. And so it's not surprising that he's chosen to make money the way he does. That's also why the little psycho gave himself that name. He thinks of himself as the product of the marriage of sex and violence."

Then Brent said "... and unfortunately, it's much worse than you may realize, Jackson. We've learned more about the modus operandi and systematic methodology in the way Deimos runs his operation."

Jackson knew little about this but had a suspicion that he was going to learn more, much more. "Methodology?" He inquired.

Brent explained, "Yes. And even under other circumstances this would still be very uncomfortable for me to explain. But in light of the fact that we believe Deimos may have Sarah, it makes the task, damned near unbearable." He looked at the mayor with a bit of visible discomfort then said, "But it must be done regardless. We've learned this morning from a very reliable source in the Berks County criminal justice system that Deimos usually starts his methodical process by kidnapping a young, attractive girl between the ages of thirteen and seventeen years old. It is believed that for the first month or so he keeps the girls hidden in places where they cannot easily be found; likely somewhere remote, private, or possibly underground; a place where their cries for help cannot be heard. And as you mentioned earlier, he has also been known to move them from location to location. He most likely transfers them quickly from the initial holding area to a site far from circulation; likely a rural farm-type of area far in the outlands."

"During this early time in captivity, Deimos gets them addicted to serious drugs, sometimes the old favorites like heroine or crack, but we've heard lately he prefers the newer, more dangerous and extremely addicting stuff like Braino."

"Ah man!" Jackson said in disgust. "No. Not Braino!"

CHAPTER 13

Braino was the street name for a fairly new drug only in existence for the previous fifteen years or so; becoming internationally known just a year or two before the plague hit. It was an extremely addictive synthetic drug derived from the combinations of both crack cocaine and heroin along several other highly addictive components. Braino was nicknamed after the old drain clog cleaner, Draino, because it did an outstanding job of cleaning out the brains of its users rather quickly, rendering them essentially mindless zombies not much different than the walking corpses which began roaming the earth a few years after the creation of the drug. It ate its way through brain cells like Draino destroyed clumps of hair and other drain remnants.

Unlike real zombies, Braino addicts often could be controlled and made to do the bidding of their handlers and they, of course, had no natural craving for human flesh. In extreme cases of Braino addiction where the person had been high for several weeks, it was often difficult to tell the difference between the living addict and the undead zombie. However, the Braino addicts didn't move as slowly and lethargically as the reanimated dead but moved much faster and as such could often be more dangerous than a zombie. Despite the fact that these poor souls were not cannibalistic, if commanded by their handlers to eat someone alive they might actually attempt to do so.

One of the reasons the plague had caught mankind by surprise and had gotten a large lead on humanity was because for some time perhaps weeks, perhaps months, those in authority thought the lumbering dead were just severe cases of Braino addiction. It wasn't until some of these so-called addicts were captured and were found to have no pulses or heartbeats, not to mention the fact that they were in various stages of decomposition, that the authorities realized something else was responsible for their condition.

Brent interrupted Jackson's thoughts. "Yes. Braino. And what we've been told is, Deimos likes to..." He hesitated for a moment, then looked uncomfortably at the mayor and asked, "Frank, maybe you don't want to hear all of this again."

The mayor stood silently for a moment, as if attempting to regain his composure, then said "Yes... um... You're probably right Brent. If um... you will excuse me Jackson. I think... I'll go over to my office for a bit. Ah... You two come out when you're finished and..." his voice caught in his throat again.

Jackson felt his own emotions beginning to come to the surface and replied. "Um... Most certainly Frank... We'll see you shortly."

Sitting silently waiting for the mayor to close the large wooden double doors between the two rooms, Jackson looked knowingly at Brent, well aware of the pain the mayor had to be feeling. Jackson then realized he had a fairly good idea of what Deimos' modus operandi was. He had learned quite a bit about just how deadly people like Deimos could be, although he never had the opportunity to actually explore the inner workings of such an operation. Jackson steeled himself for the rest of the police chief's explanation.

"Ok Jackson," Brent said taking a deep breath and returning to business. "Here is what we know. How much of it is real and how much is fictional I can't tell you. But if even a fraction of what we've learned is accurate and if Deimos does have young Sarah, then the poor girl is in real trouble. As I said earlier, Deimos has been known to kidnap young women and get them addicted to his drugs. We've heard that as soon as he gets them in his custody he begins injecting them with whatever drug he happens to feel will do the job best and most quickly. This usually goes on for a week or two."

"Also during this time the physiological and physical torture begins. It's believed that he has several of his closest and most trusted goons repeatedly rape the captive, eventually destroying her will to live as well as her self-worth. This is how he breaks his victims down and makes them feel as dead inside as the zombies walking around out there. We've been told sometimes he has his men wear masks or costumes during the rape to hide any identifying features and then he actually films the unspeakable acts to use in his various pornographic endeavors. In the case of the youngest girls, eventually the films get edited for sale on the black market as kiddy porn."

"Then once he has the girl's sufficiently mentally beaten, addicted to his drugs and basically slaves to his every command, he begins farming them out as prostitutes. That's why it's so critical that we find Sarah as quickly as possible. If Deimos really does have her as we suspect, then he will likely begin pumping her full of drugs and preparing her for a life which will be the equivalent of a Hell on Earth." Brent looked back at the closed doors leading to the main office and whispered, "To be honest with you, Jackson, Sarah would probably be better off if he killed her outright than subject her to such a fate."

"Oh man!" Jackson said with a sigh. "If that's true... I... I... just can't imagine. In my research I learned about the underground porn business as well as the prostitution, but I always thought the girls involved were runaways, druggies, or street people; castoffs who often fall prey to such ruthless men. I never imagined they might be everyday, typical young girls taken from their families and forced to become sex slaves and prostitutes. That's unspeakable! Those poor girls!"

Brent said, "You're right about that, Jackson. We don't know for sure what becomes of them after he makes them part of his stable of hookers; they simply seem to vanish from the face of the earth. But I honestly would hate to begin to imagine the hell their lives become. There've been rumors of Deimos actually selling some of his older women, like age twenty or older, into sex slavery. Such things although revolting are not unheard of."

Jackson exclaimed, "So now I guess we need to figure out what I'm supposed to do next," Jackson said anxiously. "And I'm still not exactly sure what the final results are that you want from me."

"Well... The first thing we will need you to do is to establish who actually has her," Brent said. "We need to know if it's really Deimos or if it's someone else. Whichever the case, next you'll need to find a way to locate where they might be keeping her. And that's basically it; that's all we will need from you. Once you answer those questions, we'll bring in the cavalry and take out her captors. If we get lucky we might try to take a few of them alive, but that's not really critical to the success of the operation. And to be honest, bringing most of them back dead might just send a very important message to others who are thinking of following in Deimos' footsteps."

Jackson asked, "But again. I gotta ask 'why me?' I mean, wouldn't it be better for an undercover cop or even a private detective or somebody like that to try to find her, rather than me? I'm no law man; I'm just... well I'm just me."

Brent answered, "To be honest, Jackson, I have to agree with you. You seem like a capable enough man, but I was not in favor of getting you involved from the start. I still feel this is a job for professional law enforcers and no one else. This idea cooked up between Frank and your editor Bill McCleary. We had several quite heated discussions about this."

Jackson now realized why he was likely getting the vibe of tension between the men. Brent continued, "The bottom line here Jackson is we've been assured by Bill McCleary that you have a way about you, a quality he feels is something we need to get the job done surreptitiously with as little potential danger to Sarah as possible. And like it or not, he's the mayor, which means he's the boss. Big Bill tells you have a knack for blending in and basically going unnoticed and that's exactly what the mayor believes we need here. My guess is that you can go into any corner bar, sit down, and it seems to take forever for the bartender or waitress to even stop by to offer to take your drink order. Am I correct?"

Jackson blushed slightly, "Yes that's unfortunately very true. Sometime they don't even pay any attention to me when I am sitting there with a fan of bills in my hand. It's like I'm invisible to them; like I'm not even there."

"That's what I heard." Brent replied. "That's the type of person the mayor feels we need to walk about with an ear to the ground. If people don't notice you listening or think you are irrelevant, they may be willing to say something openly they might not normally say. If we get lucky, they might say something which will lead us to Sarah. I may not totally agree with the idea, at least I didn't at the beginning. But now that I've had a chance to meet and speak with you, I think that you may be exactly what I... I mean we need."

Jackson thought about what Brent had just said for a few seconds then asked, "So where should I start and when?"

"The when is simple; as soon as possible," Brent insisted. "We need to get you to Reading preferably by tonight. You need to locate some local bars where it's likely that associates of Deimos might hang out. They may not necessarily be his henchmen but more likely lowlifes and perverts, you know, customers who buy the filth he peddles. Even if Deimos or whoever the kidnapper is has no idea you are looking for him, just being around these scumbags can be extremely dangerous. I also have to caution you, however, these few remaining seedy areas of the city will not be where the kidnappers are holding Sarah. She would more likely be held somewhere in the outlands, far away from the city; where she can be kept a convenient distance from prying eyes. The chances of you being taken right to her are very slim, but at least you may get close enough for us to find her."

Jackson thought he might have a better chance of getting to Sarah than the police chief suspected. He was already formulating a plan, but he decided to keep that to himself since it went against not only what the police were proposing but what he had promised Andrea that morning about not getting so involved. He was already starting to feel bad about some of the decisions he was making, but a young girl's life was in danger and the situation had the potential of becoming very unstable, and as such, Jackson had to prepare himself to follow his own instincts and do whatever he believed he had to do to help her. Andrea would simply have to find some way to understand that and forgive him if it came to that. At least he hoped with all of his heart she would.

To make Brent believe he was in complete agreement with his plan, Jackson said, "Although I haven't been to Reading since before... well since before this whole Zombie thing happened, I'm familiar with the kind of places you're talking about. God knows the city was full of them back then and I have a pretty good idea how I might go about blending in."

Brent said, "In that case, there's something else you need to know about the Fortified City of Reading. You may have heard stories, maybe not. It's very different than you apparently remember it. A lot has changed during the past ten years. As I'm sure you are aware, prior to the outbreak, Reading had become a virtual dung-heap of crime and poverty. Most of the residents with money had fled the city limits decades earlier for the safety of the wealthy sprawling suburbs. And as you may recall, the city was financially broke and had become a breeding grounds for criminals and low-lifes. This was how Deimos got his start. But after the dead began to rise things changed. All of the very poor people in the city suffered the same outcome of those occupants of most third-world countries. For a time they had no electricity, no medical care, and no resources to assist them. They quickly succumbed to the catastrophic effects of the plague and within a year, virtually every city resident was either dead or undead."

"Although the more affluent folks in the suburbs were well armed and able to fight off the masses of zombies, they found themselves with large properties much too spread out for them to develop any effective way to protect themselves from the ever growing numbers of undead. So groups of suburbanites formed small armies and headed back across the Schuylkill River and took back the city of Reading. They destroyed and burned all of the creatures and then surrounded the city with barricades much like we did here in Yuengsville. It became renamed the Fortified City of Reading and soon thousands of affluent, educated suburban survivors began trekking back to the city. They pumped their assets into the effort of rebuilding Reading into what has become a glorious city by the river. Within eight years almost all of the rundown buildings had been luxuriously renovated. So the Reading you think you knew has changed quite drastically."

Then Brent reached into his briefcase and pulled out two items. One was a communications unit and the other was a set of keys. "These are for you."

CHAPTER 14

"Burner?" Jackson asked looking at the CU. As with their predecessors of earlier decades known as cell phones and smart phone, CUs also could be purchased as prepaid untraceable units. There were also known to the general public as burners; a term left over from the cell phone days.

CUs weren't exactly like cell phones because the once nationwide cellular network had not yet been restored to its original strength. CU reception was often spotty at best, and the general rule of thumb was that a CU signal was only good for about two hundred miles. Depending upon the location, the distance might be a little greater, but in most cases it was often less. CUs were more like glorified walkie-talkies than true cell phones. They were fine for communicating, taking pictures and videos, like the earliest cell phones of the previous century were, but most of the high-tech features like internet access, email and the other similar advances were for the most part still unavailable.

Brent said "It's much more than just a regular run of the mill burner, Jackson. This one is very special. We can use it to track you and know where you are at all times." Considering the nature of this new assignment and the potential risk involved, Jackson was glad to hear that particular bit of news.

Holding up the CU and pointing to a black button located on the right side of the unit, Brent explained "See this black button? If you push this button you'll be able to capture and store audio files of whatever's going on around you. The device has a built in one petabyte drive, that's a thousand terabytes, so you should have enough storage space to record several weeks' worth of conversations, not that you'll need that much time. Also, as long as you're not more than one hundred and fifty miles from here, anything you record will simultaneously be sent to our command center where it will be monitored and recorded on a second, much larger drive as well. That data will also be sent to the crucial operators monitoring you in the field. To stop recording, you just have to press the button a second time. The camera on the unit works with both audio and video just like any other CU camera does, but having this black button with the audio-only feature is great for surveillance, you know for recording someone without his knowing it. For example, the CU can sit in your shirt pocket or on a table and the screen will remain dark giving no signs that any recording is taking place whatsoever."

Jackson asked, "And that red button on top of the unit, what does that do?"

"That's for you to call for help. If you press the red button twice in rapid succession it will alert us that you are in grave danger and need our immediate assistance. Then as soon as possible, help will be on the way. If you press it only once, nothing will happen, as the system was designed to take into account the potential for an accidental bump. And I really have to stress that point Jackson; no help will come if you only press the button once."

Jackson wanted to ask about exactly what sort of "help" Brent might be talking about, but he chose instead not to interrupt, as he suspected the police chief would be providing him with the rest of that information later.

Brent continued, "On the left side you'll see a yellow button. That's in case you need to protect yourself until help does arrive. If you aim the top of the CU at the intended target and press the yellow button on the side twice a sharp projectile will shoot from the top of the CU delivering a 2000 volt charge into the target. This is enough to bring down most men. If you find you need more voltage say perhaps enough to kill a man or even destroy a dead head, you keep holding in the button and the voltage will rapidly increase up to 50,000 volts. Then whatever you hit will be toast; literally and permanently."

This caught Jackson by surprise. He hadn't considered needing such a weapon before. He still had his revolver in his car, which he assumed would be all the protection he would need against man or zombie. He also knew such a thought was really only bluster on his part because although Jackson had shot his share of undead, he had never had to kill another living human being before. Come to think of it, he had never even been in a real fight in his life. He honestly didn't know if he was capable of shooting someone even if he had to. His thought was interrupted with Brent's further explanation.

"You may find yourself in a situation when you can't enter a specific area with a gun." Brent said. "We don't know for sure, but we are trying to prepare you for just about anything. If that should happen, your gun might be confiscated. But no one would likely suspect this CU as being anything more than a communications device."

"Wow. It's like you guys thought of everything." Jackson said.

Brent replied, "We were fortunate in that we already had most of this technology already in our possession. We've done our best with the extremely short amount of time we've had available, Jackson, but to be honest, even if we did have more time, no one can be assured to cover every possible contingency; only those we can anticipate."

Jackson inquired, "And the keys? What are they for?"

Brent explained, "We know your old Toyota has shall we say, some reliability issues. I wanted you to have something you could count on. I figured you would be better off with a vehicle that was a little bit newer."

"But if I'm supposed to blend in with the crowd down there, wouldn't I be better off with a beater like mine rather than something new?" Jackson asked.

"I didn't say NEW Jackson. I said NEW-ER." Brent explained. "We have a beater of our own in mind which we use for undercover work. It's a 2030 Hizan Imperial sedan. It looks almost as bad as yours but it runs like a champ. Plus it's equipped with a similar tracking device as your CU and has multiple micro audio/video cameras mounted on both the inside and the outside. We will know what's going on with you at all times."

"Big brother." Jackson said.

Brent replied, "Yeah. But this is the kind of big brother you actually want watching you. If you get into a jam any time you are in or near the car, we'll know instantly what the nature of the problem is and where you are. You will be monitored from both the ground and satellite as well."

"Wow!" Jackson exclaimed. "I really didn't expect that sort of support. I thought I'd be pretty much on my own."

"We're pulling out all the stops we can here Jackson. This is way too important." Brent said. "We realize the mayor wants us to stay in the shadows while you do your thing, but that doesn't mean we have to throw you to the wolves. In fact, our plan is for you to actually be safer on this assignment than you were this morning coming from the Ashton Cooperative down to Yuengsville." Jackson recalled his close encounter with the dead kill that morning and knew what Brent said was probably true.

"Unfortunately, I wish we had more resources to offer you, but sadly we don't. Even with focusing all available manpower to support you, we could only free up a handful of specially trained officers. We can only hope that'll be enough. The important thing is that you need to come up with some possible leads to where Sarah is being held, then notify us and let my men do what they do best."

Jackson said, "I'll do everything I can, Brent. I promise."

Brent replied somberly, "I believe you will, Jackson. I can only hope your best effort and our support will be enough to bring both Sarah and yourself back safely. I know you have a wife and family, and that makes your wellbeing even more important to us. But even with all the support we have to offer you, this is still a potentially dangerous assignment. If you find out that Deimos actually is the kidnapper, then the danger will instantly double."

No one understood that better than Jackson himself. During the investigation for his earlier story, he had heard firsthand accounts from unfortunate individuals who knew just how much of a lunatic Deimos was and exactly how dangerous he and his cadre of criminals, perverts, and drug dealers could be. Although Jackson's exposure to Deimos' criminal empire had only come in the form of fringe elements, local criminals, he did know that some of these low-level flunkies worked for people who had reported directly to Deimos, and even those seemingly unimportant thugs, although ruthless and psychotic themselves were terrified at the very mention of Deimos' name.

Jackson could scarcely imagine just how terrible someone had to have been to rise to the top of that merciless criminal empire. He had often wondered during his investigation and subsequent stories series if Deimos had known about him and about what he had been writing. Jackson suspected not or else he would likely have been killed; not to mention Andrea and Kyla as well, and it was that fear of potential danger brought on by those stories which had caused so many problems between Andrea and Jackson.

Jackson reached out instinctively and took the CU from Brent, tucking it into his pants pocket. His personal CU was still in his shirt pocket. Then he accepted the keys for his "newer" car as well.

"The car's parked right out front," Brent said. "It's the only one that doesn't look like a cop car. You can't miss it."

"All right," Jackson said, "I suppose I'm as ready as I'll ever be. Let's do this."

"Just one minute." Brent said. "There are two other things I have to show you and explain." He handed Jackson a plastic card. "This is a prepaid credit card with a balance of $5,000 on it. We certainly don't expect you to need that much but it's better to have it available, just in case. We know you won't have time to go home and get your clothes so we assume you'll be buying whatever clothing you think you'll need for the next few days, perhaps when you get to Reading this evening. They have all sorts of excellent clothing stores in the city and there are also a few roadside trading posts outside of the city limits, but I would recommend staying away from those places. They're generally second hand stores and often run by less than desirable types."

"I believe I've heard about those places." Jackson said.

Brent continued, "Yeah, they tend to be a bit seedy and we've also had reports that the owners often participate in questionable trade practices. On the other hand, despite my misgivings, they might be just the sort of place you might want to use to find the kinds of clothing you'll need to blend in with the lower class crowds. The stores in the city tend to be higher end with better quality clothing."

Then Brent reached down and picked up the battered suitcase. "We also assumed you'd need something to put your clothing into that wouldn't look too new, so we're providing you with this." As he spoke he opened the top of the suitcase and Jackson was shocked to see there was a large amount of cash inside.

"Wow! That's a lot of cash. What's all that for?" Jackson asked.

"Sometimes," Brent said conspiratorially, "You may need to grease some wheels and only cash will do. There is $10,000 in cash in this briefcase."

Jackson was shocked. "Ten grand? In cash?"

"Yes." Brent replied. "It was Frank's idea. He insisted. He wants you to feel free to use it as you deem necessary to get any information which will bring Sarah home safely. And just so you know; when we have her back again you will receive an additional $10,000 reward care of Mayor McKinney."

"What?" Jackson said with shocked surprise. "Look, I'm not looking for any reward here. I agreed to take on this assignment just as part of my job. All I want is to do whatever I can to get this poor girl home and maybe get a good story in the process."

Brent hesitated for a moment and said, "I know that Jackson. And more importantly, the mayor knows it as well. And it's because he knows it that he has decided you should be rewarded for positive results."

"But I can't promise him anything. I can't guarantee that I'll be successful," Jackson said. "Come on Brent. For all we know she might be... well she might already be dead. I certainly hope not, but we really don't know that for sure. Do we?"

"I understand completely and I'm sure the Mayor does as well. All he asks you to do is to try... and to try your best." Brent explained. "No one has any right to expect more than that." Then he extended his hand in a parting gesture, signaling it was time for Jackson to be on his way.

With that, Jackson shook the chief's hand and headed out of the office. As he passed the Mayor's desk, he saw it was empty. Jackson understood Frank McKinney couldn't allow the running of the city to take a back seat to his niece's crisis. That's why Jackson was here. Then it suddenly hit home just how much they all were depending on him. He could only hope he was up for the task.

As Jackson approached the foyer of the courthouse, he felt a strange sensation, as if he were being watched. He stopped for a moment and looked around the area. Down one of the hallways off to his right he saw a man in a police uniform standing in shadows, apparently staring at him. The man appeared to be a younger, well-built officer. Jackson tried his best to make out the man's face, but it wasn't visible. Jackson took a step in the police officer's direction and the man instantly turned and hurried down the hall.

An odd feeling suddenly came over Jackson; one of great discomfort. Although he hadn't been able to make out the man's expression, Jackson got a weird vibe from the man and wondered if it were possible the stranger was watching him. And why would that be? Was it possible the man was tailing him to report his actions to someone else? If so to whom? Maybe he was gathering information to report to someone who operated outside the law; someone like Deimos.

Jackson had no idea where such an idea had come from, perhaps it had been the man's body language; perhaps it was simply his own imagination, but the sensation was the strong type of gut feeling, which had never failed him in the past. He had been warned that some of the police might not be cooperative with him, but something about that man's demeanor went beyond a simple lack of cooperation; something about him seemed very strange.

Shaking off the disquieting feeling and walking out the front door, Jackson immediately recognized the car he was to use parked just where Brent had told him it would be. Jackson stood and looked at the vehicle, thinking about just how bizarre the day had been so far and wondering how much stranger it was going to get.

CHAPTER 15

Jackson took his CU out of his shirt pocket and attempted to call Andrea, but the call went right to voice messaging. He realized she was likely getting ready for her next appointment of the day. She always dropped Kyla off at the Ashton daycare first thing in the morning. He knew she had an appointment right after that to deal with Mabel Charles, who was in her final days. It was likely according to Andrea that today would be the day the woman might pass on. Jackson understood the stressful nature of his wife's job and knew she often liked to have some peaceful time between appointments. She'd occasionally turn off the alert on her CU so she could have a few moments to sit and relax or sometimes take a walk; anything to prepare her for the demanding task ahead. Jackson had told her many times how he had no idea how she could do her job day in and day out. He decided to leave her a voice message knowing she'd call back as soon as it was convenient.

"Honey. It's me. I just wanted to let you know I've decided to take the assignment, as I'm sure you already knew I would. I promise you I'll finish this up as quickly as possible and I'll be home safely in a few days. The police have assured me I'll have plenty of protection and will be monitored round the clock." Jackson hesitated for a moment and then said with a nervous chuckle, "See. It's already different than last time. This time I have plenty of help and won't be left to my own devices... um... ok... well... I guess that's it... I love you sweetheart and know how tough this will be for you and Kyla... but we both know... there just is too much at stake here for me to not do this. Please call me when you get some time. I love you Baby. Kiss Kyla for me and tell her Daddy will be back home soon."

He put the CU back into his shirt pocket and climbed into the car. Next, he decided he'd head over to see his friend Sean at the medical examiner's office as he had promised. He knew he probably shouldn't take the time, and if he truly was being monitored, the police might not like this unscheduled stop very much. However, Sean had said that what he needed to tell Jackson was important, and Sean never wasted his time. The cops would simply have to understand. Besides, Jackson suspected the people he would need to observe in Reading were people of the night and not early risers. Jackson was certain the slight time delay would not affect his assignment whatsoever.

A few minutes later, Jackson was walking through the back entrance into Sean Patel's forensic lab. Although this particular mode of entry was in complete disregard to government regulations, it was something he always did. Sean was hunched over a stainless steel table on wheels, apparently working on the remains of what was once a human being but now seemed to be a pile of barely identifiable decomposing flesh. The mass appeared to be a man, but Jackson was uncertain as its sex was indiscernible to an untrained onlooker. Sean was scraping bits of flesh for DNA analysis. Jackson saw Sean's digital finger print scanner next to the cadaver and understood Sean had also taken its prints.

The exhaust fans hummed loudly in the room, drowning out most other ambient noises. Jackson wondered if perhaps this very special CU the police chief had given him might be monitoring him right now, regardless of the fact that he hadn't pressed any of its hot keys. He didn't normally trust the powers that be; he couldn't help himself, it was just the way he was made. Call it paranoid, Jackson didn't care. Maybe it was his natural reporter's skepticism.

He wondered if the noisy fans would do anything to drown out his conversation with Sean in the event that he actually was being monitored. All he knew was the exhaust system was doing very little to suppress the vile stench that presently permeated the room. Jackson had no idea how his friend could stand to work in such a horrible-smelling place day after day. He supposed Sean must have gotten used to the stench, but how he had managed to do so was beyond Jackson's comprehension.

A camera was mounted on an overhead gantry capable of sliding along the length of the corpse's body and which would be used to photograph any discernible characteristics that might prove useful in someday positively identifying the remains for notification of living relatives. Sometimes something as simple as an odd birthmark, scar or more likely a tattoo would prove invaluable in the identification process. There was also a microphone on a long, extendible metal arm over the table and two video cameras mounted at either end of the work area. These were used to provide complete audio/video documentation of the identification procedure for future reference as per government regulations. Jackson noticed the recording equipment was currently inactive.

"I don't suppose you got my dead kill from this morning yet," Jackson asked matter-of-factly as he approached the table.

Sean jumped reflexively having been startled by Jackson's arrival and scolded, "Dammit Jackson! How many times must I tell you to use the main entrance and to sign in at the visitor's registry? You know that's protocol."

"Yeah, yeah, yeah," Jackson said flippantly. "But if you truly wanted me to come in the front door, why'd you give me the combination for the rear door keypad? I'm fairly certain that's not protocol either."

"Obviously it was a momentary lapse of good judgment on my part." Sean replied. "One of these fine days I'll have to change that passcode, and when I do, I guarantee you'll not be told of it. And then you'll have to use the main door just like all the rest of the rabble."

Jackson put on a look of feigned hurt, grabbing his chest, and said, "But Double I, you cut me to the quick with such horrible insults."

"Well you were lucky I'm here alone here and that I was expecting you." Sean explained, "If it were Dianado or McGinley here instead of me, you might find yourself lying on this table with a bullet in your brain. Those two tend to be much more alert and much more nervous than I. They both also have a tendency to shoot first and ask questions later." Dianado and McGinley were lab techs that Jackson had met during previous visits. Both of the men wore holsters with large caliber hand guns all the time. They never took them off.

"Well that's not necessarily a bad strategy to have these days, all things considered." Jackson admitted. "Anyway, here I am as you requested, but I can't stay long. I am in a major hurry, so you'd better show me what you have for me so I can be on my way."

Sean was not in the least offended by Jackson's brusqueness, as he was equally busy himself. He pointed to a door across the lab. "In there. Go in and check it out. I'll be with you in a minute, as soon as I finish up here. Let me know what you think."

Perplexed by his friend's suggestion, Jackson walked over to the large steel door, which he knew led to what they called 'the cooler'. It was a refrigeration unit used for short term storage of cadavers. Jackson opened the door and stepped inside. The overhead florescent lights came on automatically as his presence was sensed by the system. He hadn't been in the cooler for a long time and had forgotten how overpowering the stench of so many rotting corpses could be and how little either the ventilation system or frigid air did to suppress the odor, which was as bad if not worse than out in the lab.

The room was of stainless steel construction, about twenty feet square with rows of steel mesh roll-out shelving, which hung from all the walls. Each shelf held a stainless steel tray and almost all of them held naked cadavers in various stages of decomposition. Each body was accompanied by a bright orange digital coded flag.

The cooler was used as a staging area for PCD - RIU activities. When a dead kill was brought in for identification; it was placed on one of the steel shelves in the cooler. When Sean or one of his associates were ready to begin the identification process, they would wheel a roller cart into the cooler, raise it to the desired height, slide a corpse on the cart, and then wheel it back out to the main lab to begin their work. As this point they would remove the digital flag, sanitize it, then place it into a plastic bag in an out-basket. Several times a day, the flags were retrieved by a member of the clerical staff who then would place the flags in envelopes to mail back to their appropriate owners for reuse at some time in the future. Next, the staff member would double check to assure that the appropriate person received the correct dead kill bounty amount credited to the right bank account. Any discrepancies would usually be ironed out at this stage in the process.

Once the medical staff had acquired everything they needed from the cadaver, the examiner would attach a new tag to the corpse, stating it was awaiting final identification. Traditionally this was a toe tag, but depending upon the condition of the corpse, toes might not be available. Then the tag might have to be either tied or stapled at one of several other remaining areas as designated by the appropriate protocol.

Next, the body would be moved to a much larger long term storage facility in an adjacent building, where it would be stored until identification was complete. When a body was positively identified, any relatives still among the living would be contacted. They would then be offered a menu of options for disposal of the remains and if desired, a memorial service. If after ninety days in the long-term facility a body had been deemed unidentifiable, it was removed from storage and cremated in accordance with government regulations. Gone were the burn piles. Now each unidentified body was burned in sanitary, non-polluting cremation units. In the beginning of the plague, such a system of identification was not possible, due to the sheer numbers of undead, but now that things had become less of an issue the process seemed to work quite well.

Jackson stood in the glow of the florescent lights looking about at the racks filled with dead kills. One or two of the long bulbs blinked on and off overhead. He knew it was nothing more than a failing bulb, but the strobe-like effect in the room full of once walking corpses was nonetheless disquieting. It was like a scene from every bad horror movie he had ever watched.

He looked around and saw the various shelves stacked with corpses; each a dead kill, and as such each was accompanied by a barcoded flag. Reaching into his shirt pocket, he retrieved his personal communications unit. Jackson press an on-screen icon triggering an application called "Dead Kill Finder" and immediately heard a beeping sound coming from the front right side of the room. He walked slowly toward the noise and found a large male dead kill stuffed on a rack. And it was not just any dead kill, but his kill from earlier that day.

"Stuffed" was exactly the right words to use to describe its condition as the cadaver was so large that its chest pressed against the bottom of the shelf above it. It even appeared to Jackson as if the stainless steel shelf which held the corpse might be bowing slightly under its incredible weight. A red light on the flag lying next to the body was blinking in time with the beeping sound coming from Jackson's CU. It was definitely his flag and definitely his dead kill. Seeing the size of the beast squeezed onto the narrow shelf made him wonder how he had ever managed to remain calm enough to put the creature down.

"So what do you think?" Sean said from behind him as he entered the cooler.

Jackson replied, "It's fine, I guess. But I already saw this critter earlier today when I blew his brains out. Remember? Why in the world do you want me to look at it again?"

"I don't." Sean explained, "Your double-dead rather large friend here is not why I called you. His presence is merely a coincidence. What I really wanted to show you is on that table over there underneath that sheet."

CHAPTER 16

Jackson walked over to the table and pulled back the sheet halfway down the length of the cadaver's body and let out a gasp of surprise. Had been in no way prepared for what he would find beneath the sheet. The body was that of a young, naked woman, perhaps only twenty-two years old; her large breasts hung down slightly at her sides. Jackson could see that despite her mottled and sagging skin, decomposing condition, and the bullet hole though the center of her forehead, she had once been very attractive, perhaps even beautiful. Actually in his opinion, she still was not that bad looking; although that momentary thought disturbed him immensely.

"Whoa!" Jackson said with disbelief as he did his best to suppress a shudder which wanted to course through him. A thousand questions raced through his mind. "What... I mean who... I mean dammit, Sean... why are you showing me this? You know how I hate these freakin' dead things... and to see one... one so young... and... so... so... beauti... Jesus man! This is so wrong on so many levels."

Scan waited a beat then said, "Sorry Jackson. I suppose I hadn't anticipated your reaction. I deal with these things every day and they tend to arrive in all ages, races, shapes and sizes. They usually don't faze me in any way. But to be honest with you, even for me... seeing one like... well like her... is very disturbing and memorable to say the least."

"So what gives?" Jackson asked, confused and still with a note of displeasure in his quivering voice. He felt dirty and ashamed. The girl was still attractive enough that she stirred something deep inside of Jackson, which he never wanted to admit might occur while viewing a corpse. Feeling that way and seeing the pretty young girl in such a horrible condition made him feel filthy; as if he were no better than the rabble that took part in watching Z Porn. He felt as if he needed to go home and take a shower, not just because of the foul stench in the room but because he simply felt unclean. "So what's the deal Sean? Why would you have me look at this stinking thing anyway?"

Sean hesitated again, then said "She's not the first one I've seen... you know like this... very good looking... you know what I mean?"

Now Jackson was starting to get really creeped out. He had known Sean since childhood and had thought he knew his friend very well. But maybe there was a darker, more twisted side to Sean Patel; one he had never seen before. Or perhaps it was a case of job stress taking its toll on his overworked friend. It couldn't possibly be good for anyone spending his days dealing with nothing but rotting corpses. Jackson stared at his friend and simply nodded with bewilderment. Then he could see something else was bothering Sean, so he decided to remain quiet and see where all of this was going. He knew if there was something important to discuss, Sean would tell him eventually, in his own way.

"Look closely at her Jackson." Sean said. "Look at her neck. Tell me what you see."

Reluctantly, Jackson bent over the cadaver and glanced down at her neck. Then he saw it, bruising. It was apparent even to Jackson's untrained eye that someone had attempted to strangle the woman with something. But he couldn't imagine why. Everyone knew the only way to put these dead things down was by killing their brains. Strangulation would have done no good whatsoever. And this one also had a bullet hole in the front of her skull. He looked at Sean and said "Looks like ligature marks from a rope or something of that sort. Maybe someone had her tied up or leashed after she turned. Very odd."

"Odder than you might think." Sean replied. "Long before this woman had found her way onto my table and most likely just before she became one of them, she was strangled, murdered I suspect. Those marks were made perimortem... just before she died. Now look at her arms."

Jackson looked at the arms which lay upturned at the dead woman's sides. At the hollows of her elbows, he saw what Sean was referring to; track marks, old track marks, the sure sign of a drug abuser. "Junkie!" Jackson said with surprise. "She was obviously a user and I'd be willing to bet she was a hooker as well."

"Yes" Sean agreed. "You are correct, at least about the drug use. I would have to surmise she might have been a prostitute as well. But I believe there may be more to the story than that Jackson. It will be a while until I get back the tox screen results, but I'm willing to bet they find traces of not only crack and heroine in her body, but Braino as well."

"Braino? Not that crap." Jackson said with unabashed disappointment.

"Yep. And I can almost guarantee something else." Sean said. "If we manage to identify her, we will likely find out that she dropped off the radar some eight to nine years ago."

Now Jackson found himself suddenly paying more attention and asked, "But how in the world can you possibly know that Sean?" Then he recalled what Sean had said earlier. "You said you've seen this before. What were you talking about?"

Sean walked over and pulled the sheet back over the dead woman's head, much to Jackson's relief, then said, "Come with me."

Jackson's reporter's instincts were now on high alert. He understood Sean had stumbled onto something really important, and Jackson suspected he was not going to like what he was about to see. He followed Sean out of the cooler and reentered the main lab area where Sean walked to a file cabinet marked "Private - SP". It was secured with a combination lock, which Sean expertly opened.

"I've been noticing a pattern since I've taken over as deputy medical examiner. It has only occurred a few times over the years but enough to have made me curious and eventually suspicious." Sean said, pulling five file folders from the drawer. He laid the documents on a nearby counter and opened each one. "See the pattern?"

Jackson looked down at the open folders, each of which revealed the photo of a dead kill. Each one of the bodies depicted was that of a different young woman, all of them around the same age as the body in the cooler and equally as attractive. Also, each one had identical bullet wounds in the center of their foreheads.

"Look at the section of the report labeled 'Noticeable markings, tattoos, bruises or scars.'" Sean suggested.

Jackson read Sean's descriptions and although each girl had their own distinguishing tattoos and scars, one thing they all had in common was perimortem bruising around the neck, likely caused by a ligature. They also each showed traces of petechial hemorrhaging in the eyes common with strangulation. However, due to the varying degrees of deterioration of the bodies at the time of dead kill, a definite cause of original death could not be determined.

"Wait a minute!" Jackson said. "You mean to tell me you think each of these girls were killed by strangulation before coming back as... well as one of those things?"

"Yes." Sean said with conviction. "I believe we have a serial killer who has been using the Z43 plague and the chaos caused by the outbreak to hide his murders. If you think about it, it's almost the perfect crime."

"Almost perfect?" Jackson asked. "It sounds pretty damned perfect to me."

Sean replied with his typical abruptness. "I say almost because you see, the killer had not anticipated my involvement. He most likely assumed he could get away with his crimes because of the confusion caused by our current living conditions. Hell, maybe he still thinks everything is so disorganized that he can do whatever he pleases and no one will be the wiser."

"Man! That pretty twisted!" Jackson exclaimed.

Sean said, "Perhaps even more twisted than you might realize. What if this killer is so far gone, mentally I mean, that he simply doesn't care if or what anyone finds out? I mean, if that's the case, he is much more dangerous than I originally suspected. And for your information Jackson, there are even more similarities between the victims."

"Like what?" Jackson asked.

"With the exception of that young lady on the table in there, each of the victims has been positively identified. And although they were all from different areas of Pennsylvania, each of them had been reported missing sometime during the past nine years, and most were between thirteen and sixteen years old at the time of their disappearance."

Jackson felt a sinking feeling in the pit of his stomach as he suddenly thought about young Sarah, then a cold chill ran down his spine. "What else did they have in common?" He asked somewhat reluctantly.

"In every case, including our latest Jane Doe, each of the girls had traces of serious drugs in their tissues which were present at the time of their initial death including as I said earlier, heroine, crack, and even Braino." Sean explained.

"Man oh man," Jackson said with frustration. "Just what in the hell are we looking at here, Sean?"

Sean replied honestly, "I really don't know Jackson. But something no good I'm certain. You know I'm very proficient at putting together facts as I find them, but supposition and speculation is not my forte. But you, my man, are the ace investigative reporter, so I leave it up to you to take my facts and figure out what they all might mean."

If he were being completely honest with himself, Jackson would have to admit he was terrified about what it truly might mean. "Ballistics, Sean? Did any of the bodies have bullets still in them?" Jackson asked.

"Unfortunately not." The entry hole in the front appeared to be made by a thirty-eight caliber weapon but the entire back of their skulls were blown out. I had hoped to get lucky and find one lodged in the brain or something, but no such luck. Depending upon how decomposed these things are their skulls are often soft and easily destroyed."

Then Jackson thought of something else and asked, "Sean, these girls.... Each of them arrived here as a dead kill right? Well, who claimed the bounty?"

"Ah yes. Again, if it were only so simple." Sean replied. "Something else they all have in common is that each of them was dumped in a place where they could easily be found and reported to one of the retrieval squads. And no one ever tried to claim any bounty."

"Is that legal?" Jackson asked.

Sean looked at him as if he had just grown a second head and said, "Legal? Well no, not really. But it happens sometimes. And honestly, Jackson, do you really think an insane serial killer would care about some infraction as minor as dumping a corpse?"

Jackson realized just how foolish his question had been and was instantly sorry he had asked it. "Yeah. You're right. I guess I wasn't thinking straight. Wow! There are just many thoughts going through my mind; all at the same time."

"Well now you know everything I know." Sean said. "If my predictions are correct, that girl in the cooler will be the sixth girl in a series of strangulation murders. That is to say, at least those of which I am aware. There may be others. So you can see Jackson, this could be a real story in the making."

Jackson replied, "Yeah. You're definitely right about that. But I have to ask why didn't you just turn all this information over to the police? If there is an obvious crime here shouldn't they be looking into this?"

"On the contrary," Sean explained. "I have spoken with the Chief of Police Brent Holden himself and tried to get him interested in my information, but I couldn't seem to get him to take me seriously. He said he and his men were far too busy with 'real cases' to waste time on what he called my unfounded suppositions."

"You've got to be kidding me," Jackson said with disbelief. That didn't sound like something the Brent Holden he had met that morning would have said. Jackson was quite surprised. But then he realized he had only just met the man and didn't know him very well. It was possible that maybe on an extremely busy day he might go out of his way to avoid getting involved in something suggested by a simple assistant medical examiner. Jackson was certain the man's plate was overflowing most days. Then he thought again about the CU he had gotten from Holden and wondered if the police might be listening in on this conversation.

So Jackson said, "I just met Brent Holden a few minutes ago and he seemed like a pretty reasonable guy. Maybe when I'm finished with my current assignment I can talk to him for you and maybe get him to change his mind. But right now I'm up to my ears with work. But I'll tell you what, just hang onto these files and keep them locked up. I really want to make the time to look more closely at them. So as soon as I'm free I'll be happy to look into this further. I believe you Sean and I honestly think you have a real story here."

But back somewhere in the darkest recesses of his mind Jackson was thinking the unthinkable and hoping against hope he was wrong. He was formulating the crux of an idea. Each of these dead girls had once been attractive young teenagers who had disappeared and all ended up drug addicts, probably prostitutes, and were eventually strangled. Then each had been shot in the same way through the center of the skull. He couldn't help but notice the coincidence between their disappearances at a young age and Sarah's kidnapping. And that thought bothered him more than he cared to mention. In his gut, Jackson knew something horrendous was going on and it was very possible that Sean's discovery might actually have something to do with Jackson's current case. He just hoped to God he was wrong.

Then Sean handed Jackson a small object, which he immediately recognized as a DMSD or Digital Mass Storage Device. It looked very much like the old USB thumb drives used during the early part of the century but was much more powerful. The tiny device could store one hundred terabytes of data for starters and could be read not only by computers but by communications units as well.

"I scanned everything in these folders and put all the information on that DMSD along with anything else I managed to dig up." Sean said. "It's the smallest DMSD I could find but it's still quite large. There's tons of extra storage space still available. I figured you could use it for storing whatever you discover when the time comes. Keep it with you at all times; don't share it with anyone, and if you can find some time, please look over the files."

"Thanks Double I." Jackson said. "I'll do what I can as soon as possible. I promise."

Sean replied, "Very good, Jackson. And as soon as I have more information for you on our Jane Doe, I'll send it to your CU as well."

Jackson shook Sean's hand and turned to leave when Sean said "Be very careful out there Jackson, my friend. I don't know what your latest assignment might be, but we both know that there are many dangers out there perhaps much worse than these walking corpses."

"I know." Jackson said. He knew as well as anyone just how violent and dangerous his fellow man could be. "I'll be careful. And I'll speak with you in a few days."

CHAPTER 17

Jackson was on his way south to Berks County, traveling along Route 61 about twenty miles from the protective boundaries of the Yuengsville Free Zone, heading toward the Fortified City of Reading. There were very few towns still in existence along the route, save for a handful, which Jackson heard were located a few miles off of Route 61. The rest of the battered highway was like a no man's land. So far, the trip had been basically uneventful. Jackson had seen only a few vehicles since leaving Yuengsville.

The first had been a piece of farm equipment stopped in a nearby cornfield. The corn was tall and ready for harvesting. Under normal circumstances Jackson would not have been able to see the workers over the tops of the tall cornstalks, but the section of field behind the farmer had already been harvested and the equipment was sitting in a clear patch near the side of the highway. There appeared to be something going on with the equipment, so Jackson slowed down to try and determine if the farmer and his lookouts needed any assistance.

Gone were the days when the lone farmer could be seen riding his plow or combine across an open field. Very little farming was still done outside of the protective barriers of the towns and cities. However, though the cities had sections reserved for farming, there was often not enough farm land to go around, so sometimes more adventurous farmers took it upon themselves to farm outside of the protected city limits. Obviously, these farmers were willing to take the risks associated with this sort of endeavor, and Jackson had to commend them for their courage. Those farmers willing to do so put together teams consisting of the equipment driver as well as one or two lookouts armed with rifles, watching out for the undead.

Jackson noticed the farmer and one of his lookouts busy trying to remove something which was jammed in the sharp, triangular blades of the machinery; the other helper was still standing watch with his rifle at the ready. Jackson noticed that in addition to watching the surrounding fields, the lookout also kept glancing in his direction with suspicion.

After coming to a stop Jackson could see what the cause of the problem was. An undead creature, one which must have been randomly walking through the cornfield, had somehow gotten caught in the machine's sharp blades. Although the thing was trapped it still continued waving its arms wildly and trying desperately to get its gnarled fingers on any of the three nearby humans. The blades were now coated with a mess of torn flesh and black, splattered blood. It was obvious even from his distant vantage point that the creature was nothing but shredded pulp from the waist down, yet it still struggled to get free. As Jackson looked on, one of the lookouts raised his weapon and blew what remained of the creatures brains out, sending a shower of gore across the front of the combine.

"Farming in America in 2053" Jackson said to himself. After the immediate danger from the creature had been eliminated, the three farmers turned and looked out suspiciously at Jackson's car, not sure of his intentions. Jackson supposed these rugged farmers had encountered so many dangers in their line of work that their trust level, even for their fellow man, was all but gone. They realized he could be as much of a danger to them as the creature they were busy scraping off their blades had been. He gave them the friendliest wave he could come up with and pulled back out onto the highway.

Another vehicle he had seen along the highway had been a rescue unit, previously known as an ambulance during the early part of the century, en route to Yuengsville. It was in the oncoming lane, traveling at a moderate speed and trying its best to avoid potholes and craters. Later Jackson saw two other trucks which appeared to be some sort of mini convoy of military vehicles which turned off Route 61 and headed down some side road to parts unknown. Other than those, he saw a few other assorted cars in the oncoming lanes, but there were none behind or in front of him.

This lack of traffic allowed Jackson the time to think about his destination. He had not been to the city of Reading in over ten years; since before the outbreak. In fact, he hadn't been south of Yuengsville during most of that time either. As a result, he realized with dread he had little knowledge of what to expect when he got there other than what Brent Holden had told him. He also couldn't determine what sort of trouble he might encounter along his way. For Jackson, this was uncharted territory.

He reached over on the passenger's seat and placed his hand on his 45, enjoying the comfort it brought to him. It had served him well over the past several years and had brought down dozens of dead heads. He thought again of how he had never needed to use it against a living human before and hoped he would never have to.

Jackson likewise felt a bit more confident than he normally would have thanks to the fact that somewhere out there, out of site; someone was monitoring his movements and making sure he was safe. At least that's what Chief of Police Holden had told him was the case. He had no idea how many officers had been assigned to him or how long it might take them to get to him in the event of an emergency, but he was nonetheless grateful for at least the additional comfort the thought brought to him.

Jackson recalled how the city of Reading had once been considered a small to medium size city and was separated from the boroughs of West Reading and nearby Shillington by the Schuylkill River. The only ways to cross the river from that side of town was via the Penn Street Bridge, the Buttonwood Street Bridge, an old railroad bridge, and the Bingaman Street Bridge. Chief Holden had told Jackson that both the Buttonwood and Bingaman bridges as well as the railroad overpass had been deliberately destroyed during the early days of the plague, leaving the Penn Street Bridge as the only remaining western access to the city spanning the Schuylkill River.

Several other entrance roads on the Northern, Southern, and Eastern sides of the city were by land and were also controlled by security stations. Since Jackson was heading along Rt. 61, he had decided he would enter along that route at the northern end of town and then work his way deeper into the city from there. He recalled an area on the west side of the city and not too far from the Penn Street Bridge.

Brent had told him there was a bar or two down by the river in a still ungentrified section of the city which were places known to be frequented by the lower classes. Jackson realized anyone coming into the city from the western outlands would probably frequent these establishments rather than the more upscale inner city places, so this seemed to Jackson to be an area which would likely be as good a place as any to begin his search.

The car Holden had provided was equipped with a built-in GPS system and map display. Although somewhat limited, the map was apparently up to date because so far, every detour and closed route he saw along the highway matched perfectly with the displayed map. The system told him he was now approaching the former location of a town he recalled had once been called Shoemakersville, 'Shoey' by locals. It was now nothing more than ruins of former roadside businesses and residences. In fact, the area now looked more like a forest or jungle than the site of a once bustling community. Trees of surprising size grew wildly among the decaying structures; some as high as thirty feet.

Jackson had never thought about it before, but the trees did seem to be growing much faster than he had previously recalled them doing. Perhaps it was simply a matter of rapidly growing trees becoming more prevalent; or maybe it was something else. Ten years ago he would have scoffed at the idea of trees suddenly growing at an increasing rate, but back then he would have never believed the dead might actually arise, walk, and start feasting on the living. Maybe a few varieties of trees growing faster than usual might not be so unrealistic after all.

The wild foliage grew out through empty window frames and up through cracks in the concrete. Some of the buildings had tree branches bursting through their roofs and out through demolished chimneys. Nature was apparently determined to take over and reclaim its land as quickly as possible.

For a moment, Jackson wondered if maybe the scientists who claimed the source of the Z43 virus was actually nature retaliating against the weight of its exponentially growing population of human beings might be right. What better way to cleanse the planet of its parasites than to create a virus that would allow the dead to reanimate and eat the living? Then once humanity was wiped out, the remaining walking corpses would simply lie down and rot, acting as fertilizer to replenish the lost nutrients in the soil.

"Ashes to ashes," Jackson thought.

If this were true, then nature had most certainly gotten what it wanted, because although humanity was on its way back, at last estimate more than sixty percent of the population of the world had been destroyed by the plague.

"Talk about population control." Jackson thought.

In the distance up ahead, he could see something apparently blocking the southbound lane. Although the bad road conditions forced him to already travel slowly, he decreased his speed even further. He checked his GPS and didn't see anything to suggest a detour might be necessary and assumed whatever was up ahead must have only recently been put there.

As he got closer, he could see the obstruction was actually a large truck, which apparently had experienced some problem and skidded sideways, jackknifed, and now blocked the highway. He saw no signs of anyone in trouble or any driver waiting for assistance. He looked to the left and right of the truck to see if there was any way to get around it but saw none. There was a large four foot high divider separating his side of the road from any oncoming traffic, of which there was none and he was unable to cross over it to go around the vehicle. He stopped about twenty feet behind the jackknifed truck, took out his personal CU and called to report the situation. He only hoped a tow truck could arrive soon, as he didn't want such a nuisance slowing him down any more than necessary.

After reporting the problem over the automated system, Jackson put his personal CU back into his shirt pocket and thought for a moment about the CU he had gotten from Chief Holden which was in his left pants pocket. He decided to leave it there, figuring he had no need for it yet as he was not in dire distress. Plus, if he did have a need to call the chief at some point later it might be easier and less obvious to get the phone from his pants pocket than his shirt pocket anyway. He sat for a moment, debating what to do then letting out a sigh, reached down, picked up his revolver, cautiously opened the passenger door, and got out of the car. The disabled truck was empty, and Jackson assumed perhaps its driver had already left the scene to walk for help.

Jackson felt at first this might not have been the smartest move for the driver to make considering the current state of the world, but maybe the driver believed he had no other option. Also, if the driver was local, he would likely know how close the nearest protected town might be where he could get assistance. Jackson wondered why the driver didn't simply call for help and stay in his truck, which is what the government always recommended. Then he realized that although he had called for help himself, he had not remained inside his own vehicle either.

As Jackson slowly approached the truck, he heard something in the distance coming from behind him; a deep humming sound growing increasingly louder. He recognized the sound immediately for what it was and was suddenly filled with terror. It wasn't a tow truck coming to his aid. The sound he heard was the noise made by motorcycles, several of them. And although normal, law-abiding citizens still used such means of transportation within the towns and city limits, few would consider them out on the open road where so many dangers lurked. The only people Jackson knew of who were purported to use motorcycles on highways were the roaming gangs of outlaws. Those people; if they could still be classified as people, were reputed to be savage, ruthless, and often more dangerous than even the zombies were.

CHAPTER 18

Sean Patel stood over the rotting remains of the enormous dead kill. It was the very same creature Jackson had taken down earlier that morning. Now Sean's long work day was almost over and the sun was setting. The creature was most definitely a big one; an oversized giant of a beast. It was close to seven feet tall, with an expansive chest as massive as an ancient oak tree. Sean recognized both of the two non-lethal wounds Jackson had told him about; the one to the creature's left shoulder and the other which creased the side of the monster's skull and clipped off the top of the thing's ear. He also made note of the final kill shot which entered though the monster's left eye and blew out the back of its skull finally bringing it down. Sean let out a sigh of relief. Jackson had no idea just how lucky he had been that morning. But Sean knew. Yes, he knew all too well.

After the latest classified report Sean had read, he was surprised the single head-shot had actually destroyed the monster. He knew it was very fortunate that Jackson carried a forty-five and not any smaller caliber hand gun. Had that been the case the story might have ended out quite differently for his friend. Anything smaller would likely have required two or three head shots to prove effective and more often than not, there was no time for such a luxury.

A double tap to the head was usually attainable if planned in advance, but a triple tap when one suspected a single or double would have done the job required a few seconds more than most people had available in such a situation. Sean looked down at the huge cadaver and had to admit the creature was truly a monster in every sense of the word, and now he understood why.

When Jackson had left his lab earlier that day, Sean had warned him to be careful and had reminded him there were many dangers in the outlands and not just from the undead. He had wanted desperately to tell Jackson so much more but knew he couldn't because he was forbidden to do so. The information he had learned was highly classified. In fact, that one simple warning to Jackson, if overheard by the wrong people, might be sufficient to cost Sean his job and maybe even land him in jail for a few months. This dilemma weighed heavily on Sean's heart because Jackson was his best friend as was Jackson's wife Andrea. Little Kyla was even his goddaughter, and she referred to him as Uncle Sean. It was eating Sean alive not being able to tell Jackson at least some of what he knew, but he simply couldn't.

This was because Jackson Ridge was also a reporter and a member of the news media, and friend or no friend, Sean knew if the information which he held in confidence ever got to the media and could be somehow traced back to him, he could end up spending the remainder of his life in prison. None of what he knew could ever be allowed to leak out into the public sector until the government decided it was time to let the people know. They had public relations people for that. It was Sean's duty to just remain silent.

Both Sean and his boss, Edgar Blackwell, the Schuylkill County Medical Examiner, had the highest level of non-military security clearance with the recently formed National Center for Disease and Virus Control (NCDVC). This meant that both of them could receive up to the minute information regarding all health related issues, especially when it pertained to the Z43 virus. This information generally came in the form of special encrypted FYEO (For Your Eyes Only) emails. At their level of clearance, both Sean and his boss were forbidden by law to share anything in these updates with anyone including coworkers, friends, or even spouses or family members.

After what he had learned in the latest series of reports, Sean wished to God he had been one of the uninformed. Perhaps ignorance in this day and age truly was bliss. At the beginning of the outbreak ten years earlier, when people were being slaughtered by the millions, everyone believed that the human race was doomed to extinction. Then, as things began to turn around and mankind had managed to wipe out the majority of the undead and once again claw their way back up to the top of the food chain, attitudes began to change as well. People once again became confident and began to plan ahead for a brighter future with hope. That hope was largely the reason behind the quick return to an almost normal way of life, at least throughout the United States.

Mankind had beaten back the armies of the undead, and although everyone living knew they still had the Z43 virus lurking dormant inside of them, the virus had been all but been put out of the minds of most people. Government agencies had found ways to deal with the dead and dying to make them much less of a threat then they had previously been. However, there was one fact that most people either didn't know about or had chosen to ignore, perhaps for the sake of their own sanity.

It was as simple as Biology 101, elementary stuff. The fact was that viruses do not remain static. Under the right or perhaps more appropriately, the wrong series of conditions viruses mutate; they change and adapt to their ever changing environments. Several years earlier, when the NCDVC was formed, they made it their primary mission to study the Z43 virus and watch for any changes to its structure.

During these early years, they kept the focus of their studies on the citizens of the newly fortified cities; since they were readily available and could be tested even without their knowing it when they came for routine doctor visits or blood tests. The resulting data showed that there was little if any change to the Z43 virus, which resided inside the citizens' bodies. Scientists considered this to be a good thing because a virus that didn't change could be much more easily managed.

However, according to the reports Sean had seen, in recent years rumors had begun to spread among the civilized populations; stories about so called mutant outlanders with a variety of physical abnormalities. Since access to that population was not normally available to the medical communities, little could be done to study them.

Now, with the recent abilities of the local communities to identify the bodies of the dead kills in greater forensic detail, and with many of those same dead kills being former outlanders, the medical community was now able to study the Z43 virus as it existed in the wild. The disturbing result of those examinations was the recent discovery that the Z43 virus was indeed mutating in the bodies of the outlanders and doing so in many varied and unpredictable ways. It fact, it was mutating in many more ways than they had been able to determine or accurately document so far.

The scientists at the NCDVC had determined to the best of their ability that the reason they had not seen any trace of significant mutations among the city dwellers was because those people had normal healthy diets, practiced good hygiene, and had access to excellent medical care. The outlanders, on the other hand, were the complete opposite. They were poorly fed and had no medical care and little if any personal hygiene. They were also for the most part uneducated. The scientists believed these factors acted to create an environment which allowed the original Z43 virus to mutate and evolve, forming so many different new and unpredictable strains. Gigantism, which was present on the body over which Sean now stood, was one such transfiguration.

These mutations had apparently taken several years to manifest themselves, since rumors of strange species of humanoids only began to surface over the past few years. Sean couldn't help but think of the irony surrounding this incredible discovery. Mankind had thought of itself as completely victorious over the virus and was certain they were well on their way back from the brink of extinction, but now new, unknown strains of the Z43 virus were rearing their ugly heads and, if left unchecked, had the potential to eventually wipe out what remained of the human race either directly or indirectly.

In the past, while performing his duties, Sean had often thought about the concept of humanity and what actually qualified someone to be considered human; especially in the wake of the Z43 virus outbreak. During these times of deep contemplation Sean realized that in reality the creatures which had previously been thought of as pure human beings had in fact already been rendered extinct by the very existence of the virus. Since every living former human being now had the virus residing inside them, they had been forever changed, as had the definition of what it meant to be a normal human being. As a result, Sean had considered the all real former human beings to be extinct. Or that was to say what he thought until he read the most recent series of reports.

Sean recalled the first email he had read that told about that very special little girl. That single report had changed everything he had been previously been thinking in regards to the extinction of humanity. Of all the reports he had read, that one had been the most positive and the one he really wanted to share with Jackson and Andrea more than any other; because it directly affected them through their daughter, Kyla.

The discovery happened by accident, as many great discoveries had occurred throughout history. The encrypted report told of a young five year old girl who had taken ill and passed away at home. Her parents had been distraught to the point that they couldn't bring themselves to notify the authorities of her condition, thereby preventing them from taking any action to prevent the girl from turning and coming back as an undead monster. Then, to the family's amazement, after death, the girl didn't turn, she didn't come back. She simply remained dead. Just like humans had been doing for so many thousands of years before the outbreak.

Before the event became public, doctors from the NCDVC took possession of the body and began testing the dead girl's blood and were shocked to learn she didn't carry the Z43 virus even though it was present in both of her parents before she was conceived. Immediately, scientists began testing the blood of other young children and learned that none of the children born within a year of the initial outbreak carried the virus. They had previously assumed with two infected parents, the virus would naturally be present in the offspring. That meant it was possible and even likely that every child nine years of age and younger was virus free.

This was incredible news for Sean because it meant not only was Kyla likely free of the Z43 virus but it also meant that the human race; the real, pure human race had a chance to survive after all because some day these children would grow to adulthood and began having children of their own. However, no matter how wonderful the news, and no matter how much he wanted to share it, the news was still considered classified at this point in time, which meant he could say nothing to Jackson.

Of course, the issue of the mutating Z43 virus was such a major concern that it seemed to overshadow any joy Sean might have received from the good news about the children. Depending upon how and why the virus was mutating and what long-term effects these mutations would have, every living human being on the planet was still in grave danger, including the children. Sean wondered if these new, strange renditions of the virus would produce variations of creatures far worse than the reanimated dead which had been spawned by the initial virus. He stared down at the gargantuan beast on this autopsy table and shook his head in bewilderment.

CHAPTER 19

Jackson suddenly found himself surrounded by five road-worn, weather beaten motorcycles, each carrying a rider armed to the teeth with guns, knives, swords, and just about every sort of weapon imaginable. In fact, the bikes themselves were covered with various forms of makeshift armor and large, protruding metal spikes that appeared to be razor sharp. The blades of the spikes were stained brown with what Jackson suspected was blood; perhaps from the undead, perhaps from living victims. He shivered involuntarily.

He knew he was in deep trouble now, and for a moment he considered trying to get away by ducking down under the truck and making a run for it. He unfortunately realized the futility of such an idea as the bikers would either shoot him outright or easily go around the truck and hunt him down with their motorcycles. He held his revolver in his trembling right hand and carefully slipped his left hand into his pants pocket. He was trying to recall the details of explanation about the special CU Brent Holden had given him. His mind was blank; he couldn't remember a single thing he had been told. He wanted to silently signal for help but also had no desire to accidentally set off the Taser and fry his balls with 2000 volts. He hoped what Brent had said about the external car cameras was true so maybe he currently was being watched and his unseen police guardian angels already knew how dire his situation was.

"Now what was it Brent had said?" He thought to himself, while simultaneously fingering the CU in his left pocket. "The black button on the right is for capturing and storing audio files. The red button on the top is to call for help and the yellow button on the left side is the Taser." He was fairly certain that was how Brent had explained it, but there was something else. He remembered there was a safeguard for both the Taser and the help button; he was pretty sure he had to press either of them twice in order to get them to work and that one press would do nothing. As he studied the gang he carefully, moved his finger along the surface of the CU, trying to find the desired button and not wanting to tip them off as to what he was attempting to do.

A large man, apparently the leader of the gang, stepped down from his motorcycle, shut off the engine and stood about five feet in front of Jackson. The other four riders did likewise, taking positions surrounding Jackson, each armed with pistols and rifles all of which were pointed directly at him. Between being outgunned and having a trembling hand, Jackson realized he wouldn't be able to stand a chance at defending himself successfully against the gang. If he were one of the heroes in old movies he had seen, he would have been calm and cool and would have easily shot each of them without blinking an eye, but this was the real world, and in this world there were no such extraordinary characters. There were just real people like himself, and he knew all too well that real people died every day.

The leader of this gang was a scarred and scruffy character appearing to be in his late forties with long, grey hair pulled back in a ponytail with a matted, filthy yellow-white beard. He might have been either younger or older, but because of the man's haggard appearance, Jackson couldn't tell. He had what looked like a hundred self-administered prison-style tattoos as well as dozens of body piercings. He wore faded and ripped blue jeans and a dark tee shirt with a logo design which was washed out, soiled, and unrecognizable. Over the shirt he wore a dusty black leather vest. Several large knives were strapped to the outsides of his legs in sheathes, and one even jutted from the top of his worn motorcycle boots. His general appearance was so filthy that Jackson could smell the reek of his body-odor from five feet away. The man wore a necklace made of what appeared to be severed human ears threaded on a strap made of leather.

Jackson was still carefully fingering the edges of the CU, concerned about its orientation. He was fairly certain he had put it into his pocket with the top of the unit pointing upward. But what if he was wrong or what if it had rotated 90 degrees inside his pocket? Unlike their cell phone predecessors, Communications Units were practically square in shape. If it had rotated then the call button might be pointing sideways and the yellow Taser button or the black record button might be pointing upward.

He was carefully moving his hands along the edges of the CU trying to determine the correct orientation. If he could only find the flat bottom edge, which was the side with no buttons, and if he could then find the face of the CU, he would be able to reorient himself in relation to top, left or right, but he had to do so carefully without the gang members noticing. Plus, he had to be sure he was properly remembering which button did what. Jackson was suddenly glad he had decided to leave Brent's CU in his pants pocket after all. This at least made the chore less noticeable to the gang members.

The second biker, positioned to Jackson's far right, appeared to be in his early to mid-twenties. He had long and greasy black hair, around which he wore a faded red bandana patterned like an old style working man's kerchief. His jeans were frayed and ripped. His eyes had a strange, far off look as if the man were practically a zombie himself. He sported some sort of concert tee shirt. This one was legible, and Jackson saw it read, "Moldering Sphincter World Tour 2039". He was unfamiliar with that particular band but suspected they didn't make the sort of music which might interest him, and chances were also pretty good that one or all of its members were likely dead by now anyway. The man wearing the tee shirt was of a very thin build but appeared to be muscular; his sinewy arms sporting numerous tattoos and piercings, like his leader.

"Braino," Jackson thought. He had seen the signs many times before. The young man was obviously a Braino junkie; hence the dazed and zombie-like appearance. Jackson couldn't believe the character had been able to actually drive a motorcycle without crashing into a tree or something.

Off to Jackson's far left, a tall younger man in his late teens to early twenties stood pointing a gun that looked much too large for such a young man to handle. Although he was just as filthy as the rest of the gang, this boy; that was how Jackson thought of him, a boy; appeared less dangerous than the others. He had what someone might mistake for a wholesome, boy-next-door sort of look. He had shaggy blond hair and was tan, reminding Jackson of a surfer-boy type. He also didn't sport nearly as many tattoos or piercings as the others.

The closest biker to him was enormous; not in terms height or muscle but weight. The guy had to go three hundred and fifty pounds and was just short of six feet tall. He was wearing oversized ripped and worn jeans, which had obviously seen better days. In addition to being stretched beyond capacity, Jackson could see the pants could not be properly closed around his massive girth, so the man had tied them together with rope; and had also roughly sewed in material to allow for additional expansion. His shirt was a massive thing which looked more like a tent than a shirt, as if it had been sewn together from several smaller shirts, or maybe made from several different table cloths. It was sleeveless with deep neckline, and Jackson realized it looked like a dress or maybe even a moo moo. Jackson could tell by the frayed and ragged edges the man must have cut off the sleeves and neck area with a knife. Despite the size of the shirt, it still bulged under his incredible weight. The man was bald, but his shaved skull was adorned with a bizarre variety of hideous tattoos. The stench coming off the man was almost as bad as the reek which surrounded the undead. Jackson wished the foul-smelling man had not been so close.

Then Jackson realized he had no choice but to take the chance. None of the bikers had spoken to him yet, but he knew from stories he had heard where this would most likely end. They might rob and kill him instantly, being certain to put one in his skull to keep him dead, or else they might disable him, take his CU, and leave him lying by the side of the road until one of the roaming undead creatures stumbled upon him and transformed him into a main course. One of the bikers, the leader seemed, to be looking at him strangely, and Jackson realized there were things this gang could do to him that were worse than death; sexual things.

He decided since he was likely a dead man anyway, he would take the chance and without another moment's hesitation pressed the button on the CU in his pocket twice. He braced himself for the shock, which he feared might come but when he didn't feel any voltage coursing through his system, he assumed he either pressed the voice recorder button or if he was lucky, pressed the button which would summon help. If he chose correctly, then help might be just minutes away; if he was wrong then eventually someone would find a very disturbing audio recording of his death. Jackson wondered again about the external cameras Brent had spoken about. Were they working? Could the police see what was going on? He looked off to the leader's left to take a closer look the last outlaw.

That character was the complete opposite of the fat one. He was tall and thin, wearing a worn cowboy hat, tight jeans, and cowboy boots. He had some sort of hunting knife strapped to his leg, and Jackson immediately mentally named him Tex. He was interestingly not as filthy as the rest of the gang either, although that fact didn't make him look any less deadly. He appeared as if he could disembowel Jackson without a moment's hesitation with that knife of his.

"You!" The leader suddenly barked in a commanding voice thick with the growling, barely comprehendible dialect of the outlanders. "Drup youse froggen guun an jes putt youse boat hands weres I con seez 'em."

It never ceased to amaze Jackson how quickly these strange gangs had formulated what amounted to essentially their own bizarre language. It was some form of what was once English, but so strangely evolved; or perhaps devolved would be a better description. The coal region had always been known for its own particular accent; a mixture of Irish, Italian, Polish, German, and Lithuanian influences. However, the accents and language of these outlaws who had been mostly uneducated before the outbreak and had lived away from civilization for ten years had begun to take on an even thicker, heavier, and almost foreign quality. Perhaps it was from their lack of interaction with the educated, perhaps it was just something that naturally occurred; some sort of a reverse linguistic evolutionary process.

These outlaws seemed to Jackson to be regressing into a savage, almost animalistic state. He couldn't comprehend how such a drastic change had taken place in only ten years. Maybe it was something else; something more. Perhaps it was the effect of the Z43 virus on the society of outcasts living out among the undead and who likely received little or no medical treatment. Jackson wondered if he and his fellow survivors had not founded civilization and safe havens behind the walls, would they too have regressed so far and so quickly? His mind flashed back to the newspaper office and the smoking, drinking, and such that occurred on a daily basis. Yes, things were a lot less refined than before the outbreak, even in what he thought of as the civilized world.

Jackson looked at the gang of modern-day Neanderthals with their deadly weapons and savage appearance, realizing he was outnumbered, outgunned, and had little choice. "All right." He said as he removed his left hand from his pocket and squatted down to place his gun on the ground. "Look. I don't want any trouble here. I'm doing exactly as you ask. See? I only carry that gun with me to shoot the dead heads and not to use against the living. You have nothing to fear from me."

The gang leader looked at his associates and smiled knowingly as if they all just shared a secret joke; one to which he was not privy. "We don gives two stankin shads 'bout non of dat, pritty boy. Ain't nona us here dats ded-heds 'septn fer maybe Willie ovr dere. We ain't non too sur 'bout ol' Willy boy. Too much Braino - not 'nuf brain."

Jackson followed his gaze to the thin greasy looking character with the far-away stare. "Willy boy hab a likin' fer da Braino. We gives 'em all he wants, den he do wat we wants. We says keel sumbody Willie boy, an he keels. We says eat dat dere big pilea pig shad an he do dat too ifn we wan." The rest of the gang, except the one called Willie, laughed and nodded in agreement, appearing to Jackson to resemble a bunch of baboons he had once seen in a zoo.

Willie, on the other hand, just stood staring mindlessly out into space.

Jackson decided to try to play it safe by appearing even more harmless then he actually was; and he was well aware he was about as harmless as one could be. He thought this might help to stall for time in case help actually was coming, "Please. Look... I don't want any trouble. You see, I have a wife and young daughter at home. Why don't you just take my gun, my car and whatever you want and let me go."

The leader smiled at Jackson, revealing his missing and rotten teeth. "Don tink so. Ifn we lets youse go witout yer gun, den youse is as good as ded out here in da wild lands. Many dedheds walkin' round very hungry. Dey liks to be chompin on da brains of a pritty boy likes youse. Ifn we was ta kilt ya, weed be doin youse a favor."

"Then how about you just leave me with my CU. Then I can call for help after you go. Maybe I'll get lucky and someone will find me." Jackson said.

Then the bald, fat outlaw closest to Jackson looked at his leader and said, "Dat bee a gud one bossaman. Dis stoopid frogging Jakon Ridge tink we shud be letn him go."

The leader's head snapped around quickly as he looked ferociously at the fat outlaw and shouted, "Shutt yer frogging stank hol, Gibbler. 'An youse best does it quick, er I'll be shutn it fer ya."

But the leader's command had come too late. Jackson had heard what that man, the one the leader caller Gibbler had said. He was certain he had heard the fat one use his name. But how could that be? He had no idea who these sub-humans were, yet they somehow seemed to know him. If they did, then they likely also knew why he was on that highway and where he was going.

"He... he said my name." Jackson exclaimed aloud without thinking. "How does he... how do you... know my name?"

The leader let out a deep, foul smelling sigh and said in resignation. "Wel... it be lookin like ol' Gibbler here ain't so gud at keepin' his big flappin mout shutt. But it don madder non. Da troot is we does know who youse is an dats all dat madders. Mister Deimos wans us ta take youse wit us... ta brings youse to him an dats da onlyest reason wees is here. Enda da story. Dey ain't no mo."

"Deimos?" Jackson asked with a panicked voice. "So it's true. He is alive after all. Does he have Sarah? How did he find out about me so quickly? I don't understand any of this."

The leader raised his rifle and pointed it directly at Jackson's head and said, "Youse don haffta udderstund nuttin Mr. Jakon Ridge. Alls youse hasta do is coms wit us. An youse don be wantan ta try any stoopit shad neider. Wee only has to bring youse back alive. Deimos don give two smelly shads ifn we breaks any a yer stuffs on da way dere. Like maybees wee mite shoot offn yer neekap."

"Er mabyees we kin blows off his balls." The one called Gibbler said.

"I tolt youse to shut the frogg up Gibbler." The leader said pointing his gun at the man's head. "Jes say anodder werd and dis Jakon Ridge be ridin your bike alone ta see Mister Deimos an you bee daid ona side of dis here road. Capish?"

Jackson saw Gibbler visibly slammed his lips shut and make the sign of a zipper going across them to indicate to his boss he was done talking. Jackson stood completely still now, petrified with terror, knowing he really had no choice. If he tried to fight them he might not be killed, but he most certainly would be wounded or beaten as close to death as these mutants felt they could get away with. But if they took him to Deimos, Jackson was certain he would eventually end up dead as well, but only after what he assumed would be a great deal of pain and torture. He remained still, uncertain of what to do next as images of Andrea and Kyla passed rapidly through his mind.

CHAPTER 20

Sarah saw a rickety wooden picnic table covered with a variety of delicious looking food and desserts, all of which were spread out atop a red and white checkered table cloth. The weathered table was situated under a covered pavilion with a faded brown shingled roof, supposedly to protect it from the elements; although by the condition of the table, she doubted the roof had been capable of providing all that much protection. When she saw the tremendous spread of picnic food and her mother standing next to the table roasting hot dogs over a nearby stone fireplace, she could feel her stomach growling hungrily in anticipation.

Sarah was only nine years old, and she and her father were sitting in the sand near the water's edge. They were on a beach next to a large lake that seemed to go on forever. In the distance she could see an expansive wooded area, which surrounded the lake and bordered the beach. She loved this place, and just being there with her parents provided her with the most pleasant feelings she had ever experienced in her life. She wanted this time to never end; but then unfortunately things began to go horribly wrong.

As she and her father played in the sunshine, she noticed something strange happening. The sky above them seemed to suddenly fill with dark clouds, practically blocking out the sun. Just the slightest few rays of light were allowed to escape, making it look more like a moonlit night than midafternoon. On the top surface of the lake, she noticed a foggy mist begin to form as the air temperature seemed to drop considerably. The fog on the water began to thicken and rise to a height of twenty or thirty feet. It moved atop the water in a sort of rhythmical dance, which Sarah didn't find in the least bit pleasant. In fact, the sight made her think of a scary movie she had once seen on their home video player; one with ghosts and horrible monsters.

Previously, there had not been many sounds in the eerily calm lake; just an occasional gentle ripple of water. But now she heard splashing sounds. She looked out over the lake, expecting perhaps to see fish coming up to catch insects, but instead she saw something which paralyzed her with terror.

Sarah saw the top of someone's head rising up out of the water; first just the plastered, soaked hair, then two gray-filmed eyes set deep in withered ashen flesh. The formerly peaceful lake was now beginning to undulate. She tried to shout a warning to her father that something bad was happening, but he couldn't seem to hear her as he continued to work on the construction of their sand castle, smiling calmly as he carefully formed the structure, apparently oblivious to the oncoming peril. He didn't even seem to notice the expression of horror on his daughter's contorted face.

Then everything seemed to slow down as she turned once again to look out at the lake; checking the horrifying creature's progress. But now there were five or six of the terrible things, each in various stages of decomposition, rising up out of the water. The creatures closest to her had advanced to a point where the water was waist-high. Its shirt was soaked and hung in tatters. Its flesh was missing in places, and its yellowed ribs could be seen jutting from the rotten openings.

When she looked past the others, Sarah could see several dozens more of the wretched creatures slowly emerging from the lake, which had now lost all of its shimmering beauty and somehow had taken on a brackish and rancid appearance. She couldn't imagine how many of the despicable beasts now occupied the lake bottom and how many more would soon be coming for her and her family, but she sensed there would be hundreds of them if not thousands.

The remaining onslaught of creatures rising up from the depths, were likewise clad in threadbare, sopping clothing, and their mottled flesh seemed to hang like saturated noodles from their protruding bones. Then the ungodly things began to quietly keen as one, in a chorus of deathly moans that seemed to get louder by the second, reverberating all around her. Some of the beasts were now completely out of the water, trudging and dragging themselves through the wet sand, heading in the direction of Sarah and her family. Try as she might, Sarah couldn't get her father to hear her warning cries. She turned and looked up toward the pavilion and saw her mother likewise oblivious to the threat; still happily roasting hotdogs over the campfire.

Then strangely, Sarah seemed to be slowly moving away from her father, as if being pulled backward by some unseen force, while the emerging hoard of rotting zombies fell upon him and began ripping him to pieces. She could see his mouth open wide in a scream of agony but she thankfully could not hear him over the ever-increasing howls of the undead as their sounds continued to rise out of the lake. Her father thrashed about frantically in a cloud of flying sand and blood splatter as what seemed like dozens of the horrible creatures ripped out his insides and feasted on them before her horrified eyes. The sand was turning crimson with gore as one last time she screamed, "Daddyyyyyyyy!"

Sarah awoke with a start; her eyes wide open with fear. A scream caught deep in her throat. Sweat beaded on her skin and she was panting frantically, sitting up on the side of her bed. She had been dreaming; having a nightmare; she was sure of it now, but it had all seemed so real to her. She knew her mother and father were alive and well, but still she had a strange feeling that she might never see them again.

She slid off the bed and as her feet came in contacted with the carpet covered floor she noticed how strange it felt against her flesh. She was still in that place between deep sleep and awakening and the horrible nightmare was already beginning to fade from her memory, though the unpleasant sensations it had brought with it still remained. She had been in such a deep slumber that she had momentarily forgotten about her abduction.

Then with sudden realization, she stood paralyzed, having no idea where she now was or how she had gotten here. She remembered the earlier time when she had awoken to find herself bound and blindfolded in some damp, stinking basement. How long ago had that been? Hours? Days? She had no idea. But however long ago it may have been, that was no longer the case. Sarah thought for a moment she was back in her bedroom. Then she again noticed the strange feeling of the carpet beneath her feet and realized that although she might actually be in a bedroom, it was not her bedroom.

For some odd reason, she seemed to be having more trouble than normal waking up as the heavy cobwebs of slumber slowly cleared from her mind. Sarah looked around in an attempt to take in her surroundings. She had been right; she was in a bedroom of sorts. The sun was coming in through one of the two windows on the far side of the room, casting an unusual vertical pattern on the worn and tattered carpeting. Apparently the roughness of the aged carpet was what she had felt underfoot.

There were no curtains or shades of any type on the windows, but she could see remnants of yellowed newspaper which must have been taped over the windows at one time. Just outside of the window glass, she could see the source of the strange shadows on the floor. Each window was equipped with heavy iron bars, reminiscent of the type she had seen on old jails in history books at the library.

The walls of the room must have once been nicely wall-papered, but now they were a patchwork of faded and yellowed torn sections hanging haphazardly, showing areas where many other patterns from decades gone by could be seen beneath. In places, the plaster was missing from the walls, revealing the skeletal remains of lath beneath. There were also dark areas going from the ceiling to the floor where rain must have leaked into the room and stained the walls. Likewise, the carpet had similar, yet more ominous looking brown spots as if something had once been spilled; maybe coffee. Then she realized with terror that the stain could just have easily have been made by blood.

Sarah slowly turned and with great trepidation, examined her bed, fearful that it too might be filthy and maybe even crawling with bugs. She was relieved to see the twin-sized bed appeared to be relatively clean, although the cover was somewhat threadbare. Looking back at the barred windows, Sarah realized she was still being held captive, but at least she was no longer bound nor blindfolded. She made the assumption that calling for help or attempting to escape from this place would be just as futile as screaming would have been in the basement prison. Otherwise her captors would not have allowed her to move around untied. Then she noticed her own pungent, sweaty smelling body odor and realized she was in dire need of a shower.

The room was completely bare, with no other furnishings, lamps or wall hangings. The only light was a naked bulb in a ceiling fixture in the center of the room. Sarah tested the light switch and was surprised to see it actually worked. This meant the house had electricity. Across the room from her bed was an open doorway. Sarah walked toward it and found a small adjoining bathroom equipped with a toilet, sink and shower. A bar of soap, a wash cloth, a roll of toilet paper, a toothbrush, toothpaste, and a bath towel were sitting on top of the toilet tank. She suddenly realized she had to pee. Although she could skip the much needed shower for now she knew the call of nature couldn't wait. So she used the toilet, hoping no one would enter the main bedroom, since there was no privacy door between that room and the bathroom.

When she finished her business she flushed the toilet and washed her hands. She now knew the plumbing worked as well. She opened the toothbrush and toothpaste and smelled the paste before brushing her teeth. She didn't know what she was hoping to accomplish by smelling the stuff, since she wouldn't know if it had been drugged or poisoned anyway. She rinsed her mouth and spit the remnants of the toothpaste into the sink. She looked at the shower stall, momentarily considering taking a quick shower, but then she realized the absurdity of it, at least until she learned more about her current situation.

Sarah heard a commotion coming from outside. She walked out of the bathroom and headed over to the barred window to look out. She was surprised to see the house was in a rural area; what looked to be a farm. It had been years since she had been in a farm environment, and the sight was absolutely beautiful. There were no other houses for as far as she could see. A large field surrounded the property and seemed to stretch for several hundred yards before coming to dense wooded forest of tall trees. She couldn't see what might exist beyond the forest.

Below her window, about fifty yards from the house, she saw the source of the ruckus she had heard. It was a creature; one of the undead, which was standing and waving its arms and howling in anger. His right leg was caught in some sort of trap. Sarah assumed it was a bear trap, even though she had never seen one. The device was a large, D-shaped object with many triangular teeth which now dug deep into the creature's leg. A heavy chain went from the trap to a big metal anchor in the ground.

All around the creature, several men moved about with long poles. On the ends of the poles was some type of rope formed into a loop like a lasso. The men were wrapping the ropes around the zombie's neck and flailing arms, further restraining the creature. Sarah couldn't figure out what the men were doing or why the simply didn't shoot the thing. That was the logical thing to do and it was every citizen's legal responsibility. Even a kid as young as Sarah knew the only way to deal with those things was to blow their heads off. For a moment she considered tapping on the window to get the men's attention but could tell by their haggard and filthy appearance they were not the sort of men who would come to her aid. In fact, Sarah was suddenly certain they were likely in on the kidnapping; or at least worked with whomever had kidnapped her; possibly that man from the basement with the icy fingers and mysterious voice.

When the men had sufficiently secured the zombie in their restraints, one of them lifted a long sword and sliced the creature's leg off right where it met the teeth of the trap. The beast tried its best to break free but couldn't. The men drug the thrashing creature across the field and beyond her view. She wondered what in the world was going on and what, if anything, all of this had to do with her. Suddenly the beautiful farm scene didn't seem quite so lovely anymore. Sarah knew she was still in a bad place and was still in great danger.

Then she heard a clicking sound behind her. Someone was unlocking the door and preparing to come inside.

Sarah was terrified, having no idea what to expect next. She stood with her back pressed tightly against the outside barred windows, wishing she could simply dissolve like a ghost and float through the glass. Then she saw the knob begin to turn slowly.

CHAPTER 21

Jackson was unable to move, petrified with fear, surrounded by the gang of outlaws. The leader of the group will still smiling at him with his sparse-toothed grin. The man's rifle was pointed directly at Jackson's head, and he had no idea what their next move would be. He had already made the only move he had, but so far no help had come.

Then suddenly, without a moment's warning, right before Jackson's astonished eyes, the gang leader's head exploded in a shower of gray hair, brain matter, bone, and blood. It seemed so incredibly unreal to Jackson, as if someone had shoved some sort of explosive inside a watermelon and set it off. There were flesh and bone fragments as well as bodily fluids of all colors flying in every direction, showering the closest gang members. As the man's headless corpse became visible again amid the rain of gore, it actually stood upright for a few seconds before its knees eventually buckled and the body fell with a sickening thud to the pocked marked road surface below.

Jackson stood staring disbelieving at the horrifying sight with his mouth hanging agape. He knew what he had just seen but his mind still could not seem to come to terms with the gruesome spectacle. He had seen the man's head explode then heard the gunshot a split second afterward, followed by seeing the shower of remains and finally the body collapsing. He understood this was all too real, yet at the same time it all seemed so unreal to him.

Three of the other four members of the gang began turning frantically in circles, some of them taking random potshots at the surrounding woods, desperately trying to determine the source of the gunshot which had taken down their leader. All the while Braino addict, the one they called Willie, didn't even seem to notice either what had just happened or what potential danger still existed for him. The others understood and were in obvious disarray, having absolutely no idea what they should do next.

Jackson was still unmoving, not only terrified that one of the remaining gang members might shoot him, either accidently or otherwise, but also unsure of whom it was who was shooting at them and uncertain if he might be in their sights as well. He had heard tales of wars between rival gangs of outlanders, and he was terrified that he had just found himself in the middle of one such attack.

Then time seemed to slow down around him. Within the space of a few unbelievable seconds, which seemed to take place over a much longer time span, Jackson saw his reality shift as if it had been choreographed. It appeared to be occurring in a fashion similar to what Jackson had once seen in an ancient Sam Peckinpah movie in a museum. In the same violent, slow motion action, each of the remaining gang members met a similar fate to that of their fallen leader.

The first was Willie, his being the only one of the group not in a defensive position. He was still standing with the same strange vacant smiling expressing, staring into spaces as if without a care. It was likely that his Braino-addled mind had no idea what was going on around him. Then the top of his head-band wrapped dark slimy hair was suddenly parted along with his skull by a shot that seemed to materialize out of thin air. His head blew apart, each half falling off to their appropriate side. As the body fell forward, Jackson saw the bloody neck stump vomiting out its last few gushes of crimson as the corpse collapsed in a heap.

The tall younger man, the one who had what Jackson had thought of as a shaggy blond "surfer boy" haircut glanced at his fallen comrades in disbelief while simultaneously shooting his gun in random directions, trying desperately to hit something, anything. To Jackson, he looked like a frightened young boy thrust into a situation he had absolutely no idea how to handle, which was true. Then as Jackson watched in amazement, a projectile entered the boy's head through his right temple, caving his skull visibly inward and eventually blowing out the entire left side of his head, spraying the area with his bloody cranial remains.

The dead boy stood momentarily, as if in confusion, with blood trickling down from his entry wound and remnants of gray matter sloughing down the left side of his tee shirt. The front of his tattered pants became dark as his bladder released. Then like his leader, the boy's knees buckled as his lifeless body fell backward and thudded with a sickening sound against the blacktop. His knees still strangely pointed upward as his dead body lay prone. He looked bizarrely to Jackson like a child reclining peacefully on the ground watching a cloud formation in the sky. That was until he saw the spreading pool of ruby fluid and noticed the boy's left foot twitching spasmodically once, than twice before blessedly going still. If he managed to live through this, Jackson believed he would see that twitching foot in his nightmares for many years to come.

Jackson's attention next went to the fat bandit with the bald head and tattoos whose pants had been held together with rope. He was Gibbler, the one who had screwed up and called Jackson by his name. As Jackson looked on helplessly the man's head simply exploded just like the gang leader's head had done, although perhaps to an even worse degree, as far as Jackson was concerned. Because the outlaw was closer to Jackson than the others had been, Jackson's face and shirt became stippled with blood, bits of flesh, and globules of brain particles. Jackson watched the fat man's body collapse straight down to the ground, as witnessed through a crimson mist of gore which now covered his glasses, distorting his vision and making the scene seem as if it were being viewed from a blood-splattered snow globe.

The final outlaw, the one Jackson thought of as Tex, likewise fell to the ground, but he had blood pouring from a gaping wound in his neck. He thrashed about screaming for a few agonizing seconds, grabbing for his throat and desperately trying to breathe while arterial blood shot from his neck like a fountain of crimson and pinkish froth bubbled from his mouth. After a few seconds he became deathly silent.

Even with the danger from the gang now over, Jackson was still paralyzed with fear. Eventually, he was able to slowly begin to scan the area. At first, he was still unsure whether he was a target or not; although he realized if the shooters had wanted him dead, he most certainly would have already been killed.

He heard a rustling in the trees next to the highway, and when he turned, he saw several men dressed in dark, combat-style clothing and gear which he knew to be assault suits complete with Kevlar vests. They carried large rifles equipped with scopes. "Sniper rifles," Jackson thought. "That's how they managed to kill all those men without being seen; they're snipers."

Then he heard the roar of engines as a caravan of several black trucks and off-road vehicles converged on the scene from various direction. The doors of each vehicle flew open and more commandos poured out of each joining their compatriots. One of the commandos walked toward the first dead biker. This was apparently the leader of the squad and he walked from body to body with his hands clasped behind his back, examining their handiwork, looking like a general inspecting his troops. Before he got to the dead outlaw who had been shot in the throat, the corpse began to twitch and move slightly. Then it clumsily rose to its feet as a full-fledged flesh eating monster. The creature looked around at the various commandos as if deciding which one to attack first.

"Who in the hell did the damned throat shot?" The leader bellowed at his men. "How many times do I have to tell you candy-ass morons?" He stopped mid-thought then withdrew a pistol from its holster and while finishing his conversation, popped two rounds into the center of the creature's head. "You... always... (Bang) go for... (Bang) the head shot. It's the only way to keep them from coming back. If I find out who the numb nuts was, who did this, there'll be hell to pay. Now, you ladies get these stinking bodies loaded into the back of Walker's truck and let's get this mess cleaned up, pronto. Good Lord, these mutants smell almost as bad as the damned deadheads. Also, and listen up girls, the tractor-trailer should arrive in a few minutes to haul away all of these motor cycles as well."

The man approached Jackson, shaking his head in frustration and extended his right hand. "Mr. Jackson Ridge I presume. Are you ok sir? We saw what was happening though your car's outside cameras and got here as quickly as possible. We also got your distress signal."

Jackson was glad to know he had managed to press the right buttons on his CU after all.

The man continued, "Please accept my apology for any distress our delay in arrival may have caused you. I got a good group of recruits here, some much better than others, but all good officers. As you may have noticed, I tend to be a bit tough on them sometimes, but I do what I must to keep the sharp. They're my responsibility, which means their lives are in my hands, as is yours now. I hope you understand that sir. Sir? Sir, you appear to be a bit peaked. Are you all right Mr. Ridge?"

Jackson was dumbfounded and stood staring at the carnage for a few minutes before turning and vomiting his lunch into the nearby weeds. When he was finished retching, Jackson tried his best to regain his composure, but so much had happened in the previous few minutes that he was almost unable to form an intelligent sentence. Wiping off his mouth with his sleeve, Jackson mumbled, "Um... ah...y...y... y... yes... yes... I'm ok... I mean... I think I'm alright... Who are... I mean... what's going on... I mean... what the hell?"

"Your confusion is understandable sir," The man said. He reached into his pocket and withdrew an identification badge; the shield of a police sergeant. "My name is Sergeant David Evans from the Yuengsville Free Zone Anti-Terror Squad, and these are my men." He pointed at the others. "Chief Holden assigned us to you in order that we may assure you're able to complete your mission safely. And as you may have noticed, we take our responsibility very seriously."

"Anti-Terror Squad?" Jackson thought. He had heard of this squad and knew them by their reputation but had never seen them in action or met any members in person. He recalled a time when the need for such a force would have only been seen on the federal level, not state and certainly not local, but since the outbreak, these elite paramilitary squads had become commonplace in virtually every police department in every protected city in the country. In the smaller towns, they were primarily made up of volunteers and were like paramilitary militias, but in the larger cities, these groups were paid professionals. Apparently either Yuengsville had the budget to afford such a force, or it was possible this might be a combination of perhaps paid squad leaders and volunteers, which is what Jackson suspected was the case.

Jackson was still struggling for words while trying to keep what little might remain of his lunch in his stomach. It had only been a ham and cheese sandwich and a Coke to hold him over until he got to Reading, but now it felt as if his stomach was once again an empty cavern. The carnage produced by Evans' squad was unlike anything he had ever witnessed before. Although he had seen his share of mutilated deadheads; this was the first time he had seen his fellow human beings killed in such a brutal manner. After what he had just witnessed, Jackson supposed he was entitled to be a little off of his game.

"Sir? Are you sure you're ok?" Sergeant Evans was asking Jackson once again. "If so; we would like for you to be on your way as quickly as possible. We understand the importance of your assignment and I'm certain Mayor McKinney would want you to get back to business as well." Evans stared sternly and knowingly at Jackson. Suddenly, Jackson realized Evans was likely the only member of the squad who knew what his assignment was.

"Y... y... yes. I'm.. I'm fine." Jackson stammered, not really knowing if he truly was or not. "I mean... I suppose I'm about as fine... well... as fine as someone in this situation can be. Thank you so much for..." He looked around and the headless corpses. "... well for... you know... for coming to my rescue... At first I thought those guys were going to .... to kill me."

"They most likely were." The sergeant said matter-of-factly. "That's what those sorts of characters do. They rob and then kill people. Sometime they rape and torture their victims as well, just for fun and excitement. And that's why we do what we do and do so with such ferocity. The show of force is also important. We want to make sure word of this gets back to the bad guys. It lets them know what's in store for them if they continue to break the law. I'm just happy we made it in time to save you."

Regaining some of his composure, Jackson said, "Sergeant... Evans... is it? There's something you need to know. Something you need to pass on. I said at first I thought they were going to kill me... but they weren't. They were going to take me; to kidnap me and take me to Deimos."

"Deimos?" Evans said. "How in the world would you know that?"

"He... they told me so... they knew who I was." Jackson replied, pointing at the corpses being loaded into the back of a truck, "They called me by my name. I suspect they knew where I was going and maybe even why."

"What?" Evans said suddenly startled and disbelieving.

"Yes." Jackson said, "It's true. One of them... that fat one over there... he went by the name Gibbler... and he said my name... then their leader admitted they knew all about me."

The sergeant shook his head in confusion. "But that's not possible."

"But it is." Jackson corrected, "And they said Deimos gave them specific orders to bring me to him."

Evans said. "If someone got news of you to Deimos already, then we could very well have a leak back at headquarters; a mole within our organization. And if that's true, then we have a major problem to deal with here." Jackson suddenly recalled the strange police officer who had stood silently in the shadows, seeming to be watching him. Could that man be the one who was working for Deimos?

"Regardless." Evans exclaimed, "My job is to protect you. This information changes everything as it could jeopardize the entire operation, Mr. Ridge. And that would also put you at an unacceptable level of risk. Hell, it obviously already has. Perhaps I should call Chief Holden and tell him to call this operation off."

Jackson thought about Sarah and the horrible people who had her. He was certain now it was Deimos who had her. Then he thought of Andrea and Kyla.

"No!" Jackson said loudly, startling even himself. "I... I have to go on. I have no choice. This is simply too important. You can update Holden if you wish; in fact, I assume you must. But regardless of the potential danger I have to do this."

"I truly understand what you're saying, and I realize I have no right to detain you, but I'm certain my superiors would want me to do my utmost to try and persuade you to call this off and return to Yuengsville." Evans said with resignation. "If what you say is accurate, this could get real ugly, real fast, so please be careful Mr. Ridge. And you might also want to do something about your appearance. If they know you are coming, and apparently they do, then they likely know what you look like and what you're driving; apparently those guys did." He pointed to the headless corpses littering the ground. "And the very least I can do is help you on your way."

Evans waved his hand and one of his officers, who was now behind the wheel of the supposedly disabled truck started the engine with a roar and slowly pulled the vehicle to the side of the road, clearing a path for Jackson to get by.

"If you must carry on, then best of luck to you Mr. Ridge and God speed." Evans said as a very uncertain Jackson Ridge got back into his car and started the engine. Then the sergeant said over the noise of the engine, "Oh yes. And I believe this is yours, sir." He handed Jackson's revolver in through the still open driver's window. Jackson blushed with embarrassment, then put his car in gear and again headed down the highway toward his destination.

CHAPTER 22

Sarah stood rigid with fear, waiting for whatever was to come next. The door knob continued to turn ever so slowly before she heard a final click and the door began to ease open. After a long moment a man entered the room.

At first she didn't notice any specific details about the visitor because he didn't seem nearly as threatening as the mountain of a man who stood behind him, waiting just outside the door. At least Sarah assumed what she saw was a man, although she was having doubts about that. He was so huge, so dirty, and so hairy, with muscles bulging from his ripped and yellowed skin-tight wife beater, and she wondered if he might actually be some type of animal forced into human clothing. Then she wondered if maybe he was one of those mutants she had heard other kids talking about. She always assumed those stories were myths and rumors or simply the sort of lies big kids told in order to scare younger kids, but now the sight of the man/beast caused her to wonder if the stories were true, and that made her breath catch in her throat. It wasn't until the door mercifully closed, putting the creature out of her sight and on the other side, that Sarah was able to let out a sigh of relief and breathe normally once again. That was when she finally noticed the smaller man who had just entered the room.

He stood in front of the closed door looking her up and down in a way that made her feel very uncomfortable, as if his eyes were actually icy fingers running all over her body like dozens of crawling spiders. She felt naked beneath that invasive gaze and she couldn't suppress an involuntary shudder which coursed through her body.

The man was not large in either weight or height; certainly nowhere close to the gargantuan thing outside in the hall. He was perhaps only five feet eight inches tall and maybe one hundred and fifty pounds. He wore clean, tight blue jeans, a black long-sleeved western-cut shirt unbuttoned at the top, revealing some sort of indistinct chain. His belt had a large gaudy buckle formed in the shape of a skull. His hair was thick, black and combed severely back from his forehead. She momentarily wondered if his hair was dyed, as it looked much too dark and far too young for his pale and obviously older complexion, which was weathered, tan, and creased. She was sure the man was much older than he was trying to appear; maybe in his mid-fifties. But regardless, Sarah also sensed by the way he held himself that he was both muscular as well as strong. He had what she thought of as a tough and rugged swagger about him. The fact was, to Sarah he looked just plain dangerous.

The most disturbing features about the man were his strange smile and his piercing eyes. Sarah didn't quite know how to explain it, but she felt the two facial expressions didn't match but rather seemed to contradict each other. His clean-shaven face and cordial smile alone appeared pleasant enough although a bit forced. But his eyes bore a look unlike anything Sarah had ever seen before.

"Those are the eyes of a very bad man." She thought. "He's trying hard to look like a normal person but I can tell he is not." Something suddenly popped into her mind; an expression from a mystery or detective novel she had once read. It was a phrase the protagonist in the story used to describe a mob hit man he met face to face. "Dead eyes." Was the expression she now thought; "The eyes of a heartless, cold-blooded killer." This was exactly how Sarah felt staring into the eyes of the man across the room. He seemed to be both alive and dead at the same time. Maybe her imagination was running away with her, or perhaps she had just read one too many detective novels. Regardless, that man standing there was the one responsible for her kidnapping, so there was no way he was anything but bad.

"I hope you find your accommodations acceptable, Sarah." The man said in a soft, almost whispery voice. Sarah instantly recognized both the tone of his voice and also what the man said. It was almost exactly the same phrase he had used when she had been tied to the chair in the cellar sometime previously. Sarah chose not to reply; instead she pressed herself tighter against the window panes with her hands flat against the glass and her eyes wide open with fear, apprehension, and anger.

Once again he spoke, "There's no need to be afraid of me Sarah. I'm not here to hurt you, just to talk to you for a bit and maybe get to know you a little better." Again she noticed how his cheerful smile contrasted with his terrifying eyes.

She somehow managed to find the courage to try to speak, "Who... who are you?"

"Now isn't that interesting." The man replied without changing his facial expression in the slightest. "Here I was expecting you to ask maybe about what I want with you. Or maybe where you're being held or even why you were taken in the first place and when you will be going home. But instead, you asked who I am. If that don't beat all... I find it simply fascinating not only that you'd ask me my name but that you're not crying or hollering or begging me to let you go. Apparently, I misjudged you, sweat pea. You're a very strong young lady, ain't you. Yes, I believe I just might like that."

Once again Sarah was silent. Something was very wrong with this man. She wasn't sure what it was, but there was definitely something off with him. Sarah had never to the best of her knowledge met anyone who was really and truly crazy before. But it was becoming more obvious by the second that this man was at best very, very peculiar and at worst quite probably insane. Like his strange eyes and smile, nothing he said seemed to sound right or to make any sense to her. She was suddenly reminded of the Mad Hatter from *Alice In Wonderland,* and now everything around her seemed as strange and surrealistic as scenes from that book. The man continued to stare at her with that Cheshire cat smile and those Mad Hatter dead eyes as if he was expecting her to say something, which she of course would not. She stared into his terrible eyes and felt as if they were projecting an iciness that could chill her to the bone. She was thankful she had decided to go to the bathroom earlier, because she was certain had she not done so, that horrific stare might have caused her to wet herself.

"Alrighty then." The man said breaking the uncomfortable silence. "If that's the way you want to play this missy I'll be happy to oblige. You see, my real name doesn't much matter as I haven't been that fella for many, many years now. The name I go by now is a name I chose for myself. That name is Deimos. And for future reference, it's the name I expect, no I demand, that everyone calls me. And what that means to you, little Sarah, is I'll be expecting you to call me Deimos as well. Not Mr. Deimos, just plain old Deimos. Understand?"

Sarah stood pressed tightly against the barred windows, still not speaking. For some reason, knowing the man's name, or at least what he called himself, didn't make her feel any better; in fact, it made things seem worse. She had no idea why she had been so stupid as to ask him his name; it was just something that came out, and now wished it hadn't. She suddenly recalled something else she had read in one of those detective novels; something which now terrified her. The book involved people taken against their will, and the idea she recalled was that anytime a kidnapped character saw his abductor's face or had some other means of identifying him it always meant a guaranteed death sentence. There was simply no way the kidnapper could let a witness live. And here she was standing and staring into Deimos' insane eyes, knowing his face and now his name. In that single moment of clarity, Sarah understood she would have to find some way to escape or else she would never be leaving the house alive.

Deimos took a step closer to Sarah and said, "You might remember, when we first met the other night I said you'd be part of my little family for a very long time. Do you remember me saying that, Honey? Yep, I can see that you do. Well, I'm still hoping that might eventually become a reality, but it seems things have gotten a little bit more complicated than I had originally hoped. You might say somebody just went and muddied up the waters a bit, and it's a kind of hard to say for certain what sort of future, if any we'll be having together."

Sarah was finding it very difficult to follow the man's train of thought; unsure if the problem was something she did or simply that Deimos was a mad-man prone to rambling thoughts that made no sense to anyone but himself. She had a feeling that despite his easy going, simple man way of talking, he might be very intelligent. She also knew plenty of smart people were also very strange. Maybe that was this man's problem; maybe he was too smart for his own good.

"I can see you're having some trouble understanding me." Deimos alluded, "That's probably my fault. I do tend to ramble a bit sometimes. But to be honest with you, it's most likely your problem could be the leftover effects of the sedative I had to give you. It might be taking a bit longer to wear off than I thought. So if I can explain a bit more, as I said earlier the reason I originally had you brought to me was because I feel you're a very beautiful young lady. A fella I know in Yuengsville sent me a picture of you and figured, because you are such a good looking little girl, he believed you might satisfy both my business as well as my personal needs as well."

Sarah had no idea what he meant by that, but somehow she intuitively knew whatever it might be it wasn't something good.

Deimos explained, "You see, when we took you, I wasn't interested at all in in asking your family for any ransom money. Lord knows I got plenty of money. In fact, as far as I was concerned, I wanted your folks to just figure you were dead so they wouldn't even bother trying to find you. Like I said, I had my own plans for you. But then lo and behold I learned something I hadn't figured on; something which, to be honest, sort of threw me for a bit of loop and as they say temporarily through a monkey wrench into the works."

She didn't move nor speak, but Sarah's mind was moving rapidly as she listened to this bad man, this Deimos. Something had obviously happened since she had been taken. Something had changed and she suspected she was about to find out what that was and possibly what it might mean to her future; or lack of which.

"Well to make a long story short it suddenly seems that you do have some other value to me which could change my original plan for you after all." Deimos said. "Somebody I know who is my eyes and ears in the Yuengsville Free Zone police department has told me something very interesting about you."

Sarah must have gotten a surprised look on her face because Deimos then said, "Hum. Does it surprise you that I have friends in such high places little lady? Well, maybe friend isn't exactly the right word. He's not so much a friend as an associate of mine. See Sarah, I make it my business to have people in places wherever I find it beneficial. Anyway, I recently learned that although we both know your parents have little or no money to pay any ransom, your good uncle, Mayor Frank McKinney, most certainly does. In fact, he's got something else which I value much more than money and that's power. He's got the power to change events and people, and believe me that's something I can use to make a lot more money than you alone might be worth. No offense intended."

Sarah looked as if she had just been slapped in the face. "Oh my God, he knows." She thought. Deimos knew who her Uncle Frank was, but what she wasn't sure of was if that meant things had just gotten better for her or a lot worse. On the positive side, if Deimos had changed his plans because of her uncle's money, maybe she would be ransomed and freed after all. Then she thought, "But I've seen his face and I know who he is." No amount of money could change that.

She realized if Deimos was as evil as she believed him to be; it was more likely that he would grab any ransom money he was able to and then probably kill her and send her corpse home. Or perhaps he would simply kill her and let her wander the streets as an undead zombie. Or maybe he would collect the money and then still keep her as he had originally planned. As far as she could tell, no matter what direction her future now took, she was certain she would never see her Mom and Dad again.

CHAPTER 23

"What the hell are we going to do now?" Mayor Frank McKinney said with unsuppressed frustration to Chief of Police Brent Holden. Gone was the politician's mask of affability, replaced by a look which reflected the true anguish which McKinney now felt. "Oh my sweet Mother of God! That psychopath Deimos really does have our Sarah! If even half of what you've told me is accurate then this whole rescue mission could be in the toilet and our poor Sarah might be lost to us forever."

Brent nodded his head in resignation; thinking about Jackson Ridge and the close call he had narrowly escaped. As soon as Sergeant Evans had called Brent and told him about the incident along Route 61 with Jackson and the outlaw gang, Brent knew he had a major problem. When Evans told him how Jackson had said the criminals had actually known his name and that Deimos had sent them to capture him, Brent realized just how big the problem had suddenly become. The mayor would have to be notified that there was a spy, a mole working from inside his own police department. Brent knew he was going to have to figure out some way to deal with that situation later, but for the moment, he had more pressing issues to resolve. Brent's level of frustration and feeling of impotency was beginning to rival that of the mayor. He was unaccustomed to not being in control, and the feeling was very disconcerting. He could feel his own anger growing exponentially and he had to struggle to keep it at bay. Brent needed to stay calm and focus if things were to end the way he needed them to end.

When Brent first found out what had happened with Jackson Ridge and that the mission had been compromised, he had chewed out Sergeant Evans for letting Jackson go on to Reading and not forcing the man to return to Yuengsville. Then later when Brent had learned how Jackson was determined to go on with the assignment no matter what, and how the man honestly believed he could still proceed with minimal danger, Brent had somehow managed to relax somewhat and formulate the crux of an idea for how the mission might still be saved. He had taken a number of his own precautions prior to Jackson's leaving; some of which even the mayor was unaware, and he had an idea of how he might still be able to get Deimos once and for all.

He of course had to at least try to get Jackson and Sarah back safely, but he knew if anything were to happen to them, he needed to be sure to take out Deimos regardless. Brent had known Mayor McKinney would hit the ceiling when he found out what had happened with Jackson and had been prepared to deal with that, but just maybe if he were lucky and Jackson was right; perhaps he could still pull this off.

"I'm sorry Brent," he heard Mayor McKinney say. He was once again regaining his composure. "I'm just so damned concerned about Sarah and now Jackson that I guess I just lost my temper. And in my anger, I forgot completely about the fact that your men are in harm's way and we have a major leak in our department. Do you have any idea who this mole might be?"

"No Sir..." Brent replied. "... at least not at the moment. But I promise you I will most certainly find out who he is, and when I do he will be dealt with severely."

McKinney said, "I trust you Brent. You know I do. And I'm certain you'll figure this whole mess out eventually. I'm sure the only way those outlaws could have known about Jackson was if the information came from here; from one of our own. God it makes me sick to think that we have a traitor in our midst. And now because of this treachery, not only is Sarah in even more danger, but Jackson Ridge could end up dead, despite our best efforts to protect him. The man's cover is completely blown, and if he gets anywhere close to the kidnappers, I'd have to assume he's as good as dead. Maybe we should just try to salvage whatever we can of this horrible fiasco and bring Jackson back in while we still have a chance. I just don't know. If you haven't already done so, maybe you should give the order for your officers to bring him back."

"Well Mr. Mayor," Brent said, hesitating and using the formal address that he felt the severity of the situation demanded. "We already did try to get Jackson to come in. Sergeant Evans suggested very strongly to Jackson that he return, but Jackson absolutely refused. Jackson said he knew and understood the risks he was now facing, but he honestly felt the assignment was far too important to stop now. He stated categorically that he had absolutely no intention of backing down until he found out what has happened to Sarah."

The mayor stood silently for a moment, his trepidation subsiding, being replaced by a feeling of immeasurable gratitude. In fact, he was dumbfounded. When he next spoke, it was in an obviously controlled tone as he tried desperately to keep his emotions at bay. "Why... my God... that's unprecedented... it's incredible... I'm beyond grateful for Jackson's dedication to this, to me... and for putting himself... at such risk for Sarah. But why he would ever do so, I simply can't comprehend... and... and to be completely honest... I don't think if I were put in the same situation... I could be so... so selfless. My God, Jackson has his own family, a wife and a daughter who depend on him... It doesn't matter that we knew the assignment would be risky from the very start, because at least we believed then it was a somewhat controllable threat. But now with Jackson exposed and his mission known by Deimos himself, the danger has just escalated to an unmanageable level. Now it might even be an impossible task. I only hope to God we haven't sent Jackson on what could now become a suicide mission."

Brent nodded again in agreement and said, "I hope so as well, Sir."

"So then. Tell me what we are doing on our end to protect Jackson," McKinney asked.

"We still have Jackson under constant surveillance. He has both the car we gave him as well as the special CU. Once he gets to the city, our strategies will have to change a bit. We now plan on sending one undercover car with two officers into the city to track him, while the rest of our men remain outside the city limits. The reason for this is two-fold. First, we want to keep a low-profile inside the city and don't want to do anything to tip off the kidnappers of our presence; especially if they're watching for Jackson. I'm sure they'll suspect we're around, but there's no reason to make it easy for them."

"The second reason is, as you are aware, we are fairly certain Jackson won't find Sarah within the city limits. We strongly suspect Deimos is likely holding her somewhere in the outlands, as far away from the long arm of the law as possible. What we theorize will happen is this. If Jackson is convincing enough with whatever cover story he manages to think up, he will probably find someone in one of the seedier bars who will send him to one of the underground night clubs outside the city. This should get him closer to the kidnappers. Although I hate to admit it, in reality, their knowing about Jackson and about you being Sarah's uncle and that you sent him to find her might actually serve our purposes better."

The mayor looked at his police chief, perplexed. "How do you mean it might actually help us? I don't understand. How could that knowledge possibly help us?"

Brent replied, "Well. Here's what I've been thinking; and again this is just speculation. Normally, the chances of Jackson finding someone to lead him directly to the place where Sarah is being held would be highly unlikely; no matter how good he might be at finding out information. You recall I said that when we were discussing putting him on this in the first place. However, now that Deimos and his followers are aware of Jackson, they'll probably find him long before he finds them. As soon as he starts asking too many questions, the perps will likely identify him and then capture him and take him straight to Deimos.

"But won't they just kill him?" Frank asked.

Brent said assuredly, "If this were anyone but Deimos, that might be true. But if you recall from my report, when the outlaw gang surrounded Jackson, they told him Deimos ordered them to capture him. Although I have little doubt the gang would have killed him had they no other choice, their orders were specifically to capture him. We can only assume whatever Deimos' reasoning might be, that part of the plan will remain the same. He wants to get his hands on Jackson Ridge, alive."

"Also, now that they know you're Sarah's uncle, they will likely find a way to contact us to try to extort money. Not that I believe Deimos would actually want any money from you, but he might contact us anyway as part of some sick game he will likely want to play. Deimos is very intelligent, but twisted as well, and as such will want to make us looks as helpless and pathetic as possible. I suspect that would give him great pleasure. And if we're lucky, it might possibly help to postpone whatever sick plans he might have for Sarah for at least a few more days. This combined with Jackson' activities just might delay things just long enough for us to find Deimos' current base of operation."

"So what you're essentially suggesting is that we use Sarah and Jackson as bait to track down Deimos and his gang?" The mayor asked with great and obvious displeasure. Brent sensed they were about to get into another heated discussion and wanted to suppress any such potential conflict.

Brent hesitated for a moment, then said, "Well, yes and no. Believe me Frank, I would never suggest such a proposal or even agree to us doing such a thing under normal circumstances, as it would be far too dangerous to both Sarah and Jackson. However, this situation is far from normal. Things have drastically changed, and we're not the ones placing them in harm's way. Sarah is unfortunately already in their filthy hands, and Jackson has decided to disregard our suggestions and is continuing with the operation on his own. So yes, Sarah and Jackson have become bait to trap Deimos, but we're not directly responsible for their finding themselves in such an unfortunate situation. The fact is, Deimos will be setting a trap for himself if he tries to go after Jackson; which we are quite certain he will."

"So let me get this straight." McKinney said, "You assume Jackson will start snooping around, asking questions and when he does one of Deimos' contacts will recognize him and lead him right to where they are holding Sarah?"

Brent explained, "Yes. Once we got confirmation that it was Deimos who had Sarah, it required a change in our strategy. We all know from his reputation that Deimos is a maniac, that's a given; but he also has an incredibly large ego. There's no way he will be able to resist contacting you and demanding some sort of ridiculous ransom. And just so you understand, although at some point it may become necessary to go through the motions of agreeing to his demands, we'll have no more intention of giving him money than he'll have of letting Sarah go. It's all just a game to him. Likewise, as I said before, we don't believe he'll want to kill Jackson outright. That would be too simple for him and as such wouldn't provide enough entertainment. We suspect he'll capture Jackson and keep him alive for a while; if for no other reason than to torture him and to taunt us, letting us know how badly we've failed; letting us know that he's the one in control. And that will be his downfall and how we'll get him."

McKinney replied, "I certainly hope you're right, Brent. You're asking me to take a very big risk here. And I hope you'll be able to find Jackson and Sarah in time to save them both. You know how much is at stake and what will happen to them if you don't."

"Yes, I most certainly do." Brent replied.

Then the phone on Frank McKinney's desk began to ring. He stomped over to his desk angrily, picked up the receiver and shouted, "Mrs. Simpson, I told you I didn't want to be interrupted under any circumstances."

The woman on the other end of the line was his receptionist, Jane Simpson. She hesitated for a moment, then clearing her throat said, "Y...yes Sir. I realize that was what you told me, but there's someone on the line who insists on speaking with you... and he says it's of utmost importance... a matter of life and death... and concerns a young girl... a girl named Sarah."

"Sarah?" Frank replied. "Uh... yes... yes... please... I'm sorry... Mrs. Simpson... by all means... put him through." He looked at Brent Holden and mouthed the words "I think it's Jackson."

Then after a moment Frank McKinney pressed the speaker button on his desk phone and there was a click followed by a smooth, silky, southern sounding voice came over the speaker saying, "If I might ask, is this the illustrious Frank McKinney; most highly exalted Mayor of Yuengsville?"

"Y... yes... yes this is he." Frank replied hesitantly. He was caught a bit off guard. It obviously wasn't Jackson calling, and the Mayor was fairly certain just who it was on the other end of the line.

Frank looked at Brent with confusion, waiting for some guidance as to what he should do. Brent made motions with his hand for Frank to keep talking as he took out his own CU and quietly began speaking to someone on the other end. He pointed his index finger up to his lips then at himself to signal McKinney not to mention that he was also in the room. Frank assumed Brent has some reason for this deception and nodded his agreement.

Then the voice said again with a mocking sarcasm. "Is this the same Frank McKinney who is the uncle of my lovely latest little sweet pea who goes by the handle of Sarah Stanton?"

"Y... y... yes." Frank stammered, his worst fears now confirmed. He anger flared, "D... D... Deimos, you bastard... if you so much as.... touch a hair on Sarah's head... why... I'll..."

Then the voice interrupted him taking on a sterner, more threatening tone, as if he had not even heard a word McKinney had said and asked, "And is this the very same Frank McKinney, who thought he could get the better of me by sending some two-bit hack reporter to try to find me? And is this the same Frank McKinney who, if he doesn't do exactly what I tell him to do will get to watch a professional quality video of his precious little niece being gang raped by a group of filthy stinkin' half-retarded outlanders? And is this the same Frank McKinney who'll then get to see his innocent little angel girl being tortured and eventually killed ever so slowly and painfully? Or maybe this is the Frank McKinney who would rather watch his sweet little girl be eaten alive on camera by a group of dead heads. Is that you Frank? Do I have your attention now Frankie boy?"

Suddenly McKinney felt as if all of the wind had been knocked out of him and now he was without anger, without threats, and all he wanted more than anything else in the world was to get his niece back safely, no matter what it took on his part. He rested his hands on the top of the desk as if trying to prevent himself from collapsing. Then he plopped down into his desk chair, beaten.

"Look... I'm... I'm so sorry... please... I didn't mean anything... please don't hurt Sarah." Frank pleaded, his hands now buried deep into his disheveled hair. He was having difficulty keeping his voice from breaking. "I swear... I promise... I'll do whatever you want. Just... please don't hurt her."

"Why there you go now Frank. Isn't that much better? See, now we're talking like a couple of good old buddies." Deimos replied. "And yes you're absolutely right Frankie old pal; it's so very true that you'll be doing exactly what I tell you to do. In fact you'll do whatever I want whenever I tell you to and for as long as I tell you to as well. Because from now on Frankie boy; I own your ass."

Frank McKinney realized suddenly what Deimos' game was now. He was never going to hand over Sarah no matter what Frank offered him. Instead the madman would use her to get whatever he might need to advance his filthy criminal business into Schuylkill County, starting with Yuengsville. And there was absolutely nothing McKinney could do to stop him. His only hope now was that somehow Jackson Ridge would find her and his team might bring her home safely.

CHAPTER 24

About ten or twelve miles north of the Reading city limits, Jackson came upon a most welcome sight; at least he hoped it was a welcome sight. It was a trading post of some sort located along the right side of the highway. He had heard stories about these places and had discussed them with Brent Holden as well. Apparently some of the more rugged individuals were purported to have taken over abandoned former strip-malls, which they claimed for themselves. These entrepreneurs then converted the buildings into a combination home, general store, and fortress. This allowed them to conduct business and make money selling goods to travelers, in a relatively safe, secure environment.

These types of places were often run by characters who, although not exactly outlaws, were also not the kind of people who could function well in the confines of a fortified city filled with other people, not to mention the rules and regulations which accompanied civilization. These unique and often purported to be eccentric individuals preferred to live away from the masses, yet at the same time they did not want to be completely cut off from the benefits society offered them as the more savage outlaws did.

Their unique position acting as a sort of buffer between the civilized world and the outlands allowed them to conduct business with both worlds. Jackson suspected accomplishing this task was not an easy one and would require a certain unique sort of personality. He had heard negative rumors about some of these store owners and at present was feeling a bit anxious about what sort of person he might encounter inside.

This particular roadside fortress was surrounded by twelve-foot high chain link fence topped with concertina wire. At the base of the tall fence were masses of twisted barbed wire shaped into large balls with spiked metal poles jutting out from them at forty-five degree angles. The tips of the spears appeared to be covered with something dark reddish-brown in color. Jackson stomach clenched with the realization that the colors were likely old, dried bloodstains. He knew was going to have to be careful and watch out for himself in this strange place.

Halfway across the length of barbed wire and spike area at the end of a driveway was what appeared to be an access area presently blocked by a sliding gate. The gate was adorned with a large sign bearing a skull-and-crossbones insignia with painted blood tricking from a black circle in the center of the skull's forehead. Also present was the crudely printed warning, "All youse who has biness heer mus stopp uner pentalty of death." Jackson thought to himself how ten years ago that would most definitely not be considered an acceptable practice for welcoming potential customers to a store, but as everyone knew, that was a lifetime ago. Jackson pulled up cautiously to the gate and stopped in front of a white line on the driveway, which was marked with the word, "STOPP".

He noticed what appeared to be intercom mounted on a pole to his left. It had a red button labeled "TAK". Although the place looked as though it might be deserted, with uncertainty, Jackson pressed the talk button and said, "Hello? Hello? Is anyone there?"

At first Jackson didn't get a verbal reply but instead heard a series of mechanical whirring noises coming from above. He stuck his head out of the window and saw a camera moving on the top of the same pole on which the intercom was mounted. Then to his surprise he saw two large caliber machine guns mounted on the main entry fence moving into position, pointing directly at his windshield. He looked down at his chest and saw two red dots spaced about six inches apart on his chest. Jackson sat in his car dumfounded, unsure if he should try to back out onto the highway and just leave or if he should call for help. But remembering the carnage he had left behind him further north, Jackson decided instead to try something else.

He cautiously reached out and pressed the button again and asked, "Hello? Hello? Are you there? I want to purchase some clothing and other supplies. Can someone help me?"

A few stressful seconds passed, which seemed like hours, and with great relief, Jackson heard a crackling noise coming from the speaker. A grumpy sounding voice like that of an older man said "Yeah? Well wat in da bloody hell does yer want? An ya better makes it quick er else."

Again Jackson heard the mechanical sound of small motors as the gun barrels readjusted and both laser dots converged right over top of his heart. He assumed the proprietor of this trading post was trying to make a point, which Jackson felt he had done quite convincingly.

"I.... I need to buy some supplies." Jackson repeated, still fairly sure his life was not in danger and the store owner was simply taking the necessary precautions that were part of his doing business in a world filled with so many unforeseen variables, "I need some clothing... underwear... tooth paste... you know... travel supplies... just stuff like that."

"Ya gots money? Cash money?" The tinny voice replied over the intercom, "Cash be king in dis kingdom bucko. If'n ya got it, shows it ta me... an don go tryin nuttin' funny er I'll be blastin' yer arse ta pieces. Capish?"

"Ok... ok... all right... I get it." Jackson said as he carefully reached into his pants pocket and pulled out a few of the bills he had taken from the suitcase before leaving Yuengsville. Brent had told him he would need cash, so he pulled out a grand in large bills but he had no intention of allowing anyone to know how much he actually had; especially whoever was on the other end of that intercom and controlling those gun barrels. Jackson showed a bunch of twenty dollar bills, which he held in a playing card fan display in front of the camera. He said, "See... see... I have cash and I'm ready to deal."

A few seconds later the voice came back across the speaker saying, "Alrity pritty boy, get yer sorry arse in here an be doin it quick; jes as soon as dem gates in fronna ya opens up."

Then Jackson heard a new deeper pitched whirring sound as the gates began to slide open horizontally. "Now!

Ya dumass... now... get on in here." The voice shouted angrily through the speaker.

Jackson drove his car slowly into the parking area and before the back of the car had cleared the gates they were already on their way to closing. He pulled cautiously into a parking space in front of what he assumed to be the main entrance to the store. He tucked his revolver into the back of his pants as what he determined was a necessary precaution and slowly got out of the car.

What Jackson had not seen as he stepped onto the parking lot was a lurching, undead walking corpse, which had managed to follow his car into the compound before the gate began to slowly close behind him. Jackson stood by the driver's side of the car taking in the run down condition of the so-called trading post. As Jackson stood completely unaware of the impending danger, the rotting creature slowly made its way behind Jackson's car, heading hungrily toward the scent of living flesh.

The creature's dead eyes stared at the unsuspecting man standing next to the car with his back toward him. It could smell his warmth, his living flesh. It could sense the man's blood pumping through his veins. Its hunger for the warm contents waiting inside the man's body was overwhelming. It could think of nothing but sinking its claws into the man's belly, ripping apart his flesh, tearing out his hot, steaming innards and sinking what remained of its rotten and broken teeth into the sweet, pink sausage-like morsels of the man's spilled stomach cavity.

Jackson decided he had better head inside and see what the dilapidated store might have. He wasn't expecting much, but if he were lucky he might find something to suit his needs. Behind him the creature had cleared the left rear side of the car and with its arms outstretched, it was reaching hungrily just inches from digging its talon like fingernails into the soft tender meat of Jackson's unsuspecting throat. A steady stream of green and black colored drool seeped down from its slack-jawed mouth.

Then suddenly Jackson was startled by a loud banging noise as the front door of the place flew open and an odd looking old man ran frantically out into the parking lot with a rifle raised shoulder high and pointed right at

Jackson's head. Before Jackson even had a chance to react the man pulled the trigger and Jackson heard a bullet zing right by his left ear.

"You crazy old bastard!" Jackson swore automatically in reaction to his nearly having his head blown off. "What the hell is wrong with you? You nearly shot me, you crazy old buzzard!" Then Jackson heard a heavy thumping sound behind him. Jackson spun around quickly and saw a huge male zombie lying on the ground with the top of its skull blown off and its rotten brains dribbling brackish sludge onto the parking lot surface. Jackson was astonished and momentarily speechless.

CHAPTER 25

"Groddangit!" The strange on man growled. "Now looka wat ya went an made me hafta do!" Jackson had no idea what the odd man was talking about. And the word odd scarcely described the strange character. Jackson was having enough trouble trying to decipher the unusual dialect or language the old timer was spewing.

The man was about five foot five inches tall, average build, and was dressed in camouflage baggy pants and an untucked blue checkered flannel shirt over which he wore a fluorescent orange hunting vest. He had on bright pink running shoes, unlaced with no socks, and a bowler-style hat adorned with several long ostrich feathers tucked into a multi-colored striped hat band. His hair hung long from beneath the hat and he sported a massive crop of facial hair, which hung down to his chest, making him look even wilder and crazier than the savage gang of bikers Jackson had survived only a short time earlier.

"I'm sorry." Jackson said, not really knowing what it might be he was apologizing for. "But thank you... for... you know... for getting... that thing behind me... before it got me."

The man leaned his rifle against the front of the car and began making puppet-like gestures with his hands; first the left hand then the right, as if to suggest his hands were involved in a very important conversation with each other.

"Tank youse. Tank youse." He mimicked with his left hand. Then the right hand replied, "Oh, no. Tank youse."

Then again with the left "Oh no. Tank youse... I is in yer det ferever." And then the right hand, "Oh no. I begs to differ, but it' be me who is in yer det." Jackson realized the store owner was angry with him for some unknown reason, and that was apparently why he was mimicking and ridiculing him.

He watched silently as the back and forth mockery continued for a few more seconds until the strange man apparently grew tired of his own game. Then he looked coldly at Jackson, almost as if seeing him for the first time; all of the humor now completely gone from his face. He shouted as he pointed a gnarled finger accusingly at Jackson saying "You has costed me four hunnert dollers!"

Jackson was confused. "Excuse me Sir. You seem to be mistaken. My name is Jackson, and I don't understand what you're suggesting. I'm quite certain we've never met before, and therefore I have no idea how I could possibly owe you any money. In fact, I don't even know your name. May I ask you what your name is?"

"Name?" The man shouted. "Who gives a steamin pilea gofer shad wat me name is? Well I guesses you does for sum stupit reason. Er else ya woodn be assin me it now wood ya? Fer wat it's wort pritty boy, me name's Bob, Bob da trader. An dat's all ya needs to no. But don't go tinking dat makes us chums pritty boy. Ya still costed me four hunnert dollers, an I ain't 'bout ta ferget dat no time soon!"

"Look, Mr. Trader, I don't quite know what you are talking about." Jackson said still perplexed.

"Don't ya go callin' me Mr. Trader!" The strange little old man shouted. "Ya kin calls me Bob, er Bob da trader er even Trader Bob, but don ya never go callin' me Mr. Trader!"

"Ok. Mr... I mean Trader Bob. I'm sorry, but I still don't understand." Jackson replied. "You killed the thing. It's your dead kill. It shouldn't cost you anything. In fact, it will earn you a guaranteed hundred bucks! Surely you must know the law."

Once again Trader Bob began the two handed mockery.

Left hand: "Wat does ya means?"

Right hand: "Ya costed me four hunnert dollers!"

Left hand: "No. No. Don ya sees... I earnt ya one hunnert dollers!"

Right hand: "Butt it costed me..."

Left hand: "Suurly youse mus undderstand da laws."

Then once again Trader Bob became extremely agitated and began shouting and waving his fists in the air. "a'course I knows da law, ya stupit ijot... dead kills is wert a hunnert bucks... dead kills is wert a hunnert bucks. Even a haf-wit like you nos a dead kill is wert a hunnert bucks. But wat youse don' seems ta no is ifn I catches 'em walkin' den it's fibe hunnert. Oh yeah pritty boy. Catch 'em walking is wert fime hunnert. Now I gots to assume yous ain't so stupit as ya looks an dat ya does pritty good wit yer numers, rite? Well da last time I checked fibe hunnert takes away one hunnert is four hunnert. Dat der means... all tagether now..." He raised his hands as if conducting an orchestra or soliciting an answer from a room full of people. "Dat means dat youse still owes me four hunnert bucks on accounta me haffenta put dat one over dere down. How's dat? Simple 'nuf fer even a matt geenus like youse!"

Jackson was more confused than ever. He had been collecting bounties like everyone else in the country for the past eight or more years, but he knew nothing about any bounty being offered for catching any of the creatures alive; so to speak.

He inquired carefully as he had no idea what this strange man was capable of, "Please Bob. Forgive my ignorance. But I am unaware of any bounties being paid by the government for anything but dead kills. Why in the world would the government want them captured?"

"Gumment? Gumment?" The man shouted. "Wat sorta dimwit are youse anyhoo? Youse talk like a man wit a paper arsehole. I didn't say nuttin' ,bout no gumment. Gummcnt don't pay squat didley for non of 'em walkin. Gumment wants 'em dead as a doornail. Gumment wants 'em put down. An the gumment is a buncha cheap arses wit der dam hunnert bucks. But dem dat does want 'em walkin... dem traders. Oh yeah... dey do pays the big bucks. Dey pays fibe hunnert for dem wat still be walkin. But dat one dere on da ground... he only wert one hunnert. Dat mean youse owes me four hunnert."

Although still confused by what the odd man was saying, Jackson managed to decipher that someone, for God knew what reason, was willing to pay Trader Bob and people like him five times the going rate for a dead kill just for capturing the creatures without incapacitating them. Then he suddenly recalled the illegal games of chance that many of the outlanders ran. Could these traders be looking for zombies for these games? Then his stomach sank when he remembered the dreaded practice of Z-porn. Were these zombies being used for Z-porn as well? Jackson realized he may have stumbled onto something very important here. This was a whole new story in the making, he was certain of it. Both of those practices carried equally severe punishments from the government, yet apparently outside the cities, no one seemed to care in the slightest.

Still fishing for more information, Jackson asked cautiously, "I could be mistaken, but I don't believe it's legal to capture and sell these creatures. I'm quite certain it's against the law to do anything but put them down."

The storekeeper looked at him with distrust, and for a moment Jackson wondered if maybe he had crossed a line and the man might be inclined to kill him for his inquiry. But instead, Bob spoke to him with surprising candor. "Maybees dat mite be da case in da cities pritty boy, but incase ya didn' notice, youse ain't in no city no more. Youse be in da outlands. An out here we's gots our own laws."

Then the man lifted his rifle and pointed it once again at Jackson saying, "So youse is welcome ta come in da store an buys watever ya needs... likes I said before, I takes cash only... no checks an no frogging plastic. An jes sos we is clear 'bout tings, youse ain't leavin dis place in one piece, witout yer payin me da four hunnert youse owes me fer what I had ta do wit dat walkin maggot factory. Capish? An keeps in mind, ifn I was ta shoot ya and let ya bleed ta det, youse wood come bak an I kot ya, youse wood be wert fibe hunnert to me. Plus dat one over dere wood be six hunnert. Sos I'll be spectin ya to spend lots in here if ya gets me drift."

Although Jackson had no desire to be shot and sold as a zombie, neither did he intend to be cheated out of four hundred dollars by this highway robber. However, he also realized he had no choice but to go along with this maniac, at least for the time being, until he decided what he would do next. He also realized he needed to get the supplies regardless. He already had wasted enough time with the lunatic. He had to get his stuff and move on.

Trader Bob turned and hurried in through the front door. Jackson started to follow but stopped for a moment when he noticed the back of the man's car, which was parked nearby and was in even rougher condition than Jackson's Corolla had been. What caught his attention were the three stickers on the back of the car. They were worn with age and coated with road dust, but still legible. The first showed the silhouette of a hand gun and read "Don't worry. I won't call the police".

The second sticker was located in the center of the cracked and filthy back window and stated, "I have an attitude bigger than your old lady's ass." Jackson thought that statement was right in line with what he had seen of Trader Bob so far. This opinion was further supported by the last sticker, which read, "My other ride is your mother." Try as he might, Jackson could not help but chuckle at the audacity of the stickers.

"Hey pritty boy! Youse comin' er what?" Bob's raspy voice cackled from nearby as Jackson looked up to see the man waiting just inside the front door. "What? Ya tink I gots nuttin' better ta do all day but ta wait fer yer sorry arse? I tinks not."

CHAPTER 26

Jackson followed the odd man into the store. Once inside, Jackson walked around unassisted by Trader Bob. The place was a disaster area, with all sorts of unrelated items spread about in absolutely no logical order. The place contained everything imaginable and unfortunately it looked as if a bomb had gone off in the center of the store scattering everything in all directions. While he was looking about, Jackson saw what appeared to be the rusted ruins of some sort of small air vehicle lying under a drop cloth. It was shaped like black rounded top and had four small wings with propellers and four legs. When he saw the familiar company name underlined with the crooked smile, he recognized what it was immediately. It was one of the original drone vehicles used to deliver shipments for the internet company Amazon.

Jackson had researched the origin of the use of drones for a news story a few years earlier. It was back in 2013 that Amazon first approached the FAA, Federal Aviation Administration, with the idea of delivering packages using a newly developed system called Amazon Prime Air whose goal it was to deliver packages into customers hands in thirty minutes or less using unmanned aerial delivery vehicles. At the time, the FAA was reluctant to grant permissions even for a test run of the drones, but after years of court battles and support from loyal customers, by 2020 not only was Amazon using such a delivery system, but many other large companies were involved in the technology as well. Jackson had never seen one of the original units anywhere but in a museum. He had no idea how Trader Bob had acquired one or why he still had it. It made Jackson wonder what other interesting things could be found in the trading post. Perhaps he would return another day when he had more time and check the place out further. Although he suspected that might never happen because of the owner's insanity. Jackson's immediate concern was finding what he needed and getting out of the place alive and in one piece.

He managed to find everything he was looking for. While Jackson had been walking around the store, Trader Bob had momentarily left the building. Jackson assumed the man had done so to remove the downed zombie carcass. Jackson had been able to find several pairs of faded, worn jeans as well as a few shabby shirts a jacket and some shoes which he could tell had also seen better days. But that was all part of his plan; the one he was still finalizing in his mind. He wanted to not be noticed among the lowest element of society; the ones with whom he knew he would have to associate to find Sarah. For the briefest of moments, Jackson began to wonder about the original owners of the clothing he just selected. Had the clothing been looted from the bedrooms of abandoned homes? Had the original owners died? Or might they have been murdered for their possessions for the sole purpose of reselling them to such unscrupulous characters as Trader Bob?

Then a cold chill ran down Jackson's back as he recalled the undead creature he had downed that very morning, or the one outside currently being removed from the parking lot. He wondered if it were possible that the clothing he now held in his hands had been taken from the rotting bodies of one of those undead beasts. He had heard rumors of people who had worked at the burn piles during the early days of the outbreak, picking the corpses clean before adding them to the fire.

Jackson couldn't think about that now; he had to pay for the stuff he needed and get out while he still had the chance. He didn't want to rely too heavily on the armed escorts for help unless he had no other choice. Besides, when he needed them earlier, it had taken ten minutes or more for them to reach him. In this crazy place, ten minutes could mean the difference between life and death. He recalled how Trader Bob had shot the zombie outside and could just as easily have blown his own head off as well and no one would have been the wiser.

He had chosen not to speak any further to the storekeeper unless it became absolutely necessary, especially in regard to the four hundred dollars of which the man seemed fixated. He had decided the less he spoke to the trader about anything whatsoever, the better off he would be. Bob had just reentered the store and was standing behind the counter watching Jackson with suspicious hawk eyes. Jackson was doing his best to ignore the man's piercing gaze.

After a while, Jackson had no choice but to take his purchases up to the main counter to pay for them. It was a confrontation he had been hoping to avoid but one which he knew he had to deal with. Trader Bob tallied up his order and said "Dat'l be seben hunnert an fiffy bucks even."

"Excuse me?" Jackson asked, knowing where the conversation was heading, "I only bought these few very well-used items here. Where do you come up with seven hundred and fifty dollars?"

Trader Bob looked as if he were offended by Jackson's inquiry; as if Jackson had just questioned his integrity. Then he stared hard at Jackson and said through clenched teeth, "Tree hunnert an fiffy bucks fer all da stuff ya bought an four hunnert ya still ows me fer dat dead kill ya made me shoot. I tolt ya befer, I weren't gunna let ya leaves dis place witout payin me wat ya owes me."

Jackson knew things were about to go very bad, very quickly. He saw the trader place his hand on the rifle which was now sitting on the top of the counter, its barrel pointed right at him. Jackson peeled off five hundred dollars in cash and laid it on the counter. Then he reached his hand into his left pocket and slowly withdrew the Communications Unit he had received from Brent Holden.

He said, "There's five hundred dollars in cash. That covers my purchase and still gives you one hundred and fifty dollars more for your troubles. That plus the one hundred dollar dead kill bounty will still be a good score. How's about we call it square and I'll be on my way."

The man tightened his grip and said as he started raising the rifle, "I has a bedder idear. Why don we make it a even eight hunnert bucks fer yer pissin' me off an maybe I'll be lettin' ya leave here alive an witout any exter ledd in yer sorry carcass."

Jackson brought out his CU and pretended to be getting ready to call someone. Trader Bob became visually agitated saying, "Wat? Wat do ya tink yer doin now? Ya tink yer callin' da cops? Dunt makes me laugh. Der ain't no cops out here pritty boy. Da only law out dis way is watever gets da job don. Ain't no calvery comin' to hep you neider, bucko. Now eider add more to dat cash pile pronto er I start shootin. An wen I'm don wit ya I'll take all ya got. Oh yeah. An dunt ferget maybe I won kill yer head sos I can sell yer walkin' ded hide fer anoter fibe hunnert bucks."

Bob raised the rifle and as he started to aim it, Jackson pointed the CU at the man and pressed the yellow button on the side twice. A long projectile shot out the front of the unit and struck the trader on the left shoulder. His body began to tremble from the shockwaves coursing through his system. The gun fell from his hands to the floor, discharged fortunately not in Jackson's direction, and blew out one of the side windows. The man's eyes bugged madly from his head, and his decaying teeth clenched down tightly together as he groaned and twitched spasmodically. Spittle bubbled from the spaces where some of his teeth had gone missing a long time ago. After a few seconds of fitful convulsions, Trader Bob's eyes rolled up into his head and he fell to the floor like a rock, alive but still twitching uncontrollably.

Jackson could have easily taken back all of his money and left with the merchandise as well, while the idiot flopped like a fish out of water on the filthy, yellowed linoleum floor, but instead he chose to do what he felt was fair and left five hundred dollars on the counter. He was not concerned with any repercussions from Trader Bob, as he was likely never to see the man again despite his curiosity about the contents of the store. However, Jackson felt fair was fair. Bob had saved him from a zombie attack, and although the man's bizarre behavior might have landed him in the loony bin or jail ten years earlier, in this brave new world, such actions were commonplace, so Jackson figured the extra hundred and fifty plus the bounty on top of the overpriced clothing payment should calm the man down a bit once he recovered. Jackson retrieved his CU and placed it into his pants pocket.

Then he went out to his car and turned around to approach the main gates. He had no idea how to open them and thought he might have to search for some hidden switches. He didn't want to break through the gates with his car, as that would leave Trader Bob vulnerable to attacks. Then to his surprise once his car got close to the gates they slid open by themselves; obviously controlled by some sort of electronic eye which allowed for quick exit but no access. As he pulled through the gates they began to close behind him. In deference to Trader Bob's current pathetic condition, Jackson stopped to make sure no other creatures had managed to sneak through the gates. He would not have wanted such a fate to befall even someone as despicable as the storeowner.

More out of habit than anything, Jackson looked for oncoming traffic, of which there was none. He pulled out onto the highway and continued his journey toward the Fortified City of Reading and whatever fate had in store for him there.

CHAPTER 27

Jackson sat on the edge of his hotel bed, looking out the large picture window, watching the sunset over the tops of the buildings along the western skyline in the Fortified City of Reading; a city that, despite what he had been told ahead of time, had still proven to be quite a surprise to him.

What Brent Holden had told Jackson about Reading had been absolutely true; it had apparently gone through an incredible renaissance over the previous ten years. It had changed so drastically that Jackson could never have been prepared for what he had found. Almost every one of the old, formerly run-down row homes on just about every street had been either immaculately restored to a state of splendor or had been demolished and replaced with brand new, more magnificent structures.

Jackson stood up and walked across the room for a better look at the city outstretched below him. Although it was now almost dark, Jackson could see people walking the streets with apparently little concern about crime or danger. As he had been driving toward the city earlier that day, Jackson had imagined, based on prior impressions of Reading, that he would have no trouble finding a less-than-desirable part of town with several seedy corner bars in which to begin his search. However, he had been sadly mistaken. It had taken him a great deal of probing until he was able to locate an area in one of the few remaining un-gentrified neighborhoods not far from the banks of the Schuylkill river, which might have a chance of containing the sort of bar Jackson needed. He assumed this area had not yet been converted due to its low-lying location and the possibility of the river flooding. He decided once it got a bit later, he would venture down to that bar and see what he could discover.

He couldn't believe how different the city now looked. The Reading he remembered from eleven or twelve years earlier had been in the news almost daily for one horrendous crime or another. It had been populated by primarily lower income residents who were at the bottom of the social ladder and seemed to be killing each other on a weekly if not daily basis, as poor uneducated people had been doing for centuries.

Jackson recalled how just a month before the plague began, his cousin, Wayne, who worked in Reading at that time, had told him about seeing one such crime committed on the main business avenue and in broad daylight. Wayne and his coworkers were employed by a large bank located in the center of town along Penn Street. They were looking out their fourth floor office window one day at lunch; just basically people watching. What they had seen was an eclectic mix of tourists, business people, the downtrodden, and the homeless. It was a lovely summer day, and lots of people were coming and going about the town square minding their own business until suddenly everything went bad.

Wayne said he heard a woman let loose with an ear-splitting scream from the street below. When he and his coworkers looked in that direction, they saw a woman frantically waving her arms in response to something which was happening on the pavement just a few feet away of her. A man, who was later discovered to be a mentally deranged homeless person, was stabbing another man repeatedly. The wounded man was lying in a spreading pool of blood, dying as the woman screamed helplessly. After what seemed like dozens of thrusts with his long, rusted knife, the attacker simply stood up and began to calmly walk away, wiping the bloody blade on his filthy, tattered jeans as if nothing eventful had even happened.

Through the closed window, Wayne said he could hear the woman screaming for someone to call 911. Witnesses later said that woman had been a registered nurse, and despite her terror, once the homeless man had begun to leave, she approached the wounded man with the hopes of rendering first aid. Apparently the disheveled attacker must have heard her call out that the victim was still alive and in need of medical attention because he stopped in his tracks, turned and began walking purposefully back to the wounded man; apparently determined to finish what he had started. Seeing him returning, the nurse backed away in fear, crab walking helplessly then huddling in the corner of a nearby building, her clothing soaked in the dying man's blood. Then the madman began kicking his victim repeatedly in the head until the wounded man's body stopped moving permanently.

The attacker looked at the cowering woman who was crying pitifully and said "Now he's dead". The murderer turned to once again and casually walked away leaving bloody footprints on the concrete in his wake. Before he had gotten more than a few feet, a local store owner came running out from his place of business onto the sidewalk with a shot gun. Without hesitation he pumped two rounds at point-blank range into the killer's head, splattering bits of skull, brains, and gore all over the sides of the building, not to mention the front of the now practically catatonic nurse's clothing. The headless corpse dropped to the ground, his own blood now mingling with that of his victim. It made an oddly beautiful crimson pattern on the sidewalk as the sun reflected off the surface of the puddle. Wayne said he could see it all played out right in front of him, like a scene from some Hollywood action film; but this tragically was no movie.

So this was how Jackson had remembered Reading; a wild-west shoot em-up sort of practically lawless city where you could take your life in your own hands just walking along the street. Those days were apparently gone. Now the city was like some sort of utopian fantasy paradise. Surprisingly, Jackson felt less comfortable in this latest version of the city than the original violent rendition. Coming from humble beginnings, Jackson had never lived in such splendor, even before the outbreak and most certainly not since. As a result, he tended to be more comfortable with a much less lavish lifestyle. He imagined that was what his father meant many years earlier when he first told Jackson one of his favorite expressions. He said, "I suppose you can even get used to hanging if you do it long enough." Apparently Jackson had gotten so use to living without the finer things in life that places such as this were simply too foreign to fit into his comfort zone.

Jackson also found it extremely ironic how it had taken something as devastating as a zombie apocalypse and the near extinction of humanity to unite people of a like mind and to give them the initiative to transform such a downtrodden city into the paradise it now had become. Despite the city's current splendor, Jackson was still able to find a small area which had remained very close to the same blighted condition it had once been so many years earlier.

As Jackson sat in his room waiting for the sun to set, he recalled how he had also been surprised by the amazing condition of the portion of Route 61 leading into the city. A few miles south of that strange trading post where he had been forced to zap the bizarre storeowner, and a few miles north of the city, Jackson had noticed a remarkable change. The pitted and pock-marked roadway gave way to a perfectly smooth black-topped surface complete with glowing double-yellow lines down the center and equally bright white lines along the shoulders. He had all but forgotten what good road surfaces were like, and he wondered if even in the time before the Z43 virus the roads had ever looked that good. He didn't believe so.

Jackson had heard stories about a relatively new process known as Systematic Expansion, or SE, which he was told was being put into practice by a few more affluent cities. There was talk about someday starting the process in Yuengsville, but that might be a year or more in the future. Apparently, judging by the condition of the highway outside of Reading, the process was well underway there.

The Systematic Expansion process was a multi-phase system. The first phase was to put together a crew comprised of dozens of road workers, highway equipment, and supplies, as well as a small army of well-armed and well-trained spotters. The road workers would begin resurfacing the roadway for several miles beyond the city limits under the watchful eyes and weapons of the spotters. This was often extremely hazardous work, and the armed sentinels had to be alert for clusters of roaming zombies, especially in the more rural areas. Likewise, they often found themselves in life and death skirmishes with the savage dwellers of the outlands that were resistant to the civilized world's attempts to encroach on what they saw as their own free territory.

There was often much bloodshed involved with what at one time would have been considered the simple task of road resurfacing. Jackson had heard stories of how this type of expansion was beginning to take place more frequently thanks to the reformation of the national governments and the gradual rebuilding of the armed forces, but soldiers as well as police were still few in number, so the work was always hazardous.

Once the road had been extended out perhaps two miles, the workers would back up about one hundred feet and build a temporary entrance and security gate. Then they would begin to spread out in both directions perpendicular to the road installing tall barbed-wire topped temporary fencing along the way. They would built out perhaps a mile on each side of the highway then work their way back toward the city until they connected with the main city defensive walls. This would in essence provide a two mile wide by two mile deep area of captured wild lands known as a buffer zone, because it was no longer considered part of the outlands but it was not yet part of the city.

These buffer zones could not yet be designated as safe areas, despite the barrier of fencing; that was until they had been properly cleared. Even though many of the undead and wild outlanders usually were dealt with during the road and fence construction phase, the area was still deemed unsafe until all of the locals, both undead and living, had been accounted for and properly dispatched. Then the land could be considered cleared of danger and could become incorporated into the main community.

Once that had been accomplished, the main gate to the city would be moved out to the far end of the former buffer zone, allowing for the next level of expansion to begin. This activity took place simultaneously at various roads leading into the cities in every direction. Eventually the many cleared buffer zones would intersect, merge, and the newly located outer fortified barriers of the city would be properly reinforced. The result was a two mile expansion of the city in every direction. This was often a slow and time-consuming process. It could take as long as a year or more to create a complete ring of expansion around a large city and then another year to properly develop it.

Not all of the newly reclaimed areas were designated to be developed for housing. Certain areas were set aside for cooperative farming while still others were designated for industrial as well as business purposes. In essence, Systematic Expansion was designed to slowly take back the world from both the undead as well as the savage outlanders, while systematically eradicating both in the process.

Some might have considered this a form of genocide; especially in regards to the savages, who might still technically be considered human beings. A few more politically active types noted the similarity to taking land from Native Americans hundreds of years earlier, but if they did object, they mostly kept their opinions to themselves. This was likely because the ruling governments had determined it was the only way for a true civilized version of humanity to survive. As a result, no one bothered to raise a fuss if a few thousand wild mountain men died in the process of making their world a safer place.

While he had been driving along the glass-smooth highway, Jackson had noticed another one of those zombie crossing signs like the one he had seen for the first time earlier that morning. A few hundred feet beyond the sign, Jackson saw something that at first he couldn't believe. In the center of the road lay a decomposed hand and forearm, likely dropped there by some shambling creature; perhaps it had even been a creature's own limb which had simply rotted and fallen off. This sight, although disturbing, was not what had caught Jackson's attention. He had seen many such similar sights during the past ten years. What he found unbelievable was the condition of the appendage.

It must have landed right in the middle of the highway sometime between the time the roadway had been resurfaced and the time when the new lines had been painted. Apparently, the worker who had been driving the line painting truck hadn't bothered to move the arm from the roadway; he just drove over it and painted two yellow lines right over top of the forearm, then continued on his merry way. Jackson thought to himself as he was unable to suppress a sarcastic chuckle, "Some things, like laziness, even an apocalypse can't seem to change."

Now, as he sat on his bed in his hotel looking out at the setting sun, Jackson decided it was time for him to go. There was a young girl who needed his help, and he was determined to find her, and now he had what he thought was a good plan in mind for exactly how he was going to locate Sarah. He only hoped he would be successful and they would both get out of this alive.

CHAPTER 28

"Hello Jackson," Andrea Ridge said as she answered her CU upon seeing Jackson's picture appear on the screen. Her voice wasn't exactly cold, but Jackson could tell it didn't sound all that happy to speak to him either. He knew his wife's moods and could certainly tell she was not thrilled with Mr. Jackson Ridge at this moment. "How everything going?" There was more obvious displeasure in her voice.

Jackson hesitated for a moment, unsure of how best to go about not telling Andrea anything of what had happened to him during his most eventful day. She knew her husband just as well as he knew her, so he had to be careful how he spoke. There was no way he could let her know that he had come so close to being killed, or at a minimum severely injured, several times in that one single day. He hoped her growing displeasure with his decision to take the assignment would cloud her judgment and overshadow her recognition of any false tones his voice might involuntarily convey. Jackson decided the best alternative was to not answer her question, since he suspected it wasn't really something she wanted to know anyway. Instead he chose to acknowledge the proverbial thee hundred pound gorilla in the room, which was most likely the subject she really wanted to discuss.

"Look Honey. I told you earlier I wouldn't have taken this assignment if you really didn't want me to."

Andrea said with a mixture of sadness and anger, "And what was I supposed to do Jackson, forbid you from taking it? Was I supposed to call Bill McCleary and tell him I wouldn't allow you to do it? For God's sake, Jackson, I'm you wife and I'm supposed to support you. If I told you not to take the assignment I wouldn't be a very supportive wife now would I?"

Jackson sensed his wife was just beginning to calm down a bit. He understood what she was going through.

She was in the middle of an emotional tug-of-war. She wanted to support him, but she didn't want him in harm's way. She loved him, but she was also a wife and a mother living in a very dangerous world. She and Kyla needed him to survive. The idea of doing so without him was unthinkable for her.

Jackson said, "Thanks Sweetie. I really appreciate that. I understand just how tough this is for you. And I really meant what I said earlier, I would have refused this assignment if it weren't for the fact that a young girl's life is in danger."

The phone remained silent for a moment, then Andrea said softly with genuine concern, "And what about your life Jackson?"

For a moment he wondered if somehow someone had told her about the various near misses he had earlier that day. "No need to worry Babe. My life is just fine. I'm sitting here in my hotel room bored stiff and waiting to go out and start gathering information," Jackson lied. "This job is probably going to end up being every bit as uneventful as writing obituaries from home would be."

"Yeah. Well, you just make sure I won't have to read yours. Understand?" Andrea said. Jackson thought he could notice some more of the frustration starting to leave her voice. Perhaps just hearing him and knowing he was all right was enough to calm nerves.

"So how was your day?" Jackson asked, doing his best to divert the conversation away from himself, "And how's Kyla doing?"

Andrea said, "Well, my day was pretty much the same as always. My first client Mabel Charles passed on as we thought she would today. Jyleen was with me for the finalization procedure."

"No problems I assume."

"No." Andrea said, "No really. A minor problem with some new test equipment but we worked around it. It's just..."

"Just what?"

Andrea explained, "It's just so darned hard sometimes... you know... doing what I have to do. I mean, I know it's necessary and for the best but still... but it's so uncomfortable for me since one minute they're one of us and the next they're one of those horrible things... it feels like each time I have to... you know... put one of them down like that... I feel like I lose a little bit of my own humanity."

Jackson thought for a moment about just how profound that last statement was. He said, "I can't even pretend to know what it's like to do what you do every day, Honey. All I do know is that it takes a very special and amazing person to rise to the occasion and do what needs to be done. And you are truly the most amazing woman I have ever known. That's just one of the reasons I love you."

Andrea chuckled sardonically, "Only the always creative Jackson Ridge could take a statement about something as depressing as the act of incapacitating zombies and turn it around into a declaration of love. And that's just one of the reasons I love you too."

"So." Jackson asked, "How was my baby girl Kyla's day at nursery school today?"

Andrea hesitated for a moment and Jackson sensed the reluctance in her response and said, "Not again! Please tell me it didn't happen again"

"Yes." Andrea replied. "Unfortunately it did. This time there were three of them which appeared at the back fence. No one was hurt, the kids were all taken inside, and Jake Schwartz took care of everything."

"Dammit." Jackson said, "I swear when I get back I'm going to write a scathing piece on those morons on the Ashton Council of Elders. Why in the name of God won't they get off their lazy butts and move that daycare into the center of town? I mean... honestly? This is worse than ridiculous."

"Yeah." Andrea agreed. "I don't get it either. Both Mrs. Johnston and the Reedys have been relentless in their attempts to coerce, pressure, and practically threaten the council to move on this."

Jackson said, "Well, it looks like it's time for me to sharpen my pen and find out if it's truly mightier than the sword. This just became my top priority for when I get back home.

"Just make sure you do; and soon." Andrea said, reminding Jackson of the fact that she was still not pleased with everything going on. This made him hesitate for a moment, especially in light of what he was planning for the evening ahead. Although he really didn't think he was arranging anything all that much more dangerous than his original assignment had been, part of him wondered if this change of plans he had made the hazard more likely.

"I'll be very careful honey. I promise," Jackson said. "It may be very late until I get in tonight, so I'll tell you what. I'll set an alarm and call you first thing tomorrow morning after you drop Kyla off at daycare. Deal?"

Andrea replied. "Deal. And I'm holding you to it."

With that, the Ridges said their goodbyes, and Jackson got changed into his disguise for the evening and prepared to hit the streets.

CHAPTER 29

Jackson sat quietly at the corner table, nursing his mixed drink, rolling the torn remnants of his paper napkin into small balls while listening to snippets of conversations around him. It was at times like this he was grateful for having been born with such an unnoticeable face. To the patrons in the bar who looked as if they had all seen better days, he was just one of them; nothing more than another normal, everyday, down on his luck Joe who happened to stop by for a much-needed drink, although he had to admit to himself the ruse might have been much more convincing had he not showered for a few days. Then he would have fit in perfectly with the people around him. Several of them had staggered past his table on their way to the bathroom, and the body odor surrounding them was palpable.

He had chosen to just sit quietly for a while, observing and listening, being fairly certain what he was waiting for would come to him shortly. He was still contemplating all of the things he had experienced in the past twelve hours. That morning, he had thought he was simply going to be filling in for an injured reporter; a fairly bland and uneventful assignment, but now he was on the trail of a kidnapper and from all he had heard, a psychopath. Jackson had seen a gang of mutant would-be assailants slaughtered right before his eyes, and he was almost killed first by an undead creature, then once again by a crazy storekeeper. Jackson felt he had experienced more than his share of excitement for one day, but he knew more action would definitely be on his radar if he were fortunate enough to locate Sarah. He took another sip from his drink. The whiskey in his cocktail tasted surprisingly good for such an undesirable establishment, and the soothing warmth it provided on its way to his stomach helped to relax him.

Jackson recalled how when he had arrived at his hotel, he had asked the where he could find a local bar; not one of the high-end upper-crust types of nightclubs or restaurants, of which there were obviously an abundance, but more of an old-time corner bar. He told the man at the front desk he wanted the sort of place where a common working man could still find friends of a like mind. Even though the hotel where he had chosen to stay was the least ostentatious he had been able to find, the desk clerk seemed reluctant to send him anywhere but the high-end establishments. The concierge had written down the names of several bars on a sheet of hotel stationary for Jackson, stating snobbishly that if any of them didn't suit his needs he could always try some place the man had simply referred to as "that dive" down by the river.

The first several of the places the man had recommended were, as Jackson had assumed, far too upscale for what he needed, so he decided to venture out on his own. He stopped at a few corner bars in a slightly less desirable part of town but was disappointed to discover these places weren't quite right either. Eventually, he recalled what the hotel worker had reluctantly suggested and had referred to as "that dive down by the river". Jackson ventured along a dark side street which ended near the banks of the Schuylkill River. The place he found was the only bar in the area, and even the bar's name "The River Rat" seemed to indicate it had to be the place the clerk had mentioned, and it appeared to be just the sort of bar Jackson was looking for.

When he first entered The River Rat, Jackson had stopped at the main bar area, and as usual, he had to wait a long time for the bartender to take notice of him; despite the fact that there were only two other patrons in the bar at that time. Eventually however, he got the opportunity to order a mixed drink and ordered a double seven-and-seven. Jackson realized it was an old fashioned cocktail left over from the twentieth century, but it was also one he understood was still regularly ordered among the working classes. Back in Schuylkill County, it had been known as a "highball," but Jackson was fairly certain that name might be foreign in this place.

Years earlier, back shortly after Jackson graduated from college, before the world went the way of the dead, he had researched the name highball and learned it was originally a name given to an assortment of mixed drinks made up of some sort of alcohol and a soda mixer. It wasn't restricted to Seagram's Seven and Seven-up, but for some reason, the name highball stuck with that particular seven and seven variation; at least that is to say, it had stuck in Schuylkill County.

Jackson was sitting and thinking now about the plan he had come up with on his way to Reading. It had been the reason he had stopped at that crazy Trader Bob's store in the first place. He needed the right clothing to pull off the ruse he had concocted. Jackson wanted to dress in a way that would make him appear like one of the poorer local folks that hung out in bars such as this, but only to appear so to the casual observer. For the people who he figured he needed to get in touch with, he wanted to look as though he was actually someone with money who was only pretending to look like the locals in order to blend in. It sounded like a bit of convoluted logic even to Jackson, but it was an idea he felt might actually work.

He knew the police tracking him would be furious if they learned of his idea. They had instructed him to simply go around gathering information. Jackson thought if he had all the time in the world at his disposal that idea might have some merit, but he realized by the time he got to Reading almost a day would have gone by since Sarah's abduction. He knew the time for asking questions was long past. He had to come up with some way to get the answers he needed and get them quickly. If Deimos had Sarah, then Jackson could assume he was only interested in her for sexual reasons; either his own or for the purposes of pornography or possibly even prostitution or sex slavery.

He decided the quickest way to get close to Sarah was to present himself as a traveler with a lot of money who was trying to pass himself off as one of the locals and not doing a very good job of it. He also needed to convince the right people he was actually a degenerate; a pervert with a fondness for young girls. Jackson believed if he could connect with someone in Deimos' network of criminals, he might get lucky enough to actually be taken directly to Sarah. Although he knew the odds of this happening were slim at best, if he could at least get close, maybe he could possibly find out where she was being held.

While at the bar, Jackson tried to strike up a conversation with the bartender, who proved to be not very interested in what he had to say and was surprisingly antisocial. Jackson supposed such a man might not make it in his chosen profession in any bar but a seedy dive like the one he was now in. Despite the bartender's initial unwillingness to talk, Jackson did manage to get him to take notice when he mentioned he was a traveler visiting from the north and was interested in finding something fun and exciting to do. This momentarily caught the bartender off guard and had caused him to give Jackson a curious and perhaps suspicious look.

Then the man came over closer to Jackson and after looking around the room, bent over and asked in a quiet voice which was almost a whisper, "Jus wat sert of enertainment mite it be youse is lookin fer?" The man's breath was almost as foul as was his body odor. The combination turned Jackson's stomach and made him involuntarily pull back a few inches in a feeble attempt to escape the stench, although he was careful to do so discretely as not to offend the man, whose help he needed regardless of his pungent scent.

Now trying desperately to maintain his cover and not vomit, Jackson replied, "Uh... well... I... lct's just say... I'm a man of... of discerning tastes in women that tends to um... lean toward the... shall we say younger set?" Hearing himself suggesting such a revolting idea to the stranger behind the bar; even that one simple act made Jackson cringe with disgust. Regardless, he knew this was an essential part of his plan, and it was why he was in the bar in the first place. It was what he honestly believed he had to do in order to find Sarah.

Jackson slid back away from the bar and nodded at the corner table. "I'll tell you what. I'm going to go over there and sit for and relax a while. I'm wagering that you're the sort of man who can make things happen around here. If I'm not mistaken, and I don't believe I am, I'm sure you'll be able to contact someone who would be willing to assist this lonely traveler in finding exactly what I need while I am so far from home. Then he gave the bartender a conspiratorial wink and a nod while sliding over five twenty dollar bills and saying, "For your troubles my new friend".

He turned around, walked across the bar and sat down at the corner table. If he had correctly assessed the bartender's character, or lack of which, the man would be making a few calls, which eventually would put Jackson in touch with just the sort of people he needed to perhaps lead him to Sarah. The generous tip told the bartender that despite his common appearance, Jackson had money and was willing to part with it for what he desired, and that was exactly what happened. A few minutes after Jackson was seated, he saw the bartender turn his back, take out a CU, and make some calls, keeping his eye on Jackson the entire time in the faded and cracked mirror behind the bar.

Now all Jackson could do was to wait and see what would happen next. As he sat thinking, Jackson suddenly recalled his brief visit to Sean Patel's lab earlier that day. He reached down and patted the right spare snap pocket of his pants. The DMSD Sean had given him was still safely tucked away there. Jackson thought about Sean's suspicions and decided when he got back to his hotel he was going to fire up his computer and take a look at the information Sean had put on the drive. The more the thought about it, the more he believed it actually was possible that the same people he was currently hunting could very well be involved in what Sean thought were deliberate murders of young prostitutes. Even if they weren't directly involved, Jackson was certain they might provide some leads as to who was. He was certain once the cops finally got their hands on the kidnappers and started tightening the screws, the criminals would be looking for any possible way to make a deal to lessen their sentences. Perhaps they'd even be willing to drop a dime on whoever was killing the hookers as well. Jackson realized this too was a long shot, but stranger things had been known to happen.

He had been sitting at the table for better than an hour after initially speaking with the bartender when a man entered and took a seat at the bar. Unlike he had done with Jackson, the bartender didn't make the new arrival wait but immediately brought a drink over for him. The man was obviously a regular at the bar and someone with whom the bartender appeared to be quite familiar. Jackson watched the pair speaking in apparent whispers and noticed the new arrival glancing into the bar mirror and watching Jackson while the bartender spoke.

"Good," Jackson thought to himself. If he was correct, and he was sure he was, this was the man the bartender had called. It was also likely the man would be arriving at his table shortly to learn more about just what sort of entertainment he might be able to provide for the lonely traveler.

After a few minutes, Jackson noticed the bartender give the stranger a glass very similar to the one he currently held in front of him, which was now almost empty. He must have told the man what Jackson was drinking. Jackson assumed things were about to happen, so he set his CU down on the table in front of him, being sure to press the black button on the right side of the unit. According to Brent Holden, this would not only record and store his conversation but would transmit it to whoever was monitoring his activities so they would know what, if any information he was receiving immediately.

The stranger turned away from the bar and approached Jackson's table with the drink extended. He sat it down on the table and took a seat opposite Jackson.

CHAPTER 30

"Seven and seven?" The man inquired. "That's a bit of an old fashioned sort of drink wouldn't you say?"

"Maybe I'm an old fashioned sort of guy." Jackson said, trying his best to keep his cool but feeling very uneasy. He extended his hand to accept the drink and asked. "May I assume it is a double as well?"

"That it 'tis." The man replied cordially. "Sam at the bar told me what your preference was." Jackson had a feeling the stranger might not just be talking about the drink, but might be alluding to the sexual preference he had hinted to with the bartender as well. He was certain the bartender, Sam his name apparently was, had given the stranger quite an ear full.

The man was dressed very much as Jackson had been with jeans, a flannel shirt, and a leather jacket, all of which were well worn and showing their age. He appeared to be in his middle to late thirties and although by all appearances to be rugged and street tough, Jackson sensed there was an air of intelligence about the man he did hadn't anticipated. He had assumed anyone involved with such a deplorable group of individuals would be crass and ignorant. The man also didn't have the foul unwashed scent of so many of the other bar patrons. He was obviously something more than just a common street thug or savage outlander. This was a business man, a man with a purpose, someone who Jackson was certain commanded respect from his associates and could get things done.

"I hear you are from the north." The man inquired. "How far north?"

Jackson was reluctant to give away too much information, so he said cryptically. "Far enough north that I don't know my way around this city, but no so far as to not have heard there was some special entertainment available in this area for a gentleman of particular tastes such as myself; a gentleman with money to spend."

The man appeared to be somewhat interested in what Jackson said but was doing his best to keep his emotions in check. It was apparent this man was now moving into full negotiation mode, preparing to make himself the best deal he could possibly arrange.

"Please forgive me for being so blunt." The man said looking at Jackson's worn clothing, "But to be perfectly honest, you don't exactly appear as though you're the type of person who has a lot of cash to spare. You know, your manner of dress doesn't exactly suggest the type of wealth you want me to believe you might have."

Jackson replied, "Well, that's certainly good to hear. Because that's exactly the look I was shooting for. You see, the last thing I need in a bar like this, no offense intended, is to have the locals assume I have a good deal of money. But I can assure you my friend, I have all the cash you will require."

The man looked Jackson over carefully again then said, "All right then. I appreciate a man who likes to get right down to business. So if I may ask then, what do your particular tastes entail?"

Jackson stared at the man for a while then asked hesitantly, "As I said, I'm new to this city and I don't know you. You just walked in here, spoke with the bartender and now, although you seem to be the person I need to deal with, well I'm a bit concerned. How do I know for sure you aren't some sort of undercover cop or member of some do-gooder militia trying to entrap me? I'm smart enough to know that what I like involves activities which tend to be frowned upon by the legal community." Jackson was certain this man was exactly what he represented himself to be and was in no way a police officer, but he was playing a game of cat and mouse to help solidify his cover story while simultaneously recording their conversation and trying his best to get the man to say as much as he possibly could.

"And how do I know you are not one of the same?" The man countered. "For all I know you could be the one trying to entrap me and set me up for a big fall."

"Good point," Jackson replied, thinking quickly. "But for what it's worth, I can assure you I'm not looking to do anything but find myself some special company for the evening. I promise you I am no cop."

Then the man took a very dangerous looking handgun out of his jacket pocket and placed it on the table, resting his hand on it, his finger near the trigger and its barrel pointed directly at Jackson. His face took on an expression the likes of which Jackson had never seen and he instantly knew this man was a stone cold killer. He also suspected the man wouldn't hesitate to kill Jackson if he suspected trouble. "And I most certainly hope that's not the case, my new friend. You see, I'm well respected in this bar, and if my finger were to say, accidentally twitch and pull this very sensitive trigger and blow your hot steaming, guts all over that wall behind you, no one in here would say a word about it. Your remains would simply disappear into the dark currents of the Schuylkill River, and the mess in here would be quickly cleaned up so that no one would be the wiser. So, my horny little friend, do we have an understanding here?"

Jackson looked down at the menacing gun and felt as if his bowels had turned to jelly. He had to somehow find a way to at least appear to have regained his composure, so he could continue to play his role, but for the moment he was seriously concerned he might soil himself. Jackson swallowed hard, pulled his gaze away from the weapon, met the man's piercing, deadly stare, and said with as much calm as he could muster. "Well... um... It appears we're at a bit of a stalemate here. You don't know or trust me and I don't know or trust you." Then after a moment or two of very uncomfortable silence, Jackson said, "However, since you've got that gun and I have nothing but money, I see I'm gonna have to be the one to take the first step here. Besides, as you may have guessed, I'm desperate and apparently need to find a way to do business with you."

"Then you had better state exactly what you want and you had better do it quickly because my patience is wearing thin and my finger is beginning to feel a bit twitchy." The man replied with a deadly serious look in his eyes.

Jackson glanced down at the gun again then swallowed to get some moisture into his rapidly drying throat and said, "Well, despite my better judgment here goes nothing. I'm... I'm looking to buy sex; but not just any run-of-the-mill type of sex either. I'm looking for someone, hopefully such as yourself... who can hook me up with..." Jackson hesitated and looked around the room for effect, as if alert to potential eavesdroppers, then said more ominously, "I want a young girl. I need a young girl; a very young girl, perhaps twelve or thirteen years old. As I said earlier, I have a lot of money and I am willing to pay for what I want."

CHAPTER 31

The man sitting across the table stared intently at Jackson for a few seconds longer, then slowly lifted his finger from the trigger, withdrew the handgun, and placed it back into his coat pocket. His murderous look began to fade, replaced surprisingly quickly by a cordial albeit still somewhat suspicious smile. Jackson thought of it as a smile painted on the face of a serpent. This character was obviously equipped with an extremely volatile personality, and depending upon what Jackson said and how he said it, he feared he could find himself dead in the blink of an eye. He had been in dangerous situations before, but none quite as unpredictable as he suspected dealing with this man might be.

The man said in a pleasant tone, "There you go, my new friend. Now that wasn't so difficult was it? I hope you do understand, I need to be very careful in my line of work, I can't just accept what anyone says at face value. I don't know if you realize it or not but in this city, the penalties for what we are about to arrange can be death. That's why I needed to be certain. So... now we've established neither of us is the law and one of us is someone who can provide a service, while the other is a person with, shall we say, a discriminating sexual palate. You know what you want and I am just the man to get it, or shall we say get her, for you. I need to point out that this service will not come cheap, however. Then again, few things worthwhile in life ever do. I will, however, guarantee you complete satisfaction. And while we're discussing your wish list, do you have any specific race in mind for your little princess?" The man gave him a knowing grin, exposing several brown and rotten teeth. Jackson thought, just because the man appeared to be well educated, it didn't mean he also had access to good dental care; or even cared about such things, which was apparent in his disturbing smile.

Jackson hesitated for a moment. He had not anticipated being asked that question. Hearing the friendly; almost titillating manor in which the man spoke told him he had been playing his role as a twisted degenerate very well; perhaps too well. He was actually starting to even make himself feel nauseous.

Hiding his true feelings and continuing to play this role, Jackson grinned sheepishly back at the man, doing his best to seem as creepy as any man with such disgusting desires would be, "Well... You see, now don't get me wrong... I'm not a bigot or anything like that... I mean, I don't want you to think... never mind... you probably don't even care... what I'm trying to say is I just would prefer a young white girl... a very pretty one. You know, the type who has the potential grow up to be a real beauty someday... but at this young age... seems very innocent and... and unspoiled." Jackson let out a slight sigh to make the man believe he might be getting aroused just from their talking about what he wanted. He felt this little additional touch might help to make his act more convincing.

"I see." The man said knowingly, never taking his eyes off of Jackson. Then he inquired, "Leave me guess, you like to pretend these sweet young girls are virgins whether they are or not, and as such you get to be the one who 'spoils' them. Am I correct? Ha ha! I thought so. And maybe you like to pretend to be a naughty uncle or maybe some lecherous family friend? Or maybe you're a really weird sicko and want the young girls to call you Daddy while you are having your way with them. Am I getting warmer?"

Jackson blushed, and although it was more of a reaction of his own true embarrassment at the subject of the conversation, it worked perfectly well for helping to instill the shy but degenerated image, "Um... well... well yes... I suppose." He confessed, "In fact, whatever your fee is for such an arrangement, if you can find me... well... a real virgin... I would be willing to pay double."

"Well then." The man said with a fiendish chuckle, "It looks like today may be your lucky day, Mr. .... What did you say your name was?"

"I didn't." Jackson replied, "And I really would prefer to keep it that way. So why don't you just call me Mr. Jones?"

"Ha ha! Mr. Jones it is." The man laughed again. "And in that case, why don't you just call me Mr. Smith."

"Very well, Mr. Smith." Jackson replied, Now tell me, why did you just say today was my lucky day? Do you... have someone specific in mind for me?"

The man looked around the room then hunched over and whispered conspiratorially with rank breath tinged with tooth decay and alcohol, "Well it just so happened that we got a new arrival a night or so ago, and not only is she very young, but she is also very attractive and is very much a virgin. But that also means she will be very expensive."

Jackson backed up slightly to get out of range of the man's foul breath. "How... how expensive." Jackson said, not trying to conceal his excitement. He hoped the scumbag across the table would mistake his eagerness about possibly finding Sarah for sexual excitement. "I... I really do have a good deal of money and I really am willing to pay double."

"Well..." Smith said appearing to be contemplating price, although Jackson was certain Smith knew exactly what he planned on charging. "We had set her original price at two thousand for the night, but since her arrival... well there has been a bit more heat applied to the situation then we had anticipated and unfortunately we'll have to raise the price to three grand."

"Three thousand?" Jackson said feigning surprise. "Wow, that's certainly a lot of money."

The man looked at him slyly and said, "Well, that's the base price we set for her. And keep in mind, once she has been 'spoiled', even by a fine gentleman such as you, her price will drop dramatically. That is, until she is either of legal age or simply worn out. Then the price comes way down. Once on the market, these girls have a very limited shelf life, so three grand is the going rate; but as you may recall, you said you would be willing to pay double our rate for an authentic virgin. That means the price will be six thousand dollars."

"Oh my." Jackson said pretending to be shocked. He was fairly certain the character across the table from him was going to provide Deimos with only three thousand and would keep the additional three thousand for himself. He thought of the statement about there being no honor among thieves. "That really is a lot of money. But I did agree to pay you double didn't I? Damn, I shouldn't have spoken so soon. Apparently I'm really not very good at negotiating. So what exactly will I get for my six thousand?"

"Just about anything you might like within reason." The man replied. "We'll provide a clean room with a bed, bathroom with a shower, and whatever sort of alcohol or pills you may prefer. We'll make sure the girl is likewise freshened and appropriately cleaned up as well. We may need to sedate her slightly in order to make her more... more cooperative, if you know what I mean. You'll have her from the time we drop her off until ten o'clock the following morning. Then we'll return and take her away. During that time, you can do whatever you want sexually to her and degrade her in any way you choose as long as you don't do her any physical damage. And if you'd like, for another two hundred bucks, we can provide several digital video recorders and tripods so you can record the festivities from various angles for future enjoyment. And of course, you will have the only copy of the recordings on your own personal data cards."

"Oh... um... no... thank you." Jackson said surprised, "As tempting as that might sound, the whole video thing won't be necessary."

The man further instructed, "No problem. Whatever works for the customer. And as I said earlier, all we demand is that you don't hurt or damage her physically. In this particular case, we don't include the taking of her virginity, since that's what you're paying for. But I'm sure you do understand exactly what I'm referring to... no rough stuff. If that's something you think you want than you need to let me know now. We have other girls specifically for that purpose."

Smith chuckled and said, "Ha ha. We call them HPBs or Human Punching Bags. Ha ha. But in the case of this girl, after we get her back, we'll check her out from stem to stern, and of course if she is injured in any way... well let's just say we won't be very happy. And if we aren't happy, you'll find yourself extremely unhappy, if you know what I mean."

Jackson knew exactly what he meant. He was thinking about the big gun the man had laid on the table a few minutes earlier.

Then Smith said, "Oh, and although I shouldn't need to mention the obvious, I'll just to put it out there to make sure I covered all the bases... you can't kill her either. Again, if you want to add that option to the evening's entertainment, we'll have to likewise substitute a different girl as with the beating option; you know, a girl who is much less marketable or has reached her expiration date. And then, of course, adding that that particular feature will also increase the price. However, we do offer a substantial discount if you let us film the act for later resale."

Jackson was stunned, "What? K...k...k... kill her? What are you saying? Why the hell would I want to kill her or kill anyone for that matter? What kind of degenerate do you think I am."

Smith looked at him with an odd expression as if to suggest he knew exactly what sort of degenerate he was. Then Smith glanced around the room and again speaking softly, said, "Easy my friend... I didn't mean to offend you. But I need to put these rules out there for you so we have a complete understanding. We get all kinds in this game, and as you pointed out, I really don't know you. See... you might think asking for a young virgin for the night is a bit socially unacceptable, but in my profession, such a request is quite tame. After all, it's not like you asked me to arrange for you to have sex with a corpse or even a dead head."

"What?" Jackson said with obvious shock. "Do some people ask for that?"

"More often than you might imagine." The man replied nonchalantly. "And yes we do occasionally get some men who want to snuff the girl when they are done. So as you can see, what you are asking for although quite illegal is really pretty mild."

Jackson felt himself getting physically ill at the thought that such reprobates were actually out there walking the streets of the same world in which he was trying to raise a family. And he was revolted that people such as this character Smith and that madman Deimos were actually making money by enslaving helpless young girls. He thought of his own little Kyla and could scarcely maintain his composure. Although Jackson was not a violent man, he honestly believed at that moment he would like nothing better than to put a bullet between Smith's beady eyes.

He suddenly felt he needed to get home to Andrea and Kyla and wrap his protective arms around them and hold them close forever. His mind was reeling at all he had learned in the last few minutes. He couldn't even be certain the girl this criminal would be providing for him would actually be Sarah, but his gut told him it just might be. And if it wasn't Sarah, he would have to find some way to help that girl as well. He was thankful their entire conversation was being recorded and monitored, so the police would know he was on the right track and was getting close to finding the girl.

"So do we have a deal then?" Jackson heard the man saying from somewhere that seemed far away, interrupting his train of thought.

Jackson replied, "Um... ah... yes... yes we do. I'm sorry. I was just... well."

"Leave me guess... you were just thinking about all of the fun you're going to have with your little virgin vixen. Am I right?" Smith asked.

"Uh... Yes." Jackson replied, "You're right... yeah that was it. So... um... so when can we do this thing? How soon can you arrange it? And how do I pay you?"

The man looked as if thinking about it and said, "I believe I can make this happen for you tonight. I just have to contact someone and make sure the girl can be ready. As far as the money goes, you have to give me half up front in cash of course... and you can pay the other half to my counterpart when he comes to pick her up in the morning after.... well after you have been completely satisfied." Now Jackson was certain the extra three grand was going right into this guy's pocket. "So we have a deal, Mr. Jones?" The man asked as he extended his hand across the table in for a handshake.

"Y... yes... um... yes... we cer... certainly have a deal Mr. Smith." Jackson stammered. He really didn't want to shake the man's hand. He felt so dirty and filthy just being across the table from him, he feared that touching him might be like shoving his hand into the rotting guts of one of the undead, but he knew he had come too far to risk jeopardizing things now. He reached out and reluctantly shook the man's clammy paw.

CHAPTER 32

"Well then." Smith said, "What say we have a drink to celebrate our new... our new business arrangement." He slid over the seven and seven he had brought from the bar. He had his own drink, which was something Jackson didn't recognize; most likely some new trendy drink people preferred here in the city. Jackson raised his glass as Smith said, "To a very satisfied customer." They tapped glasses then drank heartily as Jackson tried to figure out what his next step was going to be.

He knew he needed to keep the CU which Brent Hogan gave him nearby and had to have the alarm button at the ready. Jackson figured as soon as he was alone with Sarah, he would press the alarm button and within a few minutes, the same team which had helped him earlier that day would come swooping down and take them both to safety. Then he could bring the team back to the River Rat and have them take the bartender into custody. He was certain the police would be able to get the bartender to give up the real identity of the guy who called himself Smith.

Without stopping the recording function, Jackson casually slipped the CU into his shirt pocket. He knew that from that location it would still be able to record and transmit their conversation. Smith hadn't seemed to have taken notice to the maneuver. Jackson took another sip of his drink while keeping his eye on Smith, who for some reason now seemed to be watching him curiously as well. There was something disconcerting in the man's constant gaze that Jackson couldn't identify, but he knew he didn't like it. He was happy for the warm feeling the whiskey gave him as it coursed through his system. It was serving to help to calm his nerves, and that was exactly what he needed for what he was about to ask. "So... um... Mr. Smith. Um... not to rush you or anything... but... but how soon can we make this all happen?"

Smith said, "Well Mr. Jones, it's really quite simple. You'll be happy to know that very shortly you'll be getting exactly what you deserve."

Jackson wondered for a moment what Smith might have meant by that somewhat cryptic statement, but before he could ponder it further, the man interrupted his train of thought explaining, "After we finish our drinks, I'll leave here and make contact with my source. You see, I'm not the person who actually has the merchandise you desire. I'm just a go-between, a broker for another individual. After I leave, you should wait exactly five minutes then you can go and do whatever you want to keep yourself busy for one hour. Then we'll meet in exactly one hour and five minutes from the time I leave here at a place outside the city, on the other side of the Penn Street Bridge. It's at the base of the hill leading into what was once called West Reading. Do you know the place, Mr. Jones?"

Jackson had to think for a minute. He had crossed the bridge into West Reading many times in the past, but he was having trouble focusing all of a sudden. He was getting the crux of an idea for a possible alternate plan. He could notify the cops ahead of time about the rendezvous. If Smith handed him off to someone else, one team could follow Jackson while another followed Smith. Then Jackson realized he had not answered Smith's question yet and Smith was waiting, watching him curiously. "Um... yes... yes... I know... I mean... I remember... I think... yeah... the end of the bridge... at the... base of the hill. Sorry... I suppose I'm... a bit preoccupied thinking about... well you know... tonight... with the girl."

"Yes, indeed I do Mr. Jones." Smith replied, "I'm sure the anticipation is quite exciting. Anyway, later when you get to our meeting place, I'll be waiting for you. At that time, you'll provide me with three thousand dollars in cash. Then you'll need to follow one of my associates to the place where you'll meet your special girl...."

Then suddenly Jackson realized something was wrong. He no longer seemed to be able to follow the man's conversation. He had thought at first it had been from his being preoccupied with formulating a new plan, but now he knew it was something else. Smith had just said something but Jackson hadn't understood what he had said.

"Wait... just... a second... could... could you... please repeat that..." Jackson tried to say ineffectually. He was starting to slur his words; surely two drinks couldn't have done that to him. Jackson was no seasoned drinker by any means, but he knew his limit, and two drinks was a far cry from that limit. He looked over at the man called Smith who seemed to be moving in and out of focus. "Something's... not right... something feels very wrong." Jackson managed to say in a garbled voice.

"What seems to be the problem Mr. Jones?" Smith replied. "You don't look at all well. Are you feeling ill? Should I get help? Is there anything at all I can do for you, Mr. Jones?" Then both Smith's expression and the tone of his voice changed as he said, "Or should I perhaps call you Mr. Ridge? Mr. Jackson Ridge?"

Jackson felt as if he suddenly had been thrust into a dream world. His brain was becoming lethargic and his body seemed far too heavy for him to support. What was that Smith had just said to him? He asked Jackson if he were alright or if he were ill. Jackson was suddenly certain he was not well; not well at all. And... now wait a minute... had Jackson heard Smith correctly? Had Smith just called him by his name or was he imagining that? How could this man possibly know his name? Unless...

Jackson looked across the table through blurry eyes at Smith and could see by the man's sinister smile that Smith knew he, Jackson had finally gotten it. The understanding must have been evident in Jackson's horrified expression.

"That's right, Mr. Ridge." The man who had been calling himself Smith replied. "Yes, I most certainly know who you are. My boss has been waiting patiently for you to arrive ever since this afternoon when those bumbling idiots tried to grab you up on Route 61 and ended up getting themselves slaughtered. I warned him about sending a bunch of stupid half-mutated savages to do a job which needed shall we say the sort of finesse which only I can bring to the table. But then again, that's why I'm here and why you are suddenly feeling a bit strange. My boss insists on results, and as you are now unfortunately aware, my groggy friend, I always deliver those results."

"By the way, allow me to applaud your acting skills. Had I not been aware of your impending arrival, I might actually have been fooled by your performance this evening; very impressive. So... you've come a long way and risked much to find our latest addition, little Sarah. Well you'll not be disappointed. Not only will you meet Sarah, but you will also have the opportunity to get close and personal with our leader as well. Yes sir. Deimos will be quite happy to see you, although I honestly can't say the same for you. I'm quite certain you'll find your participation in such a meeting much less rewarding. Yes, I'm afraid things will not be very pleasant for you from now on Mr. Ridge."

"But... but... how?" Jackson stammered finding it increasingly difficult to put his thoughts into words.

"How did we know about you?' Smith finished. "We know everything that goes on in every law enforcement agency for a hundred mile radius at all times. Deimos has long arms and very deep pockets my friend. He owns anyone he needs to own to get what he wants."

"But... Sarah... is she?" Jackson attempted to ask.

Again Smith interrupted. "Sarah is fine for now. She's alive and well. How noble of you to put the welfare of the girl ahead of your own. I'm sure by the time Deimos is finished with you, you will be cursing Sarah's parents for ever giving her life; as you will likely be doing with your own mother and father. You'll wish you would have never taken this assignment from that fool Frank McKinney. And the ironic thing about Sarah is we originally had no idea she was the Mayor of Yuengsville's niece. That news came later when we learned about your assignment to find her. Deimos only chose her for her looks and the future earning potential she would offer after he tired of her. Once our source in the Yuengsville police department told us all about you, as well as Sarah's relation to the mayor; then our plans had to evolve slightly, to include you as well."

Through the fog of whatever drug he had just been given, Jackson again recalled the strange police officer watching him from down the dark corridor back in the

Yuengsville police station. Had he been the mole in the police department who was Deimos' man inside? He wished he had seen the man's face or had known his name. If so, he would have found some way to form the words, to say his name aloud so that the people monitoring him would know who the mole was.

Jackson's head felt heavy, as if his neck had become a flimsy spring attempting to feebly support up a gigantic watermelon. The last thing Jackson was aware of was his forehead striking hard against the table as everything around him went black.

CHAPTER 33

Andrea Ridge walked briskly along the path that skirted the tall wire fence surrounding the northern border of the Ashton Cooperative. She was deep in thought, busy worrying about Jackson and how he might or might not be progressing in finding the missing girl. She had last spoken to him earlier the previous evening and hadn't heard from him at all that morning. She had left several messages on his communications unit message center, but he hadn't returned her call. She realized each comment she recorded on the CU/ MC had sounded more urgent and troubled than the previous, but she didn't care. Jackson promised her that he would keep in touch and he hadn't. She wanted to be angry with him, but for the moment she was too worried. Once she knew he was safe, maybe then she could have the luxury of becoming angry.

It was eight in the morning and she had just dropped Kyla off at her daycare, and since she knew leaving more messages was only going to upset her even further, she chose to do something which she hoped would help her to relax. Since she was not scheduled to start her shift until nine, she thought a few minutes of quiet walking in the lovely autumn morning air would help clear her mind and get her ready for whatever problems awaited her in the day ahead. She could always try Jackson again on her way to her first appointment, and she knew even though it might frustrate her further, she certainly would try to reach him again.

She focused instead on the beautiful day, doing her best to ignore the gnawing worry which haunted her. Likewise, Andrea tried her best to not pay attention to the barbed wire topped fence in the distance off to her left. Looking at it always made her long for the past; for a time when she could walk as far and as long as she chose without having to worry about any danger. Although she knew the fencing was there for her own protection, Andrea was sad because she understood those days of complete freedom were long gone; most likely forever.

For as long as she could recall, Andrea had always wanted to be a nurse. She possessed a natural empathy for those who were suffering and an instinctual desire to help people, and it was probably that same genuine need to help others and to fix things that were broken that now caused her so much consternation. In her opinion, she no longer fixed anything.

Each work day, several times a day, all she did was wait for someone to die, try to comfort them in their final moments, then in accordance with government regulations, she made sure they could not come back. "Government regulations." She thought. The newly formed government had nationalized all medical and law enforcement agencies. Before the plague, she had been an employee for local visiting nurses group and went from home to home providing help to shut-ins who could no longer venture out on their own. Now she felt more like the grim reaper; the angel of death who showed up simply to make sure the family's loved one didn't rise up from their death bed and eat them alive. Although she realized she was still providing an extremely helpful service, it was not the same thing. In fact, it was nowhere near the professional life she had envisioned for herself so long ago.

Times were very different now, and she understood that all too well. She was very fortunate to even have a job, not to mention a good paying job with plenty of work and great benefits. Although she felt anyone with a pulse could provide the service she was currently providing, the government required that only someone with her credentials was legally permitted to do so. She suspected this was because they didn't want any possible ramifications associated with an unqualified person erroneously pronouncing someone dead and shooting metal rods and poison into their brains. Whatever the reason, this was her job, and like it or not she had to do it. That was one of the big reasons she enjoyed these solitary walks so much. They gave her time to relax, unwind, and deal with the negative thoughts that entered her mind from time to time.

Andrea rounded a curve that she knew led to the place where she would usually turn around and begin walking back to her car. She always found this particular stretch of her walk rather intriguing. The roadway at this point began to slope upward along the grade of an ascending hill. On her left there was a space of about twenty feet comprised of dirt and weeds between the gravel path and the base of the tall fence. What was most interesting about this area was as the road went upward the fence seemed to get shorter as its base was still down at ground level. At the highest point on the path, if you were to take a long board and extend it horizontally from the road surface to the barbed wire atop the fence you would see that they were just about even. However, as a result of the inclined roadway, a deep and wide culvert was formed between the edge of the road and the standing fence.

Andrea was often fascinated by this illusion; knowing the fence was still ten feet tall and none of those horrible creatures could possibly scale it, yet at this point on the roadway her feet were practically even with the top of the barbed wire. People likely paid little if any attention to it, but when the stress of life became too much, Andrea would take a walk up the hill and when she reached this point she would fantasize about sprouting wings, jumping across the deep culvert, soaring over the top of the fence and just flying away.

However, she was a mother, a wife, and a professional with responsibilities, and the reality was there was no longer any safe place to go on the other side of that fence. Only within the protective boundaries of towns and cities was safety of any type possible. Then she thought again about Jackson, out among strangers out there, surrounded by many possible dangers from the undead, and perhaps more worrisome, from the living as well. She wished again Jackson had returned her call; she really wanted to speak to him and make sure he was safe. She would have been able to enjoy the day so much just knowing it, but unfortunately, for now, Andrea had to settle for the fact that at least she and Kyla were safe and the horrid living dead creatures didn't possess the intelligence to find a way to climb the protective fence.

Then, as if it had somehow been summoned by her very thoughts, something appeared in Andrea's peripheral vision off to her far right. "Oh my God! How did that awful thing get in here?" she thought as she realized what she was seeing. Somehow, one of those ungodly walking corpses must have found its way past one of the town's defensive borders. But she had been told such a thing was impossible and had been actually thinking the same thing only a few seconds earlier.

The creature was about ten feet away from her and was shambling toward Andrea with its head down and one withered arm outstretched, reaching. She could now see it once had been an old man. Its drooping, bald head was covered with age spots and encircled with wisps of gray hair. Its body was visibly gaunt and frail. The old man wore a yellowed, soiled tee shirt and nothing else from the waist down. Its flaccid, withered penis was scarcely visible amid its scattered thatch of white, balding pubic hair. Its legs looked like twisted sticks driven into apples, which apparently were its arthritic knees. Yet there was something about the creature which seemed familiar to Andrea.

As the thing lumbered forward, it slowly lifted its head and Andrea recognized the creature, suddenly understanding. The thing hadn't gotten past the town's defenses. It was, or had once been, old Mr. Jenkins, who had run the local pharmacy when she was a kid. He had retired and sold the business almost twenty years earlier and was most recently one of her hospice patients. In fact, she was scheduled to check up on him later that afternoon. He was not some unnamed wandering creature. The old man apparently must have passed away during the night and after turning had somehow gotten out of his house. Andrea could only hope he had not killed or eaten his wife and adult daughter, who still lived in the same house with him and were responsible for his care. She would have to contact the Ashton Cooperative police to have them check on the pair; that was if she managed to escape this situation alive herself.

Meeting Mr. Jenkins in his current undead state exemplified for Andrea how even within the protective confines of the cooperative, there was no guarantee that death wouldn't be able to find you; both regular death and un-death. She momentarily realized just how under other circumstances the entire situation might have been considered comical with the naked old man standing there with his shriveled member dangling in the breeze. That was, had it not been for the fact that he was dead, savagely hungry for flesh, and dragging himself right for her.

She suddenly realized she had foolishly left everything but her communications unit back in her car. She had no weapons of any sort, and old Mr. Jenkins was getting closer to her. He raised he head and began sniffing the air, apparently taking in her scent. His eyes were filmed over and when he opened his mouth to howl she saw he was not wearing his dentures. Score one for Andrea and at least some small bit of good luck. Yet she knew even toothless, the creature could still scratch or claw at her, not to mention overpower her and rip out her insides with his bony fingers.

Before she realized it the thing was grabbing for her arm. Andrea back-handed the creature and its head flew backward, momentarily throwing it off balance. She looked down to her left realizing she was now perilously close to the edge of the roadway. If she lost her footing she might slip and fall ten feet down into the culvert where she might be knocked unconscious or worse; she might simply become incapacitated and helpless. If that happened then old Mr. Jenkins might slide down into the ditch and rip her to pieces.

The she understood that if she could trick the creature into stumbling down into the ditch the same perils she faced would surely await it, as its bones were much older and much more brittle than hers. She saw the creature prepare to clumsily lunge at her again, and when it made the awkward attempt, she anchored her feet and dropped down to a crouch. As the thing's fragile body came over top of her, Andrea grabbed Mr. Jenkins by his shirt and one naked, bony leg, simultaneously standing up, springing with her legs, and tossing him through the air.

The undead man flew almost comically through the air, cartwheeling at least twice. Andrea had either underestimated the creature's light weight or her own strength, because Mr. Jenkins didn't fall down into the culvert as she had hoped, but flew over the entire distance, clearing the top of the fence as well; but not quite. When its body came down on the outside of the fence, its spindly arms, scrawny neck, and hairless head struck the barbed wire, where they became entangled.

Howling with displeasure, the creature hung helplessly over the outside of the fence facing Andrea; its naked legs kicking wildly at the air; its torso entwined in barbed wire. The zombie's flailing and kicking was causing its flesh to rip from its bones as the razor sharp wire became coated with skin fragments and brackish fluids. One of its eyes had been gouged out in the fall, but the remaining milky orb was focused on Andrea as its shredded fingers reached out futilely, still trying robotically to grab her from across the far divide.

Despite the horrid sight before her and the fact that she had come so close to death or maybe because of it, Andrea felt a sudden overwhelming urge to giggle overtake her. Then when she saw the old creature's shriveled penis sticking through one of the diamond-shaped holes in the wire fence looking like a turtle poking its head out of a shell, she lost control completely and broke down in fits of uncontrollable laughter.

"I'm... I'm so sorry... Mr. Jenkins..." Andrea said apologetically to the mindless being. "This is so unprofessional of me... and so disrespectful... but it's also so damn funny." She continued to laugh until tears rolled down her cheeks. Then just as suddenly, the tears of laughter changed to tears of sorrow as she became overcome with remorse for Mr. Jenkins, for herself, for her husband and daughter, and for the world. She fell to her knees and sobbed for several minutes while the undead Mr. Jenkins struggled, dangling helplessly from his barbed wire confines. She truly understood this was simply how life was now and how it would be from now on for Andrea and her family in this bizarre new world.

After a few minutes, Andrea managed to once again regain her composure. Sometimes a good cry was as beneficial as a long walk she knew. She turned away from the horrible, pathetic sight and slowly began to walk back. As she returned to her car, she contacted the local police, explaining the situation and arranging for a cleanup crew to deal with poor Mr. Jenkins. She would also suggest they check out his house to make sure the rest of his family was still among the living. They would likely send one of their rapid response units to deal with the situation.

Perhaps someone would stop by the fence in the meantime, finish Mr. Jenkins off, and claim the dead kill bounty; she really didn't care. Either way, someone would deal with the creature. Andrea got back to her car, sat for a few moments longer, then tried Jackson once again, but her call went right to voice messaging. Then she headed out to her first appointment. As she drove away, she worried once again about Jackson, how he might be progressing in his investigation and she hoped to God still he was safe.

As she drove she was hit by a strange premonition. She suddenly felt certain something very bad had happened to Jackson. She pulled over, parked her car, and dialed his Communications Unit several more times. Each time it went straight to voice messaging, which she knew would happen. This wasn't like Jackson. He was never more than a call away. She now felt instinctively certain that something bad had happened to her husband and she had to find out somehow if he was all right.

When she arrived at her client, Andrea made up her mind. If she didn't get through to Jackson after her appointment, she was going to first call the Schuylkill Daily News and ask for Bill McCleary to see what, if anything, he might know. If she struck out there, she would call Jackson's friend Double-I and see if Sean had heard from Jackson today, and if that didn't produce the results she needed, Andrea was calling the Yuengsville courthouse and would demand to speak to the mayor himself.

CHAPTER 34

Frank McKinney sat behind his office desk, staring absently down at a document that apparently needed his signature. This had been the third time he had attempted to read the blasted thing, yet he still had no idea what it was about. He couldn't begin to concentrate on such trivial matters while his mind was attempting to deal with all that had happened since the previous evening.

Frank recalled how he had been awakened in the middle of the night by a call from Police Chief Brent Holden informing him about the bad news. Frank had immediately left for the courthouse, where he met Brent to get a complete briefing of the situation.

Brent had done his best to summarize the contents of the transmission they had received from the CU he had given to Jackson. Brent explained how Jackson had entered a bar in Reading, which they were able to identify as a place called The River Rat. He had apparently tried to pass himself off as some sort of degenerate looking for underaged sex in order to possibly gain information about Sarah.

"What the hell had Jackson been thinking?" Frank had asked. "We gave him a specific set of directions to follow for God's sake."

Brent agreed the maneuver on Jackson's part was most definitely contrary to what he had been instructed to do. "Frank, you know we told him to just blend in and listen to all the conversations. But for whatever reason, he took it upon himself to play a much bigger and more active role in the investigation. And unfortunately, since the bad guys knew Jackson was coming that was his downfall." Brent had to admit though, the ruse had sounded convincing enough to him when he listened to the recording of Jackson's transmission. The conversation had seemed to be going according to what he assumed Jackson's plan must have been. However, in reality, Jackson had actually not been fooling the man who was going by the name Smith. Brent explained that by the sound of Jackson's voice toward the end of the recording, it was obvious that he had been drugged. His voice had become garbled and was beginning to slur, and it became evident Jackson's cover had been blown when he heard Smith refer to Jackson by his real name. By that time, Jackson was in no shape to do anything to help himself.

A few seconds later, he had heard Jackson collapse onto the table followed by the grunting noises of men helping to move his unconscious body, as well as the muffled voice of Smith instructing others to haul Jackson outside. After a few more moments, they heard a slamming sound like a trunk lid closing. For about a half hour there was nothing to hear but the rumble of a car's tires traveling along a roadway. Then apparently, after the kidnappers arrived at their destination, the CU picked up more rustling of clothing as if a still unconscious Jackson Ridge was being moved once again.

This sound continued for a few more minutes, and then someone must have discovered Jackson's CU, because a deep voice could be heard saying, "Look. He gots two CU's Boss. Wat he wan wit two CUs? Hum. Wat ya wan me do wit dem Boss?"

Then they heard the voice of Smith once again instructing his minion, "Give them to me. He won't need them any longer. I'll keep them with the rest of his personal items for now. Later when Deimos is finished with him, we can dispose of Ridge and everything else at the same time."

From that point on, the remainder of the transmission became muffled and garbled. That last distinguishable comment was transmitted at eleven pm the previous night. By two in the morning, Brent Holden was sitting with McKinney in his office, and although still transmitting and recording, the CU's information could not be understood. At least they believed they could use the hidden tracking device in the phone to pinpoint its location and hopefully find Jackson, and if they were lucky, Sarah as well. Most criminals had no trouble locating and disconnecting the traditional GPS devices in communications units, but this new tracker was separate and had a unique, special hidden signal which Brent Holden was happy to learn the criminals had not yet discovered.

Frank McKinney had immediately suggested to his chief of police that they had no choice now but to call in the Reading Police and raid the location pinpointed by the tracking device. He realized it could endanger Jackson and Sarah if she were also there and that it might even result in their deaths, but he felt things had gone too far for any other options to seem viable.

But Brent strongly disagreed with McKinney and asked for just one more chance to rescue them both before calling in reinforcements. "Look Frank," Brent suggested, "If you try a raid, Deimos will surely kill Sarah and Jackson and likely disappear again before they have a chance to capture him. It just won't work. I believe one or two of us could sneak past Deimos' security where a mob of police would simply not have the chance."

"One or two of you?" McKinney asked. "Are you volunteering? Are you suggesting that I let you go to Reading and try to save them yourself?"

"Well... myself and Sergeant Evans. You know David did a great job with the bikers, and I think if he and I worked together, we can still pull this off. You can have reinforcements on standby. Then as soon as we have them both safe, with or without capturing Deimos, we can signal the cavalry to come in shooting and take out as many of the bad guys as they can."

The mayor looked uncertainly at his chief of police. "Are you sure about this, Brent?"

"Yes sir, Mr. Mayor." Brent Holden said formally, "I think this may be our last shot at getting them both out of there alive."

After some deliberation, Frank McKinney reluctantly agreed to Brent's suggestion, and within a half hour, Brent had contacted David Evans, who was already in the Reading area monitoring things at that end. He had a specific location for Jackson's CU pinpointed in what had formerly been the western suburbs, now the outlands. They had arranged to meet on the west side of the Penn Street Bridge, ironically at the same location where Smith had suggested Jackson meet him before he had drugged him. By three A.M., Brent Holden was on the road, and an hour or two later, depending upon the road conditions, he would be in Reading.

It was now ten o'clock in the morning and Frank McKinney was still sitting at his desk, still trying to get some work done but still unable to focus. He was certain he would have heard something by now. If Brent made it to Berks County by four or even five and took another hour to get into position with Evans, surely he would have something to report by now. McKinney was beginning to wonder if something terrible had gone very wrong with the remainder of the operation. He realized it was just as likely that his men had run into some obstacles that they had to slowly and carefully find their way around. This was not an all-out assault but a stealthy operation. He would have to trust his men to complete this mission in whatever method they felt would work best. If that meant they were waiting and watching for just the right moment, then he too had to be equally as patient, but he couldn't help worrying about his niece and the man he had sent to find her, Jackson Ridge.

Just then the intercom on his desk communications unit sounded with its electronic chime and McKinney reluctantly asked "Yes, Mrs. Simpson. What is it?"

After a brief hesitation, Mrs. Simpson said uncertainly, "There is a woman here with a little girl out here who insists on seeing you immediately."

McKinney had no idea who or what this was about, and he was far too busy dealing with his own crisis to speak to some irate constituent. "Please ask her to make an appointment to come back another time, Mrs. Simpson. I'm extremely busy today."

Suddenly McKinney heard the sounds of a scuffle coming across the intercom and Mr. Simpson's voice exclaiming, "Please... Mam... you can't do that... you can't..."

Then an unfamiliar but stern voice came through the receiver. "Mr. Mayor. I mean no disrespect to you or your secretary but I must see you. My name is Andrea Ridge, and I need to speak to you immediately about my husband, Jackson."

Then her voice took on an air of desperation and she pleaded, "Please sir. I really need to see you right now."

The mayor let out a sigh of resignation and instructed Mrs. Simpson to show Mrs. Ridge into his office.

CHAPTER 35

The door to Frank McKinney's office opened slowly as Mrs. Simpson, a stodgy woman in her mid-sixties, reluctantly stood aside to let a pretty young woman and her small child enter. Frank was amazed at how beautiful both mother and daughter were. They both had golden blonde hair and large blue eyes. Most of the women he had occasion to meet since the outbreak bore the burden of loss, constant stress and the act of simple survival which tended to wear them down, rounding their shoulders, dulling their eyes, and wrinkling their skin. However, this woman, despite her obvious concern about her husband's wellbeing, was radiantly beautiful. Her appearance reminded Frank of how many women looked long ago before everything went to Hell; a time when women of such beauty were abundant.

Frank stood and walked around the desk to meet Andrea Ridge, putting on his best and most congenial politician's smile, despite the unpleasant circumstances. He was wearing a rumpled suit that looked like it had seen better days; almost as if he had slept in it. Andrea supposed considering the situation, he might have done just that.

The mayor addressed his secretary, "Mrs. Simpson, thank you. That will be all for now." The secretary nodded curtly, gave Andrea a final disapproving glance and went back out to her work station; closing the door behind her with a bit more than force than was necessary.

"Please, Mrs. Ridge." Frank said, pointing to one of his fine leather upholstered guest chairs. "Have a seat. And please accept my apology for Mrs. Simpson's obvious attitude. She's a well-intentioned woman who is very protective of me and is often like the proverbial dragon guarding the gates of a medieval castle. But you didn't drive all the way down here from the Ashton Cooperative to hear about my staffing issues."

Instead of walking back to his side of the desk, McKinney remained semi-standing, resting his ample backside against the front edge of his desk, attempting his best to project a relaxed attitude; even though he felt anything but relaxed. He needed to put this woman at ease. "I know you're here about Jackson. Let me see if I can accurately explain the current situation."

"Current situation?" Andrea said with undisguised frustration bordering on anger in her voice as she sat down hard in one of the chairs. "Excuse me, Mr. Mayor for being so blunt, but this is not a situation; this is my husband we're talking about and this little girl's father." She pointed to Kyla who was climbing up onto another guest chair across from her mother. She slid off during her first two attempts but eventually was successful with a little boost from Andrea.

Frank looked dutifully chaste by her remark and he took a deep, calming breath before cautiously continuing. "Yes... yes you're most certainly right, Mrs. Ridge, and I apologize if I sounded unsympathetic to your concerns. Let me say emphatically, that your husband's wellbeing is my number one priority. Jackson is an amazing man. I'm assuming he told you about the nature of his assignment. He took on this responsibility to help save the life of my young niece, Sarah and for that I will be eternally grateful."

"Well then." Andrea replied, "As nicc as that may be to hcar, I have to tell you it does very little to ease my concerns about Jackson. I've been calling his CU and leaving message all morning but haven't heard a word back from him. Needless to say, I'm beginning to have some serious worries. The last time we spoke was yesterday evening around six o'clock, just before he was planning on going out to gather up whatever information he could about your niece's whereabouts. And now I'm worried that something very bad might have happened to him."

"Y...yes... well..." The mayor stammered. "It seems we actually have had a series of unplanned and unfortunate occurrences since you last spoke with your husband... and... well... I'm sorry to have to report that we too have lost contact with Jackson." McKinney of course had much more to tell the woman, but he chose to feed the bad news to her in small doses.

Andrea's face reddened and she asked through semi-clenched teeth, "What do you mean you've lost contact with Jackson? He assured me your people would have him under constant surveillance. Was that true or not?"

The Mayor took a moment to compose himself once again and replied, "Yes, yes that most certainly was true. And we believe we know what has happened to Jackson, at least what happened to him last night when we last heard from him."

"Last night?" Andrea exclaimed, "That was almost twelve hours ago. You mean to say you lost contact with him twelve hours ago and you didn't bother to say anything to me? In other words, if I wouldn't have come in here this morning demanding to speak to you, I suspect I never would have heard from you at all."

"Please. Mrs. Ridge. If you will just remain calm for a few minutes, I think I can fill you in on everything we know and what we are doing about it." The mayor asked.

"Mommy. Where's Daddy?" Kyla said from her chair, noticing the troubled look on her mother's face and sensing the tension in the room. "Is Daddy ok Mommy?"

"Daddy's going to be fine sweetie," Andrea said to Kyla. "I just have to talk with this nice man for a few minutes. Here, why don't you play your game while we talk." She handed Kyla what looked like a communications unit but was actually a compact educational game system designed and built back before the Z43 virus hit, and which luckily was still functional.

Andrea turned to the mayor and said "Ok Mr. McKinney. I'll do my best to remain calm, but I can't make any promises other than to try. And it won't be for your benefit but for Kyla's. Now please tell me what has happened to my husband."

McKinney slowly and carefully recounted everything he knew about Jackson's trip so far. He started with Sarah being kidnapped two nights earlier, his association with Big Bill McCleary and McCleary's suggestion that he use Jackson to find out what happened to his niece. Then he told her all about the precautions they had taken regarding the special equipment they had provided for Jackson. He emphasized how well the equipment worked in alerting his men and allowing them to protect Jackson during the attempt to kidnap him on his way to Berks County.

Andrea took an audible deep intake of air when she heard the account and had to force herself to remain passive as she felt as if her stomach had turned to ice. "J... Jackson hadn't mentioned anything to me about that to me when we spoke last evening."

"He probably didn't want to worry you." McKinney said.

"So you're telling me someone tried to kidnap him and almost killed him earlier in the day yesterday, and not only didn't he tell me but he continued on with this... this thing anyway?" Andrea asked, now barely able to control her anger.

Next, McKinney did his best to explain how Jackson had refused to give up looking for Sarah in spite of the obvious danger. He told Andrea that Jackson had said if it were his own little girl who was in trouble he wouldn't want anyone giving up on finding her. Andrea's emotions were being pulled simultaneously in many directions. She was desperately worried about her husband while at the same time furious with him for not coming home to her, yet still very proud of him for continuing on and trying to find Sarah. She hated when she had these conflicting feelings; they made her feel so out of control and helpless.

The mayor then described how Jackson must have devised some plan of his own and how he had taken a more active role in the investigation then they had originally wanted him to take by trying to pass himself off as a pervert in order to hopefully get close to Sarah. He explained they had a recording of the entire conversation between Jackson and Smith including the part where the man revealed how he knew who Jackson was, and then drugged and presumably kidnapped him.

"Can I hear that conversation?" Andrea asked, not certain if she wanted to hear it or not.

The mayor declined, saying, "I don't have that recording yet Mrs. Ridge. I haven't even heard it myself. I was briefed by my chief of police about its contents. Besides, if you don't mind my saying so, I don't think your listening to such a recording would be in any way helpful to you. Listen, Mrs. Ridge. We feel assured that Jackson is still alive. We believe if this character Deimos would have wanted him killed, he could easily have had it done right there in the bar. From what we can determine, the kidnapper likewise could have easily dumped Jackson's body into the Schuylkill River and none of us would have been any the wiser. We think Deimos has decided to keep Jackson alive, as a hostage for some reason, which he has not yet revealed."

Andrea let out a sigh and then asked, "So what are you doing about this?"

Frank said, "My chief of police, Brent Holden and my police sergeant, David Evans are on their way to Berks County. They've pinpointed the location of Jackson's communications unit, which Brent had equipped with a special tracking device. Brent believes two of them can sneak into the place where Jackson might be held more easily than a large number of police. He felt the large police presence might endanger Jackson, but two men could enter unnoticed."

He assures me that once he knows Jackson and hopefully Sarah are safe, he will notify the local police, who will be standing by to raid the place and take all the kidnappers into custody. He feels confident he can do this with little risk to either your husband or my niece."

Andrea was silent for a moment, then looked at her daughter then back to the mayor and asked, "So when will we know... you know... when..."

"Hopefully soon, Mrs. Ridge." Frank replied. "Hopefully very soon."

CHAPTER 36

Jackson Ridge slowly opened his eyes. His vision was blurred and his mind felt very foggy, racked with confusion. Where the hell was he? And why was he so cold? He felt as if a chill had sunk deep into his bones; the type of chill only a long time in a very hot shower might be able to remedy. The air around him was cold and smelled horrible.

The last thing he could recall was his speaking with that slimy character Smith at the bar. When was that? Last night? A few hours ago? Days? He couldn't remember. God his head ached! He felt like someone had clouted him across the back of his skull with a two by four. Had that happened? He didn't think so, but since he couldn't recall very much at all, he supposed anything might be possible.

"Drugged!" Jackson suddenly thought, "That guy Smith in the bar must have drugged me and brought me here; wherever here is." Then Jackson remembered how Smith had referred to him by his real name, just as those biker outlanders had done.

"He knew I was coming. He called me by my name, which meant he also knew I was looking for Sarah." Jackson thought groggily.

He suddenly felt foolish. He had been certain that man, Smith had bought into his ruse about being some sort of pervert looking for a young teenage girl, but all the while Smith had been playing him for a fool. Jackson suspected Smith, or whatever his real name was, had been wise to him from the moment the man had walked into the bar, maybe even earlier if the bartender had been suspicious as well. It was just like what had happened with that gang that accosted him on the trip to Reading. These criminals had inside information and knew every single move Jackson had made. He had originally thought that having the conversation recorded and transmitted back to headquarters would benefit him, but if Deimos had an informant at such a high level, then Deimos had likely been able to use that transmitted information against him.

The room where Jackson now found himself was very dark; not pitch black but dark enough that in his current condition he was unable to make out shapes in the gloom surrounding him. He blinked a few times, attempting to focus but could still see nothing. He felt as though he was standing upright. He tried to move his arms and legs but was unable to do so. They were obviously bound. As his senses began to slowly return, Jackson realized his hands and forearms were numb and he could tell by the increasing muscle pain under his arms that they had been extended out horizontally. He suddenly had a terrifying thought which made him quickly throw back his head in alarm. This caused the back of his skull to slam painfully against something hard and solid; something which might have been heavy wooden timber. But before the thought could solidify, everything went black and Jackson lost consciousness once again.

After a time, he awoke still in the dark, fortunately somewhat less confused than the previous time but still very much uncertain of his situation. The effects of whatever drugs had been in his system must have worn off, but he was still a bit disoriented and still had a major headache. He remembered how he had inadvertently slammed his head against something hard and had obviously knocked himself unconscious. He decided it would be prudent to keep his movements slow and careful until he knew for certain what was going on with him.

Then very quickly Jackson's senses seemed to awaken at once. The pain in his head increased and hit him like a bolt of lightning. The agony suddenly rose to a previously unimaginable level, and for a moment, Jackson was certain he was going to black out once again. Fortunately or perhaps unfortunately, he didn't and managed to remain conscious. He felt nauseous, and despite his attempts to stop himself he vomited uncontrollably down the front of his chest. He felt the hot, rancid liquid on his flesh and realized he was shirtless. "I probably have a concussion or something," Jackson thought, not really knowing if he did or not.

Then his mind began to clear a bit more and he was a better able to focus through his pain. "What the hell is wrong with my hands?" he wondered. He couldn't feel either his hands or his forearms. At first he thought his hands might be missing; that some maniac had cut them off for some sick reason. Then just before panic overtook him he realized they were still there but they were probably just numb from being held in the same position for so long. Jackson was then able to imagine in the darkness what someone must have done to him. He apparently was secured to something solid and he was certain it was a large wooden object; perhaps a heavy post of some sort with a cross beam.

Despite the numbness, Jackson tried with all of his might to move his upper arms but could feel they too had been bound tightly to the cross member. Although he was worried about the lack of blood circulation reaching his extremities, which he assumed was the reason for the numbness, he realized that his arms being bound might actually have been a good thing. It had helped to support his body while he had been dangling unconscious.

Next, Jackson tried to move his fingers. At first he couldn't sense any movement, so he focused all of his willpower on getting his fingers to move. Then he thought he could feel them wiggling just a bit out in the darkness beyond his field of limited vision but he was uncertain. He had a slight tingling feeling in his fingers but not very much. The rest of his hand felt completely numb. Then he focused and tried to close his fingers into a fist but was only able to partially do so. He thought carefully about what minimal sensation of movement he was receiving from his hands and was horrified about what he imagined. Despite his terror, Jackson knew he had to find out exactly what his situation really was.

He managed to concentrate and focus all of his energy on his middle finger because it was the longest. He slowly curled it inward and touched something cold and metal located in the center of his palm. An unimaginable horror shot though Jackson as he understood that something previously inconceivable had happened to him; he had been crucified. Spikes had been driven through his palms and he was bound about his arms and legs and suspended from a cross. Every muscle in Jackson's body tensed with the understanding of his plight. Not only had he been nailed to a cross, but he had also likely been left for dead. Then he realized the situation might be even worse than that. Maybe his captor was going to return and torture him until he eventually died.

Although barely able to focus, Jackson realized suddenly he should be grateful for the numbness in his arms and hands. It helped to suppress the pain which he could only assume would have been excruciating had the numbness not been present. He tried desperately to hold back the tears of anger and frustration which were now rimming his eyes waiting to spill down his cheeks. Jackson refused to give in to the mounting feelings of helplessness, doing his best to replace those feelings with anger instead.

"Deimos!" Jackson thought with certainty. It had to be Deimos who was behind this. Who else could be so twisted as to do something so horrible to another human being? But then he recalled other stories he had heard about the savage outlanders; stories of rape, murder, dismemberment, hanging, and of course, crucifixion. Yet even if any number of the outlanders could have been responsible for his crucifixion, Jackson still believed it had to have been Deimos who had done this.

Jackson thought about how when blood circulation stops the extremities; fingers and toes suffer first, then the blood loss works its way back along the arms and legs. He tried to wiggle his toes and found that he could do so with no problem, confirming that he was indeed hanging vertically. Although his legs were apparently bound tightly to the upright post, his feet had been spared the skewering which his hands had received. In fact, he could tell by wiggling his toes that he still had his shoes on. Apparently Deimos had gotten enough warped satisfaction from driving spikes through his palms that he didn't need to spike his feet as well. Despite the severity of his situation, Jackson was grateful for at least that one small consolation. He could sense that his feet were on the ground because he could feel the soil give way under the minimum amount of movement he could manage. He thought "Soil. This room has a dirt floor."

He once again noticed the disgustingly foul stench of decay that permeated the air around him. Then he heard something, a slight shuffling sound followed by faint moaning and growling in the distance off to his far right and somewhere in front of him. At first Jackson thought he should call out to see who was there; perhaps it was Sarah being held somewhere nearby, but his instincts kicked in and told him to remain silent for a little while longer.

As he hung helplessly from his bindings Jackson did his best to remain perfectly still so he could try to identify the source of the sounds. He heard a guttural growl once more, then another and then another, and he knew for certain what the unearthly sound was coming from. It was a sound he had heard far too many times before and it also explained the revolting stench of the place. It was the sound made by those creatures; the living dead. There were zombies nearby and he was hanging bound, crucified, and completely helpless.

Somewhere out there in the darkness there must be several of the hideous things lumbering about bumping clumsily into each other like they always did. They must be able to smell him and to sense he was nearby. All of them seemed to have an uncanny ability to hone in on the living, yet he couldn't understand why, if the creatures really were so close by, they hadn't fallen upon him and devoured him already. He was unable to defend himself and was at their mercy. Then he realized something; perhaps they hadn't attacked because they couldn't get to him. As if in response to his thoughts, Jackson heard a metallic and wooden rattling sound like someone shaking a wire fence angrily as the growling intensified. He then realized that although the creatures were not very far away, something, perhaps a fence or gate, was keeping them away from him. No wonder they were all growling and sounding so angry.

The first thing he wondered was what exactly did the madman have in store for him? Was Deimos eventually going to hand him over to the horrible living dead creatures? Like most of the people who had survived the Z43 plague, Jackson had witnessed firsthand what happened to anyone who found themselves overpowered and outnumbered by the undead. He had seen his fellow human beings being torn to shreds as they screamed and died helplessly. Was this to be his fate? Was crucifying him just the beginning of a living hell that Deimos had planned for him?

Jackson looked upward and was able to see a minimal amount of light coming in through the worn boards on the roof of the place where he was being held and determined that it must be late afternoon and he was in a barn or some other sort of out building. It obviously wasn't heated, which combined with his lack on a shirt explained why he was so cold. It was the end of October, and although not yet freezing, the temperatures were low enough that one could still be uncomfortably cold in an unheated building without the benefit of clothing.

He worried if maybe shock was settling in on him. He had no idea how long he had been here or how much blood he had lost. He knew he felt very weak. Just thinking again about his deteriorating condition was almost enough to send him into a panic attack. It took everything he had not to allow those creeping feelings of helplessness to overwhelm him. He knew he had to focus. He needed to figure out how he might possibly get out of this place, but Jackson also knew such a thought was futile and he was very likely lying to himself. Attempting an escape was easier said than done, especially if you were bound with ropes and spiked to a cross. Jackson also realized by the growing weakness he was feeling that unless help arrived soon, he was a dead man hanging. He let out an involuntary sigh of frustration.

Then to his surprise, Jackson heard a small voice coming from the darkness off to his left. It was a girl's voice, a young girl's voice. She said in an almost whisper. "Hello? Is... Is someone there?"

CHAPTER 37

Deimos sat in a comfortable folding chair near the back edge of a large, deep pit in a dilapidated wooden out building not far from the barn where Jackson was being held. In the chair next to him sat the man who had called himself Smith; the same man who had drugged Jackson and brought him to Deimos. The two men were relaxing and drinking cocktails. A folding table was between them covered with a number of bottles consisting of an impressive assortment of alcoholic beverages from which to choose. There was also a large, strawberry scented candle in the center of the table that was burning, spreading its pleasant aroma throughout the area. On both sides of the two men and a few feet in front of them, a series of four large box fans were blowing the air away from them over top of the large pit. But neither the fragrant candle nor the powerful fans were completely successful at keeping the vile stench at bay.

"I want to commend you. That was a really slick job you did, Billy." Deimos said to Smith, whose real first name was Billy and whose last name, ironically, was actually Jones. Inside the unheated outbuilding the autumn air was a bit chilly, and Deimos was wearing a worn leather bomber jacket over his western style shirt. Also, the space heaters that were positioned at their feet only partially helped to keep them warm, but that was all right because they wouldn't be there very long.

"Why thank you Deimos, my friend." Billy replied, "You know I'm always happy to do whatever I can to help out." Billy was dressed casually in jeans and a sweatshirt under a worn denim jacket. He noticed on both sides of the pit, video cameras were mounted high on some sort of scaffolding pointing down into the pit. In front of the two men, raised a few feet off the ground was a large video display screen. Billy assumed it was high definition color, and it appeared to be at least a seventy inch model.

As they sat enjoying their drinks, Deimos slid a thick business sized envelope over to Billy and said in his smooth drawl, "That may most certainly be true Billy, but I'm sure this little incentive never hurts either. Am I correct?"

"Correct as always," Billy replied, taking the envelope and tucking into his inner coat pocket. He decided to inquire about the job he had done for Deimos. "So what ever happened to our new friend Jackson Ridge? If I may ask."

"You most certainly may" Deimos replied. "Let's just say I have that particular problem nailed down for the time being." Deimos was making a joke; one for his own pleasure and one which Billy, being out of the loop, didn't understand.

"And the girl?" Billy asked, even though it was really none of his business to ask.

Deimos hesitated for a moment eyeing Billy carefully, "Why are you so interested in the girl Billy?"

Billy replied, "I think you know why. It's no secret my tastes tend to lean toward the younger ladies; the much younger ladies. I was just curious... you know... if there was any possibility..."

"None whatsoever," Deimos retorted, cutting him off mid-sentence. "That sweet little prize is going to be all mine, personally and exclusively, for quite some time. Maybe in a few years when I tire of her and I decide to start farming her out I can arrange for you two to have some quality time together. Although by then I'm pretty sure she may have exceeded your age preference and it's likely you might no longer be interested."

"Understood," Billy replied curtly, realizing he had just come dangerously close to overstepping his boundaries. That sort of mistake spoken at the wrong time could mean the difference between life and death. "No offense intended."

"None taken," Deimos replied; although Billy was now on his guard nonetheless. Billy knew Deimos was truly insane, and as such, Billy understood that dealing with the man was like walking on a recently frozen pond of very thin and fragile ice. At any time the wrong move could send you plunging to your death.

In the background, growling, moaning, and groaning could be heard coming from down in the bottom of the pit. Billy did his best to ignore the sound, which he knew was the latest collection of dead heads Deimos had put into the pit for some soon to be explained reason. Fortunately the video cameras had not yet been turned on so Billy didn't have to put up with seeing the vile creatures on the screen in front of them.

Deimos next slid a plastic credit card sized thing across the table to Billy along with a set of car keys, both of which he recognized. "These are a few of the things you took from Ridge when you brought him to me. The keys are for his car, which is parked along the street outside of the River Rat, and the other thing is his key card for room 358 in the Riverview Towers Hotel. That's where Ridge was staying."

"Not a bad place," Billy replied.

"Yes, I suppose," Deimos said absently, "Anyway, I want you to get rid of the car by whatever means you choose; just make it disappear, without a trace. Same thing with whatever crap he has is up in his room. Take whatever you want for yourself, any cash, clothing, and jewelry, whatever, and discard the rest. I know I don't have to remind you not to try to use any of his credit cards, cash only. Everything else gets gone. Again, make it look like he just took off; disappeared or something."

"You got it," Billy said, now very anxious to stay in the madman's good graces. He figured anything that would take Deimos' mind off their previous discussion would be a good thing. In fact, now that Deimos had given him an assignment, Billy figured that was as good a time as any to put as much space as possible between himself and the lunatic. "Well I guess maybe I should go and take care of those things right now. You know, no time like the present."

"Yeah. Well... not just yet Billy." Deimos corrected. "I have something special I want you to see." This revelation didn't give Billy a warm and fuzzy feeling. Deimos was acting too calm, too content. He knew that was never a good thing. He liked to think of it as the calm before the storm, and he really didn't want to be around in the event of bad weather so to speak.

A moment later, Billy saw one of the large barn doors far on the other side of the building slide open several feet and a strange little man was pushed through the opening, his hands cuffed in front of him and his legs shackled. He was barefoot and naked except for a pair of oversized boxer shorts. Behind him came what Billy knew to be the horrid giant mutant creature; Deimos' personal pet, Odo. Billy hated the very sight of the creature and wasn't sure if Odo were actually still a living human, a zombie, or something else entirely. Billy didn't care to think of the creature as a human but usually as just some sort of mutation. Its massive muscles and Neanderthal forehead hanging down over its hooded eyes made it look anything but human.

"Bring him over here, Odo my friend." Deimos shouted across the distance. Even from their remote location, Billy could hear the little man's abusive protests.

The gargantuan man/beast Odo lifted the small captive by the back of his neck with one enormous hand and carried him to Deimos. All the while the man's manacled legs kicked the air as he twisted, twitched, and cursed madly, calling Odo every name in the book and then some. After a few giant strides the pair was standing before Deimos. Odo dropped the odd man to the dirt floor of the barn with a thud. Billy wisely decided to keep his own mouth shut and just sit quietly trying to remain unnoticed. He could see the storm of Deimos' madness forming on the horizon.

The video screen came to life and suddenly on the display screen, Billy could see the little man on his knees in the dirt with Deimos sitting looking down at him. Billy assumed there must be other cameras in the barn because the ones on the scaffolding were still pointing down into the pit.

"Groddang froggin' mutent!" The strange little man shouted at the beast Odo. Then he looked at Deimos and said "Ifn' ya takes deese heer cufs an leg irons offn' me I promise ya I'll rip da guts outta dat mountina pig shad over dere an kill 'em dedder den a doornail." Billy couldn't believe the outburst, as the man was in no shape to be making threats to anyone.

"Trader Bob," Deimos said with the same friendly tone he had just used with Billy. "So pleasant to have you stop by for a visit."

Bob looked angrily at Deimos again. Billy couldn't help but notice how the odd man didn't seem to be in the least bit afraid of Deimos or in any way concerned about his own life. Billy had to assume this Trader Bob character was even crazier than Deimos.

"Dis ain't no visit." Bob shouted back furiously, "Dat dere freeka natur com upta my tradin post wit yer boys an snatched me way. Den he brung me heer. Fer wat? Wat da frogg does ya need wit me anyhoo? I gots a biness to be runnin."

Deimos looked down at the man pitifully, "Bob. Bob. Bob. You can be so funny sometimes. You really don't know why you're here, do you? Don't you remember yesterday when I sent out a specific order to all of my business associates between here and Schuylkill County that if they were to meet up with one Jackson Ridge, they were supposed to subdue him and bring him to me? And didn't I also send everyone a description of the man and even a picture?"

"Yeah, yeah. I gots all dat shad." Bob said, "An I reconized him too. I tells ya I was all set ta take 'em inta custody, wen he gots da jump on me wit dat dere froggin' tazer ting of his. He done laid me out flat onna floor he did. An wen I wokes up, dat dere ugly monster was standin' over me putting cufs and legirons on me. Wat da frogg was dat all 'bout?"

Billy just sat sipping his drink, trying to sink further into his folding chair, amazed at just how stupid this strange little man was. This Trader Bob had absolutely no idea not only how bad his current situation was, or how much worse it was about to get. Billy looked between the video screen and Deimos, not certain if he wanted to see where all of this was heading.

"Well Bob." Deimos replied, "As much as I appreciated you calling us and letting us know when Jackson Ridge had entered your trading post, it appears you got a bit greedy and that was how he got the better of you."

"Greedie?" Bob said, "I weren't greedie. Dat Jakon Rigg owed me four hunnert bucks on acounta me hafinta put down onea dem dead heads. Youse always pays me fibe hunnert fer dem wen day bees walkin. Da bounty bees only one hunnert. I was jes tryin ta get wat was owed me."

Deimos said, "But Bob. Didn't you understand that I was paying five thousand dollars for the capture of Jackson Ridge. Five thousand bucks, Bob. And yet you let him overpower you and drive away because you were too greedy and couldn't let go of your need to get that precious four hundred dollars. Do you have any idea just how ridiculously foolish that was, Bob?"

"Not foolish atal." Bob insisted, "Wat's rite is rite. An no madder wat youse was offerin, dat a-hole Jakon Rigg still owed me four hunnert bucks. An dat be dat. Now take dees cufs offin' me sose I kin start kickin' da livin shad outta dat frogging mutent. Ya here? An ya best be doin it right now."

Deimos looked over at Billy, who was staring back with astonishment at the audacity of the strange little man. Deimos rolled his eyes as if he couldn't believe just how stupid the man was, then gave Billy a sly, knowing smile and a wink. He turned to the massive creature, Odo, and said nonchalantly. "Ok now Odo. You know what to do."

With that, the giant creature Odo reached down and using both enormous hands, picked up the cursing Trader Bob and without hesitation, threw him high into the air and away from Deimos and Billy. The man's arms and legs continued to thrash while he flipped head over heels. Billy thought that under other circumstances this might be a funny sight, but he could see the trajectory of Bob's decent and understood what would be his final destination, and there was most certainly nothing funny about that.

Bob's body crashed onto the dirt floor at the bottom of the huge pit and Billy heard distinct cracking sounds as either then man's arms, legs, or both were broken by the impact. He heard the little man crying out in pain while still cursing angrily. Then the two cameras on the scaffolding came to life and on the video screen in front of him Billy saw the crumbled, twisted body of Trader Bob, desperately trying to scramble to safety, one of his arms and one of his legs obviously broken as was evident by the shattered and bloody bones protruding from the man's torn flesh.

The growling and moaning inside the pit continued to increase as the creatures held there began to fall upon the defenseless man. The view went from wide angle to close up and Billy looked over at Deimos to see him working some device which obviously controlled the cameras remotely. On the floor of the pit, several of the zombies bit deep into the flesh of Bob's exposed arms and legs, tearing off pink and crimson ribbons of skin, revealing the red musculature beneath while others began digging their long boney fingers deep into the soft meat of his abdomen.

Billy could hear Bob's screams of agony while watching the unspeakable carnage live as the creatures began to pull his intestines out through the opening they had made in his belly. The growling rose to a chorus of roars as the inhuman feast of flesh continued. All the while, Deimos sat smiling while occasionally sipping his drink and adjusting the cameras for the best angle. His pet mutant Odo stood beside him, occasionally looking over at Billy in a way he didn't much care for.

After what seemed like a very long time, the screaming was finally over and the only sounds, which remained were the savage slurping, chewing and growling of the undead finishing their meal. Deimos turned to Billy and said. "Ok Billy. Thanks again for all you've done for me. And thanks in advance as well for cleaning up that Jackson Ridge car and hotel thing as well."

Billy, obviously shaken by the spectacle he had just witnessed, replied, "Y... yes... anything... anytime." Billy was a bad man, a really bad man. He had shot and killed many people in his time, but this atrocity was something he would have never considered even on his worst day. This was the ultimate in sick and twisted action of a truly insane individual. Yet to Deimos it was something he apparently did for fun. Billy had been doing business for Deimos for some time, but this was the first time he had ever been privy to one of the man's personal executions. He had heard rumors and stories about just how crazy the man was, but nothing had prepared him for a level of carnage like this.

"And Billy?" Deimos said with the most incredibly evil look in his eyes, "Be sure to pass the word to all of your associates that when I give a specific order, I expect it to be carried out exactly as I commanded. You see. I wanted you to see this little exhibition so you could personally attest to my lack of patience when it comes to disobedience. I'll be sure you get a copy of the video for your own viewing pleasure as well as for that of your friends. I just want to make sure you remember to spread the word."

"I... I... most certainly... will." Billy said as he turned without another word and walked along the right side of the pit, heading toward the door. His mind was in turmoil. He felt as if he might scream. He thought he would pass out. And he was certain he was just seconds away from vomiting. He couldn't wait to get out of the barn and as far away from that madman Deimos as he could. He realized for the first time in his life that he might no longer be cut out for this life of crime. Things were different in the old days. Even criminals had rules and at least a sort of fundamental code to live by, but things were very different now. Apparently insanity was the rule of the day.

Maybe he would take the money Deimos had given him and leave; go somewhere far away never to be heard from again. But he knew the world was likely full of men just like Deimos, and these crazy men were the sorts of characters who men like Billy had to rely upon for survival. He understood if he fled, he would soon probably find himself in the employ of another whom, although with a different name and face, would be basically the same type of insane maniac as Deimos. It was just the nature of the business where survival of the fittest had been surmounted by survival of the craziest and most savage.

As he got toward the end of the building, Billy happened to glance down into the pit. He had not wanted to, but without thinking about it his curiosity had gotten the better of his own common sense. Then to his horror, Billy saw what remained of Trader Bob. It looked as though the man had been in an explosion. His head and limbs separated from his body as inhuman creatures continued to devour his remains in an orgy of gore. As he walked out the opening in the barn door, Billy hurried to his car, stumbled behind it and vomited uncontrollably. He looked back to make sure Deimos hadn't come outside and seen him but he hadn't. Little did he know that Deimos was actually watching him on his big screen television, the signal being broadcast from a remote outdoor camera. He was laughing madly at the sight of Billy on his knees, puking his guts out. Odo stood by silently.

This had all been too much for Billy. He climbed behind the wheel of his car, retrieved his hand gun from the glove box. He was going to do this one last task. He would get rid of Jackson Ridge's car and clear out his hotel room. If he was lucky, he would find more cash. Then he was climbing back into his car and driving south. He had no idea what he would find there, but he knew he had to get as far away from Deimos as possible.

CHAPTER 38

Jackson's senses suddenly became alert when he heard the frail voice calling from somewhere out of the darkness. His head instinctively turned left in the direction from which the voice had come.

"Sarah? Sarah... Stanton? Is... is that... you?" Jackson asked, scarcely believing he might actually have found her.

Then through the gloom he heard the small voice once again, "Yes... yes it's me, Sarah... b... but... but how do you know my name. Who... who are... you?"

Jackson waited a beat, trying to figure out what he should say next. The girl was most likely terrified. Then despite his own incredibly horrible circumstances, he managed to say, "Sarah... my... my name is Jackson... Jackson Ridge... I'm a reporter for the Schuylkill Daily News... your uncle, Mayor McKinney... he... he sent me to find you..."

"Thank goodness." Sarah replied, her voice overflowing with relief and emotion. "I just knew someone would come. I hoped and I prayed someone would come and now you have and now you've found me."

"Are you... all right... Sarah?" Jackson inquired with grave concern, not really sure how to broach the delicate subject which was in the forefront of his mind. He was terrified she may have already been raped or brutalized in some other horrible way. "Did they? I mean... did... did anyone... hurt you... at all?"

There was a moment of silence, which seemed like an eternity to Jackson before Sarah finally said, "No... no not really. I don't think so... I mean... I don't remember most of what happened since they took me. They keep giving me shots of something, you know, with needles, and every time I wake up I am in a different place. And everything is foggy and confusing and I can't remember much of anything else."

Jackson thought "Thank you God for at least that small miracle. But he kept that thought to himself and then he asked her, "Have you been here... in this place before? You know... where it is... this place... where we both are now?" He was suddenly feeling drained and wasn't sure if it was from blood loss, lack of nourishment, or simply a result of everything he had been through, but he was having difficulty making sense. Yet he wanted to sound as strong as possible for Sarah's sake, but he found it was becoming increasingly difficult.

"No... no." Sarah said. Jackson had to struggle to recall what question she was answering, but then it came back to him. She explained, "The first time I woke up I was in some sort of cold, damp basement and I was tied to a big wooden chair. The last time I was in a house on a farm somewhere in a bedroom. Now I don't know where I am; where we are. Don't... don't you know? I mean... if you came here to find me I would think you'd know where this place was."

"Well... it's sort of... complicated." Jackson said reluctantly. "You see... I don't know where we are either... I was trying to locate you... and somehow the bad guys found out... about what I was up to. They drugged me too... just like they've been doing to you... I woke up here in the dark... just like you."

In the distance off to his right Jackson heard the moaning and growling sounds increasing as did the shuffling of feet which was becoming more pronounced.

"What's that, Mr. Ridge?" Sarah asked. "What's that noise? Was that you? I hear someone moving around; like feet moving. And oh man, why does it smell so awfully bad in here?"

Jackson tried to remain calm and did his best to explain, even though simply putting coherent thoughts into sentences was becoming increasingly difficult for him. "I think... somewhere in here... off to my right... there are some of... some of them... you know... dead heads."

Sarah exclaimed with undisguised terror, "Oh no! Please God not that!"

"It's ok... Sarah... I mean... I'm pretty sure... it's all right... at least for now." Jackson said, "I think they're... locked up... somewhere nearby."

"Are you really sure Mr. Ridge?" Sarah asked fearfully.

Jackson replied, "Yes... Sarah... I'm pretty sure... they can't get to us... or I think by now... they would have... you know what I mean... and Sarah... please... just call me Jackson, ok?"

"Ok Mr.... I mean ok Jackson. I gotta say... you don't sound so good to me." Sarah replied. "Are you all right? Can you come over here and help try to get me out of here?"

"No... no... Sarah. I'm sorry... to say... I'm afraid I can't... not right now." Jackson said in weak frustration. "They have me..." He didn't want to panic the girl with the fact that he had large spikes driven through his palms. "Um... they... have me... tied up to some kind of post... I can't move... or come to you... I'm so sorry... I guess I'm not... very good rescuer... apparently. Can you tell me... are you tied up or... are you free to move around?"

After a few brief moments Sarah said, "My hands are tied together in front of me but my legs are free."

"I can't see you... but I... I can hear you... off to my left." Jackson informed her then asked, "Can... can you see me?"

Sarah replied, "No. I can't. It's just too dark in here," He assumed she couldn't see him, and now he was glad to find out it was true. "but you're in front of me and off to my right."

Jackson was feeling weaker by the minute, but still he somehow managed to say, "We need to... to determine what your... situation is. Can... can you put your hands... out in front of you... and very carefully... walk... toward the sound... of my voice?"

"Yes. Yes I think I can do that." Sarah replied. "Can you keep talking so I can find my way? If it's not too much trouble; you really sort of sound sick to me."

"I'm... I'm just tired... very tired." Jackson said although not very convincingly. Then he called up all of his reserve strength, doing his best to speak in a reassuring voice to keep Sarah calm while simultaneously providing her with a voice to follow. He could hear her feet shuffling on the dirt floor, getting slightly closer to him. After a few seconds he heard a metallic rattling sound.

"There's some sort of fence and a big gate." Sarah said. "I think I'm in some kind of cage." Jackson could hear the panic rising in her voice.

"It's... it's ok Sarah." Jackson said reassuringly. "It's probably not really... a cage... Can you... do me a favor now... and follow the fence... upward... with your hands... and see how tall it is?"

Sarah said, "Yeah. I think I can do that too." Jackson didn't really care how tall the cage was, he was simply trying to keep the girl busy and make her feel like less of a victim and was actually involved in possibly helping herself get free. Then he realized in his current condition, the only chance she might ever have of getting free was of her own accord.

"I can't reach the top." Sarah called back. "It must be pretty high. "

"Good." Jackson said. "That means... there's probably a lot of room in there for you... it's likely just a ... a fenced in area... Can you follow... the fence around... and get a feel... for how much space... you do have in there?" Once again, he was just trying to keep her occupied. He still hoped that someone would come to their rescue soon.

After a few minutes of sounds of the girl shuffling about she said, "It seems to be pretty big. The floor is dirt I think and I felt something brushing against my legs that felt and smelled like hay or straw."

"Yes... That's very good Sarah." Jackson exclaimed. "I had a feeling... we might be... in a barn... it's chilly in here... but not as cold... as outside... and before those dead heads... started moving around... I thought I smelled... barn smells as well... you know... but now all I smell... is their rotten stink."

As if insulted by his remark, the milling group of undead somewhere out in the darkness began to growl even louder and their pacing seemed to become even more frantic. He heard metal rattling in the direction of the growls and was sure they too were being held captive behind some sort of wire barrier as Sarah was. He only hoped wherever they were, their barriers were strong enough to keep them there. The only thing Jackson could think of that might be worse than dying from thirst, starvation, or blood loss while hanging on a cross might be having his insides ripped out by a mob of stinking zombies while he hung helpless and unable to defend himself.

Once again, Sarah expressed her concern, "Jackson. You really don't sound very good. Are you sure you're ok?"

Even though Jackson was grateful for the girl's concern, he felt the need to do whatever it took to protect her and to keep her mind as ease. "Yes... I'm fine Sarah... and more importantly... you are going to be ok too... I promise... soon... very soon... someone will... be here to help us... someone will... be here to rescue us."

Before he had a chance to say anything else, Jackson heard a door open off to his far right and the room was suddenly awash with blinding light.

CHAPTER 39

Jackson involuntarily closed his eyes tightly against the blinding barrage of harsh light, unable to shield them with his hands, which were brutally spiked to the wooden cross member. He was blinking rapidly, trying desperately to give his pupils a chance to adjust to the brilliant illumination, hoping to see who it was who had just entered the room. He hoped it might be the police or someone else arriving to rescue them both, but somehow he knew these thoughts were nothing more than the pointless wishes of a desperate man. He was able to catch brief glimpses of two people walking toward him, coming down along a long, blurred corridor. At least at first glance he thought they were both people. The smaller person in the front was definitely a man, but the one in the back appeared so much larger than the other that it was hard to say for certain if it was even a human being.

As his eyes slowly adjusted, Jackson looked to his left to see just how bad the situation with his hands was. His stomach lurched when he saw the large metal spike jutting out from his palm; dried blood on both the shaft of nail as well as bits of the torn flesh from his pierced hand. As he had suspected, his arms had been tightly bound to the cross beam with thick, heavy rope; the kind his father used to refer to as bull rope. He didn't need to look at the other hand to know he had a matching set. He was thankful once again that both of his hands were numb, because he was certain otherwise, the pain would have been unbearable. Then, as an afterthought, he wasn't so sure if the numbness in his extremities was a good thing or a bad thing. He could also still smell the rank scent of the vomit now drying on his chest, and he wisely chose not to look down at the filthy mess.

Instead, looking out past his bloody palm Jackson could see the young girl, Sarah in the near distance behind a wire mesh covered z-rail type gate. She was on her knees and had her own bound hands up in front of her eyes in an effort to shield them from the light as well. Jackson could see now that they were definitely being held in an old barn, which had been retrofitted with bright florescent lighting and converted into some sort of prison facility. Jackson assumed this had been done to suit Deimos' twisted needs.

In the space between where he hung and where Sarah was being held, Jackson saw a small, square stainless steel medical table on wheels, standing about chest high and covered with a variety of objects. Those items which were most recognizable to him were both of his communications units, his own and the one he had gotten from Chief Holden. Also there was the digital mass storage device he had received from Sean Patel with the files containing the information about the murdered young girls.

"God!" Jackson thought, "It felt like his meeting with Sean had been a lifetime ago!" But he suspected it might have only been the previous morning. On the metal table were also several tools; a hammer, a pair of pliers, and a few additional large spike-sized nails. As if that sight alone were not disturbing enough, Jackson could also see an assortment of what looked like surgical or dental tools. These roused memories of scenes he had seen in old spy movies and Jackson instantly knew the only purpose such instruments would have in a place like this would be to inflict pain. He recalled what that man Smith had said about how when Deimos was through with him Jackson would be cursing his own mother for giving him life. This thought filled Jackson with terror as he wondered what exactly the psychopath might have in store for him.

Looking back toward Sarah, Jackson could see she was being held in what appeared to have once been a horse's stall. It was an area about six feet by ten feet, was rectangular in shape, and was surrounded by wooden cross rails. The compartment had been modified and encircled by heavy wire fencing, which had been attached to the cross rails on all four sides. Across the top another section of wire fencing had been added and welded into place to completely seal the area turning it into a makeshift jail cell. At the base of the enclosure, Jackson could see that the fencing was buried deep into the soil to prevent the prisoner from digging his or her way under the barrier. Although he couldn't tell for certain, Jackson suspected the bottom of the pen underneath the soil was likely wire fencing as well, which probably also had been welded. On the front side of the stall was an access gate secured with a heavy padlock and chain. There was simply no way Sarah would be able to get out of that prison without the benefit of a key.

Sarah slowly lowered her hands from her eyes and, after blinking a few times, saw Jackson's face for the first time. Their eyes met and for at least a moment the young girl seemed relieved to see him. That was, until she saw what Deimos had done to him. When the girl saw Jackson's spiked hands and near-death condition, she let out an ear-piercing, involuntary scream.

"No... no... no..." Sarah screamed over and over. Jackson assumed the realization of the severity of their situation had finally begun to sink in. The girl understood no rescuers were likely ever coming for them. It was apparent to her Jackson would likely be dead very soon and she would be left alone and at the mercy of whatever horrible purpose this maniac Deimos had in store for her.

"Not no... no... noo... but yes... yes... yes..." a voice said from Jackson's right, sounding inappropriately cheerful considering his current circumstances. And it was a voice Sarah unfortunately had recognized all too well. It was the same smooth voice she had heard in the basement as well as in her bedroom in the farmhouse. It was the voice of that man, the kidnapper who called himself Deimos.

Jackson slowly turned his head to try to get a look at the two approaching figures. As Sarah had done when she first encountered Deimos' bodyguard, Jackson's gaze couldn't help but slide completely past the nondescript man in the lead and instead focused on the incredible, hulking beast of a thing that was walking purposefully behind him. And "thing" was precisely how Jackson thought of the creature, as it was every bit as huge as the zombie he had taken down just the previous day, or whatever day that event had actually occurred. This was impossible for Jackson to determine since he had lost all comprehension of time.

The creature was massive in size and seemed to have far too much body hair for a normal human being. It – because that term seemed appropriate - was filthy dirty and glistened with gleaming sweat and was coated with grime. Its long hair was matted and it appeared to have a face which was almost animal-like. It had incredibly huge muscles bulging from a worn, yellowed athletic tee shirt which was also caked with filth. In fact, the only thing about it which might make someone consider it human was its wife-beater shirt and its ripped and worn jeans. Jackson felt like he was looking at a huge animal dressed in the clothing of a man.

The thing seemed to stare at him with absolutely no expression in its dark, sunken eyes, which were set deep below an overhanging Neanderthal brow. The rest of its face was covered with matted, grimy facial hair and those portions of its body which were exposed were likewise a patchwork of hair and scars. Jackson couldn't begin to imagine what manor of man-beast this thing was. Like many people, Jackson had heard the rumors of mutations among the outlanders, but he had never seen anything quite like this creature before. Even the giant zombie he had so recently shot was neither this huge nor this hideous. And now that he had seen this horrifying creature, he wished he could have been spared the terrifying experience.

"Maybe it would be a better idea for you to spend a bit less of your precious time staring at my oversized friend Odo here..." a silky smooth voice with a slight trace of a country accent said, "... and maybe you might want to spend a bit more time focusing on me; especially since I'm the one whose gonna determine how long you're gonna live and just how you're gonna die, Mr. Ridge. Oh, and rest assured at some point in the not too distant future you are most definitely going to die. It might be quick or it might be slow. It might be extremely painful or it might not hurt a bit. But ignoring me ain't gonna do much to make me lean towards the quick and painless side, I must say."

Jackson blinked back to reality upon hearing his name spoken. He hadn't even realized that he had been staring, almost entranced by the sight of the hideous creature. He realized the voice had been that of a small man who appeared almost miniscule when dwarfed by the behemoth behind him. The man was just a few inches over five feet tall and was of a slight build, wearing blue jeans, a well-worn leather jacket over a black western cut shirt, and a ridiculous snakeskin belt with an oversized buckle shaped like a skull. Under different circumstances, such a sight might have made Jackson chuckle, but he understood there was absolutely nothing to laugh about here.

The man's hair was jet black and was slicked back, revealing the weathered and creased face of a much older man than the black hair suggested. Then Jackson noticed the man's piercing eyes and his strange grinning smile; the smile of a madman. No one needed to introduce the man to Jackson; he instantly knew it had to be none other than the murdering criminal known as Deimos.

CHAPTER 40

"And, a pleasant good evening to you Mr. Ridge," Deimos said in a voice which was far too amiable for such a dire situation. Jackson stared hard at Deimos with all the fury he could manage but unfortunately he was feeling far too weak for any such look to have any real power behind it.

Deimos said "What in the world was that nasty look for? Such a hostile glare! Is that any way for a guest to thank his host? I don't think so Jackson, my friend, rather rude I must say. It appears I may have to teach you something about proper manners. Perhaps I need to drive a couple more of those spikes into you, but while your awake this time and maybe into your feet. Or I know. I could have my man Odo here start skinning you alive. Yeah that might be interesting. I have to think about that for a few minutes." Then Deimos let loose with a strange chuckle, not so much a pleasant, humorous laugh as it was the cackle of a raving lunatic.

Jackson was unsure what exactly the man was trying to prove with all of his threats of torture, and in his weakened condition, Jackson had no energy to waste participating in Deimos' twisted game. Jackson realized, not for the first time, he was already well on his way to dying. He knew he was likely going to be killed by this maniac at some point in time. Deimos had made that more than clear, but now he had a feeling because of his deteriorating physical state, death might take him much sooner than even his captor had realized. He said weakly, "D... Deimos. What... what is it? What do you... want from me?"

Deimos looked at him with a perplexed and somewhat confused expression, then said, "Hum... That's a very good question Jackson. Why... I suppose... Now that I think about it... well... I guess don't really want anything from you. You see, I'm pretty sure I already have everything I want and need. Let me think a bit about this... I got you nailed to this cross, helpless as a baby kitten, and I have my sweet little Sarah over there just waiting for me to bring her into the fold, so to speak. So you tell me Jackson, who could possibly ask for anything more?"

"But... but why?" Jackson asked. "Why are you... doing this... to me... to us?"

"Why?" Deimos said, once again smiling his disturbingly insane smile, "Why that's an easy one Jackson my man. I'm really surprised to hear such a simple question coming out of the mouth of a so-called top notch investigative reporter. I'm doing this because I want to and because I can. That's all. That's it. It really is that simple. I mean, it's not anything personal. Although I have to admit I was a bit upset about that series of articles you wrote a several years ago. Do you realize you didn't even have the decency to mention me by name? As I recall, you just referred to me as some unknown dark mysterious character. At the time my feelings were hurt, but that's all water under the bridge, or water over the dam, or water over the damn bridge. Or whatever that confound expression is supposed to be! But honestly, that previous incident has little if anything to do with your current situation. You see, all of this is just what I do. This is my kingdom and I am the king, a-ring-a-ding-ding. I'm the lord and master. And that means I can do whatever I want, to whomever I want, and whenever I damn well please."

Jackson had no idea what it might be he was supposed to say next. How could he possibly know how to respond to such madness? He had never encountered anyone like this before. Being unsure as well as exhausted, Jackson just said the first thing to pop into his mind, "But... but... it's wrong."

"It's wrong..." Deimos said looking perplexed as if contemplating the meaning of the phrase he had just heard, like it was something foreign to him or some expression he had heard for the first time. "Wrong you say? No Jackson, you're most definitely the one's whose wrong here. You see, none of this can really be wrong because I am the one who thought of it. And if I think of something, well... then it's got to be right. You have to understand something Jackson, I'm like a God around here, and a God is incapable of making mistakes. So as far as I can tell, that means I can't possibly be wrong."

"But... but what... what you're doing..." Jackson insisted weakly.

Deimos looked at him again with a perplexed expression and said, "What I'm doing is... well it's part of my grand design, if you will. It's part of what I'm fond of calling my master plan. You see, it's my own personal money-making strategy which has served me very well for many years now. Hell's bells, you're the reporter... haven't you figure it all out yet?"

Jackson struggled to come up with the words then said, "N... No. I... I don't understand... what... what plan?"

"All right Jackson." Deimos said, "Let me explain this to you. I suppose I owe you that much. After all, it's the least I can do for a man who is about to meet his maker. So just to clarify in case you didn't realize it, you are most definitely going to die tonight; one way or another. So I suppose you can think of this as my parting gift to you. And come to think of it, it's probably also important that my new pretty little sweet pea Sarah over there hears all of this as well. 'Cause she's gonna be a very big part of my plans, whether she's aware of it or not."

"Sarah..." Jackson said weakly. She was now sitting in the back of her cage trembling with fright. "Please... not Sarah... Just leave her... out of this."

Deimos chided, "You might as well save your energy Jackson. You'll live longer. Ha ha. Well now that was a real knee-slapper right there. But anyway, since you're so concerned let me tell you all about Sarah. You see, sweet lil' Sarah is a done deal and to be honest is no longer even worth your consideration. So why don't you just hush for a minute and let me explain how all this works. Aren't you even a little bit curious, mister investigative reporter? Of course you are I'll bet."

"So here's how all this works. I have me a multi-step process that all of my gals go through and it sometimes takes quite a few years for them to get from the beginning to the end. By the way, that fact is certainly a good one because all the while they're in the pipeline so to speak; they're constantly making money for me."

Jackson weakly lifted his head and glanced again at the huge monster standing behind his master in a menacing, protective pose. The thing just stood silently, expressionless, like some sort of gruesome sentinel while Deimos rambled on incessantly. Jackson tried to focus on what the man was saying, but it was becoming increasingly difficult.

"You see, I start by either finding young pretty runaways around twelve or thirteen years old. And if I can't find any strays as I like to call them, then I have my boys out scouting new talent for me all the time. When they find a gal with great potential like little Sarah over there, they let me know. I then have them follow the girl for a few weeks and learn whatever they can about her; you know her comings and goings. And then when the time is just right I send a team out to grab her and bring her to me. Once I have her where I want her then I start the process. First I like to get her hooked on one of the many hard drugs I have available to me; you know, heroin, crack, or sometimes even braino, depending upon how much they resist what I call their orientation." Deimos made air quote signs with his fingers as he said the word orientation.

Jackson looked again at Sarah. She had told him she had been drugged, but she looked fine now. That was to say he thought she looked drug free, but she looked anything but fine emotionally. He had suspected they must have given her a sedative of some sort. She didn't seem to be showing signs of someone who was under the influence of any of the other hard drugs Deimos had mentioned.

As if reading his thoughts, Deimos said, "Don't worry Jackson. I haven't officially started indoctrinating Sarah into my process yet. But I will be doing so shortly; once I'm all finished having my fun with you. That's why there's really no need for you to get yourself all riled up about sweet Sarah. Because you'll be dead as old Trader Bob long before all of that excitement begins."

Jackson wondered to himself. "Trader Bob?"

"Oh yeah." Deimos said, "Sorry. I forgot you didn't know about that. I fed your old buddy Bob to a bunch of zombies on my way over here. You see, it's never a good idea to piss me off. But then again, you know all about that, don't you? Anyway, back to my story. So once I get the little darlings hooked on my special substances, I introduce them to their new film careers. You know... you folks like call it kiddy porn; I prefer to think of it as 'child acting'."

"Whatever the term you choose to use, you understand what it's all about without me going into all the gory details. Long story short; as the years go by eventually I get them into hooking and adult porn and whatever other avenues seem appropriate based on whatever skill sets they develop. It's really heartwarming to see how they each discover their own hidden talents and specialties. But eventually all good things come to an end. So when they're either too drugged out to perform their required duties any longer or if they have simply worn out their welcome so to speak; well, then they get to star in their very own personal snuff film written especially for them. That's right Jackson. I usually have one of my boys torture them then choke them to death on film. Sometimes I even charge one of my more affluent, although severely mentally damaged customers an exorbitant amount of money to star in the film. Then he gets to do the deed himself. I suppose you could say I'm killing two birds with one stone, as the saying goes."

Jackson was beyond disgusted. He was suddenly thinking of the dead kills which Sean had told him about; the young women with the ligature marks on their necks. He didn't want to hear any more. He had heard far too much already. Then he looked again at the CU sitting on the medical cart. What if it were still recording and transmitting? It was his responsibility, even if it was the last act he did as a living human being. He had to make sure the police learned everything about what this lunatic had been doing.

"So then... I guess that's it... right? That's... the end of the line... for the poor girls." Jackson asked trying to keep Deimos talking.

"Glad you asked that question Jackson my friend." Deimos said. "Maybe you do have what it takes to be a real reporter after all. But no my friend. Death is a far cry from the end of the line for them. I mean, technically it may be the end for them as living, breathing babes to use in my money making enterprises, but it's not the end of their usefulness in making me money. You see, once they've been strangled and have been immortalized on film they now enter a whole new phase of value to me. Of course, I sell many, many copies of the snuff films to a list of very special clients who are just starving for such stuff. But there's much more than that."

"I just sit back and wait for them to return. Then once they've turned, we start photographing and filming them for my latest and most profitable marketing scheme yet. Did you forget all about Z Porn, Jackson? I gotta tell you this has proven to be a major money maker for me in pictures, magazines, and videos. Who'd of thought it? But here's the best part. Get this Jackson; I love this part. There's something new even more profitable than even Z Porn. It is something we like to call Z Love. Yep, that's right Jackson; I have an entire stable of undead former sluts of mine that I like to call my stinky little Z Hookers." Deimos waited for a reaction from Jackson, but when he received none he decided to finish his tale.

"Nothing? No comment? No reaction? Surely Jackson you've gotta have something to say. No? Oh well. So anyway, I have a whole slew of these clients; necrophiliacs and other sick and twisted freaks who are just – pardon the expression - dying to have the opportunity to stick it to one of these dead beauties. I suppose you could say these gals are drop dead gorgeous. Hey... now that's funny. So for several more highly profitable years my little dead girls are able to continue to make me money. Then one day when they become so rotten and disgusting that even the most depraved or retarded of the outlanders won't come near them... then I offer them up for any of a dozen gaming places I know about. And if none of them want to take the stiffs off my hands, well then I have little choice but to pop them, on film of course, and then leave their rotting carcasses along the side of the road for either some civil servant to find and dispose of, or for scavengers to pick to pieces. And that Jackson, actually is the end of the story."

"That's... beyond... disgusting." Jackson said, "I can't believe... you monster... there's a... special room... in Hell... waiting just for you... Deimos."

Deimos stared at Jackson for a moment with a mixture of wonder and resignation and then said. "Well. Maybe there is and maybe there isn't. Either way, it really doesn't matter very much to me. Some folks might argue that we're already in Hell. Whatever. All I care about is now... right now, and how I can get as much out of this world as possible while I'm here. And whether you want to admit it or not, Jackson, it's a kill or be killed world we live in now. Our illustrious so-called government still believes civilization can survive; that mankind can make a comeback, but not me. You see Jackson, I personally don't like to deal in fantasies, I prefer to deal in reality. And the reality of the situation is that even though we're going through the motions of rebuilding society, it's far, far too late for that. The soul of civilization, the very essence of what it once meant to be human, has been damaged beyond the point of salvation."

"I... I don't believe... that." Jackson argued feebly.

"Well maybe you should. Look at it this way Jackson. As my dear old Daddy used to say; 'if you put lipstick on a pig, it's still a pig.' And guess what? You can dress up society in all the glitz and glitter you want, but in the end it's still a pig. We all carry that damned Z43 virus inside of us and even though it may not show up until we're dead it is still got to be doing something to us. It's gotta be messing with us somehow. You simply can't carry it around all the time inside of you without it affecting you. It's slowly eating our souls from the inside out."

"So you can believe whatever you want to believe Jackson, but I believe Heaven no longer exists, if it ever did and Hell... well, Hell is right here among us; right where we live and breathe. Mankind is doomed I tell you, and as such I'm going to do everything I can to get the most out of this miserable life while I'm walking the earth."

Deimos casually walked over to the medical table and picked up the digital mass storage device Jackson had gotten from Sean. "And I thought I should let you know Jackson, I took the liberty of looking over the files on this here little device. It was very impressive. You really must have been studying my activities for quite some time, and I'm embarrassed to say I was completely unaware of it. Well, shame on me because it looks to me like you already managed to link several dead women in the Schuylkill County morgue to some missing girls who had the pleasure of working for me over the years. You apparently hadn't made the direct connection to me yet, but I can see you were well on your way. Excellent work if I must say so myself."

Despite his situation, Jackson was at least relieved to realize Deimos had not made any connection to Sean. He had apparently thought Jackson had come up with the data about the murdered girls on his own. Jackson would have hated to think that once Deimos had killed him, the madman might still be planning on going after his best friend. Hopefully, now at least all of this would end with his own death.

Deimos set the storage drive back on the medical cart then reached behind his back and pulled out a hand gun. He pointed the barrel of the pistol right at Jackson's head. In the wire cage, Sarah began to murmur "No... no... please... don't hurt him."

"Well Jackson my man. It looks like I have a decision to make. I can either leave you hang here for another day or so until you finally die and turn into one of those things or I can finish you off right now with one between the eyes. I'm starting to believe this place is becoming way too hot for me to stick around here for very much longer. As I'm sure you know I like to keep my operation fairly mobile, and staying in the same place for too long is not good for my survival. I've already instructed all of my staff to clean out the place and move to my next location. Just about everyone else is gone. All that remain here now are you, sweet little Sarah, myself, Odo, and that crop of rotting former hookers over there stinking up the pit. They've not only worn out their usefulness as living sluts but also as undead sluts as well. Now they were all waiting to be transferred to an underground casino to be used for target practice in one of their gaming areas. But unfortunately, because of my need to move quickly, that won't be their future. As soon as I put a bullet into your skull, Jackson, I'll take sweet Sarah out of here and my friend Odo will set fire to this barn disposing not only of your carcass but also those practically worthless dead whores in the pit over there. Still, it irks me to have to waste them even though they're only worth a couple of bucks each. You know what they say, money is money. But in light of everything taking place, I suppose it looks like I'll have no choice."

Now Sarah was pleading from her wire prison, "Please... please don't hurt him any more... I'll go with you... I'll do whatever you want... just please let him go."

Deimos looked over at Sarah and said, "Do whatever I say? Of course you will Sarah. You all do eventually. And I'm truly sorry, my little sweet pea, but a man's gotta do what a man's gotta do. And right now I don't see any other option. Well Jackson. It was nice getting to know you even if it was for such a brief period of time, but now it appears I have to be going on my merry way, and you have to move on to whatever awaits you on the other side."

Jackson looked away from Deimos, not wanting to have to look down the barrel of the gun which was slated to end his life momentarily. Instead, his eyes landed on the large mutant creature Odo. Jackson stared at the man/beast's massive forehead and waited to hear the final report from Deimos' gun, which he knew would be the last sound he would ever hear in life. And that was when he saw it.

CHAPTER 41

Jackson stared at the strange red dot which seemed to tremble ever so slightly in the center of the mutant's forehead. "What in the world is that thing?" Jackson wondered. Maybe it was his ever increasing weakness causing him to imagine things. The presence of dot seemed somehow familiar to him, like he should know its significance but its purpose momentarily eluded him. Then he slowly began to understand, but even before his jumbled thoughts had a chance to completely form, Jackson saw the gargantuan creature's head fly back as a black circle appeared momentarily where the red dot had previously been. Then as Jackson saw the back of the monster's skull explode outward in a shower of brains, hair, flesh, and gore, he heard the delayed sound of the gunshot echoing behind him and off to his right. The event reminded him very much of how the attack on the bikers had been. The huge man-beast stumbled backward, knocked off balance by the impact of the blast, and fell over the wire covered split rail fence and down into the pit of the now frantically growling undead women.

As the monster hit the dirt floor with a hollow thud, Jackson assumed the creatures in the pit would ignore the body. He suspected the obviously dead monster might appear to be almost like one of them. But to his surprise, they didn't leave the beast alone. Perhaps it was because the body was still warm. Jackson had always suspected there might be some sort of heat seeking mechanism present in the decaying brains of the lingering dead that allowed them to hone in on the warmth of the living. It was also possible that they had been worked up into such a frenzied state that they simply didn't comprehend the condition of the creature. Whatever the case might have been, the zombies fell upon the giant and began tearing him apart in an orgy of crimson carnage. Jackson could see glimpses of the butchery through the spaces in the fence. Intestines whipped through the air, uncontrollably spitting blood and bile as Jackson heard the creature's flesh rip and its bones break.

This had all occurred in a matter of a few seconds while Deimos was focused on preparing to blow out Jackson's brains. Deimos mustn't have even realized what was happening until he too heard the same gunshot Jackson had heard, but by then it was far too late. Almost simultaneously, a second shot rang out and Jackson saw Deimos' right hand, the one that had the gun pointed in his face, miraculously separate from his arm and fall to the ground, its finger still wrapped around the trigger as the villain's wrist detonated in a shower of spurting blood. The cherry fluid jetted from the man's mangled stump and stippled Jackson's face and chest with the ruby splatter.

Deimos instinctively grasped his severed wrist, howling in pain and holding the tattered stump close to his chest, while simultaneously in the pit, his pet Odo's remains were being ripped to shreds. His focus was now trained off to Jackson's right and the man wore an expression which within the space of a few seconds, went through a gamut of emotions starting with fury, then apparent recognition, followed by confusion and eventually terror. From Jackson's vantage, it looked as if Deimos had just realized he was a man who was about to die, which Jackson certainly hoped was true. Jackson suspected he himself had likely worn a similar expression just moments earlier when he was certain the madman was about to kill him. Sarah was on her knees now, trying to cover her ears with her forearms, her hands bound, and her head bent downward as she screamed hysterically in terror.

"You!" Deimos shouted at whoever it was standing outside of Jackson's range of sight; apparently the same person who had blown off the maniac's hand. Deimos' eyes bulged out of their sockets as he bellowed "Holden... what... what do you... think you're do..." But before he could finish his sentence another gunshot echoed through the barn as a large hole appeared in Deimos' left shoulder and he was knocked off of his feet, falling to the dirt floor directly in front of Jackson, where he lay on his back now desperately digging his heals into the dirt trying to crawl backward away from the approaching threat.

"Holden?" Jackson thought with relief. "Deimos said Holden... that must be Brent Holden... thank goodness." Apparently Brent had somehow found him; maybe he had tracked him using the CU which he had given Jackson earlier. Brent had said the thing could record for days, and maybe there had been a tracking device inside as well. Whatever method the man had use to track him, Jackson knew his luck had finally changed for the better, Deimos was down and hopefully would be dead very soon. Jackson was surprised to find himself not caring if Deimos lived or died, but he supposed even the most compassionate of individuals had their limits. And Deimos had pushed Jackson far beyond his. Off to his right, Jackson could see two shapes dressed in black clothing coming into his field of vision. Leading the pair was Police Chief Brent Holden followed by Sergeant David Evans, the man who Jackson recognized as having led the paramilitary squad which had come to his rescue from the outlaw motorcycle gang.

Jackson soon began to realize just how weak and exhausted he now was and what a struggle he was having simply attempting to remain conscious. He wondered if it even mattered any longer whether he blacked out or not. He had found Sarah, and now help had finally arrived to rescue them both. He wanted nothing better than to let go, to give in, to pass out, and then hopefully the next time he awoke it would be in a hospital somewhere being treated for his injuries. Actually, if he were to be perfectly honest with himself, he was feeling so weak that he no longer even cared if he woke up again or not. Regardless of his condition, Jackson somehow still managed to fight against the almost uncontrollable urge to simply collapse. He needed to make sure Sarah was safe first. He had come to rescue her, and he had to be certain she was all right. After that, whatever happened to him would be beyond his control.

"Help... us..." Jackson said weakly, "Sarah... Brent please... help Sarah."

As his vision blurred in and out of focus, he saw Brent Holden walking in front of him, stopping for a second to look at him with what Jackson perceived as an extremely odd expression; not the look he would have expected Brent to have, but something which seemed very strange and maybe even menacingly cold. Then Brent walked over to the downed body of Deimos, who was still alive and was still struggling to crawl away. Deimos had made it to the gate directly in front of Sarah's cage but realized this was then end of the line. To Jackson's surprise, Brent calmly walked over to Deimos and aimed his pistol directly at the criminal's head.

He smiled strangely then whispered something to the man which Jackson was unable to hear. The next thing Jackson realized Brent unceremoniously pulled the trigger, splattering Deimos' brains into the crater the gunshot made in the barn's dirt floor. Likewise, a shower of blood-soaked dirt particles flew up and rained down upon the hair and face of young Sarah who was now screaming even more hysterically then before. She dug her own heels into the dirt and pushed herself back in an attempt to put as much space as possible between her and the horrifying bloodbath taking place outside of her cage. Jackson saw the plume of crimson-colored dirt particles momentarily fly upward as if in slow motion from the craterous hole then sprinkle down over the now dead villain's face. Jackson could see the man's blood pooling on the soil's surface, forming large cherry beads that slowly settled downward, soaking into the earth.

For Jackson, everything seemed to be happening as if time had slowed to a crawl; as if it were taking place in a very bad dream. Even though Jackson couldn't say he was sorry to see the madman dead, he was nonetheless shocked at the cold and methodical manner in which Brent Holden had dispatched him.

But then Jackson realized this was Holden's job; it was what he did. He, Evans, and others in their professions were forced to deal with hardened criminals like Deimos on a daily basis and in a world where justice often had to be served up instantaneously and without remorse. Jackson supposed right or wrong, this was just the way police had to handle things like this. He could still hear Sarah's uncontrollable sobbing as she huddled against the back of her cage and he wondered to himself if the poor girl would ever be able to recover from an emotional trauma as bad as this. He had heard stories about the resilience of children to spring back from traumatic events, but something of this magnitude might simply be too much. As he barely clung onto consciousness by the thinnest of threads, Jackson tried to express his gratitude to Brent Holden but discovered he was still scarcely capable of forming the words. "Thank... thank... you... Brent..." He somehow managed to squeak out in a dry, raspy voice.

But before the words had even left his mouth, he noticed something unusual happening. Brent Holden's expression had turned even more peculiar than previously, and for some unknown reason the, man had bent down to pick up Deimos' severed hand. At first Jackson assumed he might be collecting evidence, since Holden had put on a pair of latex gloves, but there was something about the man's facial expression or perhaps his body language which Jackson sensed was not right. It was something which caused some primal instinctive fear to well up inside of Jackson. The entire situation had taken a bizarre turn and Jackson suddenly realized what it was, but by the time he did it was far too late for him to shout out any warning.

Brent Holden stood up holding Deimos' gun and severed hand in his own right hand, his finger overtop of the dead hand's finger covering the trigger of the gun. Brent quickly raised the gun, pointed it directly at Sergeant Evans, and pulled the trigger. The bullet flew past Jackson's face so close that he could hear its whizzing sound as it found its target, tearing out the front of Sergeant Evans throat. Blood spurted out like a ruby fountain as the sergeant's carotid artery was severed. Evans let loose with a gurgling, fluid-like cry as he stumbled backward, falling to the floor, his feet twitching spasmodically. Sarah's screaming started anew after witnessing this latest unbelievable act of wanton violence. Jackson was stunned beyond the point of comprehension. What the hell was happening now?

CHAPTER 42

"Wa... what... the..?" Was all Jackson managed to think. He was now utterly dumfounded, having absolutely no idea what was happening. He worried that he might be hallucinating. He had been certain Brent and Evans had come to save him. Brent was the Chief of Police. Why would he have possibly needed to kill Evans? Had Brent somehow learned that Evans was part of Deimos' crime ring? Had Evans he been the leak in the police department all along? But that made no sense. Hadn't it been Sergeant Evans who had helped to save Jackson from the gang of outlanders?

Brent Holden slowly carried the severed hand and gun back to the remains of Deimos and dropped them next to his body. He removed his latex gloves and tucked them neatly into his jacket pocket.

"There now, that should take care of that." Brent said. Sarah was whimpering in the back corner of her cage; obviously scared to death. Brent looked over at Sarah then back at the befuddled Jackson Ridge.

"But..." Jackson tried to say. "I... I... don't..."

"Yeah I know. You don't understand." Brent said, "No, I suppose that's not very surprising. I don't expect you would. You know Ridge, I just gotta say, wow! You didn't see this one coming, did you? Huh? Well don't fret much about it, Jackson. You see, you weren't supposed to. No one did. And no one will. For one thing I'm extremely good at what I do, and secondly, I've been doing this for a very long time."

Brent looked at Jackson and shook his head, saying, "My my, you don't look so good, Jackson. I was kind of hoping you would have passed on by now. It most certainly would have made things easier. But to be honest with you, judging by the way you look right now, I suspect the grim reaper is just waiting for you right around that corner over there. So it appears this story of yours has taken a turn you hadn't anticipated. But regardless, I know how important it was to you. So it only seems fair you follow it through to the bitter end. After all, that's why you took the assignment in the first place and why you're here isn't it? To get the story, am I right?"

Jackson murmured, "No... story... Sarah... to help Sarah."

"Yes I'm sure. Well that's all very good and noble, but as far as I'm concerned it's sort of irrelevant, now isn't it?" Brent interrupted. "You see, you thought you were coming here to find Sarah, but in truth the real reason I agreed with Frank McKinney to send you here was to locate that now dead piece of garbage over there; that worthless wannabe Deimos. That pretender who thought he was me. He supposed he was invincible and could do whatever the hell he wanted behind my back without any repercussions. Well I guess I just proved him wrong didn't I? Yes, I'd say splattering his brains all over the ground like that could be considered a significant repercussion, wouldn't you?"

"You... you... were... the... mole?" Jackson managed to force out.

Brent Holden looked at first surprised then insulted by Jackson's inquiry and said with obvious distain, "Mole? Don't be ridiculous Jackson. Me? The mole? That would suggest that I worked for that ridiculous fool Deimos. You really do suck at your job don't you? Man you're pathetic. Don't you understand? You have it all backwards Jackson. I didn't work for Deimos, he worked for me."

Jackson was having trouble following what Brent was saying. "But... "

"It's like this." Brent explained. "This whole thing is my operation. All of it; the drugs, the hookers, the porno, the zombies; everything is mine. I run the whole show from deep in the shadows. Deimos was just my front man. I needed a figure head, a villain; hell a super-villain. I needed someone around whom I could create a legend. Someone to be feared and who could keep the troops in line. And that was supposed to be Deimos' job.

He was mad as a hatter, but for a long time he managed to play his role well, with my help of course. The only reason he even knew what was going on with all the different police operations was because I kept him informed. He worked for me, Jackson. His was the face I used to instill terror in the hearts of my subordinates and clients alike. All of the stupid legends surrounding the evil genius of the fictitious villain Deimos are stories I created and propagated so that I could successfully control my operation through him."

"But you see Jackson, he was a fool. He actually started to believe all of the propaganda I was spreading. He really started to think he actually was some sort of invincible evil super genius or something equally as ridiculous. Look Jackson, it's like this. Any salesman or marketing guy will tell you that it's ok to lie to everyone as much as you want as long as it helps move your product and make you money. But the absolute worst thing any salesman can possibly do is to start believing his own lies. That was Deimos' downfall; he actually believed all the crap we were shoveling. He really started to buy into the fact that he was this evil genius; the brains behind our empire. And then he had the balls to think he could cut me out and take over the operation himself. Well I suppose that's not happening now, is it? You see, I worked far too long and too hard to make this enterprise a success. There was simply no way I was about to hand it over to a mindless toady like Deimos. Would you like to know what he was when I found him? Would you Jackson?"

Jackson could no longer speak; he just weakly nodded his head in response. Sarah had now gotten a bit quieter and was clinging to the wire fence at the back of her cage. She might have been listening to this wacko; the true madman behind all of this unimaginable horror; he didn't know for certain. Jackson could hear the wounded Sergeant Evans' raspy breaths hitching in his chest and could see his feet still twitching although Jackson suspected they would not be doing so for very much longer.

"The great and powerful 'Deimos the terrible' was a farm hand. A friggin' farmhand. When I met him, the idiot was walking around with a bucket and shovel mucking up after the horses. Don't you find it somewhat ironic how he went from a life of actually shoveling crap to a life of built entirely on metaphorically doing the same thing? "

Brent gave a deep chuckle. "I started building his reputation as the dreaded Deimos long before the Z43 plague started, and for a while after everything started going to Hell we thought we might be out of business. That was until I found a way to use the undead to my advantage. Thank God for perverts and degenerates, is all I have to say."

Jackson still didn't speak. Instead, he looked across the short distance to the metal table on wheels, which held the CU Brent had given him along with the Digital Mass Storage Device which Sean had given him and which Deimos had gotten so angry about. He wondered again if the CU was still recording and transmitting. If so, then as with Deimos, all of this was being monitored and recorded. He thought, even if he did die on this assignment, at least someone might know the truth someday. Jackson wondered why Brent had forgotten about the CU; since it was the very same unit he himself had provided. But Jackson suspected he would never understand a slipup like that, because he couldn't possibly fathom how the mind of a crazy man worked. Perhaps Brent was so filled with anger and outrage that it simply slipped his mind.

Brent was still ranting, "Do you know what the moron's real name was, before I created this fictitious entity Deimos? It was Stanley... Stanley Shabowsky. Can you believe that? Not a very frightening sounding name is it? Ooooh! I'm the evil Stanley Shabowsky... ooooooh. That's right, Jackson. It was all me. I'm the one who came up with the name Deimos. I'm the one who researched mythology and devised just the right frightening new identity for our boy Stanley. I created him. I taught him to kill without remorse, not that he needed much coaching in that regard. He was a natural for whatever reason. But I was the one who made people fear the very mention of his name. I gave him the power to rule in my absence, and unfortunately for him, like all fools before him; he began to believe his own fiction as truth. And that was old Stanley's downfall."

Sarah was still silent in the back of her cage. Jackson noticed that the soon to be late Sergeant David Evans' foot had just about stopped twitching, and his wheezing breaths were now barely audible.

"But... what... what... about..." Jackson attempted to question, hoping to keep Brent talking with the hopes that someone might still come to their rescue. Then he thought at least to rescue Sarah. He was fairly certain his time was all but up. Jackson guessed that Brent and Evans had been sent by the Mayor under the assumption they would find and free him and Sarah, but all that had now gone by the wayside. Maybe he just wanted to keep Brent talking for the few more remaining precious minutes of life the preoccupation might afford him. He was only half listening to what Brent was saying anyway; he was thinking about his wife and daughter. If these were to be the last few moments of his life, he wanted to spend them thinking of Andrea and Kyla.

"What about what Jackson?" Brent chided. "What about you? What about Sarah? Well that's all pretty simple really. You see, I convinced that moron Frank McKinney to send Evans and me to rescue you and his precious little Sarah; no one else, just us. I told him it would be easier for two of us to sneak into the Deimos' hideout. Then once we rescued you both he could arrange for a full scale attack with a large group. Pretty clever on my part, if I must say so myself. But alas, poor sergeant Evans is no longer an issue and I have ordered all the police to stay away from this area. I sent them a signal which indicated this was a false location and that you both were not here. So at least for the time being it looks like it's just you, me, Sarah, and those few remaining moaning dead whores back there in the pit. So now you're probably wondering just how I'm going to get away with all of this and still maintain my cover as devoted Yuengsville Chief of Police. Right? Well it's all been planned for and it's really quite simple."

Jackson was now barely hearing Brent Holden's ramblings. He was looking over at Sergeant Evans. The man had now stopped twitching. Not a good sign. Jackson didn't want to die, but if he had to choose how he was going to die, he would much rather be shot than eaten alive. He thought back to when Evans and his men had rescued him from the motorcycle gang. Evans had chewed out his men for shooting one of the criminals in the neck. He had told them to always go for the head shot so they didn't have a chance to come back. But Brent had screwed up big time when he had shot Evans in the neck, and he apparently didn't even realize it. That meant the sergeant was slowly bleeding to death and when he eventually did die, he would most definitely come back.

"So here's how the final story is going to play out." Brent explained, "When I return with your's and Evan's bodies to Yuengsville, I'll tell the mayor that Evans and I got here too late to save you and sweet Sarah. I'll explain how Deimos had already shot you, which I'll do momentarily with his gun just as I did to Sergeant Evans. I'll say that Sarah was nowhere to be found; Deimos must have moved her to a different location. I'll tell him how Sergeant Evans had so gallantly taken down the giant mutant with one shot to the head, but unfortunately Deimos, using his almost superhuman speed, shot Evans and killed him. The ballistics report for both your body and his, as well as the gunshot residue tests will confirm this. Then I'll go all humble and say I must have gotten off a lucky shot and blew Deimos' gun hand off at the wrist and then clipped him in the shoulder. Then at this point in my sad tale I may have to break down and generate some realistic tears and explain that I was so upset about Deimos killing my good friend David Evans that I lost control and shot him in the head. And that was very unfortunate because sadly, now we'll have no way to find out what ever happened to poor Sarah."

"Sarah?" Jackson asked, "What... will"

Brent said, "Oh yes... the poor, missing Sarah Stanton. Well she'll never be found. You see, Sarah has far too much potential street value to my operation to simply be discarded. I mean if at some point in the future I need to kill her, I certainly will, but I'm sure once I get her hooked on the right combination of drugs, she'll make a great little money maker for me. If the heat from the mayor stays on, I may have to sell her to one of my new off-shore clients. Otherwise she may just follow the same route which Deimos had likely planned for her. All the girls do. That is, until they are of no more use to me then... well, I'm you know what happens then. I can't imagine that arrogant fool Deimos didn't bore you to death with all the details about his, I mean my operation."

"By the way, you may not realize this, but I was monitoring the conversation you had with your friend Sean Patel the other morning at the morgue. I found it very interesting when he told me how he had managed to stumble upon those dead kills with the ligature marks on their necks. That was quite astute of him. Didn't you find it in the least bit odd when he mentioned that I paid little attention to his theories? I thought for sure that would have made that reporter's mind of yours suspicious. I assume now you realize those dead kills were all former girls of mine."

"Well, unfortunately for the soon to be late Mr. Patel, he inadvertently discovered the final results of the exact same story you were just starting to investigate. I suspect you had already determined there might be some connection between the two cases. Most ill-fated for both you and your friend, I'm afraid. Anyway, once I am finished here, I'll be returning home with the bad news for Mayor McKinney as well as the widows Evans and Ridge. And shortly thereafter, your friend Sean will be meeting with a disastrous and sadly fatal laboratory accident, which should tie up all of the loose ends once and for all. I still probably have to go through the motions of looking for Sarah off and on for the next year or so, but eventually that will die down as well."

"And who knows. Maybe a few years in the future as my operation continues to grow and flourish, I might just be able to find a special place in my enterprise for that sweet little girl of yours. What's her name again? Kyla?" Brent chided.

"You bastard!" Jackson screamed with all the strength he had remaining. "Don't you... even... ever... think..." But his voice weakly trailed off.

Brent looked at him with feigned pity and said, "Yes. Well... whatever. So, what say we get on with this and put you out of my misery?"

Brent turned to approach the fallen body of Deimos to retrieve his gun and severed hand for one final time. Then, as Brent leaned down to pick up the gun, Jackson turned to his right in response to a menacing shuffling sound he heard and saw something which paralyzed him with terror. The dead remains of David Evans was on its feet, no longer the brave and courageous policeman but now just one more undead creature craving the same thing they all craved, and that was the taste of human flesh.

CHAPTER 43

Jackson remained perfectly still, not even daring to breathe as the wretched, undead thing, which only moments earlier had been Sergeant David Evans, began to slowly trudge down the dirty aisle toward him. A light cloud of dust rose behind his left foot, which he was dragging slightly. Jackson knew the man's leg hadn't been injured, so perhaps it was a coordination problem relating to the reanimation process.

The only remaining hope Jackson could seem to come up with was that since he was clinging to life at the very ridge of death, the end might come quickly for him with as little pain as possible. He had seen what these horrible creatures did to the living, and in his bound and defenseless state there was little else he could do but wait for his gruesome end to come. He closed his eyes and gritted his teeth anticipating the walking remains of Sergeant Evans to begin tearing his stomach apart any second. Perhaps it would rip out his throat or bite his face off piece-by-piece instead. In the next few seconds Jackson imagined a thousand painful ways the beast might dismember and disembowel him. As the creature approached Jackson, whose eyes were still clamped tightly shut, he could hear its low, guttural groan just inches from his face. He made up his mind he would not open his eyes. Whatever happened to him would happen, but that didn't mean he had to see it coming.

The creature looked over at Jackson with filmed-over dead eyes, sniffing him as if savoring the meal he was about to eat. It looked down at the dried vomit on Jackson's chest and momentarily stepped back just for a second as if unsure if he wanted to eat the creature in front of him or not. At that same moment, Brent Holden was mumbling and swearing while picking up the gun still held in the severed hand of Deimos. The creature heard Brent's curses and turned in that direction, apparently deciding to choose him over the foul smelling Jackson Ridge. Later, Jackson would wonder if some part of the Evans creature might have remembered what Brent had done to him or if perhaps he had simply heard a voice that somewhere in the back of its reanimated brain sparked a memory of someone familiar.

Whatever the reason, after a few seconds, which seemed like an eternity to the terrified Jackson, he realized his insides were not being torn from his body. Reluctantly, he slowly opened his eyes just a slit to see why it might be he was still alive. He saw the back of Sergeant Evans' head pass him by, his spastic body trudging straight for the unsuspecting Brent Holden, who was still bent over, struggling with Deimos' hand and gun. Jackson had no idea why the creature had passed him by but was thankful for whatever miracle was responsible. He heard Sarah was sobbing at the back of her cage, but now she was trying to press herself even further against the back wire wall, putting as much distance between herself and the horror which was approaching down the aisle. She started moaning and keening with terror.

Brent Holden looked up from his work and into her cage. Recognizing her fear said, "There, there now Sarah. It won't be that bad. We're almost finished here. As soon as I put a bullet in Jackson's skull, we'll be on our way. I promise you'll have a nice long and rewarding career as one of my favorite special girls very soon. Don't you worry about a thi..."

But before he could finish his sentence, Brent's voice was cut off as an excruciating pain shot through his neck and shoulder. The undead David Evans had taken a huge bite out of the right side of his neck. It pulled backward savagely, ripping flesh, muscle, veins, and tendons as Brent screamed in agony. The creature dropped the chunk of Brent's flesh onto the dirt floor and immediately returned to sink its teeth even deeper into the man's blood pumping throat. Gore shot from Brent's severed artery as the Evans thing bored deeper into the tender meat of his gullet. Sarah was once again screaming at the top of her lungs.

Reacting, rather than thinking in a last desperate act of survival, Brent raised Deimos' gun, placed the pistol behind his own head, and pulled the trigger. The shot severed the right ear of the zombie and continued on until it sunk itself into the wooden post not more than a few inches above Jackson's head. The creature continued to rip into Brent's flesh until the man finally managed to get off one final lucky shot, which entered the creatures head just below the front of its ear and blew out the top of its skull, showering the area, Sarah included, with brain matter and gore.

With a sickening sounding thud the Evans thing collapsed to the blood soaked dirt floor and Brent Holden turned slowly to face the bound and crucified body of Jackson Ridge. The entire right side of the man's neck was missing, exposing the pinkish bloody meat of his torn throat and the now visible white bone of his lower jaw. The man couldn't stand but nonetheless began to drag himself closer to Jackson. Brent attempted to say something, but all that came from his bloody lips was a bubbling pink and red froth of foam and a weak wheeze which was unlike anything Jackson had ever heard in his life. The dying Brent Holden weakly lifted Deimos' gun one last time to finish off Jackson. His finger tried to tighten on the trigger, and Jackson closed his eyes once more, waiting for the sound of the gunshot, which came a second later.

But once again, Jackson realized he was somehow miraculously still alive. He opened his eyes and looked down to see the prone body of Brent Holden, face down in the mud, the last of his blood pooling not far from Jackson's feet. The only thing Jackson could imagine had happened was Holden's shot must have gone wild and he had collapsed before he was able to get off another shot. Although weak beyond his ability to comprehend, Jackson suddenly found his mind clearing somewhat as adrenalin shot through his system.

"Sarah? Are... you ok?" Jackson asked to the weeping girl huddled in the corner of her cage.

She didn't respond. It seemed as if she could only sit with her knees up in front of her face and her bound hands and arms wrapped around her legs. "Sarah... we... we have to find... some way to... get you out... of here." That was when he noticed a slight movement on the dirt floor below him. Sarah's keening began to increase as the shredded remains of Brent Holden began to slowly move. Then using its hands on the side rails of the stalls, the wretched thing stood up and looked directly at Jackson. Brent's eyes no longer carried the look of hatred they bore for him in life, but now they seemed to convey something much worse. Now there was a look of hunger in those dead, filmy orbs.

For only being dead a few minutes this creature was every bit as hideous as any Jackson had seen which had been rotting for weeks or months. Its head hung at an odd angle to the left as none of its neck muscles existed to support it. Jackson wished David Evans had bitten just a bit further and maybe he would have severed the spinal column and essentially decapitated Brent Holden. If so he would have remained dead. But now apparently some of the nerves in its spine still existed and remained intact enough to allow for reanimation. As a result, the creature was still able to stand, move and as such still was driven by the same insatiable desire to feed they all had, and Jackson was the only easily accessible food source in the barn.

Sarah's keening sound had risen to a full-fledged scream of horror at seeing the incredibly hideous beast now standing and mobile outside her cage. Hearing her cry, the creature momentarily forgot about Jackson and clumsily turned toward the gate of her prison. It grabbed the wire fencing and began shaking it, howling angrily as Sarah screamed even more uncontrollably. Although it could not get to her she was not more than ten feet from its hungry grasp and that alone was enough to push the terrified girl over the edge.

Jackson's anger grew; not only his anger toward the dead Brent Holden but his anger toward all that had happened. He was helpless, crucified, dying. Sarah was a prisoner screaming with futility as a living dead, nearly headless creature was shaking the entrance to her cage trying to get to her. In the distance, Jackson could hear the pit full of walking corpses raise their groans and howls to join those of the Holden creature. The frustration and helplessness became more than Jackson could bear.

With one final burst of energy he couldn't spare and didn't even know he had, Jackson shouted, "Over here... you stinkin' maggot motel... You want something to eat? Well eat me you undead douchebag." No sooner had the words left his mouth than Jackson realized how stupid he had been. To someone looking on, the act might have seemed heroic, but now in the face of what was to come, Jackson simply felt ridiculous. The creature turned slowly and began once again dragging itself back toward him. Jackson had accomplished nothing with his outburst, because surely as soon as the creature was finished with him, it would simply return to the cage and continue to try to get to Sarah until she eventually either starved to death or died of thirst. Once she came back as one of them, the Holden thing would just walk away, and Sarah would stay locked up until bugs and scavengers eventually consumed her living dead remains. Jackson was filled with sorrow at what a mess he had made of things.

And with his latest outburst, all he had managed to do was prolong the inevitable. Their future was certain now. Jackson saw the creature approach him with its strangely cocked head and exposed neck and vertebrae. He wondered what it would take first; his nose, his lips, or his eyes. Or would it simply sink its fingers deep into the tender, exposed flesh of his stomach and rip him open like an eager child opening a present on Christmas morning. Then would it pull out his hot, steaming innards like Jackson's mother used to do with their Thanksgiving turkey.

Brent Holden's now snapping jaws got closer to Jackson; just inches from his face. He had his answer; the creature was going to take his face first. It raised both of its hands, one grabbing the left side of Jackson's face, the other grabbing the right. Its mouth opened wide, ready for the bite. Jackson could smell Brent's foul breath, already starting to putrefy with the stench of death. Just when Jackson was certain his nose was about to be devoured, he heard a loud bang and the Holden creature released its grip, falling to the floor in a heap.

Tears, a combination of frustration, weakness, terror, relief, uncertainty, and a thousand other emotions seemed to pour from Jackson's eyes. Then as if beyond his ability to control, he started to feel the world around him go black. He was going to pass out he could feel it; maybe never to wake again. The last thing Jackson believed he saw before the world around him went dark was the image of his friend Sean Patel walking down the aisle way toward him.

CHAPTER 44

It was all so strange, so surrealistic, and so bizarrely irregular. Jackson was standing in the darkness, silently staring at his own partially visible likeness looking back at him from deep inside the reflective surface. This mirror-like façade was reflective yet not quite exactly a mirror; not seeming to have exactly the same property of glass. This was something he had never seen before, and the harder he stared at it he was not even sure its existence was even possible. It appeared to be almost mercurial or liquid in its composition, yet it was still part of a wall existing in an impossibly vertical state. All around the reflective surface was blackness, and there was no comprehendible outside edge to the mirror; it simply seemed to feather outward until it became one with the blackness.

Jackson sensed he was standing in a room of complete and utter darkness, he looked down, and although he could feel his feet and knew they were present, hidden somewhere in the gloom below, he couldn't see them. A black fog swirled all around him, obscuring the lower half of his body. Jackson couldn't comprehend how all around him was a world of pitch blackness yet this small area of pulsating liquid mirror was not only visible to him but it seemed to cast a radiant, silvery light out toward him so he could see at least part of his body.

Looking at as much of himself as was visible, Jackson could see he was shirtless and quite possible naked. His chest appeared to be uninjured, but he did feel a cold chill passing through him, and at that moment he would have given anything to be dressed and warm once again. Jackson felt as if it had been a very long time since he had been warm. He also noticed a smell. It was something strange, something medicinal and antiseptic. He couldn't comprehend why such an odd place would have such an odor. And he could hear something in the distance; a humming and whirring sound as well as a steady beeping and perhaps a thumping, beating sound as well.

For some reason he didn't fully understand, Jackson found himself lifting his two hands upward in front of him palms facing him, feeling the need to examine them. They seemed to be fine although he did sense a dull pain radiating out from the centers of his hands. He tried to close his fingers into a partial fist and the pain seemed to intensify. Jackson felt he should know why he was having such a pain, but for the life of him, he couldn't recall.

"For the life of me." He thought absently. He felt as if that statement might actually mean more than he realized and was not just a figure of speech. Then he opted to leave his hands open. There was no point in causing himself any undue discomfort. Again, for reasons he didn't understand, Jackson turned his hands with his palms now facing his reflection in the undulating vertical silver surface. At first he just saw his own apparently naked reflection looking back with his palms raised, but then the likeness slowly began to change. Jackson felt an odd sensation of uneasiness forming in the pit of his stomach, as if he was in some way aware the chain of events he was currently experiencing was about to take a very bad and horribly frightening turn.

In the mirrored surface, a tiny, round hole no bigger than the head of a pin suddenly appeared at the center of each of his palms. Jackson stared at the black reflected dots for a moment, unsure of what their purpose might be. Then slowly the two holes began to increase in size to about a half inch in diameter as they simultaneously turned from black to red. Still Jackson couldn't understand what he was seeing or what it all might mean, while at the same time he felt he somehow should know.

Next, from inside the ruby holes a thick, transparent, crimson colored gelatinous substance began to overflow, pulsating and dribbling out of the orifices, crawling almost snake-like down the reflection's wrists toward its elbows. Although completely repulsed by the revolting vision, Jackson was also far too transfixed by the utter wonder of the sight, and as such he was unable divert his eyes from the obvious horror unfolding before him.

Then the upraised hands in the reflection seemed to age and wrinkle as their fingernails rapidly grew, springing forth and hooking down around the fronts of the fingers, turning disgusting shades of yellow, brown, and even black. The flesh on the hands continued to shrink and wither changing from pink to tan and finally to a translucent brown then grey color while revealing vivid outlines of the shapes of the bones beneath. As Jackson looked up at the face, which was supposed to be his face, he saw instead a zombified version of himself staring dead-eyed out from the mercurial reflecting wall.

The hair on the head of the image was disheveled and appeared to have gone mostly grey. It had fallen off of the creature's skull in clumps, revealing large patches of liver-spotted, withered flesh mapped with large, blue throbbing veins. The skin of its face seemed to cling to its skull. Clouded, soulless eyes bulged out of black-rimmed, flesh-bagged sockets, and his mouth hung slack jawed below a thinned, hooked boney nose. Inside the open mouth was a hideous graveyard of tombstone-like broken, missing, and rotten teeth.

A thin stream of crimson drool leaked over top of its withered, shrunken black lips and slowly trickled down along the thing's chest. Large areas of flesh were missing from its torso as if they had either been torn off or had simply rotted away. Jackson could see exposed yellowed ribs jutting haphazardly out of the open areas. Small strips of flesh and muscle hung from the broken, pointed bones.

Jackson looked again at the thing's hands with their oozing wounds and noticed with revulsion how just below the translucent surface of the red flowing gel crawled some sort of worm-like creatures skittering about. It was as if the filthy creatures lived within the sickening gelatin and were using the viscous fluid to transport themselves from inside the Jackson-thing's decaying body for whatever reason. Jackson's thoughts were confirmed when he looked down at the end of the crimson stream and saw several small maggot-like creatures, which seemed to fall from the mirrored surface into the black fog on his side of the mysterious reflection.

Jackson began to suddenly realize this all had to be some sort of horrible nightmare. He had to be dreaming, because something so bizarre, so ungodly, and so horrendous couldn't possibly exist in reality. But at the same instant he also knew that train of thought was no longer true. Things as hideous as the creature in the mirror and perhaps even more repugnant did exist in his world and had existed for the past ten years. Ten years ago, this might all be impossible, but no longer. Although he could still not understand what this illusion might mean, he instinctively sensed that perhaps in the waking world, he might have just been through something as bad as what he was now seeing or perhaps worse, because it would have been real. However, he couldn't recall what might make him feel that way.

Then the image in the reflective wall opened its mouth wider and began to howl like a banshee. Its sound started out as a low guttural moan, but with each passing second it increased in volume and intensity until it reached an ear-piercing screech. As it bellowed, the creature raised one of its now visible boney arms and pointed its long clawed boney finger at him. Fearing not only for his life but for his immortal soul, Jackson wanted to turn and run from the horrible approaching living-dead abomination, but his feet felt like lead weights holding him captive and at the mercy of the hungry flesh-eating thing. He closed his eyes, not knowing what else he could do, praying with all of his heart that he could awaken from this horrifying fantasy. It was then he felt a cold, hard fingernail scraping down the side of his face.

CHAPTER 45

Jackson's eyes slowly fluttered partially open as he let out a loud sharp breath. He realized to his surprise he had been on the verge of screaming, but somehow he had managed to suppress the cry. Nonetheless, he was disoriented and confused, in that place between slumber and waking. He could determine he was in some sort of dimly lit room. The horrifying dream he had just experienced was already fading from his memory, but in its wake the event had left Jackson with a feeling of extreme uneasiness; one that he couldn't seem to shake. It must have been a bad one, because he recognized this strange feeling, which he had experienced after nightmares previously.

The first thing Jackson noticed as his mind slowly began to return to consciousness was the strong scent of flowers permeating the air. Then he realized he felt as if he were lying down on his back. Jackson became momentarily horrified as his creative mind took the floral smells and combined them with his reclined position and produced a mental image of his lying in a coffin awaiting his own funeral. For some reason which he couldn't bring to mind, this image felt like one which could actually have been a reality. His eyes flew all the way open with horror.

Fortunately, as his vision came into focus, Jackson realized he was not lying dead in a coffin but was actually in some sort of bed. Yes, it appeared to be a hospital bed, and Jackson was not lying flat on his back but was propped at a slight angle. He slowly turned his head glancing to his left and saw a tall, chrome tubular pole with an intravenous drip bag connected to a transparent tube feeding some clear liquid into a syringe connected to a port installed in his left arm. Several other tubes led into the main tube. He was apparently being fed medicine, likely pain killers as well as essential nutrients. Why this might be necessary he still couldn't remember.

Looking down along his arm, Jackson saw his left hand was bandaged around the palm area but his fingers were still exposed. He could see his hands had been injured somehow but had no memory of how it might have happened. He tried to wiggle his fingers and found he could do so slightly but with great difficulty, and doing so caused a dull ache to radiate out from the center of his palm.

He looked down at his right hand and saw a similar situation, but movement of his right arm was not confined by any I-V tubes, although when he tried to lift his right arm he found he didn't have the strength. Strange how something as simple as lifting his arm could prove so difficult. He looked down at his chest area and saw he was dressed in a hospital gown. There was no mistaking it by its bright yellow color and tiny red and blue floral pattern. Where did hospitals buy these things anyway? There were a series of wires leading out from underneath the gown to some sort of monitoring device, which he assumed was tracking all of his vital signs. So unless he was having another dream or otherwise hallucinating, he was obviously a patient in a hospital somewhere. He knew there was more he had to think about, but his clouded mind still was unable to focus very well.

He saw a white, gripper shaped object with a red button on top and a wire coming out of the bottom resting down near his right hand and realized it must be the nurse call button. Jackson decided he would try to press the button, if he were able to effectively use his fingers, and then he might be able to find out where he was and what in the world was going on. He carefully managed to inch his right arm over and guide his hand around the device. But when he attempted to press button he found he was unable to summon the dexterity necessary to do so. Also, when he tried to move his fingers, the dull pain returned, shooting through his hands into his fingers. As bad as the ache felt, Jackson realized why it was not more severe. The pain medicine he was being fed through the I-V tube must be some really top shelf stuff, although it did seem to be clouding his mind.

Then a memory suddenly flashed into his mind in vivid detail like a scene from a movie, and Jackson recalled what had happened to him in Deimos' makeshift chamber of horrors. He now remembered every horrifying moment of his awakening and finding himself nailed to the cross beam. His hands began to tremble at the painful memory and he began to worry if he would ever regain full use of his hands again. How could he ever hope to recover completely from such a physically traumatic ordeal? Then, like dominos falling down one after another, all of the horrible events which Jackson had experienced in the previous few days came flooding back to him like a tidal wave of terror. He recalled every moment of every painfully frightening ordeal he had gone through; the biker gang, Trader Bob, Smith, Deimos, and finally Brent Holden.

Then at last, Jackson remembered something else; something he had at first thought was part of some distant dream but now he knew was actually the very last image he could recall seeing just seconds before he had blacked out. Jackson was certain it had been Double I, his friend, Sean who had finally come to save him in the end. But how could that have been possible? Once again he began to doubt himself. Had it really been Sean, or had it simply been his imagination? Jackson knew he had come frighteningly close to dying in that barn, and it was possible and maybe even probable he had been hallucinating then as well. But the image had seemed so real and so clear even now that he believed he hadn't imagined his friend's presence. Somehow Sean had tracked him, followed him, and eventually saved his life.

Jackson suddenly realized his breathing had become shallow and quick; more like panting then breathing. He knew he had to regain control, had to calm down or he might start hyperventilating. So he decided to take a few deep, cleansing breaths and to try to distract himself by studying his surroundings. From his inclined position, Jackson had a fairly good view of his small, private hospital room. He could see the shadowed shape of a large window off to his left with a thick, room darkening shade pulled down. At the base of the window he could see a slight bit of daylight peeking through a small opening below the heavy tan shade. The window had a deep sill that jutted outward and appeared to be practically covered with baskets of floral arrangements all hidden in shadows. Now Jackson at least knew where the floral smells had been coming from; one less thing to be concerned about.

He looked past the foot of his bed and saw several guest chairs, all currently empty. Off to his far right was a large white door which hung partially open, allowing a small amount of light to enter. He could also hear the sounds of busy hospital workers outside in the hallway as the noises filtered into his otherwise silent room. Across the back of one of the guest chairs he saw a welcome and familiar sight; it was Andrea's coat. On the other he saw several of Kyla's favorite books as well as her book bag.

Jackson was overwhelmed by how just the sight of his wife's and daughter's possessions had suddenly made everything in his world feel all right. No matter what had actually happened to him, no matter what had almost happened, and no matter how bad things had been, everything would be better now. He breathed a sigh of relief, realizing his wife and daughter were somewhere in this hospital. Most likely they had just left for a moment and would be returning shortly. He was alive and back with his family. Jackson believed there could not possibly be anything in the world better than that.

Then as the series of pleasant thoughts passed through his mind, the door to his room was pushed slightly open and Jackson saw the most wonderful sight he thought he would ever see in his entire life. Andrea was trying to sneak carefully into the room, remaining as quiet as possible, not wanting to disturb his rest. She was holding Kyla's tiny hand and gently whispering something into her ear, most likely reminding her to be quiet, but once his little girl saw him, nothing on earth could have kept her quiet.

"Daddy!" Kyla suddenly shouted at the top of her lungs. Andrea was about to scold her for her outburst when she looked over and saw her husband awake and looking back at her, wearing a look she knew was that of pure joy.

CHAPTER 46

"Jackson, oh my sweet Lord in heaven! Jackson! You're awake." Andrea shouted as she ran across the room following Kyla to Jackson's bedside. She threw her arms around his neck, fearing she might hurt him in her exhilaration. "Oh thank God! Thank God!" Andrea repeated as tears streamed down her cheeks.

"Daddy's awake! Daddy's awake!" Kyla shouted.

Jackson was unable to utter a word, finding his own voice catching in his throat. Tears poured from his eyes. He wanted to hug his wife and daughter more than anything else he could possibly imagine but was still unable to lift his arms. So instead he simply enjoyed the sheer pleasure of their embrace and finally said with a raspy, cracking voice, "God! I love you both so much... I thought... I would never... see either of you again."

"We thought we'd lost you too." Andrea said tearfully.

Kyla said, "I missed you Daddy."

"I... I missed you too, pumpkin." Jackson assured his daughter, bending down and kissing the top of her head.

When Andrea and Kyla finally broke their embrace and stood back alongside the bed, he said "It's just so... amazing to be... well to be alive and with you both again." Then he asked. "How... how long was I... was I out?"

Andrea took a deep breath, trying to regain her composure and said through tear-filled eyes, "Well... you gave us quite a scare... you were out for a couple days..." She thought about it for a second. "Two and a half actually... it was... really... touch and go there... for a while..." She stopped speaking and her shoulders started shaking as she sobbed uncontrollably.

"It's ok Mommy," Kyla said. "Daddy's ok now Mommy."

Jackson looked down at his wounded hands for a few moments, then when he heard Andrea's sobs stopping, he looked back at her and could see she had managed to calm down a bit. She said apologetically, "I'm sorry... it's just..."

"Yeah I know," Jackson said, smiling at his wife. "I know exactly what you mean... me too." Then after a moment of hesitation, he said. "So... I assume this is a hospital." He was hoping his reference to the obvious might allow Andrea to switch from worried wife mode to professional nurse mode. His assumption was a good one.

Andrea explained, "Yes. It's a hospital in Reading. They brought you here when they... when they found you. The doctors gave you all sorts of medicines, several pints of blood, and pain stuff for... well for your hands." She hesitated again for a moment trying not to cry then said, "A couple time while you were out, the doctors thought you were going to wake up... and you came close, but then you would just faded back out again... they told me it would just be a matter of time... but... I didn't know for sure... It was really terrifying."

Jackson looked down at his bandaged hands again and shook his head with frustration. His hands were how he made his living. He wondered if he would ever be able to type another story again. As if reading his thoughts, as only a wife can do, Andrea quickly said, "The doctor told me there was no major nerve damage done to your hands. He said in a week or two you'll be able to start physical therapy and soon they'll be as good as new. In fact, he said it's a good thing you're a writer because eventually, using a keyboard will probably be a great form of hand and finger exercise as well."

Andrea hesitated for a moment, then said, "When I heard... what had happened... what they had done... you know... to you... the nails... oh my God I couldn't believe it." She almost broke down again but somehow managed to hold on. "Do you remember? I mean... do you know... what they... I mean what happened to you?"

Jackson looked like he was deciding what to say, as if unsure how much he wanted to recount to his obviously upset wife. He said reluctantly, "Yeah... I know... I remember... well... pretty much everything. It was a... well... it was a really close call... not at all what I had anticipated... or else I wouldn't have... you know.

"You wouldn't have taken the assignment?" Andrea asked.

"Yeah." Jackson replied, "Maybe I wouldn't have."

Andrea looked at her husband for a moment then said, "No... I don't think that's true Honey. I think once you found out that Sarah had been taken, nothing could have stopped you from trying to help her."

Then Jackson looked at Andrea with a sudden awareness asked with obvious concern, "Sarah! Oh my God. I can't believe I forgot all about poor Sarah. How could I be so insensitive? Is she... is Sarah all right? Did someone find her and get her out of there too? I forgot... maybe it's the meds they're giving me... God, I feel like such an idiot."

"It's ok Jackson," Andrea said consoling him, "Don't worry... Sarah's fine. Physically there is nothing wrong with her... but emotionally... well let's just say she was a bit traumatized by everything she's been through, but from what I've heard there were no indications of any long-term psychological damage. I think once she if back home with her family, things will quickly get back to normal for her. In fact you'll be happy to know Sarah's still here, in a room not far from here. I believe I heard she may be going home today. She's been asking about you as well. She wants to see you when you're feeling good enough for visitors. It seems as far as she's concerned, you're her hero."

Jackson looked confused, "What? Hero? Me? No... I don't think so. Sarah must really be confused... Some hero I am... I'm pretty sure heroes are supposed to do the rescuing... and not supposed to be the ones who need to be rescued. All I did was screw things up royally."

"But Jackson, you are a hero. You found her. You did it. You were the one who found her when no one else could," Andrea said.

Jackson explained, "But it was all a setup.... I was set up, Honey... he... Brent Holden used me... like a fool... you know... to find Sarah and locate Deimos... but not to help her... he had his own reasons... bad ones... very bad ones... oh man... I was such an idiot... I am such an idiot."

Andrea looked at him with the knowing eyes of a wife and said, "Maybe so Honey. But you're my idiot, and you'll always still be my hero."

They looked at each other for a moment, and then both burst out laughing. The humor seemed to melt away several days' worth of stress in one joyous moment. During the course of the next hour or so, Jackson recounted for Andrea all that had happened during his time on assignment. She informed him he was currently in one of the best hospitals in the city of Reading and now that he was awake, it probably wouldn't be very long before they were able to head back home.

Jackson asked, "Now wait a minute. We can't afford the best! We can barely afford the worst. Who's going to pay for all of this? It has to cost... oh my God! It has to cost a fortune for me to be in here. I know your insurance is pretty good... but it can't possibly be good enough to pay for something like this place... can it?"

"Relax, Jackson." Andrea explained, "It's all been taken care of."

"It has?" Jackson asked, "But how? What do you mean?"

Andrea then told Jackson of how she had traveled to Yuengsville the day after he failed to call back, and how she had met with the mayor. Jackson had to suppress a laugh, knowing how when Andrea was on a mission she was a force to be reckoned with. He was quite certain even the mayor of a small city would be no match for a troubled Andrea. She explained how the mayor had been extremely grateful for everything Jackson's had been doing to find Sarah. Then once everything was over and Sarah was safe, Frank McKinney had volunteered to pay any of the medical expenses that might not be covered by Andrea's health insurance, including his upcoming physical therapy. She told him the Mayor was also paying for the hotel room where she and Kyla were staying.

"Wow! That's amazing!" Jackson exclaimed. "But... but... oh man... I just realized... I'm going to probably be out of work for a long time... I mean... I know I don't earn all that much... but it's something... and it's still better than not having any extra income... you can't be expected to carry the load yourself, Babe... I really messed up bad this time."

Andrea just smiled then explained that the Schuylkill Daily News was going to pay his weekly wages for as long as it took for him to be back to normal.

"The Skook? Bill McCleary? Paying?" Jackson said shocked. "You've gotta be kidding me. I'm not even their regular employee. I'm just a temp. And besides, Big Bill is normally so tight he squeaks. Why in the world would he be willing to pay me for nothing? Are you sure about that?"

Andrea said, "Well yes; strange as that may sound. I also met with Bill just yesterday and worked out all the arrangements." Jackson once again imagined just how persuasive his wife probably had been. He guessed she had Big Bill wrapped around her little finger. Andrea continued, "You see... well... you've actually been their feature story for the past several days. I've saved copies of all the newspapers. I'll read the articles to you later. They've been selling more papers than they have in years Jackson, both physical papers and digital copies as well. So has the Reading newspaper. And it's all because of you."

"Me? Jackson asked. "But I was supposed to be the guy who wrote this story. And now my story's been handed over to someone else?"

"Yeah." Andrea explained, "And there's a real good reason for that, besides the fact that you've been unconscious for several days." Jackson noticed a slight scolding tone to her voice, something which might not be noticeable to everyone but something a husband wouldn't miss. She said, "You may have originally been promised the story, but that was before you became the story. Once everything broke and you ended up in here, the papers had no choice but to have someone else write the story. You're the biggest news event to hit Berks and Schuylkill County in many years. In fact, the story has made it to the wire service and gone national and international. You're a celebrity."

"Me? A celebrity? But for what?" Jackson said again, confused. "I'm no celebrity. All I managed to do... is to nearly get myself killed... several times. I didn't save anyone, I didn't help anyone and ended up having to be rescued by... well... who did rescue me anyway? I think I can remember something right before I blacked out... I could have sworn I saw Sean walking into that barn with someone else behind him. But I'm not really sure. Was I dreaming that or what?"

"I think you must have been hallucinating." Andrea said. "I pretty sure Sean was still back in Yuengsville when you were rescued."

Jackson asked, "But who... I mean... how... I mean... what happened? If it wasn't Sean... then who saved me."

Andrea replied, "To be honest Honey, no one seems to know. The police were monitoring your CU and heard everything that was going on, including both Deimos' confession as well as Brent Holden's. I'm told they sent in a rescue squad, but by the time they arrived, you were freed and lying on the ground. They found that someone had bandaged your hands and had cleaned out the wounds and treated them as well."

"But what about Sarah? Didn't she see anything? She must know who came to help us."

"The rescue squad said they found Sarah huddled in the corner of her cage. The door had been opened, but she hadn't come out. She was apparently in shock. The police have been questioning her about what she remembers, but she's blocked out most of what had happened. She remembers talking to you and she can recall Deimos pointing his gun at you, but after that, everything else is a blank."

Jackson's eyes opened wide and he said "Smith. What about that guy Smith; the guy who drugged me? He was the one who arranged everything. Did he get away?"

Andrea replied, "No he didn't. He came close, but no. We later learned his real name was Billy Jones."

"Smith's real name was Jones?" Jackson said, recalling how the man had chuckled when Jackson told him his own name was Jones. He must have found it humorous to use Smith as an alias, especially knowing he was actually dealing with Jackson Ridge and knowing what fate awaited him.

"Yep." Andrea said, "The police caught him in your hotel room going through your things. He was trying to steal all the cash you had been given for the assignment. He got into a gun battle with the Reading Police and was killed. And after getting a call from the officers who had listened to the recording of your abduction, they raided the "River Rat," arrested the bartender, and closed the place down."

Jackson said, "Wow. That's amazing. But you know it's still so weird about Sean. I would have sworn on a stack of bibles I had seen Sean. And there was someone else too. Someone I didn't know or even see very well, but something about his body language seemed familiar."

"Well as nice as that would have been, you can safely assume it wasn't Sean. In fact, he can tell you himself when he stops by to see you."

"Sean's in town?" Jackson asked.

Andrea said, "As soon as I called him and told him you were found, he headed straight down here. He's staying in the city at the same hotel as us and has stopped in almost every day to check on you. He apparently took some vacation time. In fact, I'll give him a call shortly to let him know you're officially among the living, and I'm sure he'll be here before you know it."

Jackson shook his head, "This is all so weird. I just wish I would have had a chance to tell the story, the whole story. There's so much more I'm sure I could add."

"Well... you most definitely will be getting that opportunity very soon." Andrea said. "You'll have to brief the police, as I'm sure you know. But what you don't know is you'll also have the opportunity to have your side of the story; the complete story published."

"What do you mean?" Jackson said.

Andrea replied, "You were right about Bill McCleary being stingy. But I worked on him and got him to see things my way. So in exchange for the Skook paying your salary for the next several months, you'll be sitting down with one of their staff reporters several days and week and co-writing; dictating actually, detailed accounts of the entire story. You'll share a by-line with their guy, and you'll have final approval on the story's content. The only thing you won't be doing is physically typing the story. The plan is to get the story nailed down with all the required facts as quickly as possible while all the details are fresh in your mind and while the topic is still hot."

Jackson looked at Andrea with amazement, "That's a great plan. Did you think of that yourself?"

"Well... I had some help from Sean." She said. "But there's more."

"More?" Jackson asked.

Andrea smiled and said, "Yes. Much more. The initial stories will be concise and designed for daily newspaper and online publication. But I've been approached by a national publisher who wants to take advantage of your new found fame and have you work with one of his ghost writers on writing a book about everything. They agreed to provide you with an advance, and you can begin working with them on it as soon as it is convenient. The sooner the better."

"What?" Jackson asked. "This is all so weird."

"Maybe so. But I guessed that once you woke up we would have a tough road to recovery ahead of us, so I thought quickly and managed to negotiate several really good deals for you. I hope I did well. None of them will make us rich, but they will certainly help to keep us financially above water until you are back on your feet again."

Jackson looked at his beautiful wife with his mouth agape. "Andrea. I always knew you were a beautiful, kind, and extremely intelligent woman, but I had no idea you were a genius."

"Well." She said smiling back at him, "I guess you know now."

CHAPTER 47

As Andrea and Jackson were talking, the large white door to his hospital room slowly pushed open and Jackson could see the front end of a wheelchair making its way into his room. As the chair cleared the door he saw Sarah smiling at him with a look of gratitude he felt he most certainly didn't deserve. She was dressed in jeans and was wearing a sweatshirt covered by a light fall jacket.

There was an average looking man in his forties with a receding hairline pushing the wheelchair. He was accompanied by a woman of around the same age. The woman was carrying a bouquet of get well balloons and there was a large plastic bag hanging from the handle of the wheelchair, which Jackson assumed held gifts from well-wishers. He imagined a slew of stuffed Teddy Bears populating the bag. The couple was looking at Jackson with expressions of adoration similar to those Sarah was offering. Jackson assumed these two people were Sarah's parents. Jackson also noticed the family resemblance between the woman and Frank McKinney.

"Jackson! You're awake!" Sarah shouted as she leapt from the wheelchair, raced over to him and began hugging him tightly around his neck; possibly too tightly. Jackson couldn't help but smile at the young girl's enthusiasm. It made him happy to see she was apparently recovering well.

"Sarah! For Pete's sake. Be careful!" Mrs. Stanton said. "You don't want to break the poor man's neck after he saved your life, do you?"

"But... I... I... didn't." Jackson started to say. He was caught by off guard. He still felt he hadn't saved anyone, and the idea of being thought of as a hero was as foreign to him as any he might imagine.

Mr. Stanton came forward and touched Jackson lightly on the arm. Jackson could see tears rimming the man's eyes and suspected this man was generally a stoic sort of man not prone to showing such strong emotion, "Mr.

Ridge... I... we... Lizzy and I... are so grateful for what you did... to save our Sarah." His voice caught in his throat. He glanced down at Jackson's bandaged hands and said, "I'm... I'm so sorry about what you had to go through... your hands... and I look forward to the day when you are better so I can properly shake the hand of the man who brought our daughter back to us."

Jackson didn't know how to respond. Despite his discomfort, he understood that like it or not, to these people he was a hero. It was as if they needed to think of him that way. It seemed to give them some unspoken but much desired comfort. He simply said, "Please call me Jackson. And this is my wife Andrea and our daughter Kyla."

Elizabeth Stanton stepped forward and similarly touched Jackson's arm, "You can call me Lizzy and this character over here is my husband Jim. We've already met Andrea and sweet little Kyla many times in the past several days. We've tried to stop by to see you every day... but you were... well, you were still asleep. In fact, we were hoping you might be awake today but to be perfectly honest we really didn't have high expectations. We really want to get to meet you and speak with you before we left. And now I have to say I'm so very happy we had the opportunity to do so."

"I'm going home today Jackson. Isn't that great news?" Sarah said, beaming with joy. It was obvious to everyone that the young girl had developed a bit of a crush on her hero.

"Yes." Jackson replied. "That's excellent news for sure. I'm also glad I got to see you all before you went home."

"Me too." Sarah said, and then she began to cry with pent up emotions that might have been from happiness or the relief from knowing now that Jackson was going to be all right. Or maybe it was simply pent up stress from everything that had been building inside of her for the past few days. It might have been because for the first time, Sarah had the chance to release all of those feelings in the presence of the one man who could truly understand what she had gone through now. It was as if seeing Jackson awake and on the road to recovery meant the long ordeal was really finally over and the healing process could begin.

Jim Stanton explained, "I'm sure you understand it's been a rough week for all of us, probably the roughest week we've ever had in our lives. And that's saying a lot considering the condition of the world we live in. But I also suspect the next several months are going to be tough as well until we're all back to normal."

Jackson looked confidently at Sarah and said, "But we're strong and I'm sure we'll all make it through this just fine." He was not just referring to Sarah and himself but to everyone in the room because they would all be affected for a very long time over the events of the previous week. He turned to Andrea and said, "Honey, can you make sure Sarah has my CU number and all of my other contact information?"

Andrea reached into her purse and took out Jackson's wallet where he kept his business cards. She handed one to Sarah and one to each of her parents. Jackson said, "Sarah if you need anything at all, even if it's just somebody to talk to please call me anytime." Then he looked at her parents, "The same goes for you both. I want you to know you can count on me for whatever you need to help you all get over this." Then he realized something, "Oh yeah, it might be a while until I can answer any calls on my own but Andrea will help me with that."

Mrs. Stanton looked at Jackson with tears now streaming down her cheeks, "I can't believe this Jackson. Here you are just waking up from a coma, you can't even use your hands and the first thing you think about is what we might need. And you wonder why we consider you a hero? It's because you are a hero."

CHAPTER 48

Sean Patel watched from the hospital room doorway as Jackson lay in his bed with his back slightly elevated. Jackson's hands were bandaged and lying at his sides while a series of tubes and wires led from his body to a variety of machines and monitors. The curtains of the large window had been drawn back, letting light filter in from the outside. The day was overcast, cold, and rainy, but Jackson appeared to be staring contentedly into space, perhaps enjoying whatever minimal sunlight did manage to peak through the gloom or maybe he was just staring at nothing and thinking. Sean supposed after what Jackson had just been through he had a lot to think about.

It was all so strange. Sean and Jackson had been friends since childhood and were as comfortable with each other as any two friends could be, yet now Sean was feeling uneasy, as if the man in the hospital bed was someone he was about to meet for the first time. He wanted to say something clever, maybe even something funny; anything to break through this wall of uncertainty that seemed to separate him from his friend. Not having any idea what to say, Sean simply said, "Jackson?"

At first Jackson didn't respond, and Sean wondered if he had either not heard him or something else might be wrong. Then slowly Jackson turned and looked over in Sean's direction. Initially, Jackson's expression appeared distant, as if he were looking but not really seeing. Then after a few seconds, Jackson's expression was replaced with his normal wide, boyish grin. Sean felt the wall of uncertainty crumble to pieces as his friend returned from his world of deep contemplation.

"Sean... Jeezus Double I. Get over here." Jackson said as he uncomfortably tried to lift his right arm to welcome his friend. He was still too weak to even accomplish this simple act. Sean hurried over to Jackson and embraced him tightly.

Jackson said, "I've been waiting to see you... to talk to you.... to find out. It was you... wasn't it? You were the one who saved me... I'm sure it was you... don't try to deny it either Double I... I mean... that's a major thing man... how did you... I mean... what happened."

"No... sorry Jackson, but it wasn't me," Sean replied. "I wish I could say that was true, my friend. But sadly, you are mistaken. The fact is I was nowhere near Berks County when you were rescued. I was all the way back in my lab in Yuengsville."

Jackson looked at him disbelievingly and said, "But... but wait a minute... I was certain it was you... I know I saw you... and if I'm right and it was you... I can't figure out for the life of my why you wouldn't accept the credit you deserve."

Sean waited a beat, then said, "Look Jackson, there's simply no credit to accept. I had known you were missing. Andrea called and told me, but I had no way of knowing where you were or how I could even begin to find you. Even if I were the heroic type, which you know I'm not, I had no way to track you down."

"But I would have sworn I saw you coming into the barn, just before I went unconscious. I thought it was you and there was someone else was walking behind you." Jackson said. "I didn't see his face but I'm pretty sure he was wearing something dark. In fact I thought you both were wearing dark clothing."

"Well." Sean said jokingly. "As flattering as it might be that your potentially last thought on earth was all about me, I'm sorry to have to disappoint you. Andrea told me you had been through a lot and looking at your condition now, she was apparently right. So I suppose having a few hallucinations was something to be expected. From what I've been told, you came very close to winding up on a stainless steel table being examined by the Berks County equivalent of me."

Jackson shook his head and said, "It's so hard to believe all of this really happened to me. It's like a bad dream. You know? No, it's worse than a bad dream because here I am awake and yet I'm still living it." Then he looked down at his bandaged hands and said "But the condition of these hands tends to serve as a constant reminder that it all really did happen."

"What do the doctors say?" Sean said, trying to keep the conversation moving in a direction away from him, "How bad is... you know... the damage."

"It appears I got off pretty lucky." Jackson said looking at his hand again and then adding, "They said the nails didn't cause any permanent injury and there appeared to be no significant nerve damage either. I'm told whoever the mystery man was who rescued me; he did an excellent job of treating my wounds. The doctors said he must have had medical or paramedic training. So that, at least is a good thing. In a week or two I have to start physical therapy for however long that takes."

Sean said as if deep in thought and only half paying attention, "Good... That's... that's good to hear."

"So." Jackson said, "Now what?"

"What?" Sean said, coming back to reality.

"I said so what happens now, you know what are your plans. Are you heading back home now that I'm back to semi-normal?" Jackson asked.

Sean thought about this for a moment then said, "Well, yes, I suppose. I guess my vacation time is over. Now I suspect I'll head back up to Yuengsville and go back to doing my part to help keep the wheels of society turning. And I suppose you'll be heading back to Ashton with Andrea and Kyla and starting your therapy."

Jackson contemplated for a moment then said, "Yeah. I guess that's all we can do. It's kind of what we've been doing for the past ten years. We just keep putting one foot in front of the other and carrying on. It's so strange living the way we do now isn't it?"

"Yeah, I guess it is." Sean replied, "But it's all we have and all we can do. That and wait for things to get better I suppose."

As if sensing some uncertainty in his friend's voice, Jackson asked, "Things are getting better, aren't they Sean?" Jackson knew Sean was privy to information that he was unable to share with anyone, but he was still free to give his personal opinion.

For a moment Sean recalled the last reports he had read about the mutations found in the Z43 virus and was naturally hesitant to answer. Then he remembered the positive news about the virus not being present in the blood of younger children and he said with a genuine smile, "Yeah, Jackson. I believe things are getting better. I suspect we still have a lot to get through before things are eventually back to normal. Hell they might never get completely back to normal, but they're getting better. Yeah, I think so."

"Good." Jackson said, "That's good." Then he yawned and shook his head, saying, "Man, I'm really getting sleepy. Must be the meds they're giving me. I've been in and out of it all day. You'd think being unconscious for several days would have been enough sleep for a while but you know... better living through chemistry and all that."

"Yeah, I understand." Sean replied. "Look Jackson, I checked out of my hotel and I have to head back to Yuengsville as soon as I leave here. I'll keep in touch through Andrea and stop by to see you when I can after you get home. You just focus on getting better my friend and do whatever the doctors and physical therapists tell you to do. Ok? If you do as you're told you should be back to normal before you know it." He patted Jackson on the shoulder and turned to walk away.

"Sean?" Jackson called.

Sean turned and looked back toward Jackson.

"Be careful out there. It's a long way back to Yuengsville and the roads are still not safe, as I can personally attest."

"Not to worry Jackson." Sean said, "They've arranged for me to have a police escort all the way home. I'll be safe enough."

Jackson smiled sleepily as his friend left his room. He had only half heard what Sean had replied, but deep in the back of his mind as he fell back to sleep, he was replaying the supposed hallucination he had experienced back in the barn. He saw Sean walking toward him followed by someone else. Then the sleep overtook him.

CHAPTER 49

Sean walked down the long hospital corridor and turned into the area where a bank of four elevators waited to take him down to the hospital lobby. His thoughts seemed to be a million miles away. He had a lot on his mind. As he rounded the corner, he saw a young police officer in the uniform of the Yuengsville Police Department sitting on a cushioned bench waiting for him.

"So." The officer inquired "How did it go?"

Sean looked up and saw his young friend, Officer Anthony Kelly, looking curiously at him. He took a deep breath, sighed, and said, "Ok. I suppose. He is still a bit doped up from all the pain meds."

"But what about... you know?"

"I'm honestly not sure yet." Sean replied. "He swears he saw us Tony. At least he thinks he saw us. I'm pretty sure I've managed to talk him out of the idea for now, but you know he's a reporter and I'm sure he's still a bit suspicious."

Anthony said, "But he has to realize he was in really bad shape Sean. He probably can't trust anything he believed he might have seen. You have to make sure you convince him of that every chance you get."

"But it's not like we did anything wrong Tony," Sean said. "We did manage to rescue him and the girl and rounded up of a whole bunch of bad guys in the process. In fact, it sounds like something we should be proud of and not something we're trying to cover up."

"Maybe so." Anthony replied, "And it's not exactly like we're really trying to cover it up or anything. But... well you know it's complicated. I mean, this was an unsanctioned off the books operation, which as far as the world needs to know, never happened."

Sean hesitated and then said, "I understand. But.."

"But nothing Sean. You know this could have very easily gone the other way and would have blown up in our faces."

"Sean, we can't admit to anything that might reflect back negatively on either the police department or the Mayor's office. You know the powers that be are like thin threads, which barely hold our cities together and keep us from plunging right back into total anarchy. Look, everything worked out for the best and let's just leave it at that. Jackson and the girl are safe, the bad guys are all dead or in jail, and a major ring of drug pushers, pornographers, and sex slavers has been destroyed. Plus, your friend Jackson is now considered the hero of the day so all of the publicity will be focused on him. No one will be looking at us for anything. It's a win-win situation."

Sean took a deep breath and said, "I know. You're right. But I just feel so bad keeping all of this from Jackson. He's been my best friend since we were kids."

"Maybe so." Anthony said as the door to the elevator opened and they stepped inside, "But as you said he's also a writer and a reporter. Don't you ever forget that. If he figures any of this out, he won't keep it to himself. Believe me, he won't be able to."

Sean knew Anthony was right, but that didn't make him feel any better. The true story behind the rescue and his involvement would wait for another day. For now it had to remain a mystery. The elevator door opened to the hospital lobby. Sean and Anthony walked out to Anthony's car and prepared to head back to Yuengsville. Sean turned and looked up at front of the hospital. He was surprised to see Andrea Ridge standing at one of the windows looking down at him. She nodded her head in a fashion that led him to believe she might have her own suspicions about his involvement in her husband's rescue. Sean nodded back and then climbed into the car and with Anthony driving, pulled out of the parking lot.

EPILOGUE

Jackson Ridge gritted his teeth and bore down with all of his might as the sweat beaded on his brow and his eyes squinted against the dripping perspiration. He was doing everything in his power to squeeze the rubber ball. The infernal thing had been just one of the many tools and gadgets the physical therapist had given him to strengthen his hands. He had completed his exercises with his right hand and was now just finishing up the workout with his left. In fact, Jackson had done twice as many repetitions as the therapist had recommended. He was a firm believer in the idea if one was good, then two must be better. This was his philosophy for most things in life whether food, drink, medicine, or whatever. Although the pain he was currently experiencing was great, the feeling of weakness, which was still present in both hands, was extremely frustrating.

If there was any bit of good news to be had, it was that Jackson realized since both of his hands had started out with almost no ability after his injury, they seemed to be progressing at a similar rate together. He recalled how, being right-handed, that particular hand always had been the stronger of the two. However, now he was starting to believe by the time all of his physical therapy was over both hands might end up equally as strong.

After the final squeeze, Jackson let out a long deep sigh of relief and reached out carefully, lifting a small hand towel to wipe his face. During the previous several weeks since his ordeal, Jackson had managed to master such minor skills as lifting small objects, holding his toothbrush, and even pressing the buttons on his communications unit. However, actions involving more strength such as lifting a full coffee mug by its handle or using his revolver were all mountains to be climbed at some distant time in the future.

Jackson looked up at the clock Andrea had hung on the wall in their basement where he did his therapy workouts. It was eight-thirty-two. He was right on schedule, even with the additional repetitions. It looked like he must be getting better at this therapy stuff. He saw he still had time to get his morning shower and dress before his new literary partner and ghost writer Brian Arthur arrived from New Times Publishing to begin their daily work.

During the previous several weeks, Jackson and a reporter from the Schuylkill Daily News named Emmett Glenn had spent several days a week working up articles for the newspaper. They had started out co-writing articles just for the Skook but soon learned their pieces also found their way onto the various wire services as well. This initial writing work only lasted for a few weeks or so before the furor and public interest began to wane. During that time, however, the newspaper's circulation grew dramatically.

Now that the newspaper article portion of his responsibility was over, Jackson was working with Brian Arthur about seven hours a day, usually from around nine-thirty or so in the morning until about four-thirty or five in the afternoon. They were working on the book version of his story for New Times. Andrea had managed to negotiate a deal involving both The Skook and New Times while he was in the hospital. The book was to take the form of a first person narrative novel told in Jackson's own words, with the hopes of providing a firsthand account complete with all the same joys, sorrows, fears, and other emotions he personally experienced during his ordeal.

Because of Jackson's condition and her new responsibilities, Andrea had taken a leave of absence from work for a few months. This also allowed her to take Kyla temporarily out of daycare. She hoped that by the time Kyla was ready to return to the school, the daycare would have relocated to a new, safer location. At least for the time being, they were not hurting financially.

As Andrea had told Jackson back at the hospital, the Schuylkill Daily News would continue to pay him all the while he was at home recovering in exchange for exclusive initial rights to his story. In addition, he had received a ten thousand dollar reward from Mayor McKinney as well as the remainder of the cash that was retrieved from the hotel after the police shoot-out with the now deceased Billy Jones.

Acting as Jackson's agent, Andrea had arranged for a number of phone interviews with a variety of different magazines and newspapers. She also took Jackson to several press conferences and a few local television and radio interviews. These interviews were then transmitted all over the world via a variety of internet type links and as a result had been seen by millions world-wide. They also got a substantial advance from the publishing company for the rights to his book.

However, the whole recounting of the event and rehashing them over and over for the novel was proving to be quite a stressful tribulation for Jackson, perhaps even more so than the simple newspaper articles had been. This was because in the case of the novel, Jackson was required to pour more of his own personal emotions into the work, which he found draining. He was so thankful the work was scheduled to be completed within the next month. Then he would only have a temporary reprieve while the book was published and released by New Times, who already had a deal to distribute it through several national book wholesalers, each of which had client lists containing some of the biggest book retailers in the world. Because of the media blitz Andrea had arranged during the previous weeks, the buzz about the upcoming book was strong as was the public anticipation.

Jackson was relieved Andrea had managed to negotiate a nice royalty option for him, because if the book sold as well as everyone hoped it would, their financial worries would be over, at least for a few years. Andrea was also presently fielding offers from a number of major film studios. Financially this also had the potential to be very rewarding, but it too would require a lot of work on Jackson's part. As soon as the novel was completed, Jackson and another yet to be determined writer from the movie studio would begin working on the screenplay.

He was also happy Andrea had been able to get the leave from her job. He knew none of his recent opportunities would have even been possible without her active participation. Andrea loved being involved and had great organizational and management skills. She had no problem juggling multiple projects simultaneously. Also, with her actively running the whole show, they had developed a new closeness they had not experienced in many years.

Taking a shower was Jackson's way not only to get clean but to unwind and to think of both nothing and everything. He found he was able to relax and let his mind wander under the hot steaming spray of the showerhead. Jackson stood calmly thinking about not only everything that had happened and everything that he had accomplished so far, but also everything he still had yet to do. It boggled his mind how much his life had changed as the result of that one assignment. It looks like this truly had been the story of a lifetime.

Then suddenly he thought about Sean. He hadn't seen his friend since the day Sean had visited him at the hospital. He knew Sean was very busy and he too had been just as busy and as such felt equally to blame for their lack of communication. But Jackson sensed there might be more to Sean's noticeable absence. He was starting to wonder if Sean might be avoiding him because of something he, Jackson, might have said. The only thing that came to mind that Sean might have found disturbing was when Jackson mentioned he thought Sean and someone else had been the ones who saved him.

But surely Sean wouldn't have let something as trivial as that bother him. Especially since at that time Jackson had been barely clinging to life and was likely hallucinating anyway. In fact, Sean had been the one who helped to convince him that he had imagined everything. Sean had even sworn he had been in Yuengsville working at the time and he never lied to Jackson. Even though at the time Jackson's illusion had seemed real enough, now that he had time to think about it and to relive the events in great detail over and over, he wondered how he could have been so foolish as to even think a non-violent intellectual like Sean could have been his mysterious savior.

Jackson supposed that particular puzzle would have to remain a mystery until sometime later when he was fully recovered and might have time to investigate further.

Although as a reporter, he hated loose ends and not knowing the complete story, as a fan of all things mysterious, he thought there was something very special about not being able to answer all the questions his potential readers might have. The idea that somewhere out there lurking in the darkness was a shadowy figure, the true hero of the story, was actually starting to appeal to Jackson. And the fact that this person's identity was and would remain a secret just added more intrigue to the whole story.

He reached down and turned off the water in the shower, another new obstacle surmounted, then began to carefully dry himself off. He walked over to the bedroom window and looked out across the expanse of the Ashton Cooperative, seeing the barbed wire topped fence barriers in the distance. Jackson let out another contemplative sigh. The world was certainly a different place than it had been only ten years earlier. He had no idea what the future had in store for him, but he had little doubt it would most certainly be interesting.

A Rather Lengthy Comment From The Author

Like writing the book wasn't enough ... sheesh!

Potential Spoiler Alert: If you haven't yet read the book, you might not want to read this section until you do. It assumes you've already completed the novel and might want to learn a bit more. You know, the whys and wherefores of my writing of the book. Although I don't intend to give too much away, why take the chance? Who knows what I might say... I certainly don't. With that being said, let's continue...

A few years before the legions of zombie apocalypse enthusiasts had reached the level of rabid fandamonium to which they'd skyrocketed by the end of 2013 and 2014, I had already been planning to write a zombie apocalypse type novel of my own, but one with a unique approach. Unlike many of the novels which were and are out there, I wanted mine to be one with a completely different take on the whole zombie apocalypse thing. I needed to create a story that had enough going for it so it would hold up on its own and maybe even after the zombie craze had finally fizzled out as all such fun things often do.

I wanted my story to not be just another zombie story but to be a thriller which would take place in a world a few dozen years in the future; in my brave new world of 2053, ten years after the zombie apocalypse had occurred. However, unlike most novels in the genre, in my book the predicted apocalypse had not wiped out humanity or completely destroyed our way of life. I didn't want to portray a world where humanity had been plunged entirely into a primitive and savage Darwinian state of existence.

I realized I was taking a bit of a literary risk since a world of total destruction and rampant flesh-eating zombies was exactly what all the doom-and-gloomers and most zombie fans usually like to see portrayed. I also didn't want the aforementioned apocalypse to result in the end of mankind, but to just to become something of a bump in man's evolutionary highway and one which would temporarily wound humanity before we all once again were able to rise up and take our rightful place at the top of the food chain.

In my idea for the novel, the zombies would have come very close to taking over the world and as such humanity would be driven to the brink of extinction before eventually making a comeback. I would have like sixty or seventy percent of humans destroyed before mankind began to take back the earth. When the surviving humans did managed to get their act together, the living dead would be wiped out by the millions and after ten years these undead would end up being less of a threat and instead would be relegated to the ranks of being nothing more than a nuisance; albeit a deadly one. So my story had to take place at a time after mankind was on the road to recovery and was well on its way to rebuilding the world.

My goal was to write a story which was actually a thriller set in that post-apocalyptic world where although zombies still existed they wouldn't be the main thrust of the story. Instead, they would be an exciting backdrop; interesting color if you will. Although their existence wouldn't and couldn't be ignored and would in actuality still be a major contributing factor in the insane murderous villain's modus operandi, this couldn't be just another zombie book, and the undead couldn't be the main focus of the story. That being said there was no reason why I couldn't still have plenty of zombie-related fun in the book; which I most certainly did.

I personally felt that by 2012 the entire zombie genre had been done to death if you will pardon the pun. Yet during 2013, as I was writing this novel every day dozens of zombie based books seemed to be flooding the market. Since I don't have time to read other authors' works I have no way of knowing if someone else had a similar idea to this. I can only hope they haven't. (I really like being the first to do things and hate it when I learn that someone had the same or similar idea. But I digress.)

So I decided to do as I had done with several of my previously written zombie-based short stories such as "Dinner With Andy And Meg", "Happy Valentine's Day",

"Bright of The Living Dead", "Call Him Maury" and "A Love Best Served Cold"; and that was to come up with something different and not just another "me too" type of living dead story. I figured if I were going to take the time to write a novel with zombies in it, the book would have to have a significantly different approach, hopefully something new, something fresh and something never done before.

So I began to do the proverbial "What if" scenario to get my creative juices working. I thought of questions like what if the zombie apocalypse actually did occur? And what if mankind came close to the brink of extinction but then made a comeback? What if mankind used his intellect and technology to defeat the majority of the armies of the undead? And what if only after ten years' time, the zombie threat was suppressed to the point that life began to continue in a direction heading as close as possible to the way things were before the apocalypse?

And what if zombies still showed up from time to time, but not by the hundreds but just one, two or a few dozen at a time? And what if the reformed government had placed bounties on their heads which resulted in an organized way for the citizenry to earn some part-time cash, while simultaneously helping to eliminate the problem? How would the new world have changed in this recreated environment? How would the apocalypse alter professions such as the legal or medical fields? Needless to say the questions kept coming and the creative juices began to flow.

And then there were of course many more questions. What if there was a counter culture; tribes of wandering criminals who occupied the areas outside of the protected cities? And what if an insane sociopath who made his living catering to the wild outlanders chose to use the cloak of zombie activity to disguise his own sick and twisted underworld enterprises? With millions dead, undead, and missing, how easily could he mask his activities and literally get away with murder? And what if a small town free-lance investigative journalist with a wife and young daughter, who was simply trying to make ends meet in the strange new world, was given the opportunity to help find a missing, kidnapped young girl? And What if this provided him with the opportunity write a story which would lead him deep into the depraved underworld where the psychotic was master?

What horrible secrets would he learn? And what if our reluctant hero was anything but a hero? What if he was just like you or me? How much danger would he be putting himself and in with his investigation? And in a world where enforcing law and order was at best questionable, who could he turn to and how could he hope for protection?

Before I knew it, I had the crux of an idea for the novel. I decided to call it "Dead Kill" because as you have learned in the prologue, this is a term which I coined to refer to the elimination of a zombie; in other words the act of "killing" something which is already dead. Of course the living dead cannot be technically killed but destroyed.

As always, once I started writing the story evolved and eventually resulted for better or worse in the novel which you have just read. But then as stories often do, this one kept evolving, as did the never ending list of 'what if' questions which constantly haunt my mind. So after I was about three quarters of the way through with writing this book I decided that one novel would not be enough to tell all of the tales which could possibly occur in the new world with my new cast of characters. And I really liked the character Jackson Ridge. He was a non-hero hero. I have been asked by my devoted readers for years to write a series sometime. And although I had never actually considered writing a series before, I realized that quite accidently I had created a world and a collection of characters that were all perfect for a series.

Two words I try to avoid when discussing or planning my writing endeavors are 'never' and 'always'. (You may notice I didn't even say I never use them or always avoid them.) I find as soon as I say I'm never going to do something, I often end up doing it. And likewise when I say I'm always going to do something, I often stop doing it. Yeah, I know it's weird but so am I. So I decided late in the game (December 29, 2013 to be exact) to not just complete this novel but to create an entire series of Dead Kill books instead.

So, since this was not just going to be a once and done novel, I had to change the title of the book slightly. Instead of simply calling the book by its original title "Dead Kill", I decided to add the subtitle "Book 1 – The Ridge Of Death". (Like that clever play on "Ridge" as in Jackson Ridge?) This way the reader would know there was more to come in the continuing adventures of Jackson Ridge, ace investigative reporter.

Ok. So I suppose I've rambled on long enough. I most certainly hope you enjoyed the three-for-one benefit of a fresh approach to the zombie horror genre mixed with a good old-fashioned psychological bad-guy thriller and the idea that there are more adventures to come in the near future.

As always, thank you for taking some of your precious time and using it to read my book. Some people believe the act of buying a book is one of the greatest compliments a reader can offer an author, but for me it's the actual reading the book which is truly the greatest gift. For what is more valuable than our time?

Thomas M. Malafarina, March 2014

www.ingramcontent.com/pod-product-compliance
Lightning Source LLC
Chambersburg PA
CBHW050124030726
47505CB00007B/2022